TULL

THE GUARDIAN

THE FIRST NOVEL FROM

GRIFFIN WRAY

114 | 31

Tull the Guardian

Second Edition Hardback ISBN-13: 978-0-9993776-0-4

Released by Uskoa Press on March 25, 2021.

Wrap cover design and illustrations created by
Yannick Bouchard at illusorydreams.com.

uskoamythos.com

First and foremost, may all my works bring glory to the Lord, for He is more deserving than my imagination can reveal.

"Do not oppress the widow, the fatherless, the sojourner, or the poor, and let none of you devise evil against another in your heart."

Zechariah 7:10

The Holy Bible, English Standard Version®

"Now to Him who is able to do exceedingly abundantly above all that we ask or think, according to the power that works in us, to Him be glory in the church by Christ Jesus to all generations, forever and ever. Amen."

Ephesians 3:20-21

The Holy Bible, New King James Version®

"Amen" is an affirmation that means "so be it," "verily," or "truly."

The Second Creation of Yah—the characters in this and other Uskoa Press novels who do not exist in our time—abide by a varying translation of Scripture that does not deviate from the core meaning but is fitted to the language of their land.

Contents

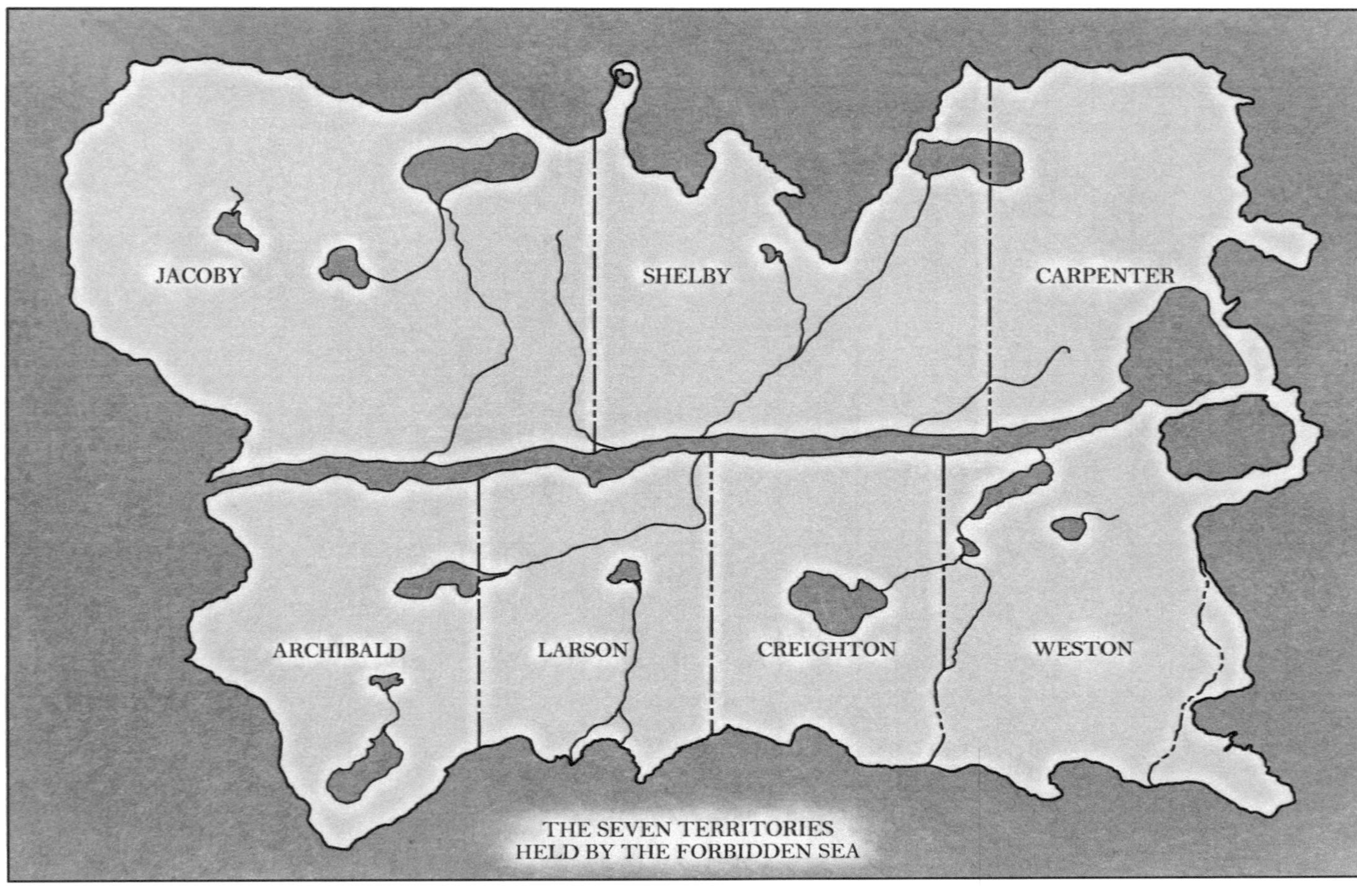
JACOBY
SHELBY
CARPENTER
ARCHIBALD
LARSON
CREIGHTON
WESTON
THE SEVEN TERRITORIES
HELD BY THE FORBIDDEN SEA

I. | Guardians

One

The 10th Morn beneath the Moon of the Drifting Leaves
The 14th Gathering Season of the Accession
In the Blessing of I'Esh, who tends the harvest.

Ghost's Breath Rim
The northernmost point of the Jacoby Territory
Where the wind chases the shadows across the Forbidden Sea . . .

The Last War of the Second Creation ended without a victor. No army declared triumph, and no cause proved superior to any challenge. The oppression that created conflict and the pride-filled arrogance that led to war withered long afore ammunition dwindled or the flow of blood sickened the dueling forces. When the dust of war settled, troops gathered around no great leader who ushered in peace; in point of fact, no leader emerged from their ranks at all.

Two armies, once aroused by pride of hatred, agreed upon mutual surrender when the light fell unto a darkness not imagined by them. What they saw when light returned rid them of every conflict. Once-embittered forces then united and threw their weapons and the designs for those weapons into a *new* sea. Those on the battlefield, and the land around them, found the nations reformed, in remembrance of the psalmists, *unto a multitude of isles*; seventy-four well-isolated isles scattered upon a single, unending sea.

Afore violent tides settled on the isle numbered *fourteen*, the Accession redefined the power structures of creation. What was spoken of only in books paled the written word. A new conqueror descended from Tai'evas on billowing fire and battled a foe that pushed open the terrane and crawled from the waters. Figures of brass and light swatted terrifying creatures of putrid deformity back unto Ki'eoppa—*the Pit.*

Those creatures who descended from the sky-fires, called *Ministers*, warred against their fallen siblings, called the *Fallen First.* These mighty siblings warred till the ash of their battle blotted out the stars. The only light that rose vaulted from the shed forms of those who fell evermore in war. Those shed souls carved a new path in the skies that let the sun return, though less formidable in magnificence.

Time faded, and the winter that froze the harvest thawed unto a new bounty. Still, the firstkind's war raged across a visible arena for one hundred twenty-two of the secondkind's spans. So mighty was the battle that none born of warmakers challenged Yah's firstkind. The earliest witnesses made choice souls Advocates and Guardians, who kept them from disobedience and saved them from trouble.

In time, souls who stayed in their troubles blamed the old fathers; those who surrendered and survived the warring. Though their choice ended the Era of Despair, peace brought no guarantee of satisfaction. A weakened belief oft threatened division among the witnesses of both wars. They called this time the Era of the New Fathers.

Lamentations and prayers for mercy littered every conversation. Those with wisdom set new laws, new teachings, and new technologies into motion. The fables of old held no candle to the realties anew. Absolutism replaced belief and the tangible, knowable creatures bore the faith and fear of once-proud souls.

The souls born in the Era of the New Fathers proved the weakest lot. They seldom rose from their repentance, and never bettered their souls in the presence of those who warred. They composed their books and laws till they grew too weak, then relied on brass hands to take compassion on them. They starved beside lush gardens and withered in thirst alongside racing brooks.

Those whom the Ministers elected flourished. They clothed their bodies, kept their souls clean, and learned their way. Their progress rested upon the backs of laborious trades and care for their elders whilst their mourning wore trenches along the graves of those who scoffed at their example. In disregard for their lineage, the Era of the New Fathers withered till all that remained was the Era of the Reformers.

Those who led the second era of the Accession named the warring creatures The First Creation and those they protected The Second Creation—as all affirmed their createdness. They sought richer familiarity of the firstkind, and even learned the language those marvelous and horrifying creatures spoke. Their parents had surrendered fast to fear. This era wanted more, and sought idea-makers, builders, scholars, and technicians to lead.

Female souls matched the number of male souls, at first, but survived their counterparts till a three-to-one ratio set them apart. Even so, the dominant and the submissive thrived *as one*. The secondkind flourished. Creation of technology, medicine, and culture mingled with the ways of the Ministers through obedience. These *cousins* entrusted each other, and harmony flowed as never boasted afore by their ancestors.

Ministers lavished affection on the abandoned souls of the first era and took them into their care. They instructed the wise and, together, rid the land of every disease and illness. No soul suffered betrayal by the body. Though the established government and the corporate Church withered like their ancestors, the secondkind bettered others afore their own desires.

Joy gushed from every soul, and Yah blessed all plenty. What they created, what they shared and learned, exceeded hope. Souls who never observed war or suffered sickness found their paths vast. They labored hard together and for one another. For the first time, they embraced the plan of the Triune.

Those who performed trades wrote detailed journals and collaborated with other trades for combined success. They put away their parents' books of grief and terror. Their writings filled shelves and minds with ideas that those minds bettered too. All provided, all found purpose, and all enjoyed an abundance that saw them exceed their parents and maintain peak levels of memory, musculature, and ability.

Yet, even in a time of such blessing, there arose a throng who sought upheaval and gave into lusts and corruption. They kept to the shadows and the dark. What they wanted, they took; possessions, food, and fashion, till such a time when what they wanted were *others*. They took their fellow members of the secondkind as offerings unto those creatures whom Yah punished.

The corruption continued, and a division struck the secondkind. They turned from obedience, and redefined good as oppressive and wicked as fragile. Their contempt—also at a peak—suffered no limitations. Hatred fed hatred till they turned spoiled and sour in their gluttonies. They introduced fear into the land again; though, the sensation exceeded the vileness of their elders.

TULL

The blameless of the Era of the Reformers chose pridefulness and unhemmed the works of their parents and elders. Most let vainglory taint them and delighted in their awfulness. They destroyed creation as an expression of their purposefulness. Delight fell with promise and hope. Then the fruit of mighty trees replaced all with terror that knew no name.

They defiled bodies, lay with beasts, and violated the blameless. Their voices rose against the Mighty Creator and declared the Fallen First victims of Yah's unkindness. So, the Triune rebuked both creations *again* and shook the lands to open eyes and turn souls from their wayward deeds. This time was the Era of the Falling Lands, in which those who boasted in the vile took the title of the *Partakers*.

The isles lost portions and souls. Buildings, bloodlines, and choice endeavors fell unto the sea. The fourteenth isle lost three-fifths of what they kept. Still, the defilers would not repent.

The Partakers subverted judgeships and forced new laws. They infected Believers, enticed away the weary, and used pleasures to embolden their message of defiance. Families fell apart. Even the Ministers turned from what they saw.

In the darkest eves of the secondkind, a tarnished soul worthy of a Minister's sorrow gave birth to a blameless soul of distinctive might. Afore mother first nourished child with milk, she swore his purpose to goodness. She saw how peace arrived too oft through fear and not oft enough through inspiration. She desired that her son learn the ways of a soul that never lost hope in Yah's grace.

"Hear your fallen daughter again . . . proszę . . . i'ea poi kani tuo'da Yah toi'evoa . . . si'ella i'esena kuain Yah o tuo'da minûlle toi'evoa i'ea lupauk si'e."

She who forsook her name—and that sorrowful Minister—sighed with renewed belief for her hope in her son's purpose and her recognition of Yah's promise. Time passed, span upon span, till the blameless babe rose amid the lot of the secondkind. He possessed a fairness that attracted Ministers and strength that did not fail. The Minister, called Enke'loi, swore an oath to their Creator never to let the babe fall till all the Triune's plans for the Second Creation unfurled. As a soul who had lost droves of siblings, she proved determined, and kept safe a soul deemed agreeable and noble. But, even the most upright soul needed a helper.

TWO

The 1st Eve beneath the Moon of the Sower's Hand

The 122nd Sowing Season of the Accession

In the Mercy of Yah, who gives the rain, the seed, and the bloom.

Beacon 083.38.814 recognized at 16 Sevier . . .

Identifier confirmed—Nelson James Tull.

Purposed to serve the Second Creation as 19th Guardian.

Now in the Era of the Guardians, the Crater of N'Ach Shi'an and the Valleys of Mechh'täva hid beneath the hem of shadow on the moon and taunted a scarred iris to find their shape. By the fourth rising, the moon's adornments would show their depths in full. Still, those scars on the lunar surface meant much to a soul who oft fell unto slumber beneath the First Creation's warring. He lost count of the eves spent watching innumerable fires erupt far above his reach.

In his blamelessness, he stood in the shaft that Mechh'täva created when the tempestuous spirits of Ra'ab Shi'ekah pummeled the Warring Minister into the mountains of the eastern hem. The memory produced a smile fourteen spans later and revealed three scars upon a bearded face. His eyes—one scarred, like his cheek—reflected the brilliance of the sky-fires and the disfigured moon. By the Moon of the Reaching Sea, now fifty-five moonrises from this eve, the hues would change, and the effects of the legendary Ministers would no longer hide from the eye but boast with definition.

"I'll miss seeing that. Even so . . . better that I bring Yah praise this time."

TULL

Nelson James Tull, scarred son to Kara Doe Nelson and Patrick James Tull, suffered twenty-nine deaths—what the secondkind called *ends*. Not bad; if counted against a territory. But one soul? On one soul, so many ends took their toll. He got the pun, not that he laughed. He enjoyed the relationships he had cultivated here and had planned on staying longer.

"All hinges on time."

Those ends? All his. Not that he murdered—*ever*. They were *his* deaths; including one that marked the end of his purposelessness. His first end. That one, though spiritual, set loose the flood that followed.

The rest fell in service to the Second Creation. He met his end for friends, for strangers, for foes. One end for a dog. Well, ended to preserve the blamelessness of the soul who *owned* the dog. He considered that choice worthwhile then and now.

Ended by stabbing—four times. Ended by impaling—three times, including one by tree limb. Ended by broken neck—once. More than enough. Counting the end of selfishness and his heroic dog rescue, that made ten.

Ended by drowning—eight times. Ended by fire—three times. Ended by collision—twice. Twenty-three. Ended by falling object—also twice. One of those *accidental*. That made twenty-five.

He once dropped from a bridge, strangled by a pylon cable, and fell into the sea. Blaming one cause over the other proved difficult. Twenty-six. Then there was the time an arrow flung him onto an iron trap. Twenty-seven. One end by trampling. Twenty-eight.

There was only one end that he had no recollection of. In his mind, that end must have proven pleasant. Maybe he went in his sleep. Maybe he went in his lover's arms. Maybe he slipped in the shower. Still, number twenty-nine, but not his twenty-ninth end, evaded him.

By showing up to the setting where the Loy River flowed into the sea, he invited end number thirty. Against orders and common sense, he stood on the cusp of harm. If ever a moment existed when *all things* deserved undoing, though, this was that moment. In light of that, he proved the fearlessness in his purpose.

The mere *thought* of seeing Enke'loi, who kept him from eternity, steadied the Jacobian. Though a Minister in design, the creature who appeared to him in feminine form warred like no other that he observed afore. Her body appeared as one fluid burnished brass piece that kept pure flame. Flowing fire created the train of her form and her eyes shimmered like melted gold. She *reached* higher than any among the secondkind and imparted grace mightier than any wind.

Enke'loi revered her lessers with immense love and kept Tull from each end that he might keep worse creatures from hurting Yah's treasured Second Creation. Ministers, being the First. Animals, being the Third. Those *worse creatures* were the siblings of she who kept him: the Ministers who revolted against the Triune and the creatures who existed in the living veil of constant shadow.

By now, Tull sensed when Enke'loi might reappear. For the past two eves, his gaze seldom strayed from a sky filled with the fire of celestial warring. Though she never descended in his sight, he watched. In the same way that he avoided stifling his gift and grieving his Creator, he remained ever watchful. Such obedience made him renowned as a Guardian and feared as a Believer.

Other than that, he learned not *why* Enke'loi selected him above any other soul. He protected Believers but was no healer, no teacher. He fought hard for every soul. These were not worthy traits that set him apart.

In measure of stature, his was taller and broader than most, but no more heroic than weary. In terms of wit, he listened more than he read books. In terms of kindness, he showed more than he received. He had a handful of friends. More than some, he realized.

Despite the look of him, with scars on his face and terror-induced silver strands in his hair, he bore the most serene stare of any born creature. Too beautiful to be born by chance. And, be certain, he realized how best to use the advantage. Most times, he said more with his eyes than his mouth ever conveyed.

"You're sure you ought to go against Olley this time?"

How could he not? He half-smirked, and the glance he offered a sloe-eyed soul softened his penchant for recklessness.

"*She* isn't going to forgive this."

"I'll speak to her." He glanced over his shoulder, as though fear-filled.

"On which side of getting swatted?"

As he sensed the nearness of his thirtieth end, he knelt to face one of the most resistant, most cunning, and most startling creatures—as all are creations—known to him. This creature of beautiful ferocity held no fear in the shadow of his reputation, his build, or his scars. Already in her twelfth span, Hazel-Sue, oft called *Hazy*, never budged. So, he leaned closer.

TULL

Hazy surrendered not one breath nor one wavering glance; too proud to even wipe the tear that agitated her poise. She knew what awaited, and she hated the aftershock more than a child should know about hate. He considered their nearness to her thirteenth span and the uncounted tears he had chased away in that collection of moons. When he smoothed her silky tresses in comfort, she turned her moist cheek against his scarred palm to remove her tear.

"I must do this, whirlybird. You believe me, do you not?"

She had the brilliant eyes and broad cheeks of her mother, but her impression of Tull's smirk deserved applause. Brave face or not, he rubbed the tear from her cheek and tasted the salt on the pad of his thumb. Her head proved heavy with thoughts as she dipped toward him but the seat belt around her shoulder suspended her. He kept to one knee and straightened a blanket till he hid her rigid feet.

"Don't be fearful. Your mom won't forgive me."

She sniffled and nodded, but wiped away the next flow of tears with her own palm. Tull took hold as her fingers fell toward her thigh and kissed across her knuckles, despite how she squirmed when the whiskers of his beard prickled her skin.

This time, her whole hand squeezed his fingers and reminded him of the first time he held her. Every hurt abandoned his heart. He never told her of that power she held over him. Now, he knew he must; lest he leave her wondering.

"I'd ask that you be helpful and be respectful while I'm away."

She *was* a wonder.

"Will you?"

"Yes."

Tull leaned in and kissed her smooth forehead and kept every thought. Hazy latched onto him as best as her arms allowed and wept. The sound made the boy beside her gasp and drew Tull's full attention. When that blameless soul remembered his pouting, he turned and resumed his silent treatment toward the Guardian.

"Don't be ornery, Q. J." Hazy proved a mighty defender of stubborn fools.

"Worry not." Tull reached across the bench seat and rested his hand, covering the boy's hand and knee. "As to afore. I promise I'll never tempt you into eating soured leeks again."

He who proved bold for towing six spans behind him, yet proved no match for Hazy, tilted his crown of curls and looked on the weathered soul with scarred pewter irises. "Give me your word."

TULL

Tull's expression went blank. "My word is yours."

"Or peas."

"Or peas. *Sure.* I'll ask that our judges ban both from the territories!"

Hazy laughed and inspired he who mimicked her in every habit to do the same. Tull fed on their song and reached into his pocket for a memento that once belonged to Beau Itzal Zeck; highest among cherished Jacobians and Guardians. The memento, part of a soldier's campaign medal, was a keepsake of the Last War and a parting gift entrusted to the territory's fourth Guardian by the first. Now worn and smooth, minus one bent edge of the copper disc, the medal represented how far the secondkind had ventured since their warring ended. The weight of significance burdened Tull and captured Q. J.'s immediate interest.

"Guardian Zeck entrusted this to me when I was named scion. He told me, 'Keep safe my brother . . . from the Last . . . from my father.'" Tull stretched out his hand and let the boy take the medal with small fingers that teased his scars. "Would you keep this till I come back?"

The boy protected the memento with two cupped hands but wasted no time peeking at the worn face up close. Tull spent little time as a teacher; as something more than a traveler through their lives. The land brimmed with wonders, but nothing compared to blameless curiosity. If the Jacobian saw the moonset, he would do more than protect them in the morrow.

Again, he hesitated. "I thank you, partner."

"I thank you." Q. J. spoke fast, and his lower lip slipped behind the upper till he exaggerated the shape of his mouth and turned his button nose.

"You'll mind the girls for me, will you not?"

He offered a *shurg*. Not a shrug, which relied on two shoulders. A single-shouldered *shurg* expressed obedience while foretelling the terms remained conditional and certain to be forgotten on a whim.

"Well, I s'pose that's a good enough answer for who the answer's for. When you see Vic, let him teach you how to put a proper shine on that medal, but don't let him convince you that I was lax in my care. Let him tell you of the ice caps till again you see the bears that belong to them."

Q. J. nodded as though he listened well, and Tull ignored the burden on his heart as he rose, then shut the door. Hazy twisted at the waist and clung to the door handle with a clutch that might turn jealous the worn, hand-sewn bear she kept near in times of sorrow. The gentle soul who faced Tull and knew Hazy's secrets smiled at her, but the child remained stone-faced in the presence of a ruse. Her eyes pleaded for an outcome that kept the four souls together long enough for their favored Guardian's senses to reach him.

Jules Baker Shannon towed the same hope, and looked from Hazy's eyes to the sky-fires for help. "Dad oft tells how this moon brings trouble."

The secondkind lived by the *moon*. Their calendar counted one *span* of thirteen distinct *moons*, each of which cycled for twenty-eight risings and settings. The measure of time began with the moonrise—the *eve*—followed by moonset—the *morn*—and the highest point of warmth and light—the *peak*. The Moon of the Sower's Hand marked the second moon since the most recent six-moon winter—which ended the three-moon gathering season and thawed unto the four-moon sowing season.

"Far and slow till morn."

"We've suffered worse."

"Here?" Her brow arched, but her gaze met Hazy's burdensome watchfulness.

Tull shielded Jules from expectation, though he proved as vulnerable when she set her amethyst irises on him. "Remember the loose stones in the road after you cross the old covered bridge near Violet's grave house. Carl and Bea will meet you there. Remind him to avoid—"

"The Shelby Territory."

"Head north, along the mountains, but stay off the hem of the—"

"Salt lodes." She grinned well, but her sadness returned. "You could—"

"No other cares for these blameless souls as you do, J. J."

"I—I wonder. They're cute runts, but soured leeks remind me of home."

He exhaled, and Jules turned toward an axe propped against the rear wheel. Like the pre-Accession campaign medal from Zeck, her father had gifted the weapon to Tull as alms. She seized the worn handle, but met the Guardian mid-hike and just shy of the overcoat that swayed from his fingers.

"Momma's still the best cook in all the Carpenter Territory."

Tull grinned and let her ramble. They traded, and he lifted the axe overhead, then set the weapon in a leather harness strapped around his shoulders. Jules reached beneath his arm, took hold of the worn handle, and tugged downward. The motion released a trigger mechanism in the butt of the handle and set two silver spikes outward and perpendicular to the axe handle and along the contour of his back.

TULL

"Remember the times you scared me with tales of werewolves?"

"Indeed."

"Well, they seem fluffy about now."

Tull mouthed the word *fluffy* while Jules circled and reset the spikes. She ran her fingertips across the blade's broken tip and straightened the hem of Tull's vest. As she circled back around, her best grin spent on reassuring Hazy, she caught the look in his eyes and stared at his unmoved lips.

"You should have let Dad replace that handle when he—"

"The handle is fine."

"We should have—"

A wail unlike any siren punctuated the air with the force to devour sound and divided Tull's reach between the door handle and Jules's forearm. The pitch forced Jules's hands against her ears and her teeth bared as she bit back a squeal of pain. A second roar shook the cobblestone path, then an explosion in the distance produced a ripple of stillness. In the aftershock, her rig shook on both axles and widened the eyes of the blameless.

"Their little ears can't take much more of that."

"You should go."

"So should you!" She cinched his suspenders and leaned on him till the weight of her rested on his chest. "Don't break our hearts. All of you come home."

He glanced from her purple-hued irises to her mouth, then back to her eyes. Though he loved the trio well, and she above all, from them he kept compassion. "Soon, I'll see you."

"You had best."

She swatted his backside and buried her hands in the pockets of a jacket she had borrowed into her possession two spans afore. Letting pass her terms of a loan, she opened the rear passenger door and volunteered Hazy's keen grip and stern eye for the safekeeping of Tull's coat.

"Tell your—"

The blameless grew wide-eyed at her sudden silence and weaved around her shape to find Tull gone from sight. Jules wasted no time searching, but upheld the duties entrusted to her. Once, the Guardians rescued her from harm. Now the blameless deserved as much from her.

TULL

1610 VINER'S WAY

THE LOWEST POINT ADJACENT TO SEVIER IN THE ARCHIBALD TERRITORY
WHERE THE LOY RIVER'S MUD MINGLES WITH THE FORBIDDEN SEA'S SALT . . . .

The headlamps from Jules's rig shone across the remnants of storefronts and the tramcars crushed by seawater and fallen masonry. The creatures that bubbled up from the tide picked clean those drivers and passengers, shopkeepers and patrons alike. Then, true terror visited Sevier and the Guardians swooped in to counter the bringers of dread and bereavement.

Tull observed the battle damage and the eeriness that loomed along seven avenues of high-priced ruins. That he remained unspotted only made him a bigger target; bold, since the Liar knew his name and hungered for his end. The *Fallen First* would not take the Guardians as trophies. They would leave them displayed.

End the protectors and frighten the protected. This foe sought another *end* then death, and the secondkind should have prepared their souls better. Four brief lines of text and a warning from eras long passed. The *meaning* baffled scholars, bristled clutch-fisted Believers and provoked the cynical into bouts of laughter. Now, all learned the words of truth, and their fear *grieved* Tull's heart.

He ascended the cobblestone trail toward the waterfront, not letting any surface go unchecked. Those who could, *fled*. The Guardians led the rest away. They set fires along the banks, in the mouths of caves, and in the tunnels beneath their feet. Only the plots from Malachi's Vine to Pender's Chance remained accessible, as far as the coast allowed. The rest stood atop bluffs.

The lantern from the Bellflower Signal House swept across him and drew the Guardian's eye. A charred shape soiled the tan column of a building to his right and spread outward with a starburst pattern. He *sensed* an example, and rushed toward the burn site. A familiar scent of ethane gum and body fat filled his nostrils and stole his breath. Muscle and bone turned to ash, and only the torso and one arm remained unburned near a kettle lantern. That arm, identifiable by a scarred bicep, covered the charred face of a hardened soul.

The first body Tull discovered marked one less Guardian: Robbie Rudat Pine. For a eunuch, he *brimmed* with rage; then again, perhaps *because* of his truncation. As

Guardians went, none proved meaner. That their foe proved him a cautionary tale spoke to their perverse tactics, for they set fire to the soul who wielded a blowtorch.

Fire, crystal, and ore destroyed the First Creation's fallen; those who tore away their brass shells long afore the Providence of the Second Creation. The *stains* of four creatures told Tull of Pine's bravery. He was not a tender soul, by any measure, but Pine spared Tull from harm time and again. In turn, the Guardian took the blowtorch and set a protective fire around his fellow's remains.

"We were meant before a better purpose than this. No?" He looked Pine over a final time. "I'll seek you in the next land, friend."

He strayed from eulogy, his firm belief rooted in the idea that every soul of the secondkind existed to care for one another and to increase the Triune's glory. All the Guardians needed to do was keep the land *safe* from corruption. In his heart, he believed Pine kept true to his purpose till his end seized him.

Every cancer upon this isle cured. Every historic disease of the body and mind cured. Every debt paid, every need met. They were a better era—a *purer* era—than existed in the Era of Despair, but they were not all *whole*. Where *want* of *any* form existed, sin and foes awaited.

The current foe wailed and cast Tull onto his back, where he still found the wit to cover his ears. He then rolled onto his side and felt less restricted. A shaft of wood and graphite composite rolled the other direction. Beneath the weight of him, the axe handle snapped. All that remained where he fell was the blade and not enough handle to prove of use.

Though obscenities arose in his mind—most riled by his stubbornness—his first action was to look toward the place where he stood with Jules. The vacant space soothed him; still, he took a knee and touched the ruined gift from her father. The sky-fires no longer reflected in the face of the blade, just as the whisper of the Helper did not reach his ear to guide him.

Few would fault an unarmed lone soul who faced an all but certain end if that same soul ran. Few, but one. That one rose to his feet, brushed down his trousers, rolled up his shirt sleeves, and followed the trails of lightning and destruction. Though he set his jaw and his focus, his internal voice recited a passage that oft brought him comfort.

He continued his search for friends and reached an overturned plate of glass marked with the symbol of the Archibald Territory Chief Inspector's outpost—an outpost seated near the top of a smoldering hill to his east. He touched the symbol and let steam rise from his fingertips. Fire had scorched much of that hillside, then flash-boiled when seawater battered the remains. The now-charred setting produced a dank backdrop for another well-known victim.

"Myra?" Tull's voice drifted across the still intersection.

Even afloat atop charred cobblestone, Reformer Myra Sorrel Hont looked restful and adrift on ashen plumes. Her purpose kept her far from the outfit's woes, yet she helped them as her father had too. Her eyes now absorbed the sky-fires, and her lips parted from the absence of her soul. Tull pressed against her jaw and shut her mouth, lest wandering spirits convert her into a vessel of wicked intent.

Evils in this time corrupted the internal that other souls might fall victim, and Tull believed the Reformer made a tempting vessel. He took the scarf from his neck and concealed her face. He then gave thanks for her soul and that she had found peace with their Creator. Joy, not tears, lit his eyes for her sake.

"Now take rest, sister, and greet those who follow you this bitter morn."

THREE

When Tull staggered back with Myra's body and estimated the count of heads her attacker stood in height, his heel slipped. Beneath, a crimson smear that collected ash coagulated. The road he set Myra upon proved clean, and he sought yet another body of a friend. Ten paces toward the shore, he found one in the form of Holston Lucius Buckler II, an inventor of *peculiarities.*

"That's what a fire-rig does to an upper-cruster. His blood's as thick as mine."

Tull turned toward the distinctive laughter of Timothy Todd McCrea, an abettor like Jules, who made trouble like a Guardian. He watched Tim run bloodied fingers through his beard as he scratched at the skin close to the jaw. A flow of blood like a drizzle of honey caught the firelight from a nearby shop and Tull's eye. He who rebuked the Triune and criticized his Guardians seldom served as an upright example to any soul.

"I dragged him from the next set of treads, but he doesn't get my scarf."

Tull checked the coastline and reached into his pocket. "Flip you for who advances and who minds the perimeter."

"Why should we use your alms?"

"When do you travel prepared?"

Tim wrinkled his nose and spat.

"Fine, precious. My alms, your flip." Tull fished out three alms and tossed one toward him. Tim withdrew his hand, as though afraid, and let the alms follow the incline toward the sea.

"Not that one. Give me another one."

Tull set his jaw and tossed him another silver alms.

TULL

This time, Tim caught and held up the alms toward the firelight with an approving nod that cast his bangs over his eyes. He then stood, cracked his back, and stretched his shoulders. "This'll do. I should have enough for fare on the last trolley *and* a hot towel. Lucy's on the hem."

The western perimeter, where the sea and snow clashed, proved invisible from this ravaged locale, given the setting's sharp descent. Glass barbs sprang from the beach and buildings fell into the tide, then formed a false horizon that kept them divided from the most distant Guardian, Lucy Bright Moon.

"S'pose she caused that explosion?"

If she drew breath.

"Bet she did." Tim peeked at the alms he held. "But not a *big* bet. I called heads and . . . *look*. See?"

Tull nodded; not over Tim's attempt at humor or his cheating at an alms flip, but at the conditions around them. "Indeed."

He looked and saw how, in a moment, timeless evil upended eras of blood, pre-War architecture, relics from the Era of Despair, and a purpose that this current era never knew. The aftershock formed a perimeter against the Fallen First and rerouted the Loy River, which flowed now across the three-lane avenue, flooded two blocks, and crept toward the bodies of those the Jacobian had guarded.

Without an offering of help from Tim, the actual Guardian lifted the body of Buckler the inventor and set him against an overturned copper post. Buckler spent his inheritance on the design that cast frequencies through the land and reaped a fortune greater than his father's. He proved useless in chaos; inept in basic ways, squeamish toward the unsanitary, but no coward. Salt-laced ash, the sort that made Tim weep from discomfort, collected upon his remains and preserved him from their foe.

Rather than skewing Tim's purpose, regardless of a *rigged* toss, Tull acted on an urge for advancement. "Look for a perch to settle on while I—"

When he turned toward Tim, he found absence. He looked first in the direction of the hem. Then, behind him. In a faint smudge of color amid the salted snow, he saw Tim walking away from the battle. The Guardian's jaw went slack. All the spans he had kept the Guardians miserable whilst he pined for their title, and now he abandoned them.

"At times, I imagine he was the best reason for our pact."

TULL

An affable, confident voice drew Tull's attention to a well-shielded nook behind a fallen clock tower. There he noticed a blackened pool that shimmered with the reflection of one whose impeccable build and fashion sense set him apart from all other Guardians. Even the sweat-riddled reflection looked full of swagger. Olley Hendrie Falk deserved the title of outfit leader and, though his end circled him, he offered a light-hearted sneer for his barb against Tim.

"Then the giants came, and we realized we needed a runt to face them." Olley had the delivery of a soul accustomed to speech-giving, and of being listened to when he spoke. Still, even a simple soul noticed that he cast blood across his chest when he laughed. If he saw the moonset, his endurance would surprise both souls. "Correct me if I'm wrong, but I believe he took joy from an *upper-cruster*'s death. He shares your sense of inverted snobbery."

Tull kept silent, even as he tightened a bandage around his friend's arm.

Olley's murky, pearl-hued irises sparkled with realization as he fixed his gaze on Tull. "You weren't purposed to be here, let alone to *handle* field command."

"I've since felt regret."

His leader's square jaw set with gratitude. "You broke from my plan."

"Yes."

Olley sighed as Tull took the kerchief from around his neck and covered the wound nearest his heart. "You're impossible to reason with."

"'Impossible is an idea designed by the fear-filled to keep us from proving our dominance over them.'"

Both laughed till Olley groaned in pain. "Citing *Lefty* the *Apostle*? End me now, lest you mean to further cite him when you scatter me."

"I do have his collection of sonnets."

"All six deckled scraps!" Olley laughed and made the new arrival do the same. "We have lost George. Who else?"

"Pine, Myra, Buckler, and I've not seen Marko."

"You've towed the ash of my abettor by now. And, I fade." His nod of admission proved his feebleness. "Do They not know the help we need?"

Tull said nothing against his leader, the Ministers, or the Triune.

"Have you seen my bride this eve?"

"No."

TULL

"I heard a brutal scream toward the shore." His hand twitched as he pointed, but he no longer had full use of the limb. "The sound lacked her *chill*. Don't you tell her I said so."

"I would never. Lest I would." Tull held Olley's wrist, and the twitch of damaged nerves ceased. "I'll advance. No need for you to settle on a perch."

"Are you telling me?"

"I would never."

"Lest you would." Olley lifted his head and stared at Tull. Peace fell upon him and he confessed a flaw in his plan. "I let us stay too long. I believed They would help—"

Tull calmed him with another squeeze to his wrist.

The sensation of pressure reset Olley's focus and perked the clarity of his thoughts. "The blameless? You took them away?"

"Jules took them away. We're the last souls here. What say I find the doves and we get, too?"

"I thank you. Nelson . . ."

Tull listened, but Olley's next words and breath never flowed. He buttoned his friend's coat and wiped down his face. Olley would want his bride to see him in the best way, even at his end. The Jacobian spoke a prayer over the Archibaldian's body, then removed a knife from the blistered knee-high boot that settled in the crimson pool. He set the hilt in a still hand and adjusted the shoulder. "A gentle scoundrel till your end."

He let each fleck of ash and tear muddy him but kept his word to Olley and advanced. Toward the shore, he counted sweeps of the lantern against the buildings and listened for sounds of struggle. Doves or not, the two female Guardians fought in ways that made the most virile male shiver. None ever needed rescue them nor blush when they provided rescue.

Twenty paces nearer to the shore, Tull found the first of the pair. He knelt and touched the slender neck of Nita Naomi Ozul. Still warm, though her wide eyes spoke to her condition. Once as bright as fire, they now glazed over in her soul's absence. The bones of her legs pierced the fabric of her trousers in five places. Her dominant arm pierced the sleeve in two more places. Even broken, she would not cry for help.

With her unbroken limb, she had pushed a dagger into the low side of her abdomen, ruined their foe's scheme, and still clutched the hilt. Between her teeth, a leather sheath dulled her perceived scream. Tull held a scream of his own and applied a sure hand that removed the blade from her body. He returned weapon to sheath and fastened the clip to her belt.

He took the time to shut Nita's eyes, brushed down her face, hoisted her in his arms, then carried her uphill and placed her alongside her husband. He rested her head upon Olley's shoulder and straightened their legs afore them. The pose seemed worthy; at rest after spans spent running toward harm.

"Soon, I'll see you both."

Tull watched over his friends an added tick, gathered Nita's bow and quiver, then sought the second of the doves. Lucy Bright Moon, of the former Erori Territory, lumped raillery and injury on all. Olley, who professed a lack of imagination and an inability to resist Nita as his failings, believed Tull would meet his end a thousand times to keep safe the blameless. He designated Tull to oversee the last evacuations of his Archibald Territory whilst he and the others upheld their purpose at a tremendous cost by having Lucy serve as a scout in Tull's stead.

Their current foe bore the name *Seko'tae*, and boasted their purpose outshone all creation *beneath* the sky-fires. Scribes who saw their end afore the Era of Despair used names like *giants*, *titans of might*, and *Nephilim* as titles. The sons of the Mighty Creator *went into* the daughters of the secondkind, and those daughters bore fruit. The Seko'tae were the *fruit* of those pairings; two creations alive in one *new* form: an outcast creature that despised their own uniqueness.

Beneath the Moon of the Burning Morn, ten of thirteen moons ago, the Seko'tae awoke to take *more* brides and *more* daughters with help from traitorous conscripts. Thirteen hundred thirty-three fruit-bearing souls went missing from the territories since. From a population of five hundred eighty thousand, and those pummeled in the Seko'tae's wake, the loss devastated.

A foe who sought the secondkind's daughters entered unto death without hands or tongue. Tull held up the latter and inspected the jewel-tipped arrow that pierced through from the underside. The tongue's brass-coated, scarred edges showed the wear marks of lion-like teeth. The surface stank of acid-impregnated iron, which dissolved the arrow's pristine edge and stole his breath till he flung both muscle and weapon away.

He shut his eyes and sought guidance from one-third of the Triune. That member, called *the Helper*, dwelt within the secondkind yet oft went unheard by unsealed souls who pleaded for still more proof than all that surrounded them in the visible. Doubt, disbelief, rejection, and even commotion muted the purest voice. Tull learned to keep an attuned ear long afore he was named a scion to Guardian Perry Wallace Rudat.

"Seek the place where you last traveled with your mother."

The Jacobian exhausted his breath and opened his eyes. The Helper reminded him of the first soul who mystified him and she who turned his blamelessness into brokenness. Throughout his resets, he had lost count of how long he went through his everlasting purpose without her care. He let eternity hold their reunion, then thanked the Helper for he learned Lucy's present whereabouts.

"I give thanks and trust your guidance unto the Bellflower Signal House."

Though the judges forbade sea travel, the secondkind constructed signal houses that cast frequencies and a sweeping lantern to other potential survivors of the Accession. In Tull's time, no proven signal originated from outside the seven territories. Still, the Seko'tae wanted the signal houses destroyed. No soul proved why, though Buckler suspected the frequency cast the mingled creatures unto madness.

Weather's abrasiveness cut through every fiber with similar madness as Tull headed for the isolated coast. The voice of the wind howled at him and the stones that formed the town wept the tears of the ages—the tears of fallen souls who sought comfort. Such tears flowed black and dense like serpents and leeches; upright against gravity. In better times, when no creatures warred, Squires bottled those tears and offered them rest.

The haunting wind struck Tull like a hand, the terrane jarred him, but he kept onward. No longer distracted by such wonders, the Jacobian kept in prayer. Even with salt-stung eyes, he followed the path toward the place where now-blinded Noble Joe Massey last saw Tull's mother. With sound heart, Kara Doe Nelson's son marched toward a place he feared.

Where false light failed and sky-fires shone over the water-bloated glebe, he discovered a fallen Seko'tae member; feminine in shape, absent of hands and tongue. Opal ribbons blew from her scalp, and he tilted his head as he sought an identity. Then, the fallen lantern's light washed over him as flakes of snow pelted him and rinsed ash from the face of a foe. That same light reflected off the brass-inflected flesh along the nose and brow.

"Daughter of Ibn Ezra. *The First.*" There ended his eulogy.

Great silhouettes moved through the reflective brass and turned him toward the signal house. The tower sat toppled and flooded, with a still-working lantern. He shielded his eyes from the harsh light and tromped through the undertow on mire-blistered soles. The silhouettes cowered, chased away by a change in the wind's course and not his nearness.

He struggled with each breath as he waded through floating fires and let the elements adhere to him without risking his footfall. The glebe shook with such violence that the signal house tower rolled toward the tide and crushed the glass blossoms created by the wrath of the Ministers. Another disembodied howl saturated the air and made him brace. As the silhouettes fled, the change in path of falling snow directed his eyes to the place where Lucy Bright Moon battled.

"Lucy!"

He choked for breath as he scaled the broken back and shoulders of a creature three times his size, then discovered a headwound that sheared the skull. The lamp from an overturned floodlight pierced the creature's dimmed eye. He prodded the *spongy* eyeball, run through with a weapon that cauterized the wound tract. The Guardian perceived the *force* required for the feat and, for the first time that eve, appeared uncertain.

"Lucy!"

The sound of his voice provoked an outright scream, then the wind entwined her till she cast a red, phosphorous plume like firelight hemmed in lightning and *electrocuted* a third great creature, still unseen by Tull. He recognized little of his fellow Guardian. Amassed in scars and open wounds, the *remnants* of power that she bottled grew more ferocious than he imagined a body might withstand. The effect circulated beneath the ashen snow and brought the body of Ibn Ezra's daughter two heads off the ground when struck.

The aftershock burned away the ash and sent a tendril of lightning from the glebe. Identical tendrils arose and kept back the Guardian who went against orders. Lucy's eyes met his and showed recognition of the Jacobian. Then she bared her teeth and raised another fence of tendrils certain to stop a heart on contact. As he clutched his borrowed bow, movement in ash and smoke drew his eye.

TULL

His gaze shifted upward, where he expected the appearance of his foe's face. Then, he directed his gaze further up. His head tilted backward with such steepness that balance forced him to surrender one step. Tull fell on his knees in the presence of unblemished radiance shaped into the form of a creature who captured every worry of his heart.

"Enke'loi."

On the face of the Warring Minister, the scars of boiled tears from an ancient heartache absorbed the light that shone from within her brass form. No tears welled in her eyes, but she towed a sadness for the secondkind's plight. The fiery train of her form boiled the waters and isolated Tull's position on an island of cobblestone. Then a yowl of pain, like a mewing lion, made her bare her teeth as a swing of her fist reduced those stones around him to grit.

Tull looked upon the forearms scarred by the fingers of her siblings who once clawed for salvation to spare them from hope's abandonment. Her long fingers flowed without seam into the handle of a sword of fire and the shaft of a mace fitted with seven curved blades. Each blade dripped fire. Both weapons extended from the Warring Minister's forearms—not as separate devices, but as solid parts of her form.

He retained uncounted words, poems, proverbs, and prayers. Her presence kept him from every syllable. He looked away from her and across the field where the signal house once stood. Dizzying snow sought to blind his view but when he pawed at the flakes, he caught glimpses of Lucy's battle.

Between creating and hurling plumes of fire, her long motions glided not unlike a troupe of dancers. One limb slipped around the other, yet each performed a specific move; contrary to, but complemented by, the other limb. The steam that rose from her heated skin mingled with the vapor of her furious breath. She spared nothing for the moments that awaited *after* she eliminated her hated foe.

An unnatural gale upset the tendrils, forced collision, and created thunderous explosions that lit the eve and stung the eye. Lucy weaved from hips to shoulders, threatening and lethal. As the gale intensified, the snow and ash fell away from Tull and cleared a perimeter of exquisite circumference and cleanliness. Only then could he lament a pact between the Guardians that rolled away like the sea.

FOUR

"O Mighty Creator, strengthen my hand and forgive my aim."

Tull's voice, plucked from his lips by the chaotic winds and deprived of sound, drew the eyes of *his* protector. Her shoulders fell, and the sheen of her forearms ran dull. Her spirit settled her purpose for battle and the absolute compassion she lauded toward the Second Creation softened her flame. Her hand of burnished brass, now absent of weapon, rested atop the Guardian's head and kept him from harm.

She shielded him from every icy blast but made him observe Lucy's deeds. Tears filled his eyes and he longed for *blindness* rather than seeing even a foe fall. He wept as he prodded at his chest with his palm, expectant of what was to come. He dwelled on the next ticks of time's swift arms and imagined the land that awaited.

When he glanced unto Lucy's position, he saw a mammoth sword rise from the debris. The blade burned with fire on one edge and dripped brass upon the shore. A silhouette moved across the reflective metal and a veil of smoke billowed against the winds. Amid the distractions, any wielder went unseen.

Enke'loi reacted against the threat and raged with fire to defend Tull. The Warring Minister battled in rightness as their mutual Creator defined rightness. She deflected the sword with her mace and roared into the funneling wind. The veil of smoke and shadow screamed back at her then Lucy's voice followed.

"Pian Vi'emane horä!"

All this because she abhorred another's fruit.

"Pian Vi'emane—"

From the darkness along the coast, a sea of wailing voices cried out with a pain-filled shriek. The collar of Tull's shirt ran red as sudden and complete deafness *saved* him from the songs of war. Ash and snow accumulated as he shivered, and blinded him from what his heart could not bear. He reached out and plucked a blue monkshood flower from a sprout of grass and laughed with what little joy remained in him.

Plumes of light and fire filled the sky and a tentacle slammed against the fallen signal house tower. The percussive blast knocked the Jacobian sideways, but not off his knees. He collected instruments designed to defend the secondkind and latched the nocks of two bolts onto the string of Nita's bow. Whilst on his knees, ready to sacrifice purpose and foe, he spoke words he no longer heard except from his heart.

"Lord of the Poet King, from Your goodness You have allowed me a purpose of fulfillment." He rested both bolts between his index and middle fingers. "I thank You for Your unending mercies."

Tull rose, that he might see if Lucy stood, but his foot slipped on ice and pain shot upward from his knee to his hip. The abrasiveness of salt, sand, and ash battered the petals of the blue monkshood flower but could not upend the roots. He raised his shoulder, drew back on the bowstring, and held the arrows steady as his instincts aimed into the heart of smoke and shadow.

"I thank You, that You stifle the fires of my heart and make me anew."

Fire flashed like lightning from within a swirling funnel of snow and he let loose both arrows. A wave stood on the shore, like a figure in the shadows *daring* attention. As the sea crashed with the ferocity to wipe clean every trace of the secondkind, peace abounded. Between the crushing pain of falling droplets, a voice broke through the chaos and the Guardian's deafness.

"The Creator wills that you be spared, that you bear witness to the coming age, and prepare your siblings. From the Triune's great mercy, back you shall return; to a count of past breaths that number my brothers and my sisters."

Enke'loi's serene face changed as she arched her back and cradled him to her chest. She roared like a lion, and the mouth of the beast replaced her soft countenance.

"Do not be fearful, Son of Mighty Maidens, for the whole of heaven sings over you as afore and afore. But remember that the land shall not be for you as once you knew."

The scars of teardrops on her cheeks were all that remained. Such marks proved forgotten when she let loose a roar that consumed the great cry of death. Wandering spirits fled from her in fright. From will and promise, Enke'loi shielded Tull and delivered him backward into his past lest his end sealed the Era of the Guardians.

TULL

The oft-vilified sting of death neither broke the skin nor stole the breath. In that still and sudden last glint of time's measure by the secondkind's count, where the soul shed the finite body, the creature of divine fire kept safe the weary Guardian and held back eternity's tide. Her might shook the terrane and cast back the falling elements as she relocated Tull unto another time within his span.

Enke'loi transported neither a physical body, nor a mind. Rather, she harbored the soul, upon which the lessons and wisdom of a land he already knew, and a time he already endured, were written. There, the character resided. That she could rewrite that knowledge upon his younger soul in whatever instant their Mighty Creator willed offered him a chance to please the Triune.

She kept Tull from the judgment and in her obedience, she pleased their Creator. The body he shed no longer mattered, and the soul he overwrote gained a richness that other souls never imagined. Even if the land changed, hope abounded that the pains of that previous land were no more. His return to an earlier time let him steer others away from the choices and the changes that destroyed them.

So, she kept the Guardian's soul within her hand, protected by her brass exterior. There he gained no knowledge withheld from the secondkind, nor learned the ways of her mind or her heart. What pain he suffered and what heart he lost, she mended. This protected others he faced again from reprisal of uncommitted sins and unchosen paths.

As to her own travels, the land, like the sea, responded to the lick of Enke'loi's fiery train and extended them passage through seasons and changes past without tiring. The rotation of land increased in measure, as determined by the secondkind's sense of measure. Time fell back like granules, for such measure meant nothing there. She lived for the deliverance of one soul—approved by grace—and not the insight of souls who reveled in unbelief.

The Fallen First pursued her, so she took on a form like a lion. She girded her body with armor that no bite, no sting, and no thorn penetrated. In this form, she terrified those weakened spirits and those fallen siblings who feared the mere thought of her name. She traveled and never slowed.

TULL

Gales and storms sought to undo her path. A rush of wind nudged her, and rains washed away the established paths. So, she closed her eyes and trusted the Helper. She shed her distractors and pressed into the promise that the Creator she served and feared spoke unto her ear.

Yah, the Mighty Creator, formed all and reigned over all as head of the three-part *Triune*. He Who Pleased the Creator, I'Esh, also called the *Forever King*, traveled too, on an incomparable journey as the purest and most victorious example to the secondkind. From the Forever King's goodness flowed the third figure of the Triune. Reformers taught how the spirit of the Heir flowed like a mighty brook or a changing wind, but the Helper proved hardest of any voice to hear and the easiest to deny.

Why Tull found approval from the Triune went unanswered. Enke'loi and her siblings found the Jacobian slow to learn and quick to withhold. He who suffered nineteen resets afore he appreciated peace needed another nine till he practiced patience. He might see twenty-eight more till he accepted forgiveness. She remained watchful, nevertheless.

In silence, her actions proved her regard for the slow and stubborn Jacobian. She listened for her Creator and the chance to obey. She awaited a sign from the Forever King. All the while, she sensed the wisdom offered to her by the Helper who imparted purpose to her celestial traveler:

> *"Where you go, the path will not grow tender beneath your feet, but you are not abandoned on your journey. You will see this time from afar and will find the tools to forge a clearer path toward an unseen morn. Remember the promise, treasured soul, and trust. Stand prepared for the light's rising, and in the dark, lean upon your Creator, for He surrounds you evermore."*

Where Good Fell

An Interim

THE 23RD EVE BENEATH THE MOON OF THE OLD EMBERS

THE 114TH GATHERING SEASON OF THE ACCESSION

IN THE BLESSING OF I'ESH, WHO TENDS THE HARVEST.

BEACON 083.46.102 RECOGNIZED NEAR BLOOMING COPSE . . .
IDENTIFIER CONFIRMED—OLLEY HENDRIE FALK.
PURPOSED TO SERVE THE SECOND CREATION AS 21ST GUARDIAN.

"Tull, are you near?"

Olley Hendrie Falk—fearless, unmarred, and seven spans younger—smacked the ledge of a transparent glass composite layered with copper wires and contacts. Three small lights near the plate's belly went dim, then two more burned brighter. One flickered, and he smacked the device again. A map appeared on the face of the transparent screen and the lights earned names. From where he stood, the northernmost light showed the name of the soul he sought.

"I found an ancient tree that yielded decent plums and I picked us enough to chase away the taste of all this bitter ash we've swallowed for our judges. I must first see to this dust cloud to the south. The plume holds the strangest colors. How about you follow my orders for a change and stay where you are?"

He then sighed. "I believe we near a new morn. That's ten for you, old bear, and two less for me. Pine is going to be ratcheted up a few notches more than oft. He's down by three eves! Soon, I'll see you."

Olley pocketed the device, cinched the goggles around his face, and stared upward at a cloud of red granules that swarmed like gnats around the eyes of a young child. The leader of Guardians and abettors tightened the shred of a blouse that belonged to his bride around his nose and mouth and tucked the pointed tail into the neck of his shirt. His eyes seized on the formation, which held together so well that the surveilling projection-gliders could not penetrate.

"Only in Gutefiel."

Where good fell, the Fallen First flourished. They turned a once-pleasant settlement into an ash-trampled, drought-ridden plain. In that place, a thicket of burned-up trees formed a hem skirted by mountains to the east. The skies that loomed seemed never to shine in full portion but absorbed the firelight and battle scenes as easily as they stifled the sound of a scream with an ash blanket. Gutefiel withered that the secondkind might forget the place existed.

"Next time, *I* want to choose where we spend our offering."

Olley's handsome face soured with contempt when he stepped in something too malleable for inspection. He heard a hollow pang against the drought-struck ground, reached toward his hip and held still. A creature adorned in blistered skin ran at him with outstretched hands and twelve fingers sharpened to ragged claws.

With his right hand, he swung a sabre and cut away the creature's forearms. He then reversed, swung on a backhand, and sliced an angular neck. The creature fell to a knee, but the head struck a fallen, petrified branch and ricocheted backward. Olley turned and kept the loosed skull from impacting his groin or the satchel where he kept the plucked fruits.

"Best mind the plums." His thick brow arched when he inspected the fruit. He then remembered his soiled boot and smeared the blistered surface over the creature. The success of his cleaning impressed him. "I thank you."

The secondkind lived as spectators and eventual fodder in the firstkind's war. When an attack reached the surface, or the wayward fled in retreat, they turned against their *cousins*. In those moments, the secondkind relied on the Guardians to save them. Few relished their sense of purpose with more aplomb than Olley Hendrie Falk. In point of fact, all who observed the Guardian knew he kept one love above his love for attention.

"What say you, my bride? Fancy a trip to some hot pool where we can soak our wounds and I can revel over your unflawed skin?"

Nita offered no answer. That seldom kept him from conversing with her, though. Every Guardian from Lucy Bright Moon back to Beau Itzal Zeck conversed with some unseen soul. What raised concern from their audiences let them maintain their wit. For all they witnessed, with proved as precious as water and light.

The Fallen First haunted, agitated, possessed, tormented, and infested as means of distraction, ambushing their mighty siblings and preying upon the Creator's *lesser* works. They also warred with one another—fallen sibling against fallen sibling. They reveled in madness the way Olley reveled in adoration for his bride. His all-consuming love *deserved* every attention from him, even in her absence.

Those who flourished in harm's way invited trouble from oft-reckless, seldom cunning rabble-rousers. The judges referred to them—the flourishers—as *Guardians*. From time to time, these trouble seekers corralled the fallen into prisons, trapped them with archaic symbols, shackled them with ancient ores, and deafened them with forgotten prayers. Elsewise, they left them to the Ministers and Squires.

Olley preferred sharp weapons and long-winded tales that oft heaped praise on his own head. He set a lofty gauge for his ability to boast and to wear down foes—and some fellows—through ceaseless storytelling. By his fourth morn in Gutefiel, every soul trapped in the offering disengaged their listening gear; save the soul he shared fruit with. Even his bride cut him off after the second eve, too fearful that he might take his mind off his duties to flirt with her.

He swatted at the branch of a petrified tree and cast loose a hobbyist's projection-glider. The noise the lightweight copper craft made against the hardened roots startled a creature of size comparable to popular house pets. The Guardian from the Archibald Territory flicked his wrist, sliced upward, and cut the tattered wing from that same creature.

When that now wing-less creature hissed at him, he answered back, "I believe I know your sister. Light-hearted lass. Shiny complexion."

He then withdrew a railroad spike from his dangling suspenders and hurled the sharpened fastener at the belly of the creature. The flame-and-hammer-sharpened edge pierced one tar-black gut and rank, lemon-yellow bile poured out. Even with a shred of Nita's blouse covering his nose, he pressed his hand tighter across his face.

"Worse than watching a Partaker feast!"

The smells never improved. He loathed the stench of the unclean. Those who opposed him bore a list of names from those who fretted over pristine surfaces and rotted within. Olley disliked that group, though they proved most meddlesome to the ways and means he guarded them.

TULL

He thought no more of smells nor privileges; nor his bride's unflawed skin. He stood at the hem, where an unseen force tore open the terrane and cast granules upward into a cloud. Within that cloud, he might find the Fallen First or *Partaker*, *Infested*, *Wanderer*, or, most cast away of all, *Forsaken*. None frightened him, and he maintained his barrel-chested swagger as he stepped into the formation.

The Infested were the most tortured amid Partakers. As proof of their stance against the Triune, they let into their bodies the wandering spirits of the Fallen First. Most were too innocent and too immature to discern the perils of their choice. Disobedience to their purpose brought pain and cast them unto a darkness wherein rejecting their Creator seemed good. Few realized the count of spirits a lone body held.

When a wandering spirit fled, destruction and disrepair marked the spent vessel. Wanderers forced a way out of every orifice with a violent punch. The flesh of the Infested creature ripped apart from within. They gnashed their teeth hard enough to fracture them. Even the tear ducts, sinuses, and saliva glands failed.

Two survivors of the infestation stood beneath the red, granular cloud and in a garden of ash and petrified woods; as bare as the moments of their births. Their marred bodies turned the stomachs of more than they aroused—at least in their true form. She, and two-fifths of the territories, was born of two of their three races. She blanched her hair and her skin to bury all she hated about her mother and her mother's blood.

The pair of trousers she fitted around her long legs belonged to a willowy admirer–not the soul at arm's length—who favored the version of her that he knew; a version *masked* by the illusion of si'ir touomo granules and an ironclad will. Her spine and shoulder blades jutted when she bent down for her boots, and her long tresses scraped the blades of trampled grass.

She towed hundreds of scars upon her body, but only one sickened the soul who watched her dress. His hand, broken, set, and rebroken on an uncounted cycle during his own infestation, traced a scar beneath an ink print. When he touched her, goose pebbles filled the gaps between the other scars.

"I'll miss the look of this face."

"I can't remember her." She rose and let her hair conceal her torso.

His blood-red eyes shifted onto the scars that adorned her ears. "You say that to hurt me, do you not?"

"I've forgotten the way you once looked. Why should I remember me?"

He mewed and kept her from kissing him. "Time proves impatient. Help me, won't you?"

She found the bandages in his hand, unfurled the first, and started masking his face. The fabric, singed by mire and stained with decay, had lost elasticity. "Soon these will fail. You'll need a better disguise."

He took from her belongings a long, hand-knit scarf and smiled at her with broken teeth and blood-flaked lips.

"I remember when I made that."

"As do I. I watched and imagined what thoughts troubled you."

"My own end." Her own lips held their form better, though their scars muddled her ability to pronounce a crisp *S*-sound. Though she loved him, she held onto a wickedness that delighted in prickling his belief in her affection. "I oft feared I would live so long."

"Is that a regret?"

She squeezed his jaw till she stilled him, smoothed down the bandage, and looped the last feathery drape over the crown of his wavy hair. One pass, then a second. Midway through the third, she let free her answer. "Most oft."

He tweaked her breast and snagged her tresses on a sharp bone tied around his wrist. A tooth from his own mouth gathered strands of her hair and drew another curse from her lips. He pulled away from her by arching his back and finished covering his face without her. If able to produce tears, she still refused.

"You believed elsewise?" She pulled the first of two blouses over her head and adjusted the sleeves against her lean forearms. She trapped the billowy fabric in a beneath-the-bust corset fitted with sheaths of hiltless knives. "I've dreamt of my end since my blamelessness ceased."

"Lucy?"

Lucy Bright Moon spun on her heel and, with a splayed hand, pushed her concealed lover toward the shadows beneath the tree.

Not one for dismissal, he stepped back into the open and observed her lithesome admirer. "Celibate Marko Glenn Stran! What's he doing here?"

"I haven't a clue." She nudged past her lover and approached the intruder, whose trousers she wore. "You're not a Guardian. You're not allowed here."

"I . . ." He hesitated and looked upon her true face, forgot his words, then propped his stance with a coward's valiance. "I feared for you."

"Who asked for such regard from you? *Get!*"

"Did you see my face?" The voice behind her rose to an indecent pitch and threatened Marko. "Did you see my face? Tell me!"

"I saw."

The trio spun toward Olley, who stood with goggles and saber in hand. His handsome face never appeared more solemn or dissatisfied. Lucy cursed in her mother's tongue and her lover swelled with rage.

"A regret I tow as much as any mirror you pass. I counted three actual rats fleeing from you as I set foot beneath this cloud. The scarves are an improvement. Dreadful by their own design, tacky even by your low standards, but truly an improvement!"

Only one pleaded, "Please! Olley, sir! I feared—"

"For *her*. Yes, I did hear. I warned you long ago that she had no interest in you, Marko. As my abettor, you should've heeded my word. Now, here we stand." He looked toward Lucy's riled lover. "*Again.*"

Lucy panicked. "He'll bring others!"

"Why would I involve others"—Olley tossed aside the saber of an ancestor and rolled up his sleeves—"when I can turn that mash you call a face to pulp and not lose my breath?"

When her lover—a dirty and rough fighter—stepped toward Olley, Lucy pulled back at him.

"Release the fool! Before I end him, he can tell me how he goes uncounted on my display plate."

Lucy regarded her fellow Guardian's might and, more than once, admired the look of him when he went without a shirt. The arm she seized pushed her backward and Marko kept her from falling.

Her lover scolded her. "Deal with *him!*"

Lucy and Marko watched the exchange of punches till the sounds of pummeling fists sickened them. The abettor lunged in defense of Olley, and Lucy found her desire to keep safe her lover. Marko's arms proved smaller, softer, and she wrangled him with ease. When he resisted, she leapt upon his back and proved she too fought dirty.

TULL

With her forearm around Marko's neck and her thighs against his sides, she contained what breath he held. She then hammered the side of his head with a closed fist. He wept. They fell into the ash and she kneed him along the spine as she crawled toward the pack she had discarded when she met her lover in the garden of ash.

Red grit went airborne as she opened the flap and took a rolled sleeve of cannisters. She drove a knee into the small of Marko's back, clutched his neck, and unfurled the sleeve. Her hand swatted at the grit and ash that all the activity churned, and she struggled to read the labels on every cannister. While the two brutes wrestled on the ground and kept one another from reaching Olley's saber, Lucy plucked a single cannister.

"I know this won't comfort you, Marko, but I like you. Blame your poor timing; that you found me when I've devoted too much to waste on a simple abettor."

She separated the lid from the cannister with one hand and pulled back Marko's head with the other. The strain on his neck forced open his mouth; the intended target. She held the cannister to his teeth and a forceful gust knocked her away from him. Her hand bled from the shredded cannister, and she gathered the waste into her satchel while the abettor flopped in a cloud of ash.

Her eyes beheld the overpowering of the weaker soul by the wandering spirit that remade Marko into a vessel. She went through the same fight, but the way that the abettor buckled and submitted chilled her. He had no threshold for pain, and she showed no regret over what she forced upon him.

The mind perceived a scream so horrid that most overpowered souls broke their bodies in an effort to flee what took over them. During her transformation, she broke her hips and her hands. Her lover broke his collar bone, his arm, and his foot. The curiosity over what damage awaited Marko elated and sickened her. Then, she received her answer.

"No more! Let me hear no more!" With more strength than she accredited him, Olley's abettor tore away his ears. The first ear she shrugged off, but the way he tore off the second ear garnered her respect.

"Marko!"

Olley's guttural lament for his abettor and the way he cursed Lucy cost him the advantage in his own fight. Her bandaged lover claimed the saber and sliced. The muscular torso of a boastful Guardian split open and Olley fell.

"*Nita . . .*"

TULL

Marko's screams almost deprived Lucy from hearing Olley's call to his bride. In turn, she gathered a handful of ash and sought to choke the sound. She packed her victim's mouth with the ash and clasped shut his jaw with all her might. The teeth within broke and she hid her face rather than see the plea in his eyes.

"If you wake from this, remember, I know what you hold closest to your heart." Olley's foe then used his weight and severed the ring finger from the Guardian's hand with the saber. He collected his trophy from the flow of blood and kept the saber, too. "O, Marko . . . Marko."

Lucy stared at her lover as he crouched down and toyed with Marko's wounds.

"There is a mirage. Can you see? There, *within* your Guardian, I tell you, is water. Drink from him. Drown the screaming." He tossed the saber aside, clutched the abettor's lapels, and flung him toward the Guardian he served. "Drink, till your gut bursts! Marko . . . *Marko.*"

Lucy stood still in the aftershock whilst her lover selected what relics he wanted besides Olley's saber and ring finger. The soul ashamed of his own face kept a peculiar habit of trophy-taking. He even kept the spoiled cannister that cut open his lover's hand. Though he spurned her without a farewell—driven mad by her imagined infidelities—she chased after him. They turned Olley defenseless against his now-corrupted abettor, who believed him an oasis for the ash that Lucy used to stifle him.

NELSON JAMES TULL

Tull's inkwork paraphrases verses of the Old and the New Testaments and tie an ancestral thread between two souls found in the Scriptures, Psalm 62:1 and Matthew 28:20. Our tale's hero began out of appreciation for an unnamed anti-hero from a famous novella that inspired the dream of time travel. This character's purpose is to serve as a traveler through a genealogy that connects the paths of seven primary characters and hundreds of supporting characters across an interwoven mythos. Aided by Tull's wisdom, we who travel alongside will meet creatures of monstrous and magnificent sorts in this time of the Accession.

31

FIVE

THE 23RD MORN BENEATH THE MOON OF THE OLD EMBERS
THE 114TH GATHERING SEASON OF THE ACCESSION
IN THE BLESSING OF I'ESH, WHO TENDS THE HARVEST.

<u>SEVEN POOLS</u>
A FORMER LAKE TURNED DRY BY THE GUTEFIEL FIRES.
SHELTERED FROM THE ASH PITS OF THE FALLEN FIRST.

Enke'loi stopped *between* moments of turning and increase in Tull's purpose. Though she stood far from the warring of that previous land, she remained there too. The soul of the secondkind shed the body, but the firstkind *divided* and existed across time—entuned evermore and held together by their Creator. She neither vanished from nor existed in a single land, but in *every* land.

Her form changed again, and she twisted till she protected the Jacobian from harm in his thirty-first reset. A scarred hand flowed between the threads of his clothing and touched his chest. Brass ran across him like a trickle of water and created a path of light upon his body as the soul she towed entwined with the soul in present form, overwriting and honing a *refined* soul. Truth corrected memory, hope mended hurt, obedience replaced sin, and wisdom educated pride.

Whilst held by an unseeing eye and an undiscerning spirit, the bandaged soul who swatted Olley approached in a cloak of shadows. He observed the body that rested, and pecked the hilt of the saber with the split nail of his thumb. Though the Guardian made an easy target, this cruel foe withheld. Whatever debate raged within him, he let the feel of the saber satisfy his fingers.

TULL

The mere hint of trouble made Enke'loi's lower teeth jut from her mouth. Her free hand formed the shaft and ball of a mace, but not the fiery blades. A bed of fire flowed from her train and she set her eyes upon those siblings she found *within* the trespasser. Her open hand never fell from Tull's body, but fire rose in her eyes as her voice settled the breeze.

"Jäi'toä, vyli'eni."

Though she remained hidden from him, his fingers rested on the hilt. "Time to rise, brother."

Enke'loi roared and snapped her teeth near his face. The wandering spirit that agitated Enke'loi took form and seeped from the scarves that disguised Lucy's lover. In response, the winds swirled and the rocks cried out the name of their Creator. The Infested spirit retreated into the body, the trespasser retreated, and Enke'loi finished the amendment of souls.

Departing footsteps pounded ash and called for Tull's instincts to stir him. The brass that shielded his soul returned to Enke'loi and her mace retreated into her other arm. When she clapped her hands, every speck of dust settled and an isolated flame surged. Afore the sound of her clap ceased, the fourth soul who guarded the Jacoby Territory opened his eyes on this land. Light surged in him and his irises dimmed, like cooling bronze, as his soul was rewritten and reshaped by that previous land for a truer interpretation of this land.

"Only You return my soul." Tull kept the unfinished prayer of that previous land upon his lips. With that prayer, the past seven spans stood anew, awaiting his choice in living them again.

While he considered his choice, he watched the ocean of fire in the sky where warring siblings swam in battle that would follow I'Esh's return and seal Ki'eoppa at time's end. In this age, the sparks of war burst as flecks of brilliant light within the sky-fires; better than any display seen by the created eye. This era never witnessed light's absence in the eve. They never witnessed the blotting of the sky-fires, the tide that never found shore, or the stars that waited beyond.

He dragged his palm across his chest and wiped down his face. A crackling of flame drew his attention toward his washed, bare feet and a small fire, burning without wood, that warmed him. In the shadow of a myrtle tree, opposite a trail of boot prints, a choir of brass figures smiled upon him and ascended with Enke'loi without disturbing one branch or one flake of ash.

TULL

Blood-curdling voices wailed and creatures fell on their bellies in response. Tull marveled over that feat till his nostrils stung. The stench of tart mire and bitter ash confirmed his whereabouts, as certain as any map. "*Gutefiel.* Bleeding on Ebbe Demesne was more pleasant to me than Gutefiel."

In his thirty-first span, beneath the Moon of the Old Embers, the judges ordered a celebration for their *serving* the secondkind. An *offering* for their enjoyment set every living Guardian—save one—in the place where they suffered their worst defeat. Few learned that the judges also *arranged* the offering as payback for the thorny behavior of the Guardians and the rule they—Tull included—oft criticized.

Considering thorns, a sting in Tull's hip throbbed. He groaned as he shifted off the meat of his leg and claimed Guardian Beau Itzal Zeck's campaign medal from his pocket. Still in his possession in this land, and intact enough that an embossed face remained distinguishable, the medal produced more than an ache in his muscle. Tears formed in his eyes for the tender soul who waited on him in that previous land, and he kissed the face of the memento.

"Soon, I'll see you, partner." A screech in the distance took away his breath and gave him cause to pocket Zeck's medal. He then fitted his socks and boots onto his bare feet. "Of all the ticks in my time. . ."

A harsh light blinded him in response to his deep voice, and he bowed sideways till the branch of a once-proud, now petrified, myrtle tree shielded him. Cheers erupted in the distance and the sound of applause followed like a thunderhead. An aerial projection-glider broadcast the activities of the Second Creation nonstop, as if an extension of the warring above, and as proof to the secondkind that their Guardians protected and entertained them.

He knew not the count of eves that passed since his entry into Gutefiel, nor the whereabouts of his friends. He bore the memory of entering Gutefiel alone on the first eve of the offering. The memories of this time caught up to him, though, and mingled with those memories he kept from that previous land.

Enke'loi compared time—the secondkind's declaration of time, anyway—to grains of sand on the seashore. Relocate one grain and the sea still found the shore. Moving one soul through time, despite the secondkind's amusing certainty, played little effect on creation's longevity. His relocation—the resetting of his time—allowed more time for the secondkind to accept Yah's purpose, to seek their Creator, and to prepare the hearts of other souls for what awaited them in lands Tull observed.

TULL

He remembered the crashing tide at Malachi's Vine; more abrasive than the ashen field beneath him. The softness of Q. J.'s voice teased his ear, much like the haunted breeze that cooled him. Even the salt from Hazy's teardrop reminded him of something purer than the mire he breathed. He missed their arms around his neck and their laughter in his ear. He missed the amethyst pools of Jules's eyes.

Seven Pools made him pray that, in that previous land, the trio reached safety together. *Without him.* In this land, Hazy enjoyed her fifth span; not thirteen moons till Q. J. arrived and turned her reign contrary. Even now he found memories of them worth chuckling over, but their *absence* produced an invisible grip within his chest.

"Be still and discern."

The Guardian trembled but the Helper's unheard voice, a wisdom that spoke to his soul, brought him peace as the flame brought warmth. Stillness fell on him like the crashing wave that took his body from that previous land.

"From Firstborn to last, preserve all who reason.
In this you please your Creator."

Tull needed time to perceive the scope of the Helper's guidance but focused on the grace that kept him *from* his end. He called his purpose *everlasting*. He aged, he suffered injury and shame, but he never entered eternity. In gratitude, he wept for mercies anew as the words but not the stillness of the Helper faded.

When he wept no more, he discovered a meal awaited him. Every time, he awoke to find a cup of the cleanest, coolest water and two fragrant cakes—no larger than the palm of his hand in measure—set upon a warm stone. The cornmeal and honey nourished him in full, gave him awareness of his choices, and washed away the sting of every mistake from the previous land.

With his first bite, another single wail pierced the eve and brought to Tull's mind that previous land. The sound haunted; still, he smiled. Another remained in Gutefiel with him; at least one. He needed now the strength to find them and chewed the first fragrant cake.

He heard a muddled voice, but his perception of the words spoken failed. A silhouette in the falling ash loomed, as if unsure of him too. Tull finished the first cake in three large bites, drank down one-fourth of the water, and took an anticipatory breath. "Aan'a aromoa lu'ok seni . . ."

A cold-eyed soul with silvering hair cropped close to the scalp and hands blistered in scars approached the fire. As he welcomed the heat, Guardian Robbie Rudat Pine never noticed an absence of firewood. "I tell you, 'Eight more eves till Hivi'ern!' S'pose you can sleep till then? I can! That prickly misborn soul who devised our offering best choose a more derelict hole than this to challenge me!"

While Pine grumbled against the locale chosen by Judge Hansel Ornlam Hofnarr, Tull performed basic subtraction in his mind. Eight eves till the Feast of Hivi'ern meant his less-changed soul entered Gutefiel seven moonrises ago. Even after all that ended his stay in that previous land, he remembered entering Gutefiel in this land. He remembered, too, that this Hivi'ern marked the first for Hazy to wear a gown of purple fabric in observance of her fifth winter.

Pine sniffed and spat. "I tell you, that weak-kneed, velvet-bellied excuse of a judge who imagines he's our better has nothing on the *wastes* of space, the *products* of inbreeding, that made this place their home."

Tull sipped more water but kept from his next bite of dense cake.

"You ask me, we ought to make our judges spend an eve in this ash."

The ever-modest Robbie Rudat Pine appeared lighter in spirit than in that previous land; not that Pine enjoyed much distinction across lands.

"I tell you, old Cameron Lou Fenner ran for the gates midway through his first eve! More like *limped.*" He missed the wood but noticed the cake. "Whilst you passed this eve baking!"

"Keep from that."

As he oft proved, Pine followed his whims and snaked the rest of the second cake from the stone anyway. What tasted as sweet as honey in Tull's mouth turned astringent on his friend's tongue. Soon, the thief's bite burned his mouth and throat like poison. The talker fell to one knee and forced vomit to salve the pain.

Tull laughed with delight. "If that's not a testament of your way."

"What's that—"

"Fall!"

Tull flung the warm stone and Pine dropped into his own vomit. The stone struck a spider-like creature, once a herald in the Triune's court. Two of six scorched wings entangled the herald's broken feet, and the weight of the stone toppled the creature upon the ash field. A spasm of the wings strove but earned no escape.

The force of the stone pinned the befallen creature and caused a shrill, pained wheeze. Tull noticed the once-beautiful creature's eyes, now gouged out and scarred along the socket rims like spent candles. The creature writhed against the ground in a desperate attempt to flee but the weight of the stone entangled those deformed wings in drought-struck grass. Only Pine laughed.

"Look! The worm can't lift the rock. That trick never ages."

Tull discovered and stuffed a portion of uneaten cake into his mouth. Rather than chewing, he filled his mouth with the remnants of water and swallowed. With that one portion, he gained discernment and insight worth another span in his purpose. For that reason, he used caution when he brushed crumbs from his lips and into his mouth.

"Why you won't end these wretches reaches beyond my wit.." Pine plucked a glass lighter from his pocket, lit the wick, and tossed the open flame over his shoulder, which burned the creature. "Does our purpose excite you no more?"

Tull offered him his canteen over an answer.

"What? You can't handle the smell of puke-breath?"

"Your tongue's gone to tar."

"Ah! All this bitter ash we've sucked in—"

The Jacobian let his clean tongue waggle over his ash-dusted chin. "I told you not to eat the cake."

Water spilled down the mouthy Larsonite's face and neck while Tull pulled the warm stone from the burning mire. Neither the fire nor the flaming innards burned his bare hands. He placed the flat stone down, then slipped a knife from the sheath strapped around Pine's ankle.

With the butt of the knife, he broke the rock into seven pieces; each one bite-sized when compared to the size of the two cakes. He flung the knife upward, caught the tip, and watched Pine's reflection move along the blade. As one sheathed the weapon, the other pocketed the seven stones. The Jacobian then shielded his ears, nose, and mouth with a worn, red balaclava.

"If you've rested, we should see who else we can find."

"If *I've* rested? I landed a kill!"

"Hence my offering you rest."

TULL

"I don't need rest."

"Then why are you standing still?" Tull's cheeks shifted the fabric around his face when he grinned. He led Pine through abandoned Gutefiel, outpacing he who entered the offering three eves after him.

Pine caught up to him, but struggled to match his stride, given he stood one head shorter than Tull. "Where are we headed?"

"I heard a scream from over that way. Our kind."

"I didn't hear—"

Pine dove sideways and Tull hooked his limbs around a tree branch. An imbued elk ran through the path they followed. The creature's eyes shimmered with brilliant, orange hues offset by the rich, cocoa-hued coat that rippled with firelight as the spirit within stirred. Even the twisted antlers suggested an evil vying for control and cleared a path as four proud hooves stomped through the ash fields.

"That beast's made passes at me the last four eves." Pine dusted his knife and watched Tull land with a crouch. "Imagine if that beast ended up on George's farm!"

Both chuckled, and the sound drew the befallen closer. Five depraved creatures, each of once-unflawed shape, encircled. Their twisted bodies, mangled by falling and warring, corrupted their beauty and gave each a deformed visage. Thirteen orange eyes dripped tears of mire.

"My turn!"

Pine swiped, lunged, and knocked down each creature while Tull set a stone piece upon every back. Not one retained the ability to discard the stone and remove their burden. The spirit-infested elk charged back toward Pine, but Tull rammed the hindquarter with his shoulder and toppled the creature sideways. As he too stumbled away, he placed a broken stone atop the ridged head of Pine's taunter.

"I said—"

The legs trembled, then the jaw and breast of the elk scraped the ground and folded the creature's body into the ash alongside another of Yah's creations.

"I ought to—"

"Put away your knife." Tull chucked aside the last stone piece. "Lucy . . ."

Pine waited till he passed, kept his knife free, and ignored Tull's instruction a second time. He kept the blade gripped whilst Tull checked the length of her spine for injury. His gentle touch jolted her and startled Pine, who gasped and shook off his fright till he circled around with mock composure.

TULL

"Turn away."

Pine delayed till a stern glance reinforced Tull's request. He scoffed, but heeded him. Tull plucked a teardrop-shaped glass from the ash between his feet and the hand of she whom he saw last in that previous land. The tart, synthetic odor of a cosmetic salve wafted and he saw the scars fade from her slippery hand. Lucy's eyes gleamed like an eve without the moon, then with one breath, she lifted her torso from the ash. When she slung her head back, she revealed a fresh imprint of a fist across her jaw; which Tull compared to Pine's hand size by eye.

"Keep your barbs and trinkets," Pine protested with all his charm. "I wouldn't waste the water needed to wash her off my knuckles."

As Pine spat more of the tar-like bile that coated his mouth, Tull caught a mindful glint in the eyes of the insulted soul afore the imprint vanished. Her skin turned smooth, then her brow, eyes, and lips appeared unflawed. Three si'ir touomo granules lasted two moon cycles but cost one thousand alms and a hike into the mountains above the Taotáva and their knotted caves. A synthetic substitute cost thirty alms and lasted one moon cycle; lest a soul spend time in a place like Gutefiel. She, whose abettor purchased an ampoule for every moon of the span, stayed too long, and her *true* face resurfaced.

As her structure settled, she looked upon the face she had scarred with her fingernails afore he knew her name. "You stare."

"Your nose bleeds."

The fearsome huntress wiped the effect of too much salve and disturbed the small ceramic hoop in her septum. Neither spoke of what brought them to their reunion.

"Are you well?" Tull's voice soothed even Pine.

"Unlike you, I've never desired a mother, Nelson." Without gratitude, Lucy nudged him away, dusted off, and walked alone. Still, she behaved better whilst on the salve.

"*Friend?*" The mouthy Guardian's throaty voice, imbued with a shrill, creature-like grumble of humor, teased the response. Pine then flicked his brow. "Good to see she doesn't shed her bristles when she blooms."

Lucy retorted when she stooped and flung Tull's cast stone piece and struck Pine's lowest rib.

"Has to be the head shock." Still, he rubbed the spot she struck.

TULL

Tull inhaled against Pine's barb but remembered Lucy's rage, as he had witnessed in that previous land. "Be merciful."

"No time!"

The way the trio clustered enticed a swarm of other creatures. Though they had used the ploy to tremendous success in the past, this time found each of them addled. In no mood to deal with the swarm or the looming ash cloud, Lucy proved why others allowed her unsavory insolence. Tull heard her first, the way she muttered in a language she seldom spoke, then pulled Pine to one knee.

The terrane shook, and a gust of air sprang from her position. Her grief-filled scream blasted outward like a gale, which upended the swarm and cut a path in the ash field. Even the now-visible spectators who watched from outside the fenced-in remnants of Gutefiel braced their stances, with more than one knocked down. Then, in balance, Lucy fell backward like a cast leaf and the one who returned to this land caught her as unconsciousness silenced her.

Pine went from throat to throat and collected kills from Lucy's exertion. "I'd like to use this time and call bull—"

"No."

"Well, I do! I tell you, she brims with head shock from letting in what-all! Makes the creeps rush over me. Imagine how the honored ones must want to be rid of her!" Pine looked over at Tull. "By *honored ones* I mean our judges."

SIX

Tull proved his soul's patience and ignored Pine till his subordinate took notice of what interested him more than rambling. The ash and red, granular haze above lingered, but never blocked the path out of the offering. In point of fact, nothing moved against them on foot or breeze. Tull shook his head, as his eves and spans from other lands mingled, and looked upon Lucy as he considered her behavior at the Bellflower Signal House in the previous watch and, now, in Gutefiel.

"What do you make of that?" Pine looked mistrustful of the stillness.

"Depart from this place."

"I said—"

"We've stayed too long." Olley's regret haunted Tull from that previous land. Heartening their legends or leading the outfit well in the eyes of the judges meant nothing versus shielding his fellows. "The time's come when we walk out now."

"I tell you; keep running *from* the battle and souls might say you resemble Barton Blinken Ganix."

Tull overlooked the barb. "The three of us will leave now. In your heart, you—"

"My heart? My heart! You s'pose I do any of this by what's in my heart? This is where I belong. I'm not you. This is who I—"

Tull sucker-punched him. No warning, no compunction, and not even a prayer of repentance. The Jacobian proved his own short fuse this time, however justified his hot-headed friend made him. "And, that's your flaw."

As Pine fell toward him, he swept him away and protected Lucy. Though both remained unconscious, he spoke to she who saw him last in the previous land. "Still somewhat woozy. Should I drop you between here and there, I'll let pass your anger toward me. I needed both cakes."

A remote-operated projection-glider fitted with nine intrusive bulbs hovered and drew a scornful glance from the Jacobian. Nothing gave away a position better than shining lights. But, at least those *outside* Gutefiel found amusement. The lenses focused, and the microphones shifted to accommodate his posture.

"Keep talking to your own ears; let the territories imagine you've turned loon."

Woozy or not, he draped Lucy across his shoulder. The cove of her hip bone rested against his collar bone and she shielded his expression from the pair of projection-gliders that now concentrated on his activity. He held onto the ankle of her boot, then clutched Pine's wrist. True to form, the Larsonite still held his dagger.

Tull obeyed the Helper and proved his *use* in assisting two troubled souls away from further agitation. He ignored the gathering projection-gliders and trusted he walked a path that would not let him stumble or find harm. As the fallen sensed his obedience, their jeering voices arose. Other spectators who watched from the foothills that bled into Gutefiel cheered him on.

If he fell, his belief meant nothing. The elusive and ever-critical naysayers would invest in ways to disprove his belief and affirm the rightness of their criticism. His belief held him; not the other way around. He knew what awaited and recalled who trembled.

Every soul knew of the First Creation. That some saw and still refused belief divided souls from purpose, acceptance, and their families. On this eve, amid their amusement and screaming, all watched a *known* Believer haul one stone heart and one *former* member of the Infested from harm. At least one judge would hate him for that.

Tull cast an eyeful of anger toward the *fourth* projection-glider that surrounded him. The added light, mingled with a noisy propeller, drew the eye of a creature that slithered over the broken rocks that formed the glebe. A bloated gut pressed against two sets of hind legs and dragged the rock, which produced an odor of spent matchsticks. He still towed no regret for his strike against Pine.

Squires—creatures of a scale smaller than the Ministers—moved like darts across the sky-fires. They pushed back against their fallen elder and cleared a wider path for the Guardian and his fellows. The breath of a roaring beast withered the shell of one glider. Tull nodded in gratitude and made use of the opportunity.

TULL

When he saw the keepers pull open the triple gates, his obedience lightened the weight he hauled. He represented an end of the offering. With Gutefiel to his back, he faced the purpose upon him and his thirty-first chance to right his way. He believed that he proved his usefulness, and he cast out the disturbances.

Tull's eye sifted through the ash cloud that rose from the opening gates and fixed upon what looked like a mirage. The purest smile ever to grace the secondkind swayed with a praise-filled sound of laughter deep from within a slender belly. That jovial soul—taller than Tull remembered him—had a gleam in his eyes that not even Gutefiel dimmed. Such a sight brought joy to the Jacobian.

"George!"

"My friend! I see you have watched over our fellows."

Tull considered Arthur George Green the most honest soul in the territories and kept their friendship with gladness. The Guardian from the Weston Territory—who answered to his middle name—stood as the first soul cast from the offering. Not that he was weak or fearful. Rather, George possessed tremendous empathy, and the Fallen First preyed on empathy. That he lasted more than an eve served as a testament to his bravery and loyalty.

He dragged Pine across the threshold of the gate and through a fragrant bath that cleansed the surface of attached spirits. When no danger fell on his soul, and once Pine was on the other side of that gate, George looked to the Jacobian who slipped Lucy's body down his arm and placed her on the wet ash. By the law, George never reached back across the barrier of Gutefiel.

"I have water for you both." He tossed Tull his canteen. "Drink!"

Tull sipped, but used the rest of his portion to clean Lucy's eyes. Heavy, red grit sullied his fingertips and brushed against his pant leg. His eyes met George's, and the Westonian offered him a clean cloth as a rag. Neither spoke of the red grit.

"Guardian Tull!" A voice powered by thick, flapping arms rose and cast away his caller's integrity. "Guardian Tull! I am Charles Campbell Upson. I am Thesp Phinn Derek Wade's intercessor! My benefactor—"

"This isn't the last of them!" An interruptive bystander fielded a stern glance from the oft-upbeat George, who pulled Lucy through the same bath as Pine and noticed the sullied waters as Tull pushed her.

"Guardian Tull! I say, Thesp Phinn Derek Wade sends—"

Tull took a half-step backward. "Who hasn't come through?"

TULL

"Guardian Tull!"

"Olley remains, but Marko appeared within this eve." George tossed a transparent display plate detailing their whereabouts to Tull. "I lost his beacon when he passed under the red cloud."

"Who prepped him?"

"No soul dares."

"I say, your friend Phinn Derek Wade sends alms, Guardian Tull!"

Tull sighed with a profane harshness. "Upson, you said?"

Acknowledgment silenced the pest.

"Your benefactor proves his persistence and, I see, demands the same of his agents. If he wishes to pay alms, then he can honor my friend, Arthur George Green, protector of the counters who will maintain our storage cities this winter."

"But, of course. I'll extend your *suggestion*!" Upson eyed the least dashing of all the Guardians and feigned a smile.

George turned chalky and spoke toward his fellow. "I imagine you enjoyed that."

"No cause to imagine. *Believe*, George."

"If we follow the perimeter, in obedience to the laws, we can reach our friends afore the peak."

Tull bared his teeth and kept profanity from his lips; still, the intrusive onlooker and Phinn Derek Wade's proxy cowered. He reared back and looked over his shoulder. "If an already sullied idiot walked a straight line from this gate, George?"

"You would see the glimmer of new morn, lest the Fallen First—"

"In a straight line I go, then. Are you well enough to see to these friends of ours?"

"As you say. *Burua*." He laughed at Tull's mutual sickness.

"Get your hands off me!" Pine hollered and shoved away onlookers, then noticed Tull's feet versus his location. "I trusted you!"

"Olley remains. And now Marko."

"Olley?" Pine shoved Upson and stepped toward the gates. Others pulled him back. "Let go of me! Spineless misborn ingrates!"

George calmed the hothead with a hand upon his shoulder. "No soul may enter twice or risk infestation, lest they face our judges."

"Then let our judges come down here and stop me!"

TULL

As others closed the gates between the Guardians, Tull lobbed back George's device and lulled with his smooth voice. "His words need not offend. He deserves rest and alms for his bravery."

The gates locked and Tull turned his back on the idea of rest. Pine fought against the crowd, striking two who blocked him, but *not* against George. The taller of the pair stepped aside and let the shorter fuse hurl his best pack over the gate. Weapons rattled as they landed and drew Tull's attention, but not his hand.

"Tull!" Pine clutched the gate and buried his bootheel in the gut of one who tried keeping him back. "You take that pack! None of your ruses. Cut down whatever crosses unto your way. You end them all!"

"Discern, child."

Tull trusted his peacefulness above Pine's agitation and listened to the whispers mingled in the winds that crossed the peaks. He then tossed back the offering. As the ranking Guardian, he confused those who watched for mere entertainment and emitted a phrase to those fellows who knew the language he spoke. "Haja'la an'tua."

Pine's ears perked like a dog that recognized a command but felt trained to react to the sound of retreating hooves that dizzied the air. His lips parted, but then he set his jaw and responded with a half-nod that turned into a swift glance toward George. The gentler soul offered the same nod, weighed down by compassionate eyes, and hoisted Lucy. Pine then tapped the gate and let Tull depart but eyed lingering Upson.

Scatter and be watchful. To an unpracticed ear, the language of the firstkind meant nothing. Even the gliders' relays filtered the language as garbled speech. That Tull spoke the language so soon in this land meant that he recognized the warning on the wind. His two fellows understood and did not debate his authority.

"Olley and I will see you soon."

The Guardians and their territories loved Olley. He brimmed with charm and swagger, loved the secondkind, and shunned belief in unconquerable foes. Above Tull and the other four in the outfit, he alone possessed an ability to coddle and submit to the judges at the same time without sacrificing in the eyes of either side.

He lacked George's trembling superstition, Lucy's unkempt rage, Pine's contrary disposition, and Tull's penchant for suffering. Nita, who approved of few, refused better offers and stayed at her husband's side. The outfit fought harder for them, that the pair might enjoy their purpose together more. Even the abettors—like Marko—gravitated toward the soul he served and set their souls in harm's way for belief in Olley's headship. In fairness, Tull sought Marko with the same regard he heaped onto Olley.

Now, the way the soul from another land trekked across this forsaken town and *found* the missing without incident added to his legend. He tracked no better than George and strategized no better than Nita. He walked toward a massive cloud of red granules unchallenged by the creatures and spirits that haunted Gutefiel's rot. *That* ability mystified others most.

The jaded, the stiflers, and the Partakers said his guilt-tormented soul pushed him toward madness. Those who praised their idea of him counted him blessed; chosen by the Triune above all others. He ignored both sides with impartial fervor. They did not appreciate discernment. Still, in their times of crisis, they relied on him and what the Helper spoke to his heart.

"Be of caution, for you have not counted the souls that reside in one body."

"As You lead me . . ."

Possessions by wandering spirits turned his stomach, but he pushed on beneath the ever-watchful eye of a projection-glider and into the granular cloud. His presence churned that cloud, and the wandering spirits that filled the voids squealed and gnashed. They taunted him; accused him of weak faith and all their usual *tricks*. Soon enough, they fled from the sound of his prayer.

When he found his friend, whose end he witnessed in that previous land, he wanted to forsake impartiality. What remained of Olley's expression captured an emotion that few eyes needed witness. The disfigured flesh that once made him so attractive clung from one side of the skull and sagged like a limp sail against a sea of tangled hair. His eye offered no response to pain or light, but fixed on the ash beyond his abettor's shadow.

"Marko."

Next to Olley, from what seemed at first a position of prayer, Abettor Marko Glenn Stran knelt with his back toward Tull. The Guardian winced as a wave of bitter ash struck him. The winds challenged the tart haze, but the granules clung to him like the residue he washed from Lucy's eyes. He roared within but never trembled.

TULL

Olley flailed, not from his own energy, but from the way that Marko tugged at his thigh and ankle. A torn pant leg swayed from the work and scraped at the blackened ground. Then Tull heard the sound that confirmed his suspect thoughts, put to light by a projection-glider caught in the petrified branches. Marko's head jerked to one side as he forced the leg downward and away.

Tull picked up a fallen branch, and Marko's shoulders then rose till they hid the bloodied sides of his head. A throaty sigh fell from his lips and he tried his hardest to remain still. That sigh produced a violent twitch in his arms and the bones of Olley's ankle ground under Marko's hold. Tull flung the branch, not at Marko, and struck the limbs of the tree.

Other branches fell. One struck the circular disc around the stuck glider and freed the craft from entanglement, lest the territories see his friends in their shame. The shift of unkind light angered Marko, who rose to his feet and shouted in a muddled voice. Blood and ash stained him from mouth to breastbone and dripped from his fingers. His own outburst upset him, made him beat his temple with bloodied hands, then he wept like a furious, heartbroken soul.

"You sought to hush the screaming, did you not?"

The microphone built into the hull of the projection-glider adjusted toward the sound of Tull's voice. For the first time, Marko noticed him. He leapt over Olley's body and bent at the knees and hips as he urinated in fright. His limbs trembled, and his mouth sought a form that allowed coherent speech. When that failed, he splayed his hands toward the Archibaldian he served.

"I must report that Marko's infested and has turned on Olley. I'll prep them for transport and bring them to the gate. Have Response and Rescue meet me."

There were few souls past their blamelessness gentler than Marko. He served Olley with unfettered loyalty. He made humble choices without fail. Now, the aide adorned in his leader's blood looked toward Tull, and a sight like electric current pulsed in his eyes and fluttered beneath his skin.

In their land, there was no greater sign of weakness than the soul who knew of the Fallen First but could not withstand them. Marko knew every scripture. He knew every law. Still, the wandering spirits filled him.

Tull spoke a prayer for him in three tongues: first in a philosopher's tongue, second in a warrior's tongue, and a third time in a shepherd's tongue; not for the abettor, but for the Fallen First. A grotesque chorus of voices rang from Marko and provoked the surrounding creatures that leered from the shadows. He offered their distraction no audience but repeated his prayer and let them wail with the possessing spirits.

In that moment, he might have marveled over the way the winds toppled the former Ministers and cast their faces into the dirt. In wonder's stead, he kept a cautious eye on Marko. Olley's abettor gasped in fear, then fell sideways and vomited. Tull looked away, a horrible expression on his face, and shifted at the hips to soothe his own stomach.

Marko's purge drew the contents from his stomach, but not the wandering spirit. A geyser-like burst of sediment sprang from the glebe—a common occurrence when a spirit fled—and Marko stole the idea. He erupted onto his feet, thrashed at the air, and ran from the Guardians and the glider's light. His course led him *into* the heart of Gutefiel, when south offered a more peaceable destination.

"Shelter him, Merciful Creator."

Another voice rose softer than their whisper. "Nelson . . ."

The Jacobian fell to his knees and took hold of Olley's hand.

Olley blinked with declined function and struggled to focus. "End me . . ."

"And face Nita alone? I thank you, no." He refused to lose his friend twice in what he counted as one eve. "Best we leave this place to the ash."

"Ash . . ."

Tull grinned when he caught Olley's eye on him, but the Guardian who oft spoke without ceasing said no more. His rescuer checked for back and neck injury, then turned him onto his shoulders and surveyed the frontside. The sight of the chest wound provoked a fruitless visual search for the outfit leader's saber. The Jacobian who found him never lost the hope-filled reassurance in his eyes, though.

He smoothed loose skin across what remained best undescribed of Olley's composition. That Marko retched again—even from a distance—told enough. Like the face, Tull tended to the leg and forearm too. The Guardian also discovered Olley's wedding band, near a damaged hand, and held the well-weathered ring for him to see.

"Worry not." He spoke a blessing over the band, as he had with the warm stone that trapped creatures, then pressed the ring onto Olley's middle finger. The Guardian assessed his friend's mass and sighed over the stiffness in his back. "You couldn't have followed George's eating habits? His shadow hasn't changed since the ninety-ninth winter!"

The Jacobian stripped off his outer shirt beneath the approaching morn's chill and pulled Olley's left arm through the sleeve. The covering of a chest wound cost him warmth and nothing more. When he reached for the arm tucked beneath Olley, he noticed a clutched hand. First, he pulled an arm through a sleeve, fitted the shirt over his leader's shoulders, then inspected why he clasped his right palm.

Olley revealed for a trusted friend a torn cloth piece that matched nothing of his own ensemble. A token pinned to that cloth said all that he could not. The small copper pin, forged from a mine owned by second era Guardian Buster Roderick King, bore the mark of an antiquated number seven. Tull recalled the glimpses he took of Marko and remembered the pin upon the collar of the abettor's shirt.

"But a soul we regard . . ."

Olley shut his eye, Tull exhaled, and both understood. Those who wore the pin boasted evidence that they enjoyed the fierce protection of *all* Guardians due to risks they took to help the outfit with a need. Guardians would disobey their judges, their plans, and time of mending to defend those who possessed such a pin. The simplest souls in the territory grasped the ramifications of harming a wearer, so the trinket's presence bore true deceit.

"How a small token changes much."

Tull stored the pin in the pocket where he kept Zeck's campaign medal. His instincts brimmed and tinged his care with agitation. He removed the shred of fabric that covered his face, secured Olley's foot and ankle, then fastened the fabric with the strap of a sheath. He took from Olley his cravat and a strap from a forearm sheath and secured the last open wound.

"We travel now. Ours won't be a short walk, but I won't give up on you."

Olley shed a red-hued tear that gathered Tull's attention.

"O Mighty Creator, increase our strength and let the voice of the Helper guide my feet as I tow my friend away from the wicked." He then clasped Olley's hand and remembered a remark made to him in that previous land. "Relax your heart. They know how we need Them. They do not fail."

SEVEN

Blooming Copse

83 cubits from the southern fences that keep Gutefiel.
In a parched grove that smelled of rot.

The eve broke as Tull reached what he considered the halfway point in the journey. The added weight on his back reduced his gait and changed both his center of gravity and the scope of his vision. To the latter, the ash and wind mingled till the sky-fires hid from his eye. He never stumbled. The Jacobian minded Olley's breaths and recited a melody of praise.

He sought specific markers; this cluster of burned rigs, that collapsed foundation, and remnants of former roadways consumed by fire. Charred remains bled their once-proud colors and still gasped the screams that once filled Gutefiel. That hauntedness brushed against the wind but never attained breath. Still, the place worked on Tull's conscience.

"Remember how the smoke drove out the peak, Olley? O, the count of eves we pondered if we'd see light again!" He adjusted his leverage and took cautious steps over broken tiles. "Now our judges make us return to our dishonor to esteem and amuse them. They've never heard the cries beneath the breeze. Much like the pylons' song, are they not?"

He stared at the skyscape of a town that crumbled underfoot. The crooked peaks, collapsed towers, and fallen steeples spoke to the depravity the Guardians witnessed and the way their failure weighed on them. "The way we haunt this place... we owed them more. In our hurt, we let what befell her tear us apart when we should've stayed—should've named that beast and made fear our weapon."

TULL

The winds blew downward and cleared the land of threats and gliders with a might like Lucy's scream. Ash rose from the trampled ground, awakening a stench of decay and surrounding the pair in a cloud. Tull's anger rose, but not above the mechanized roar. Light bled through and cast them in misshapen silhouettes.

"Wretched beasts of the sky!"

Affixed to the hind end of the light, Tull witnessed a drab, hollowed-out beast with whirling blades and a skittish hover. He relaxed his shoulders and crouched to protect Olley from the percussive roar. A blizzard of ash blinded, but a rescue medic adorned in goggles and an illuminated helmet rushed to aid him. The medic's mouth moved, but the voice never rose above the rotors, not that he abstained.

Tull brushed him away when he tugged at Olley and kept hauling his friend. His scion, Ingram Franklin Kemp, interceded, and helped tow the Archibaldian toward the rotorcraft while the rescue medic stood shunned. Tull nudged his scion and eventual replacement on board next but remained on his feet. Marko was still there, and Tull bore the responsibility of finding him despite how Olley's fingers motioned for him to board too.

The rescued medic screamed in his ear. "We take him to—"

"You take him to the Corban Outpost!"

"Our judges order us—"

Tull broke the helmet light with his grip. "Who keeps you safe in the dark?"

The rescue medic wavered then Ingram, who looked refreshed and untested, wasted no time. He set his hands upon Tull and snaked him off his feet like a farmer plucking a carrot from the garden. The shunned medic swatted out the ash, which the pilot took as a command to lift off. This happened fast enough that Tull never challenged the use of a rotorcraft. Though the noise and frustration silenced the Helper, his distrust screamed at his soul till Ingram distracted him via a transparent plate that displayed a pre-written notice:

THE OFFERING HAS ENDED.
JUDGES NAME YOU OUR VICTOR.
YOU PROVIDE OUR HEADSHIP NOW.
MENDING PROTOCOLS UNDERWAY.

Tull splayed his open hand toward Olley and tilted his head.

TULL

NITA RELAYED COORDINATES.

Tull accepted the answer and let the medic work, lest Olley suffer and Nita take offense at every soul in the rotorcraft. He wiped grit and ash from his eyes as he sought a sign of Marko but failed in his attempt. A fleeting moment of eeriness ushered in the light of sky-fires and let Ingram share new instruction.

I AM TO USHER YOU TO JUDGE HOFNARR.
FOR YOUR OBEDIENCE, HE LETS OLLEY TRAVEL WITH YOU.

Tull weighed the message, then looked out the door as he calculated foot travel and Olley's need to reach a chamber house for mending. Whilst he debated, the rescue medic tethered him into the cabin and then washed Olley's wounds. Tull found a button discarded from his leader's coat, which he slipped into the same pocket that held other mementos. He then resumed watch over the sky-fires.

Colors beyond the scope of describable vision burned clean and vivid above the ash. The breeze offered a swell of warmth with such intensity that the rotorcraft trembled. As pure light washed over the Guardian, the ash and sediment on him dissolved as if he never carried them at all. He grinned from the sensation, and invited the wonder they experienced.

The less-enthralled pilot turned the craft away from the gates, south of the perimeter, and across the Loy River. The arrangement of settlements, fields, and structures twinkled beneath the sky-fires and false light. He had no idea of the time. He only knew by sight that hundreds of souls celebrated out of doors—celebrated the offering, the Guardians—and *him*.

He pondered the whereabouts of his fellows and prayed that Pine, George, and Lucy scattered from Gutefiel with better success than he and Olley. Nita remained mercurial, but such a nature suited a Shelbian. His friends survived. The emotional and spiritual exhaustion from that previous land mingled with all he endured in this land and stirred him as the force of light shimmied the craft.

The projection-gliders followed, but only as high as their programming allowed. They then hovered above the shrinking lights and grid-like arrays of the seven territories, he assumed, toward the Creighton Territory, though he preferred to watch the sky-fires. No befallen creature stopped him. Still, the method of departure uneased the outfit's new headship.

The secondkind no longer took to the air, for the skies belonged to the First Creation. He reasoned that Enke'loi would allow him more than a few watches in this land and resigned his apprehension. He remembered the decree that banned flight and sea travel then realized the irony of his lawbreaking at a judge's invitation. In his heart, he struggled to understand why Yah let His Creation suffer beneath the rule of corrupted and vulturous judges.

While an answer escaped him, the altitude let him see the lay of the land. Whether he set his eye on the timbers to the north, the desert to the far south, or the clusters of light along the western coves, he committed the landscape to memory. The shimmy of the craft's tail took away his breath, and the medic who saw to Olley stared at him as if he suspected a cause. The Guardian let the soul he shoved have his fill now.

More spoke the name of Nelson James Tull than had met him. Few who had met him knew him. After all, Olley was the face of the outfit. A name was enough to tow a legend; the greatest burden a soul might carry shy of outliving a beloved soul. Walking from Gutefiel unscathed had not aided his cause toward peaceful trespass through the territories in pursuit of his purpose.

Ingram tapped his shoulder and pointed toward the east. The peaks obstructed the sunrise, but once the rotorcraft cleared the summit, the remnants of four more territories proved visible to both travelers. For the past twenty-three spans, those territories—Damaris, Erori, Othniel, and Perlin—sat beneath the surface of the Forbidden Sea. Steeples, chimneys, and even a few well-built monuments remained upright as grave markers in an ever-flowing field. In the morn's light, however, and at their position, the land that once existed shimmered like a mirage and stirred a haunted fog above the tide for the two Jacobians to remember.

The secondkind considered the peaks and everything above the foothills off-limits, for there the firstkind dwelled and took rest from their warring. A few creatures staggered from their caves in confusion as the pilot ascended. Some rabble-rousers hurled rocks. One rash creature even took flight and looped around the nose of the craft.

In response, one of the crew released a pair of levers. The tail shimmied as the lightweight canopies retracted and let the winds awaken small foil gliders designed for interference. Dozens of devices swarmed the nose of the craft, providing a buffer that congested and entangled the limbs of the creature. The pursuer swatted at the trespassers and cast broken pieces of the craft toward the nested beings below.

Those creatures gathered and examined the components. Their voices rose in chatter and intensified the breeze that flowed across the peaks. That wind, in turn, shook the rotorcraft. The one that challenged them delighted, as if the craft played, and offset their flight path with a nudge to the craft's nose.

The intake wheezed and the propeller spun off-balance, but the pilot succeeded. Even as the rotorcraft steadied, nothing prepared the souls on board for the sudden, blinding gleam that confronted them. A flock of Squires drifted in formation, then swooped down to meet the trespassers. Their figures shone with an intensity that ruined the eyes of the secondkind and the befallen, but their magnificence captivated.

The pilot redirected and arced away from the mountains and around a trio of silos. Those creatures that challenged them retreated into their caves or elsewise covered their faces from the Squires. The flock cried out in praise to the Triune who created all things, and the first that flew with them circled back toward the mountain. In unmarred symmetry, two Squires at a time flew away till none remained near the foothills.

The mist on the fields spread as the rotorcraft raced between barns and farmhouses, sending horses, sheep, and cattle into a frenzy. Both landing skids clipped the branches from a few treetops, then the entire tail swung as the clock turns and cast away the fog. In all, the landing devolved into a running slide across uneven terrane.

Ingram leapt out first and surveyed the field on wobbling knees. He counted silos with a shaky hand, then covered his eyes and staggered. One winged creature remained watchful of the craft. The brilliance of light against his seamless edges burned away the mist. That same brilliance cast his solemn face and massive chest in shadow that reduced elegant limbs to slivers of gemstone-like clarity.

The Guardian poked his head from the door of the craft and squinted toward the watcher. "Araemo illi'nen sera-aekku."

A smile as warm as any friend's lit the Squire's face and his alit eyes focused on Tull. He waved in receipt of the name bestowed upon him, that of *gracious cousin*. The light glistened as he raised his head toward the sky-fires and radiated till he reduced their shadows. The creature vaulted away in silence, disturbing not even the dew that remained unsettled.

One of the crewmen cursed. "What did you say to that *thing*?"

"I asked for ten ticks of patience afore he calls fire upon this beast." Tull whispered the truth in Olley's ear, added a promise betwixt brothers, then leapt onto the stable glebe. He then looked toward his scion, whose warm skin looked clammy. "Need a tick?"

Ingram fell to one knee as the rotorcraft returned to flight.

"We can rest."

"You said nothing of patience or fire."

Tull hid his ornery smirk and angled his focus toward the sky-fires. They never ascended close enough to see warring creatures, only the effects, so he expressed simple gratitude to one creature for good will. In a canvas of explosions, lightning strikes, and combustions, mere gratitude toward those who warred for the secondkind's betterment paled. The side he rooted for held their advantage and kept the other side from consuming them, and his heart brimmed with gladness.

Ingram coughed into a rotorcraft-spoiled patch of field grass. "Almighty!"

"My water's run out." Tull drummed his hollow canteen. "Sorry."

"Gah! Wicked, wicked—terrible—landing!" Tull's scion spoke with an aristocratic diction, like Nita, marred only by his nauseous belch. "I applaud you on your victory, my benefactor! Both in our flight and in the offering. Bittersweet, though, I'm certain that must—"

"Taste?"

Ingram vomited again. "Truly, you are a legend. Ten eves in Gutefiel!"

Tull helped his fellow Jacobian to his feet and patted his shoulder, casting bitter ash into Ingram's pristine coat; a coat adorned with a copper pin. "*Seven* eves."

"I attest, I counted all ten moonrises and the moonsets that followed."

Tull then realized that Pine sought an advantage over him when he cited *eight* eves till the last moonrise of the gathering season, when they celebrated Hivi'ern.

"I can tell you, I also saw Olley and Marko on the display plates. You were right to save them."

"Olley has an asepsis phobia concerning the mending chambers."

"Better unclean than buried, I imagine. Why was Marko there?"

TULL

Tull shook his head, took one glance toward the rotorcraft's path, then prompted his guide. Ingram served as Tull's scion—*successor*—so his proximity to odd transports and Tull made sense. A scion oft knew matters reserved for judges, Guardians, and chiefs. Still, the Guardians passed a decree of their own and freed their scions from service to the territories. Each of them, Ingram counted, refused the dismissal and sought to change minds through loyalty and presence.

"All the paltry branches! No plumes of color. I remember how, in the gathering seasons of my blamelessness, these fields roared with splendor. I watched them from our lavish bluffs. Paltry, Creighton!" The scion laughed like a creaking stove and cast moisture around his head.

How the scion remained blind to their setting troubled his benefactor. Any soul raised near enough to Shelby to gain a Shelbian accent who still failed to recognize how the wickedness of their neighboring territory bled downward seemed a fool. The middle territories on this side of the Loy turned toward rot. That oppression trickled further, till decay forged a desert from the southernmost pool.

Tull crossed behind his scion and marched seventeen paces nearer to the foothills. The angle of Ingram's curious brow took time that the Guardian imagined better spent on other matters. "You said we're to see Judge Hofnarr."

"Yes."

"Now we stand in his territory."

Ingram looked around, confirmed the coordinates of the Creighton Territory on his handheld display plate, and turned from the Weston Territory. "I exited from the wrong side! Say, what device model do you hold? I prefer the accuracy of yours."

Tull huffed and led the way. "I don't own a handheld."

Ingram cradled his stomach till he caught up and reclaimed a half-gait lead. "Unlike the others, I recognize the charity in your coup; most of all, in these moments. That said, I'd ask that you recognize that my father prepared me for the season when I might defend the territories as fifth Guardian."

Despite contrary upbringings, the pair shared views on a gamut of topics and spoke at length about any number of them when occasion allowed and when the Guardian proved talkative. He realized how well Ingram kept a one-sided conversation and appreciated that talkativeness flowed from a well-read, dignified mind. While his scion rambled, Tull kept a corrected path southward and prayed for wisdom afore he faced the most erratic of the seven judges. In those previous lands, he never met with Judge Hofnarr lest his fellows joined him and only then by rail.

"I fancy our esteemed *jester*'s luxury." Ingram motioned toward the new morn's light. "Not one glider in sight. Can you remember when last you traveled with no glider spectating?"

Judge Hofnarr inspired disloyalty. The Creightonian's advocate, oft-draped in falsehoods and notorious as an inconsiderate drunkard, adorned his tree with *spouses*: female, male, animals, and one blameless soul. The most peaceable of the six Guardians detested the judge and set Ingram on guard. The least peaceable bore a scarred knuckle that matched the judge's now-bejeweled incisor for the judge's blameless spouse; however *legal* Hofnarr made his vile perversions and sickness.

"Can you?"

"No."

"I fear he watches, and I cannot say why."

Not a soul learned from where Hansel Ornlam Hofnarr originated. The way he spoke, the way he bragged on an ancient fortune, and the way he never mingled with those he ruled, made him seem enigmatic; not that the Creighton Territory thrived on hospitality. He clutched his judgeship whilst the Guardians mourned a respected fellow. Since then, he sought ways to agitate their grief.

Hofnarr achieved recognition as a thesp. Some boasted that he never emerged from a role or showed his true character at all. The more his audience dug, the less they found of him. Why an elusive soul chose such power contradicted the image—the performance—of his reclusion.

After an era immortalized him on reels, the one that followed saw he had a belly that looked like a wineskin and flat, black irises that spoke to the condition of his soul. Naysayers dismissed him for his lack of convention and his eccentric cruelty. His routine bored them, and his proclivities disturbed their hearts.

Tull, and those loyal to the Jacobian, kept a close eye; after all, the secondkind relied on him for such choices. Hofnarr attempted assassinations upon four of his fellow judges. He failed every time, oft due to his preening. Still, the judges kept him in place for reasons unknown to the Guardians, the scions, the abettors, their scions, the chiefs and their deputies.

"Wait."

TULL

Ingram responded to Tull's hush and found the Guardian crouched on one knee. He dug a shard of broken rock from a rupture in his boot after rummaging with his index finger till he cleared the brittle arch support.

"High arches."

"You're aware they make and sell *new* boots, are you not?"

"These are just right."

Ingram sized up the hole in the side. "As you say."

"Perk of being a Guardian." Tull patted him on the shoulder and assumed the lead in boots tailored to his feet and gifted to him the morn he was named a Guardian.

Tull came from nothing. He was an orphan who held little memory of either parent. What memories he kept confused him, and he feared they never belonged to his mother and father at all. Still, he seldom complained. He feared his Creator too much to resent Him for keeping him from his parents, whom he should have joined afore and afore.

Both he and his scion proved their patience as a sultry figure approached from beneath the shadow-rich groves. She produced no shadow, which tempted her habit of playing the sneak. Though the smile she bore looked as fake as the costume lashes that kept the light from her eyes, she tried her hardest to feign genuineness. Tull sensed the wickedness amid the *absence*, and let his stillness guard Ingram's position to the right of him.

"Congratulations on your *victory*, brother. Truly, our *Creator* favored you." She wrapped her hands in a prayerful pose and draped her arms toward her thighs. "Ten eves and not one kill. What an intriguing strategy!"

Her false praise landed between where Tull's shadow fell and where her toes dug into the field. She used the words—the tokens—of a Believer, but the intentions twisted on her tongue. Tull kept his opinions buried, but remained cordial. "Are our judges here, Steward Leflore?"

Ingram stepped back when they heard her purr. Her grin stretched nearer to the spangle earrings in her stretched lobe, defiant of her instincts. "Well! I was unaware I followed my own reputation; least of all from the lips of he who burned the Wilkołak nests back into the sea."

"You are to answer my benefactor, who guards even you, Shelbian."

Hofnarr's steward scoffed at Ingram and teased like a feline craved attention; only for the chase as she led them. "You'll see who we've gathered."

TULL

Tull remembered her from that previous land, though she no longer gravitated around the judges. She *sympathized* with the Fallen First and bowed knee to the Seko'tae. She entertained spirits and magick; as though she honored what the Guardians fought. The laws called her a Partaker. She claimed a Believer's nature as part of Hofnarr's deceit.

The Guardian knew the cruelty of those who shared her practices. He still saw the phantom bodies of Believers they hung from trees; bodies he found and cut down. Bodies he prayed over and buried. His hands withdrew into fists and his eye captured a sight that provoked him as much as her falseness.

"Stand right there."

Tull stripped a hiltless knife from Ingram's boot, abandoned the pair, and approached a captive bound and stripped down to his hips. His frail torso splayed from the angle at which his bindings held him to the exposed root of a withered plum tree. The stench of decayed fruit and old sweat irritated his nostrils, but he towed an unflinching shadow.

Another used the tree-bound soul as a punching bag. His left side collected welts and discolored flesh that deformed the look of him, but his sense of hearing kept him alert. The way he trembled and turned from Tull's approach strained the bindings and gave the Guardian an opportunity to slice them from the tree. He caught and kept the freed captive from a mash of blood and urine, where most of his front teeth rested intact.

"Do not be fearful. I tell you, you've survived this. I am Nelson James Tull. Do you believe me?"

One eye strained till the full iris showed in his anxious gaze. He noted the scars on Tull's face and nodded.

"The soul with whom I travel is my scion. He'll take you to mend."

His working eye shot toward Hofnarr's steward.

"Don't look to her." Tull fished through his pocket, removed a copper alms versus the pin that Olley clutched, and set the coin upon the root, where he marked the face with Ingram's blade. He offered the distinctive alms to the beaten soul, who accepted. "From this morn onward, you're beneath my protection. This token is proof of my word. True, Ingram?"

"Indeed. Come, friend." Ingram approached and noticed his new charge as much as his damaged blade.

TULL

"I owe you a knife."

"You owe me nothing, benefactor." He steadied the one he took in hand but kept eye contact with Tull. "Soon, I'll see you."

"You've no idea how insulting your choice might prove." Steward Ivy Camille Leflore warned the soul who lasted ten eves in Gutefiel.

Tull's unbothered smirk spread even as he collected teeth from the mash. The morn's light caught the ledges of Ivy's teeth and backlit the worm-like creatures that swam behind her eyes when she grimaced over his cold shoulder. Seven spans of *learning* aided him now and made him inflict scorn upon his character for not seeing what she was the last time he walked this land. Time also taught him to better filter his thoughts and to hold back most of what he wanted to say. Others, not so much.

"Tull!" The voice of Judge Marvin Elam Katch met the ear like a winter's wind. Katch played jailor to creatures, escort to those who provided information to the Guardians, and was a crude technical genius.

"Marvin." The Guardian pocketed the loosened teeth and hurried to greet the judge whom few would touch. "How are you?"

Unnerved by concern, the soul who ruled the Larson Territory wavered through his handshake. "Fine, fine. Walked out early, didn't you?"

"*Tull.*" The second voice came like a screech. Then, a putrid creature who dressed as one of the secondkind appeared at the other end of a chain and manacle affixed to Katch's wheelchair. By his ragged build, boil-covered skin, and lacking height, Vernard Voler needed no introduction. He cried out in mock dread and his misshapen hands covered his murky, amber irises.

"Enough." Katch yanked the toad-like nuisance away.

"Honorable One. You mentioned *plans.*"

"Meet me at the rig." Katch ended his visit with a firm slap of the hand across Tull's backside, forcing the Guardian to set his jaw in agitation. "I'm on the north road!"

"His visit—"

"I'll wait for you!"

Voler waved his bulbous fingers and offered a smile of ragged, stained teeth. The steward, who observed all, glowered and resumed escorting Tull.

"You might've told him about Ingram."

"I haven't the right to tell any judge whom to offer a ride in their rig."

"But you'll ride with him, knowing he did nothing for another soul?"

TULL

A wheelchair-bound body further outnumbered by Hofnarr's creepy entourage and Voler. The logic seemed obvious.

"And, say we collect Ingram and the *thief* again?"

"There are simpler ways to spend the morn tied to a tree, Steward."

She laughed from deep within her core, cackling and twisted. She then called out to a soul Tull failed to notice. "Did you hear him?"

A barrel-chested lug, never called handsome, stared with the enthusiasm of a corpse. Bearer Doherty Arnold Peake pushed the tip of his tongue through a gap of three missing teeth but ignored the steward. Nerve damage to one side of Peake's face and neck caused him to wear a permanent sneer, as though a retort for whatever stared him down. "Tull. Be glad that Nita *weren't* in the fight. Elsewise, she might've proved more accomplished than you."

"Look who's learning their big words."

The judge's caretaker and errand runner offered no comeback, only a rattle of his head and a tremor in his jowl, and a slight peek from side to side as though he searched for another soul that Tull referenced. Pine caused Peake's nerve damage, but Nita took his teeth. He was another reject; a brute deemed unfit for upright purposes. Tull recalled some of the embarrassing, vile, and brutal ends that Peake suffered across other lands. Such memories made him smirk.

EIGHT

II Molder Grove

The home of the Creighton Territory's Advocate.
On a plot rich in decay.

Tull noticed the ember of a cigarette smoked inside a derelict greenhouse positioned away from the morn's arrival, and practiced patience in lieu of decorum. As with the surrounding fields, every plant within the greenhouse withered from neglect and malnourishment. Their limp vines and insect-riddled leaves mimicked the condition of the territory's judge. Like them, his frail limbs trickled from a moth-eaten silk robe that fell away from his discolored abdomen.

"When last I demanded you kneel in my presence, you broke my feet." The judge noticed the boots Tull wore; fitted with protective flaps that preserved his feet and shins. "I s'pose we'll let dignity suffer in my stead this time. Nelson James Tull, Nelson James Tull, that's a cruel streak you tow."

Even when he spoke, Judge Hansel Ornlam Hofnarr never lost the carnivorous smile that reshaped his toxin-bloated face. The esteemed jester traced a scar that curved along the lay of his distended gut. Hofnarr never averted his eyes and seldom blinked. He taunted with a smile that caught the glint of a false incisor that disappeared when a waifish girl with sores on her legs snaked her hand in front of his mouth and fed him.

He ate rotted meat and drank vinegar-mingled wine between puffs of his salvia-based cigarette; all of which fermented in glass jars that dangled from the ceiling. Worse, he *thrived* on such a diet. Given the level of damage he inflicted and what attacks souls unfurled on him, he needed the oddities to create a boundary that prevented trespass.

"Nothing to say then?"

"I tell you, I've never tortured a soul I kept restrained."

The judge set his flat, glib eyes on Peake.

"He stole from you."

Hofnarr waved his hand, then giggled till wine trickled over his chapped lips. "And *you*. Top scarecrow, these next thirteen moons, given your victory. As voice of all scarecrows, tell me how you intend to honor me. I am a *fair* advocate, after all, and worthy of praise. Did I not see to the needs of the Archibaldian? What tribute do you offer me, *scarecrow*?"

"My tributes to you ended when I stopped at the bones in your feet."

"Bold words for a soul who stands alone." Steward Leflore's heels never disturbed the dust as she approached Hofnarr and draped a hand across his back in a way that exaggerated the curve of her hips.

"Perry Wallace Rudat gave me the first lesson of my purpose: *Get stuck, you're on your own*. I've never been on my own." His gaze skirted the hem of the sky-fires, visible through the vented ceiling. "I could invite them down and prove my word, if you please; though, tributes mean little in their eyes."

Hofnarr's steward stooped and whispered even as the judge's eyes remained flat. All the while, Tull kept his eyes trained on the hands of the heartless soul who had called for him. Peake watched a horsefly ascending the back of the waif's left leg and the waif counted pieces of meat with hungry lips. When spoiled meat appetized, and bugs chose a living body in rot's stead, the avarice Tull felt toward the advocate seemed passive.

"Ki'ellä mi'enun vii'hano, Luoja. Oapeta mi'enulla rauhaa." Tull's prayer for peace versus wrath landed short of his host's ears.

"The Creighton and Archibald Territories have lost their scarecrows. Depending on Nita's willingness to fight, Shelby risks an identical plight. That leaves four scarecrows to patrol seven territories. Even with your mangled face, you must sense the approaching chill. Lest you accept the Advocates' strategy for—"

"Replacements."

"Reinforcements."

"Like the one you sent away."

"I'll take on Olley's labor."

"You and your missing abettor?" Peake dug too.

Hofnarr exhaled in a manner that filled in every curse, every insult that he might have spewed, were he fifteen spans younger and able to fight.

"The pact holds. Despite your hope."

The six Guardians agreed that each would fight—though outnumbered—till none of them remained. They would not force another into their purpose.

"A soul kept in Yah's favor ought not seek tributes from his fellows."

"I can pass laws—"

"And I can call down creatures of fire."

The waif urinated where she stood.

"All that you had, all that you were, and you choose vileness over purpose. How you prove Yah's Word true by acting as He foretold."

"Mind your tongue!" Steward Leflore's shrill voice tore through the air and the waif fell into her own mess.

Hofnarr ran a blunt nail across her scalp and full strands of hair fell away. "What I am is the penalty of your fealty. These territories belong no more to the Believers and the Reformers. They are not Yah's. The time for—"

"Partakers? Infested?" Tull belly laughed as a taunt to them. "I'd forgotten your comedic timing. I thank you for the performance."

"You would do well to still your tongue. My bride hungers, as you've noticed." He fed her a mealworm as if she were a house pet and she ate with the same obedience. "You cut loose her next meal. Now we'll have to find her another. Say I order Falk delivered here, that my little bride might feed on what remains of his face!"

The muscles in Tull's arms twitched and his lungs disagreed upon taking in more air and powering a rage-filled scream. In the meantime, he who held authority drove in another dagger.

"You scarecrows will bend in tribute; either with respect, or with my heel to your necks. I will not be railed against."

Tull ignored those who demanded reverence, plucked one of the discarded teeth from his vest pocket, and held the chipped bone toward the roof vents. He admired the slightness with such devotion that the words of this lot, their vileness, no longer weighed on him. They foretold how they might leverage each of the Guardians and how they would savor body parts of their *feasts*.

TULL

As they boasted with vile tongues, their guest settled heart and hand. Then an opportunity arose with the pitch of Steward Leflore's cackle. He hurled the tooth, and, on instinct, she put up her hand to defend her face. She caught the tooth and then the burden of her act, but the Guardian rushed and seized her wrist lest she discard the bloodied bone.

"Release me!"

"If you didn't starve this blameless child or help beat the one whom I've already released, you'll open your hand, and his tooth will fall to the ground."

She cackled and squirmed, but never bent his arm.

"In the name of I'Esh, if you've hurt her, the weight of that tooth will drive your hand to the ground like an anvil on a feather's back."

"You—"

The Guardian released her and stepped back as the weight of a single tooth stole her strength. Steward Leflore fell to one knee and used her other arm to prop up her trembling hand. She tried to sling away the tooth, but only aggravated her plight. The bone's weight forced her hand down till the hardened glebe broke around the shape of her. She howled as she raked her knuckles over soil, unable to lift her limb.

Tull bent at the hips and teased her ear. "Ask forgiveness."

Hofnarr's steward shook her head in refusal and turned from the waif. She seized her wrist and tried to force her body upright. Every muscle tensed. She gnashed her teeth. Even when she cried out, the extra lilt of might failed her. In a matter of seconds, she went from furious to helpless to desperate.

"No other can help you." He moved the bone back and forth with a brush of his nail, each time making her cry out. "Now you try."

The pretender cursed him in a tongue that none of the others spoke.

"Remember how I offered you a way out."

He spotted a dehydrated pit from a plum that stuck half-buried in the parched glebe. Once the pit broke free, he surprised Peake with a hurried toss. The brute fell backward and crashed through a greenhouse panel. His boot caught on the frame and the shorn hair of his head grazed the terrane the structure sat upon.

"Judge Hofnarr, you're surrounded by souls whose conduct sets you at risk. As Guardian, and for the solace of the Creighton Territory, I'll have them removed. I'll contact *Chief* Katch at once, you needn't fear. By the eve, you'll know solitude in this place again."

TULL

"This is trickery!" Another shrill scream passed the steward's lips.

Hofnarr stirred on soiled, velvet cushions and considered his ability to fend off Tull's next *perceived* trick. When the Guardian deprived him of his cue and walked away, the judge fell beneath a spell of nervousness that exposed his weakness. In that moment, his fear of ridicule got the better of him. "A moment will come for you! A moment none of your beliefs or your trickery or your legends will keep you from!"

Tull hesitated at the doorway, almost pivoted, but kept his feet planted. "You beguiled the innocent and cursed fruitful terrane. Worry for your soul and remain upon this withered orchard. I cannot promise your safety should you stray."

"Be of use."

Tull held breath and tongue behind a dead-eyed snarl. He heeded the internal voice of the Helper and surrendered a shred of what compassion he buried. He reached into his pocket and took a pair of alms. He set one of high value upon the threshold.

"Blameless soul. What I leave you is yours alone and will not harm you. Once you see that I'm clear of this place, collect my alms. Go to the nearest farm in my name and ask to have your wounds cleaned and to buy what food they'll sell you. Do remember to thank them, even though you've paid. After that, the food and any spare alms belongs only to you."

Tull departed from the judge and his entourage, past the tree where he cut loose the bound soul, but away from the spot where the rotorcraft delivered him and Ingram. He glanced along the horizon for signs of Ingram and the beaten soul, neither of whom remained visible. He never looked back, never debated whether Peake wanted revenge or Hofnarr wanted more meat. The resets cured him of the what-ifs that kept other souls awake.

He admired the colors across neighboring farms, rich with purple and golden leaves. Another soul burned a fireplace and the chimney smoke created a veil across the sky-fires. The moment his feet touched near green grass, he brushed the dust off his sleeves, set foot on the lush field, and breathed deeper. The skin-crawling sensation that teemed on Hofnarr's orchard stayed, and the Guardian forged a diagonal path toward the north road and his promised ride.

Tull

<u>68 Charlton Sage Way</u>

10 Cubits across the Larson Territory border.
Not far enough away from the stench of II Molder Grove.

The Jacobian found a crusty, detached Judge Katch *enjoying* an indecent reel of a Shelbian whom he met once and a sybaritic novitiate in a hand-ripped violet middy, who arched her back to kiss the older soul as a reward for his asperity. The second time the judge watched the middy ripped open, Tull stepped onto the passenger's riser of a slender-bodied, high-axle rig. Less enthralled by the reel, he set his attentiveness unto the territories that withered beneath two judges.

"With breasts like hers, she could rule the territories! If Gus catches Berwin knowing his daughter that way, though, neither will see the winter!" Katch laughed. "He has a short fuse! And she has a twin who looks just like her . . . well, *bigger*."

Tull proved he lacked the interest required to loosen his jaw and respond but recognized the given names of two overseers; both of whom oft gave in to their tempers. Most who learned of Katch's delights strayed from contact with the eunuch. He *collected* proof. He studied inclinations and thought nothing of scouring every tick and deed of a soul who turned his head.

"Look at that form!" He admired how she cast off her middy. "Ha! Ha-ha! Does she look like a novitiate to you?"

Katch manipulated the flow of information through the territories like rocks in a brook and kept *unpolluted* archives he shared with no other. He dispatched data to abettors and chiefs, but seldom looked away from the information he doled. The power of others' secrets manipulated him. In turn, he preyed upon those he anticipated as threatening the power of the judges and their system of rule.

"This will keep in a jar till I need Berwin's fealty." He then laughed as he glanced around the setting. "Her mother shares an occasional bed with Hector. That's *three* fools with more concurrent pissing contests than—well—you and Cyril!"

Tull shifted in discomfort. He detested Judge Cyril Adair Mumus aplenty, but liked when others tracked his resentments even less. "Have you happened upon any word of Marko?"

"They'll find him in a treetop or given back by the thaw." He crouched closer to the novitiate's image and teased the chapped corner of his mouth with his milky tongue.

TULL

"About that ride."

Katch caught the Jacobian's averted gaze and laughed. "That's what I like about you, Tull! You're gentle enough not to admit you suffer arousal like the rest of us, and cruel enough to enjoy the frustration."

"My purpose is easier with admirers."

"Ha!" He swept the passenger's bench seat with his forearm and waved his hand. "Which way do you travel from here?"

"If you can drop me near the Shelley Signal House without traveling far from your way . . ." His appreciation drifted beneath the engine's grumble. "I thank you."

"I'm headed further than that!" Katch adjusted the transparency of the screen and released the brake lever near the steering column. "There's a nest I seek to visit along the No. 4 Steam Tram. This slimy dollop I'm towing emits an odor that attracts harvesters, see, and I'm angling to lure one in and have my fun."

Tull said nothing. Voler earned worse than a trip to Katch's ossuarium. Still, he disliked the *slimy dollop*'s ability to watch a judge in a way Tull needed not to bear knowledge about either.

Katch tapped the glass with two fingers. "There's a saloon for silica-miners and *Heretic* cooks where this dove would gather a heap of alms! With those pert—"

The front tire struck a sizeable obstruction in the road—bone or stone—and forced Katch's concentration from his seedy mind to his skeletal hands. Tull shifted in his seat, jarred by both.

From behind him, the toad-like Voler ran his prickly tongue along Tull's neck and tasted his sweat. "What did you do?"

"Do that again, I'll rip your tongue out and tie a knot around your throat."

Katch intervened and shut the compartment. "What *did* you do?"

"The Partaker with Hofnarr. *Leflore*."

"Mmmm?"

"I gave her a keepsake to hold for me."

Katch laughed and pointed behind them. "She turned Voler in. Ha! The little dollop owes you a favor now! Ha-ha!"

While his driver spewed insults toward Voler, Tull settled in the seat, took the brunt of every bump in the road, and prayed for stillness in the judge's tongue. If his sense of direction proved true, the rig sat ten ticks from the nearest banks of the Loy

River. With nineteen ticks of the reel unplayed, he wanted for a still moment to see his surroundings, as he witnessed them in multiple lands.

When a breathy plea faded in volume, not pitch, his eyes opened in surprise. The cab, now dim but for the dash gauges, offered him the chance to exhale in peace. Still, he extended gratitude toward their Mighty Creator. Over the next three ticks, not one sound rose above the hum of the engine.

"Good, you're back. I find I'm *negligent* of not remarking sooner. I needn't tell you, Marko's an idiot, but I've oft counted Falk likeable. Between you and me, I thought Nita would murder them both anyway."

Tull offered a peculiar expression.

"You and I should get together more oft. I'll show you the reels you ought to see. Nita has a foul streak! All the things these fools take for granted. But, I like seeing the lives they live. Those like us—who truly *see*—don't interest the Fallen First. They like the gravy, but not the marrow."

Tull found the odds more favorable that most souls in the territories lacked the stomach for the details. Katch experimented, studied, hacked, and sewed back together more parts than any soul counted. His compulsion stemmed from his own circumstance. He saw beauty in what others called hideous, and wanted what others called beautiful to be fractured like him.

"In what territory does the lottery say you'll mend?"

"Your own. Sister Lois Westmore offered me a room." He spoke fast, as if afraid the judge might corner him with an offer to stay at his home.

Katch gauged the tone but hid his awareness behind a sideways grin. "I imagined she might!"

"You need a hand with that harvester?"

"Worried I'll meet my end?" He grinned at his passenger. "No, but I thank you. Let those chaste doves make a fuss about you!"

Tull wanted to coax the judge's motives away from him but learned against riling an elder—and a free ride—long ago.

"If you traveled toward the storage cities up along the northern hem of the Carpenter Territory, afore all that rock turns to glass and ice, there's a medical response outpost. Not much else; some fueling stations, a service road for the dam, and a well-pecked mine. Some brash fool ended a morgue worker named Monteith, but the grains and crops remain untouched."

TULL

Tull kept still while he coaxed his mind to supply context to the familiar name.

"Falk's dove went and had a look-see. I delivered the message, or you might have faced that harvester I'm after during Hofnarr's damned offering. I picked up the stench once. Now I need to make up for lost time.

"I'm crass, but you won't blush when I tell you we lost only time mourning. O, he kept to his way through a novitiate's duties, then upheld his purpose with his benefactor's consent." He then burst with laughter. "Imagine! That *necro* gets turned into a plaything for a soul he trained to behave as him!"

Had his choice about ending the offering *two* eves sooner created such a rift? Had he spared a confrontation with the harvester but cost another their purpose? He witnessed greater rifts from lesser choices. A *yes* versus a *no*. Stillness in action's stead.

"Can't I buy you a meal? Plenty seek to celebrate with their scarecrows." He scoffed. "*Guardians.*"

"I ought to keep moving."

"Avoid temptation, you mean!"

Tull leapt from the rig onto parched terrane. "You've not heard from Ernie, then?"

"Not one forsaken word! No surprises thrive in that old bone bag! Keep an eye out, won't you? I hear that McCrea's looking for you." He scrunched his nose. "Hard to say that name and not check the underside of your boot."

The Guardian's smirk gave the advocate his response.

"Tull."

"I thank you, Marvin." His passenger reached into the cab and shook the judge's extended hand, but withheld his remark till the rig departed. "Truly You are mighty, Most High, but as far as righting souls, I believe You needle Your patience with that one. Shoo!"

Tull watched the reflection of sky-fires against the copper bands of the Shelley Signal House. Once he checked Marvin's course, he crossed the main road onto a narrow road worn into the terrane and headed further from the mountains, the storage bins, the two judges, and Gutefiel. As he traveled with the Loy's flow, a bead of light beneath the skin of his neck pulsated and relayed a signal onto the copper bands that communicated his whereabouts to the secondkind.

Abettor Way

An Interim

The 24th Morn beneath the Moon of the Old Embers

The 114th Gathering Season of the Accession

In the Blessing of I'Esh, who tends the harvest.

Beacon 089.86.218 recognized at 8711 Mornside Lane . . .

Identifier confirmed—Jules Baker Shannon

Purposed to serve the Second Creation as Rescue Medic.

"Welcome back, most precious owls of the eve. I am Conveyer Ginger Faye Olley bringing you the facts you need, every eve, all eve and into the morn, here on WAM Radio. I sit with Thesp Phinn Derek Wade. He is one of the ensemble members we watched in last span's gothic terror film, *Scarecrow*. In that film, you portrayed the victor of the offering we celebrate, and the new headship of all Guardians, Nelson James Tull."

"Right, Ginger, you're absolutely right. Well, except for the word *portrayed*. My work was no mere portrayal. I *became* a soul who's already living, already known, and already adored by an era. He keeps us safe and fights real monsters for us, don't forget."

"I've *not*."

"I struggled to become him, Ginger. I refocused my purpose to believe, to exist, to be this tremendous hero of ours. That required a honed skillset to survive and to perceive; not just to react, not just to get by. I, hear me, I believe those were the toughest two moons of my purpose, Ginger."

"*Indeed.* You spent time with Guardian Tull, then?"

"Well, *sure.* We talked. He's so exact in his purpose. He's so *set* on what he seeks. Truly? I was the only soul who could be him, and even I imagined, 'Was I him or was he me?'"

"*Well,* since the film, you've oft reminded us of your support—admiration, even—of his efforts."

"My absolute support! There's no bigger supporter than he who is seated here with you now."

"*Mm-hmm.* You aren't surprised then, that he returned to Gutefiel and won the offering?"

"In no way, Ginger. In no way! Listen, I know this soul as I know my own reflection. I count him a friend. What I didn't learn from him, I learned from within when I went into the mountains and meditated the way that he did after he won the original victory. What I learned—"

~

"That isn't at all why he went into the mountains!" One who knew Tull growled at what she heard and tore away her earphones. "How can one so beautiful sound so idiotic? Your pretend scars went the wrong way! As did your hair."

The eve responded with silence and turned an outspoken soul kinder toward the pompous boaster. Jules Baker Shannon seldom missed Ginger's shows, and even paid alms for extra listening privileges. But she would sooner donate one moon's salary than spend another tick listening to a buffoon like Phinn Derek Wade. Blushing—for her outburst and her preferred conveyer—filled her cheeks, and rekindled memories of an awkward blamelessness when she could not disguise her emotions so well. Even so, she gave thanks that no other soul watched her rant whilst out of doors.

Nineteen ticks afore the fourth watch reminded her how she hated the silence. She loved peace and stillness, but not the silence. With the outfit running silent too, she had no one to talk to who grasped the shorthand of her secondary purpose. So,

TULL

from a breezy perch outside a chaotic house where wonder and normalcy mingled, Jules watched the neighboring homes across the tart, chipped road whilst her benefactor, Lucy Bright Moon, slept through the aftershock of the Gutefiel offering.

A projection-glider hovered between the copper posts at the corners hem of the yard and watched Jules as she watched house number 8710. At first, she stared into the lens. When the encounter devolved into a contest, she balked. Then, the moment further devolved into a creeping machine guided by an unseen eye in an unknown head. A chill rose on her skin and produced a shiver along her spine.

"Get!"

A moment later, three heartbeats at most, the craft heeded her and drifted away; but not in the typical, parallel course that most gliders followed. This one ascended near 8716, then raced toward the deserted territories beyond the mountains. She could not specify why, but the intrusion felt vile. She retreated into the front room of 8711 but watched for the glider's return.

As she plucked her feet from ash-singed shoes, she counted the times a glider had stolen her from a private moment; a knack she could not give away! One more glance, then she turned her back on the street and stripped off her hooded shawl. Even then, she hesitated and turned out the nearest light and lingered on watch till her heart settled. When the tension passed, she straightened her empty shoes with bare toes and stooped to neaten the arrangement of a child's boots and their strewn laces.

"We must work on your knots, Snuggle Runt. First, the new data reels."

The data reels, part of her responsibilities as an abettor, contained the threats against the secondkind that deserved a visit from one or more Guardians. Next to lurking drones and twice-a-moon visits to a synthetics-dealer, who kept large dogs in a cramped home and oft stared too long at her breasts, reel-monitoring marked Jules's least favorite portion of her work. Though she had not yet learned who performed the data culling, she settled into a chair surrounded by display plates to honor them and to help the Guardians. Idleness held the wrong sway on her thoughts.

Her former benefactor, Otto Meynell Chessy, oft denounced that flaw. With him in mind, she chose the jovial Advocate Scion of the Weston Territory as her first beacon review of the new morn. She admired the love Otto found from his study of laws and belief. Most oft, she caught him asleep in his chair or rummaging in the kitchen. His habits that tormented her during the first season she had spent in his provision now served as ways she kept the future judge in proper step and kept a tether on a lonesome soul.

"Best not let me find you canning again, Otto."

618 REELS LOGGED.
DO YOU WISH TO VIEW?

"Tim..."

She pursed her lips and trapped the vulgarities Timothy Todd McCrea fueled. She then repented, as the secondkind feared rebuke for even a hint of blasphemy. Her fellow abettor shirked his duties the way she surrendered privacy to gliders. Four watches of reels to review from *his* shift preceded her own duties. The way he doled out his workload, his frustrations, and his routine thoughtlessness upon her stung, for he knew how far she traveled, and how she counted on sleep between shifts.

"Start viewing." She slumped onto one hand.

Her system chimed and a gray, rectangular box appeared in the belly of every display plate. A friend with a silver beard and shiny scalp awaited her response.

"Another morn, Syd. Do forgive. I'll owe you double when next we talk."

As she declined an opportunity for distraction, she received a priority alarm from the data sift. She entered her access protocols, let the display plate map her right hand, and even spoke her full name into the microphone attached to her earphones. Her heart pounded, and her instincts prepared her for the worst as she wrapped her fingers around the curved edge of her chair.

"*Don't be him. Don't be him. Don't be him.*" Her face then went slack as a figure appeared. "Samuel?"

> Under a mask of welts and abrasions, Carpenter Territory Advocate Samuel Herbert Gwynne drew Jules nearer to the fourth display plate. She knew this judge, and her heart hurt for him. The longest-seated of the seven, who befriended Guardians and abettors, suffered a beating worse than she had observed in a long while. Her heart ached for her judge and she tensed as she accepted her duties to him and to her territory.

TULL

The slope of the foothills limited the range of the projection-glider and offered coverage for the creature who assaulted the judge. Tendrils of black hair extended from the scarves that overlapped and disguised the face and ears. With gloved hands, the attacker twisted a saber and tightened the restraints. Samuel gasped what air remained trapped in him and his head drifted against suffocation.

1 BEACON MAPPED.
1 RESULTS IDENTIFIED.
DO YOU WISH TO VIEW?

"Yes." She revised the parameters. "Search all line of sight beacons."

INDEXING RESULTS WITHIN ESTABLISHED PARAMETERS:
207 MUSE TERRACE.
SHOWING ALL BEACONS WITHIN LINE OF SIGHT RANGE.

ADVOCATE SAMUEL HERBERT GWYNNE
NO ADDITIONAL RESULTS.

"No addition— They're right afore me! Remove all parameters. Remap."

INDEXING RESULTS WITHIN ESTABLISHED PARAMETERS:
NO ADDITIONAL RESULTS.

"How can this be?" She leaned nearer to the display plate, then sprang upright in posture as she gasped. "Thirty-one! This is thirty-one."

Nearing fifty moons ago, the Guardians tasked the abettors for evidence that few advocates or chief inspectors believed existed. They hunted a single soul for an amassed thirty "fright-related" crimes; from trespass to destruction, to theft, to brutality, and worse. The crimes betrayed the Triune, the secondkind, and the laws of the old judges.

TULL

Her favorite Guardians, Tull and Falk, stopped Myriad, who bore an ever-changing body and had haunted the Archibald Territory for seventeen spans. Guardians Ozul, Pine, and Green trapped the Shadow Charmers, who had terrorized the southern territories since the Era of the Falling Lands. The Red Horde, who vanished like the morning mist, could not escape the Guardians either. They bested foe after foe, yet never produced a fleck of proof of this aggressor's presence or identity. Till now?

"I—I see you!"

> The onlooker showed no fear of Jules, the projection-glider, nor Judge Gwynne. He kept his hands, his torso, and his waist guarded by a heavy coat; almost too heavy for the season. The scarves about his head, detailed by their muted colors, proved his selfishness for secrecy over breath. He covered his crown with the hood on his coat and stood with his back against the wind, even as the glider changed positions.
>
> The wind upset Samuel's body, which shook the pike that held him. His attacker drove a saber into the terrane, then charged downhill and planted the full breadth of his heel across his prey's stomach. The strain on Samuel made Jules pool with tears. As judge and abettor felt anguish, the attacker proved calm enough to set fire to leaves, which he cast above head. The glints of light confused the glider, and the lens's nauseating effort to focus resulted in a gap of useable footage.
>
> SURVEILLANCE ALERT!
> PROXIMITY SWEEP: INCOMPLETE.
>
> NO ADDITIONAL RESULTS.
>
> When the lens settled, the cruel attacker stared back at Jules. The scarves he wore concealed the span between his eyes, his ears, and even the contour of his face, but he gave the projection-glider ample time to map his posture and frame. Then, he slipped his

gloved hand free and waved at the projection-glider the way a bully mocked a helpless soul. In his other hand, he produced a dull object, no bigger than his lighter. He depressed a spring-loaded lever on the head and the projection-glider flipped sideways and careened against the terrane.

"Nine watches ago."

Jules drew a breath till her ribs ached and her trousers slipped. She considered Samuel's dearest, but the judge wrote laws that required that she first appeal to the territory's advocate scion, Guardian, and chief inspector. She opened a vocal frequency for the system and held still while the lens recognized her face in low light. A blue light turned green, flashed twice, then held without a flicker. She let out her breath, thinking through her response and the words she needed to use without stammering, and stared into the lens.

"Abettor Jules Baker Shannon seeks authorization for Urgent Secure file relay from system SDM830302. Locate active beacon and open frequency to authorized devices for Carpenter Territory Advocate Scion Harding Dwiazda Meeker and Carpenter Territory Chief Inspector Dermot Eoghan Gensch. Passcode: Gypsum Two-Five, One-One Fog."

"INTERFACING. SEEKING AUTHORIZATION . . .
AUTHORIZATION GRANTED.
STATUS: URGENT SECURE.
PINPOINTING ACTIVE FREQUENCY.
FREQUENCY: DISCOVERED."

"Relay reel"—her eyes glanced toward a file catalog—"11131933, eyes only, triple verification. Attach header: Advocate Samuel Herbert Gwynne Attacked. Get!"

"FILE 11131933 LOADED.
RELAY LOADING.
RELAY COMPLETE.
REEL DELIVERED TO:
CARPENTER TERRITORY ADVOCATE SCION

TULL

HARDING DWIAZDA MEEKER AND
CARPENTER TERRITORY CHIEF INSPECTOR
DERMOT EOGHAN GENSCH."

"Of all the times to fail the Creation, Tim."

While Jules absorbed what she had witnessed and considered how she should help *more*, she took a broader view of the display plates and exhaled the pent breath in her chest. As her eyes adjusted, she noticed the glimmer of light in two beautiful lenses. Like the glider and display plates, they too sought Jules's attention. The observant little soul who slept less than eight full watches proved victorious.

"So soon, Snuggle Runt?" She brushed the button nose on her visitor's face. "Did I—I wake you?"

Her eyes closed tight, and she shook in objection hard enough to cast her teddy bear from her hand. The sewn-on eyes and coal-black nose scraped the desk and made her socked toes curl. Her reaction proved she roamed from more than a bout of sleepwalking. Against her nature, she stared at the bear's fuzzy hide and debated retrieval of the one she seldom let from her reach.

"Nelly-Belly's fine down there."

The sleepy-headed soul responded with raised arms and fell toward the abettor. Jules scooped her up, and the blameless soul melded against her body like a malleable shell. Her arms found Jules's neck as she rested her cheek against the soul she loved more than any bear. Lucy's abettor sighed as her heart fluttered and rested her jaw upon a small crown.

Jules shut down the fourth display plate and further shielded little eyes by rotating in her seat. After the terrors and adrenaline, her heart pounded *through* the little body that lay on her and moved her toward a change in scenery. Without a groan, she rose from the chair and moved on sure feet into the kitchen.

While she pulled open the refrigerator door, Hazy raised her head from rest. "Which do you want, partner?"

Hazy pointed past a covered water pitcher to the glass bottle of milk. While she watched with a sober face as milk chased emptiness from the glass, her fingers stroked the wing of a bluebird insignia on the breast of Jules's sleeveless blouse. Jules took the first sip, as per their habit, then held the glass as the sleepless soul drank. All the while, Hazy never abandoned the bird's threads.

She drank two large gulps, then a third, till breathlessness seized her. Her pupils reflected the false light of the room and she sighed heavy enough to cast her bangs across her brows. She swept her hand across Jules's breast and patted her own tummy. After she caught her breath, she took another long sip, by her measure, then offered the glass to Jules.

"All done?"

She nodded and lifted the glass toward Jules's chin. Rather than waste, Jules drank the rest of the milk, then rinsed. Hazy propped her forearm onto the dishwasher's muscular shoulder and observed in silence while she scrubbed the set of mouth-prints and dried the glass with one hand. No complaints, but a single nod of approval when they checked the glass under the kitchen light.

Jules sat the glass in the steam bin and spoke as soft as cotton against the child's ear. "Only *four* more eves till Hivi'ern."

Those sleepy eyes widened and her whole body turned rigid as she tried her absolute best to keep her excitement contained. Jules matched her expression, and the duo *pretended* to scream for joy without emitting one note beyond throaty exhalation. Lucy's abettor held the blameless soul tighter and swung her hips till two little feet swayed enough to produce a laugh the child buried against Jules's shoulder. For that, she received seven kisses to her neck and one to her crown.

As a real treat, Jules unwrapped a pocket-sized chocolate from a waxed paper and bit the candy in half. She chewed one bite and held out the other for the sleepless soul. What she loved more than chocolate was the way the little one kissed her fingers each time she took those shared treats. They chewed together, purred over the fragrant cocoa, and sighed.

"Want to sit with me a tick afore you go back to beddy-bye?"

A full cheek swept in agreement across Jules's shoulder. In response, she shut out the light and patted a slender thigh. Mid-step, she gathered the worn bear off the floor, then tucked him between their torsos. Hazy pinched his leg with her own and patted his forearm the way that Jules soothed hers. The trio returned to the seat with an easy sigh, too unnerved to relax and too relaxed to move. Jules offered a rhythmic sway but yawned ahead of her best mimic.

"Are we to have one of those eves, you s'pose? No, we don't s'pose. Lazy bones *s'pose* and we are *not* lazy bones."

Hazy shook her head and brushed Jules's forearm with a socked foot as her toes settled against the desk's ledge. Jules rested her elbow on the same desk, shy of little toes, but with an urge to evade protocols and duties. She winced toward the nearest closed door, recessed into four panels and painted the color of shadows. Her gaze fell toward the tarnished knob, fitted with a deadbolt above and another below. The one beneath the knob faced outward and half-tempted the Guardian's abettor, but in annoyance's stead, she spoke into two mismatched little ears.

"I must wake Lucy now."

Hazy pinched her lips between her teeth and buried her chin against her bear's crown as Jules set her down and scooted away from the desk. The unforecastable temper tantrums of the Guardian who slept in the next room worried the trio—for Hazy oft counted the bear's opinion on all matters. As Jules approached the door, the child tucked her bear behind her, certain to keep her fellow shielded from what awaited. With three swift pats against the wood, the abettor roused her benefactor.

"Lucy. I need you to wake."

The blameless soul watched with wide eyes as Jules grinned, then followed her fist as she knocked again. Her attempt proved considerate versus the scream that came from the other side of the door. A heavy object struck the plank at eye level, then another that shattered like a drinking glass near the upper bolt.

On a mad dash, Hazy rushed toward her bedroom. She forgot her place in the room, though, and struck the back of Jules's chair with all her might. The chair held, and the blameless soul fell onto her backside. The reaction startled her, and she trembled in pain without uttering the cry that pushed toward her throbbing mouth.

Jules cooed her from afar and blocked the unanswered door. Her eyes gleamed for Hazy, and she patted at the air, as though she coddled her. The sleepless soul half-crawled toward her room till a barrage of foot stomps scared her into another attempt at running. By then, Jules bristled.

When the door swung open, the abettor used her whole body to keep Lucy back. Of matched height, Jules's better-developed shoulders and thighs defended any sighting of Hazy from the ill-tempered Guardian. That same Guardian stood barefoot on shards of broken glass and never winced. The veins in her arms showed and her teeth moved like small blades along her pale lips as uncounted tongues aligned to form a lone, discernible voice.

TULL

"I told you to let me mend!" Her raspy breath sounded vulgar and her eyes fluttered as if whispering voices fed her words to speak. "Do you not remember where I've spent the past four eves?"

"Every soul remembers," Jules challenged and slowed her speech. "*I* seem to be the first soul to discover an attack on our judge."

Lucy gasped a dry breath. "Is that all?"

"Samuel's reel is on display plate four. I'll look in on Hazy."

"Don't wake her!"

Jules found Hazy crouched alongside her sunken bed, hidden by a protective mound of hand-sewn stuffed animals. Almost all joined her collection as gifts from the Guardians—who doted on her with tokens where their abilities to connect with a blameless child failed them. She of two purposes, whose instincts thrived at an early age, made the art of soothing her seem effortless. As she held her in her arms, Hazy bawled and trembled, cautious not to let her voice betray her.

The abettor wept with her, sniffling above the child's best efforts to go unheard. So changed their hopes for a peace-filled eve and a pleasant morn. Jules liked Judge Gwynne; she liked that he looked out for families. Now, with Olley and Samuel incapacitated, and a plan she arranged afore the offering in ruins, she needed a new strategy for the sake of the beloved and blameless soul she kept close.

II. | Traveler

Nine

The 24th Eve beneath the Moon of the Old Embers
The 114th Gathering Season of the Accession
In the Blessing of I'Esh, who tends the harvest.

<u>The Corban Outpost</u>
A prosperous fruit ranch kept secluded by almond trees.
Within the hearing of the Divided Falls.

Tull mended far from the modernized settlements and well-lit places. He hid in the fog-draped lowlands where projection-gliders lost their way, and few traveled in the eve. Auditory sensors tracked sound, but the optical feeds went dormant once visibility fell beneath two-fifths' potential. This late into the gathering season, and so near to the Feast of Hivi'ern, the fog provided immeasurable isolation.

The Larson Territory offered simple comfort that most failed to experience due to fear. As a traveler headed away from the mountains through the Weston Territory and across the Creighton Territory, fear turned palpable. In Larson, fear and terror matched the withered and barren Creightonian fields. The fog represented the territory's last breath and little more.

The Guardian's new headship rested amid Reformers; a populace devoted to the Triune and practitioners of charity. The laws did not touch them. They were fruit growers, planters, and gleaners who broke their backs in humility yet opened their arms to strangers. The distractions of the offering interested them little, and they worried more about the coming winter and the howling that nestled in the fog.

TULL

When locals found Tull on foot, they offered him a ride without fear of his appearance. Once he settled, they gave him fresh water and apples picked from the tree that morn. Two parents, two sons, and two daughters. They offered him no names, for they sought no credit from the secondkind for their deeds.

The daughters held to their Larsonite upbringing. The sons offered guesses for his travels till their mother hushed them. Their mother expressed *curiosities* over the soul who kept the outpost he traveled toward. Then, the family's head hushed *her*, and they traveled in silence; none treating Tull as though his timing or presence troubled them, even unto the moment when he chose the cover of the eve in their care's stead.

At Sister Lois Westmore's outpost, the Guardians resided in legends *whispered* like the tales of old. So, when one of the four allowed members visited, the air buzzed with giddiness and expectation. Tull earned his invitation by his conduct and his host's trust by his secrecy. The nineteen in her care, aged twelve to fifty-six spans, worked as hard as any Guardian. They never sought protection, yet found they enjoyed an extra defense more than once in fear's stead.

After he endured the tests against possession, suffered an indignant examination of his body, prayed, and fasted, he vanished into a chamber kept for favored guests. Nothing lavish, though decorated in shades of burgundy and ivory hues, and nothing above or beneath the furnishings of all who made their home in Sister Lois's care. The chamber offered comfort without inviting laziness as he offered mystery for the wit and fantasy for the eye.

He mended among souls who nurtured widows and orphans. They too buried those who had no other. Upon land willed to her by the territory's first judge, she who provoked the curiosities of the modest made a haven from the cruel. Thus, the acquaintance of scarred rabble-rousers betrayed her character.

One resident, a witness of twenty spans, sneaked into the chamber and admired Tull in a manner frowned upon by belief and benefactor. Still, curiosities and sin-filled whim tumefied at the sighting of the secondkind's guards. Though hidden behind two walls of opaque glass that reached no higher than the tip of his breastbone, the soul who lasted ten eves at Gutefiel gleamed amid a steam shower while the steadiness of fire from the copper stove reflected against his musculature and scarring. With no potential husbands, this spectator wrestled her curiosity with prayer-chapped lips and wide eyes.

TULL

Like the steam that cast outward from Tull's cleansing, the fog that crept into the chamber through open windows provided a third barricade for wandering eyes. As if alarmed by a prowler, his onlooker held the hem of her skirt against her legs like a shield and tested that the hood of her robe remained against her crown. She who heard tales of the hand-shaped marks upon the Guardian's shoulders, where a fiery Minister plucked him from harm and changed his bones, felt the slithering fog's betrayal as her sharp gasp told of her intrusion.

"Do mind the shadows! Lest you're a water wraith, in which case, *do* mind your nearness."

She giggled but stayed hidden. "You are He Whom Ministers Adore!"

"*She* calls me the Son of Mighty Maidens. *He* calls me slow to learn."

"*She* whose unflawed handprint rests upon you?"

"That tale! Ministers burn with the brilliance of fire but remain gentle to the touch. In their presence you'll know peace that you've never imagined, not harm."

The sound of his easy laughter, more tired than practiced, possessed the warmth to draw her across the chamber's open floor. She wrapped her fingers around the wooden frame that held together the outer fence of opaque glass. The interior wall, nearer to the shower and rigged to confine the mess, kept her innocent even as the fog and steam drifted between. Still, she angled for a better look.

Tull swung and cast steam in her direction, if only to provide a startle. "I might've resisted. Do guard your eyes, but say what's worth the risk to you."

"The others say you've no abettor; only the scion who awaits your fall for his chance to boast the purpose that is yours. Truly! Our Creator would not purpose you to labor with no aide. Does no soul tend to you?"

"Sister Charlotte!" A new voice provoked one of them. Not the Guardian.

Like a scolded soul, she spun to a dizzy standstill. "Sister . . ."

In the doorway stood Tull's pristine hostess. Sister Lois Westmore looked over her charge first, then the Jacobian, who never once covered his nakedness nor stopped cleansing. Her eyes, keen and dark, showed regard for the opaque glass and the fog retreating into the eve. As she inhaled, she drew her eyes toward the blushing soul. "Were you not present when I declared this room off-limits, Sister?"

"I returned his boots." Her claim wafted like steam and met the briskness of fog.

"A task I did not choose for you. Were he a soul of similar ability and contrary intention, he might have snapped your neck." The rebuke cast shame upon her charge and humiliated the Jacobian, too. "Weep over your fortune later, and tell me why you disturbed our brother's mending."

Tull increased the steam and let the accompanying hiss mock them as Sister Charlotte flitted through another excuse. Enke'loi restored him and sealed him when she delivered his soul back to this span. She who invited him into her home considered such claims blasphemous. So, he stilled his tale and went along with the allotted mending time required of all Guardians after the offering, lest the territories fear their protectors plotted against them.

As for appearances, if another of the outpost's residents entered the chamber, they would reflect the ratio by which females outnumbered males across the territories. Had his hostess not endured Gutefiel or combatted suffering, and had she not the skills of a surgeon, she would find one less guest to correct. She proved brisk in word, work, conduct, and—oft to her discredit—affection. Tull respected this friend to his elders, but disapproved of her coldness toward those she deemed *less* or *contrary* in their belief by her expectation for them.

In soberness, Sister Lois approached the opaque wall with a second towel, as if to chastise her guest, and never ceased from dressing down Sister Charlotte. "—never spend an eve in the place where he has spent ten. Thanks to the Creator for His mercy. Amen, Sister?"

There came a whispered amen; then, the reminder of Tull's deeds as the flow of steam ceased. "Our Jacobian Guardian drove out He of Dark Hearts with fire and cast him into the crater in temptation's stead."

Sister Lois huffed and looked to the cleansed Jacobian for an answer as he stepped between the two walls of glass, then blotted his face and beard, his crown, shoulders, arms, and chest. "Your territory's Guardian set that fire. Nadl—*He of Dark Hearts*—mends in a sanitarium. He, too, fears the fog."

"Our sister reveres the tales of your work above the care she gives her own." Sister Lois watched him cast aside one towel and matched Sister Charlotte's flush pallor when he girded his waist with the second. "She will fetch our brother soup and bread. And fruit."

"Yes, Sister."

"Innocent Sister." Tull called to her and offered correction to her prior moniker for him. "The Ministers love every soul; even those they battle."

TULL

The reminded soul's joy-filled grin proved her inner gentleness; however, her curiosities moved her. She acted in obedience to her benefactor and departed as the Guardian dressed in trousers and a sleeveless undershirt.

"She too grows curious."

"I oft attract the meddlesome."

Tull took the barb with an aware grin. "Hofnarr starves his child-bride. I tell you, I would not weep if she turned him into her next meal."

"You see how they torment those who disrupt their laws. Her father set his voice against his Honor. That was his only interest in taking the child."

"I believe his Honor's laws torment our Creator."

"You cannot touch him."

"They told me as much the last time, too."

"Though now you are the soul who walked from that place after—"

"I know my purpose without legends!"

Sister Lois raised her hand and hushed him that she might make her point. "Our ancestors destroyed their purpose on accusation. From them, the Era of the New Fathers sought judges to rule. No soul since has shown the resolve to right that rule."

"Zeck would—"

"Beau Itzal Zeck was a simplistic brute. You establish your legend with resilient silence, and, like your tremendous belief, your name suffers from what you consider lowliness. From that, any truth or any lie can be spun by any soul that speaks in your stead. If the territories knew of your discernment or your displeasure with the laws of corrupt judges, you might lend them the courage of speaking out in *their* belief."

"Olley's our talker."

"And what does he need you to be for him now?" She offered him a laundered shirt prepared while he mended. "Nita remains silent. Your *subordinates* mend. As you are required to mend. We needn't our Guardians failing when we—"

"Don't mistake me for one of *your* subordinates. I thank you." He took a measured breath as he considered Nita, put on his vest, then set his towels in a copper steam hamper. "You've not heard from Ernie, then?"

"Nor have I the expectation. We have heard of *disturbances* along the southern hem." Her words sounded breathless, more elected than free. "*Commotion* in the shadows; near the observatory that Olley adores."

"Commotion favors the shadows."

She oversaw the lay of his suspenders across his broad shoulders. "They've tucked a church nearby."

"Near Judge Rogers' memorial?"

"*Near*; at the divided falls." She watched him roll the sleeves of his crisp shirt. "My mother called the place the Church Amid the Shadows. Her era comforted the diseased and the starving there; when such conditions befell this land.

"Just this eve, a traveler, from whom we purchase our tools, spoke of the commotion, and observed two souls—blameless, he suspected—moving about the church. He's old and did not investigate, for the glebe proves unstable there; unsafe for dwellers. Perhaps a Guardian could offer passage? We have place and purpose for any soul who seeks them for the winter."

"As you say; now that I've mended."

"You've another morn and eve yet. There are souls eager to serve in your stead: Ingram Franklin Kemp, Cameron Lou Fenner's daughter, even Timothy—"

"An unpardonable choice." His tone invited her chuckle. "What happened in the territories during the offering?"

She crossed the floor toward where the gift of a new scarf hung and pinpointed her answer, though she knew far more and withheld. "All prepare for the winter ahead. Partakers hanged more Believers. A tank failed at the exposition in Sevier. Another two travelers went missing in the Carpenter Territory near the Shelbian border. Some blame Marvin's troubles with keeping watch over his creatures.

"This produced chatter of the *Devourer* returning; like every gathering season! O, why do such tales arrive afore the onset of winter? I s'pose to give the blameless a tale to keep them in on blustery eves. Odd spinsters, too.

"Scion Kind Hand suffered a medical crisis. She's with child. They suffer sleep-terrors of such an extreme that their hearts bear too much strain, though I fear her allowance of Partakers into her home proves as great a risk." She snapped a vine of passionflower from a fresh wreath in the corner of the room and her tension broke. "Do you dream yet?"

"No."

"No, I imagined not."

Sister Lois's scoff cut worse than her correction. Reformers dreamt during natural sleep cycles. In this time, they communicated with the Triune. The rest of the secondkind, deemed too conflicted by the Reformers, remained void of their gift.

They *needed* the guidance of the Reformers like the rule of the judges, lest they fall captive to the Fallen First.

She folded the vine of passionflower into the scarf and set them with a pack of supplies he kept with her as a reserve. He looked from her ever-trembling hands upon the column of seventy-four buttons that kept her gown fastened along her spine and admired the contrast between the ivory fabric and her rich hues separated by a crease of pinched flesh at the jawline. She lived further from the grip of judges than any other soul and restrained every moment with a caution that he imagined needled even their Creator.

"I'm reminded!" She took from her pocket a gold alms. "The traveler who delivered you to our door returned. He feared you'd lost your last alms."

Tull saw in her hand the alms he had *tucked* into the bench seat as repayment for random kindness.

"When truth proves untold, or a soul's purpose, a mind creates another."

He ignored her intentions. "I'm sure you'll find reason to buy apples soon."

She accepted his gift with a solemn nod.

"You despise the uncounted intrusions of our judges, but I'll remind you that their advancements still benefit you. Your outer wall could use fortifying. Should Edvard Böhm Bartosz near this place seeking his daughter—or you—your Guardians will learn of his trespass and come right his path."

His host swooned not from chivalry but sickness at the mention of Bartosz. "I'll see what keeps Sister Charlotte from bringing your supper."

When the silence settled on him again, he found his boots, though damaged, next to a chair and awaiting his feet. Sister Charlotte or another had polished the ash of Gutefiel from the soles and laces, either to bring the Creator glory or to keep memories of that place from Sister Lois. He rose and put on the new scarf, moved toward the open window, then climbed over the sill and leapt without eating or taking provisions or vine. Better his hostess kept a supply of weapons, should Edvard Böhm Bartosz prove more cunning than Tull found him.

TEN

<u>BARKAMENA LEA</u>
A PLACE OF INTERMENT FOR LARSONITES.
WHERE THE FIRSTKIND BARGAIN.

The amber haze of false light from Sister Lois's outpost proved the last invention that Tull needed that eve. The Moon of the Old Embers shone amid the distant sky-fires and cast a wave of brightness over the field that he would cross for the next watch; lest his foot slip and cast him unto the shadows of creation. Away from the souls of the secondkind, he provided an ear for the wailing of creatures who remembered the moon beneath their feet and not above head. Sister Charlotte, though, might have wailed, too, at the shallow pool of fog that the Jacobian waded through.

The lea due south of the Corban Outpost drew his pity. No other site rivaled the forests of the Jacoby Territory, for the forests there stood taller, sturdier, and loftier than all others. He felt his memories needled in this sallow place. In a previous land, Tull ended the one hundred fourteenth span in the sparse forests along the northern ledge of the isle, where he sought Deacon Richards Vernon Shield, a Partaker, for the burning of a Reformer's outpost near the Carpenterian foothills.

After the Guardian tracked, captured, and towed Shield to the judges, he rode one last time with the arsonist. He had delivered him to this same field, where Shield joined a revolving crew of sixty souls who atoned for crimes and pulled the fragments of the Larson Territory's wasted trees from the glebe. While he could prevent Shield's tragedy, to stand here afore that time again humbled Tull.

"Too many trees uprooted."

TULL

Through their atonement, the convicts ushered another purpose upon the field. The Last War ended without resolution, but the Accession claimed more souls than either army. The firstkind's arrival took one-quarter of the population in what stood as the territories at that time. The wood from uprooted trees served as markers for the buried secondkind. From where he stood, graves stretched beyond his vision.

"Too many grave markers."

By the time the storms caused by the Accession passed, another one-third of the population had fallen. Five hundred fifty-five thousand members of the secondkind remained throughout the isolated territories that the storms also reshaped. Even in the one hundred twenty-second span, the Carpenter Territory made discoveries of lost settlements. Their ancestors resided still in overturned homes, water-crushed vehicles, and states of dread.

When the lastborn of the Era of Despair passed, the secondkind's numbers *scraped* above four hundred forty-four thousand. At the end of the Era of the New Fathers, the populace decreased another one-eighth. Then started the Era of the Reformers; Tull's grandmother's era. Juanita Gene James inspired uncounted souls, led Reformers, judged twelve territories, but treasured one soul above all others.

"Truly, no voice but yours could make our Mighty Creator hesitant to keep me from my eternal rest. I miss your soul the most, J. J."

The Reformers labored with the mercy and knowledge imparted to them from the firstkind. They cared for the orphan, comforted the widow, mended the broken, and lifted the spirits of the weary with rejoicing—evermore with rejoicing. They succeeded where the Church of old, the enterprises, and the government failed. Through their obedience to Yah and labor for His glory, the population improved, along with the abundance of provision and progress but the secondkind cultivated fields of graves larger than most farms and the sight shamed him.

"Would I change this even if I returned a thousand times?" He climbed a lone wall that stood since the Accession and remembered a face amid those who labored with Shield the Partaker that resembled he whose reel Marvin kept *for fealty*. The tethers and sites that once fascinated now wearied, and though he longed to understand Creator, siblings, and cousins, better, he straddled the wall as a name amid the grave markers registered in his mind. "Kovács."

"Tell of your troubles, *cousin*."

TULL

The gentlest voice filled Tull's ear. One of the First Creation sat beside him; longer and leaner than the Jacobian. The creature's voice hinted at a *grace* unseen in this land, but the brass body bore the scars of uncounted battles.

"I will not judge thee."

Tull ached for what he had in that previous land. "I regret what I remember."

The Minister remained patient as a doe trotted into the field and grazed unafraid.

"There are so many pieces to see but each tow a burden."

"Better that the sins of this place be forgiven, buried as vessels in the Forbidden Sea, lest pain stifle the flame that burnishes the soul." The breeze settled. "Now, tell of your *troubles*."

"Did I choose the wrong priority? Did I confuse purpose and headship? All that I was too proud to set my heart upon. I turned from them and they are unguarded."

The words of truth flowed from Tull's heart without his pride's reshaping them. "I have failed more times, across more lands, than I ever care to count. I've gone back on my word, forsaken my promises, turned shallow the heartfelt claims that drove me to my knees. I can't imagine why the Triune finds use of me.

"His mercy spares me. That makes the *aftershock* of my foolishness hurt more. *Knowing* that I can do better, but falling into traps over and again, as afore and afore. How could such a fool as me deserve mercy? I failed them."

"All who fill the throne room of the Most High hear your heart's cry, cousin, and They are your peace. I leave thee to carry such precious tears to our Creator's phial."

Tull glimpsed the Minister's face, collapsed on one side by battle. The creature smiled and exuded the warmth of his care in the same moment he then vaulted into the sky-fires. Not one hair upon Tull's head scattered from the others, nor did the gust cause him to squint. Such elegance and strength humbled the unworthy secondkind.

Another moment, then Tull leapt to the other side of the wall and continued through the territory judged by Marvin Elam Katch and guarded by Robbie Rudat Pine. With each step, the pain he towed lessened; not vanished, not absolved, but reduced in scale. He ran his fingers across the coat of the doe's back and shared her pulse as his last tether to the lea. The grazing creature then watched the Jacobian who entered the dank timbers and vanished unto the fog.

Directed by the breeze on his lips, he pivoted clockwise and passed under the intertwined branches of two honey locust trees. Hidden from the eyes of those creatures who nested above, he measured every step, certain that no unnecessary sound betrayed him. Forty paces in, he stooped and patted the glebe till he touched an exposed root. That root he followed toward a boulder cracked open from the terrane upward.

On the other side, he discovered a path of singed grass that ran toward the Archibald Territory. Tar-like strands cast a rotted odor and made him change his course according to the wind flow. He stayed to the north of the brook and strained his neck as he followed a trail of brass flecks that rested beneath the surface, lest he agitate his heart by entering the waters. Till the terrane changed underfoot, slick from surface mildew and unforgiving from withheld rain, he let his prayer dwindle.

"Child! Come to me, child!" A maternal voice pierced the darkness. "If you hear my voice, call out. Let me find you!"

None sought a blameless soul. Rather, a luring spirit baited those who travelled near to the shadows. Those foolish enough to respond opened their bodies to harm, their minds to madness, and their souls to undoing.

"Child?" The voice drifted further into the darkness. "Child?"

Tull held still, then the breeze rustled leaves and silenced the lure. "Yah-valo sävuttä vari'eoi'hin i'ea käppä Pi'meyttä."

In response, the voice that lured squealed in lament and cast leaves and nuts down on Tull. As one fled unto the shadows of branches, the other committed his path to the mildew and tar. If he traveled far enough, he might see the creation of a new vein in the glebe. The judges considered lone exploration of the veins a crime; still, the Guardian traveled deeper into the woods.

ELEVEN

8 GORATZEA PLOT

A ONCE TRANQUIL SETTING.
NOW ABANDONED.

When the Church of old fell, the Guardians of the era spent a season boarding windows, bolting doors and gates, and preparing every abandoned house of worship for a time of drought. Such was the law of Judge Brooks Howie Rogers. Devout in his love for the Word and the law, he wanted every building preserved and ready for a time when the secondkind returned to their way. His decree held now for more spans than Tull witnessed in all his resets.

He saw what coming terror drove the proud to their knees, and the fear-filled cries of the forsaken stung his ears and doubted Lois's tale of trespass. Where the tar-like strands ran into pools of shadow and broken terrane upheld moss stood the Church Amid the Shadows. Any closer to the southern ledge and the structure's shadow might have fallen into the sea. Letting pass his doubt, he approached the squatty, single-storey design.

The shadows that lent the locale a name fell upon the easy slope of the roof, cast down by massive trees too muddled in darkness for identifying. Eras-old growth dropped into the sea on a whim there. The foundations proved too brittle to bear *this* era's burden and remained an ever-changing contour. Whilst the glebe rotted from beneath the surface, the church walls stood.

No active sign of trouble kept away the Guardian, nor a need for fearlessness. The roar of the divided falls—a waterfall separated by a grove of trees—buzzed in Tull's ear like an insect about his head. He spotted the mist to the east and the sea to the south. Ten paces further south awaited the sea; lest the plummet broke his neck first. Given his penchant for drowning, falling, *and* breaking his neck, he kept twelve paces from the ledge.

So, when a bay of small lights above head redirected and veered toward him, he took notice. "Why keep a holding pattern above this place?"

A lightweight, triangular copper frame fitted with a silent engine and navigational fins hovered over him. A cannister of lights, microphones, projector lenses, and a viewing screen fitted to the belly focused on the Guardian and his surroundings. The gadgets distracted from the emblazoned logo of the tech outfit that designed the glider, then a mechanized voice greeted him.

"RECOGNIZING. GUARDIAN NELSON JAMES TULL.
ACKNOWLEDGING . . ."

"Declare ownership and patrol settings."

The glider shimmied in resistance, as if programmed against revealing such information. Still, the craft proved intelligent enough to recognize Tull's authority. Whoever kept an eye on the church hid from the Guardians. So, the Guardian proved his ornery streak against the secretive owner.

"Override. Guardian Nelson James Tull requests use of glider number"—he squinted at the low-lit underside—"CTQ840429 for single-frequency relay. Passcode: Traveler Zero-Eight, Zero-Eight Abide."

The craft strained with palpable violence till the onboard lights flickered. A spark of light rippled in the display plate and the landing feet extended, then retracted, then hammered the trio of bays that kept them tucked away during patrols.

"INTERFACING. SEEKING AUTHORIZATION . . ."

Tull shivered when the disembodied voice of the glider's operating system spoke. Committed to laws or not, in an age where the *wind* spoke, he preferred machinery that did not. "Switch to visual interface."

"ACKNOWLEDGING . . ."

TULL

The glider's fins adjusted, then obeyed Tull. A beam of emerald light mapped his height, gauged his eyesight, and shifted into a readable position shy of his reach.

"ENTERING SILENT MODE . . ."

"I thank you. Locate Judge Ernie Purcell Bliss of the Jacoby Territory."

AUTHORIZATION NOT RECOGNIZED.

"Listen to me better, you rejected—"

The glider fluttered and drifted, which prompted a change in tone.

"You're correct, you're correct. Not about my authorization, but I must mind my tongue. I thank you for the reminder. Now, list all current Guardian abettors."

IDENTIFYING ALL CURRENT GUARDIAN ABETTORS . . .

ARCHIBALD TERRITORY ABETTOR
MARKO GLENN STRAN—BEACON INDETERMINATE.
LAST ACTIVE 68 WATCHES AGO.

"Seek but do not rile. Pass."

CARPENTER TERRITORY ABETTOR
JULES BAKER SHANNON—BEACON IDENTIFIED.
TRAVELING WESTWARD ON NO. 8 STEAM TRAM.

"Know that I seek you . . . but not through a plate." He fretted. "*Pass.*"

CREIGHTON TERRITORY ABETTOR
TIMOTHY TODD MCCREA—BEACON IDENTIFIED.
HELD AT 84 PENDER'S CHANCE BY ARCHIBALD TERRITORY
CHIEF INSPECTOR LODI STEVEN HONT.

One brow arched high above his cold, pewter iris. "Pass."

TULL

JACOBY TERRITORY ABETTOR
VALERY LETA KOSLOWSKI—BEACON INACTIVE.
LAST ACTIVE: 19,392 WATCHES AGO.

"You would have watched Ernie." Tull's missing abettor represented why he despised the shadows. His scowl worsened. "Continue to seek. Pass."

LARSON TERRITORY ABETTOR
JOSHUA BLAINE ROYCE—BEACON IDENTIFIED.
IDLE AT 22 MCNEELY CENTER.

"I forgot Royce. Pass."

SHELBY TERRITORY ABETTOR
FARRELL WAYNE HAMER—BEACON IDENTIFIED.
ACTIVE AT 47 SNEEDEN RANGE.

McCrea stood a better chance of hearing Tull ask for help. "Pass."

WESTON TERRITORY ABETTOR
VIOLET GREY PINNEY—BEACON IDENTIFIED.
IDLE AT 110 CELE FARMS.

"Idle? Pass." Violet, in George's absence, maintained their farm of crops and cattle, and Tull respected her right to rest. Without an available abettor, he considered the schedule of his scion. "*All is well*, Lefty. Request to pair—"

The glider raced away from the Guardian and across the brim toward the sea. Tull stood leg-locked and jaw-slacked and watched the device crash into the tide, as visible beneath the sky-fires and by the disappearance of onboard light. More plagued the church than two blameless souls breaking the perimeter. Now, he stood detached from all his fellows.

TULL

"I imagine they'll withhold my alms for that glider, too. Truly! Your humor prevails. I would enjoy laughing along with You, O Mighty Creator, but I will step onward without the ease of tech. Pardon my laziness."

The branches rustled on a calming breeze and he pressed onward across the shadows. A derelict prayer garden welcomed him with bristled ferns and a cracked footpath that fell into open rifts in the terrane. Neglect teemed from the once-holy place as Believers worshipped out of doors, where the First Creation oft joined. Churches devolved into mausoleums, much like the mass graves and eroded lands that surrounded them.

He discovered two planks removed from the door and estimated their gap let in a trespasser of slight build. Jules with her musculature, Nita with her height, and Sister Lois with her rigid demeanor would not pass through. Hazy would pass. Q. J. would carve a tunnel through a crack in the stones. Tull could have crammed Tim through. The Jacobian ripped loose two more planks and straightened the stack till all looked removed by the same hand. He then entered the church.

Loose dirt shifted beneath his foot, two steps across tile. There he paused and looked into the dark at the *removed* furnishings. Another soul had gutted the entirety of the sanctuary. No pews, no floor tiles beyond a two-tile perimeter, not even the foundational belly. Every board formed a wall set to the east, holding back the dirt dug up from the surface and turned the refuge into a dig site.

A lattice grid of braided-steel cables partitioned off the interior, minus a ledge of tile no more than a stride's breadth. Eyelets in the walls of the church offered anchor points. No fragment of the slab foundation remained. Draperies covered the stained-glass windows, backed from the outside by planks like those that covered the door. Disturbers *tried* hiding the dismantling from sibling, cousin, and Creator.

The achievement, depending on hands, consumed two, maybe three, discreet moons. He considered every aspect deceitful, letting pass how purposeful the process seemed. He peered into a hand-dug pit that ascended deeper below than the steeple rose above the entryway. A breeze blew from the pit and the cables swayed till they created a musical sound.

A hand-drawn glyph on a pile of dirt caught his eye and produced a scowl. An open heart, topped by a dove and absent of the pitch of a roof since he last saw the design in that previous land. Like an artist signing their creation, the glyph marked a claim on the dig site and filled him with angry breath.

TULL

"This is beneath you, Anya. And you, Sister. *Blameless!*"

Anya Nora Rains surfaced along Tull's path as oft as the moon went dark. The arrangement of the dig site spoke to her *designed* meddling and the idea of her nearness made him uneasy. Sister Lois Westmore knew that. A possible end to avoidance provoked him with a fire that rivaled Enke'loi's train.

"What has this to do with my purpose?"

He turned from the site and his attention fell on a rope ladder that draped from the surface into the pit's bleakness. The rungs matched an adventurous, if not slight, gait. Anya, who stood five heads high, distracted with her walk. The gap between rungs hinted that the blameless soul spotted in her company matched her height. She possessed a knack for luring the unwanted, too.

"We share her sting, runt."

He tuned out the divided falls and shut his eyes from the setting. His long fingers curled around the grooved texture of a braided-steel cable. When he plucked the cable, sound reverberated across the opening and a scraping noise stopped.

He rose and followed a small pair of boot prints across dirty tile. A second pair of shoe prints, sized larger and tapered inward, trampled the smaller feet and stoked his curiosity. If one trait held true across his every reset, Anya worked the watches in solitude. Worse, she worked them whilst most souls—Guardians counted—slept.

If she uprooted the place where hunger, disease, and contamination ceased, then she forfeited the expectation of a respected workspace. The Reformers did their work *afore* a new church rose and the judges found a way to bind their hands. They gave the secondkind a future, and Anya took away the reminder of them.

In the place he imagined he might find a cubbyhole where she napped, he found what created the scraping noise. His concern faded with a smile and an easy laugh. "Are *you* the Devourer?"

A raccoon with a twisted ear and a filthy coat feasted on a mesh bag of overripe avocadoes. The steely-eyed creature stared at the Guardian and chewed the husk. Gnashing tiny teeth, the furry creature tossed aside one piece and chose another with a softer underside. Tull cocked his jaw and exhaled his frustration.

"Much of that last bite rests on your chin" He watched the well-ripened creature toss aside another fruit. "I agree. Wrong consistency."

TULL

The mesh bag confirmed Anya's presence at the church. Her glyph, her shoe size, her method of laying out a dig site, and now one of her favorite foods. From the stench of the spoiled fruit, he reasoned a moon or more had passed since her last visit.

The Guardian shook his head and conversed with the avocado bandit. "If you're ever in a position to keep a soul from their end, pause and consider how much of a pain that soul might become to you."

The racoon's jaw stopped, as though the beast contemplated the advice. A spirit-possessed elk was a pardonable foe. A raccoon gorged on avocadoes was not. Tull backed down from the altar without further intrusion and spotted folded newsprint.

The since-departed soul who founded the publication detailed the isle's history with caution and adoration; as he treated his lastborn granddaughter. Of course, she still read his work. Tull imagined Philip Clapham Tarry's supernal view of Anya dimmed now. As he tossed away the rag, a distraction of light caught his eye. Without thought, he grabbed at a tri-folded slip of paper that fell from between the newsprint pages with one hand.

In his error, he forgot the nearness of the cables that formed the grid across the pit. The same layer of leather and embedded steel that protected his feet and legs allowed for one braided cable to slip beneath the frayed hem. The snag turned the Guardian's leg into a lever and thrust him headlong into the hole in the floor. His voice rose as his body fell, and he kept a tighter hand on the papers than the raccoon kept on his snack, which rolled along the altar and chased after the Guardian.

TWELVE

Tull's shoulder broke loose the first plank, his head the second, and his hip the third. A pile of brittle timber cushioned his fall, and he landed hard enough to break the pile and cast upward a cloud of aged dust. An avocado struck his left eye, but he never lost his hold on that tri-folded slip of paper, even as he wiped away the residue of wet fruit. No, in pain, he wrung the sheet and crumpled the crisp edges.

As he made the *pat* check for breaks, he snapped a bone. He held that bone up without contest and without pain. His broad chest then swelled with disapproval as he closed his eyes. The odds of timber breaking his fall dwindled.

He turned his head and stared into the orbital socket of an abandoned skull. To his credit, he never screamed. He never cursed. Some sudden shifting of his full body occurred, but even that *seemed* understated. The way he kicked away the overlapped remains till he found solid footing and thrust his whole body upright in a panic, however, embarrassed him.

He flung down the broken bone and remembered the slip of paper in his other hand. His muscles squeezed a groan from his lips when he arched his back and examined his fall. No blood or broken skin. In gladness, he cherished that the projection-glider and the rest of the territories missed his descent. He lifted a hand to brush cobwebs from his hair and crammed the scrunched paper against his brow.

"Almighty!"

The winds retreated at his utterance. Above him, the braided cables trembled like plucked strings and cast their percussive groan over him. As he collected his thoughts and dusted down, his knees, one hip, and an elbow cracked in relief. The air stank of another *relief* but, with nose and mouth covered by a new scarf, his senses focused on the distant sound of fracturing.

"'Yah, our perfect Creator, makes war in my name, so I must keep–'" His final word went unsaid as a gale struck his back and made him step further unto the darkness. "Not so still, then. As You say."

Tull unfolded the paper Anya kept tucked in newsprint. The sight of the Mumus name on the letterhead produced tears in his eyes. In his heart, the fragments of regard and concern he held toward the Gierigian meddler plummeted. He kicked one of the skulls into the shadows and wadded the paper.

From the hand-dug floor, he collected a glass jar that smelled of chicory, a leather strap like one found around a tool handle, and a frayed wad of twine. Anya wasted her alms on the best chicory root for she brewed fetid muck. She mishandled her tools, too. With her discarded trash, and an old knife he fashioned from a rail spike, he cobbled together a lantern.

In need of fuel, he trusted his sense of smell and headed toward the source of mire. *When* next he faced Anya, he wanted her to explain *why* she again added her hand to the Colonel's meddling. *How* she let that vile wretch sink his crooked teeth in her exceeded his wit. If she lied, he now knew *where* to toss both souls.

Mire burned purest when ignited through contact with iron–like the iron rail spike he heated and hammered down to a knife edge in a season when he traveled lighter than George. The glebe oozed with mire in areas of focused traffic as if the builders tapped into Ki'eoppa–the Pit. Thicker than syrup, more potent than ethane gum, the liquid held a lime-green hue and a bile-like froth. According to *experts* who encountered the Fallen First in pristine conditions, with the creatures sedated, mire aided in the digestion of glebe and ores.

Guardians knew the *balm* of the Fallen First. Every defiant member of the First Creation stripped off their brass armor and let their poisoned souls reshape a new and hideous outward appearance. The friction of an other-realm body that moved through this land created lesions and open sores. Mire, however foul to the secondkind's senses, acted as a salve against physical damnation.

The Guardian screwed the knife-punctured lid back onto the glass jar and watched the frayed twine-wick burn into the mire. The leather strap he tied around the mouth of the jar and to the trousers' belt loop near his hip. If he set the mire pool on fire with anthracite, he risked suffocation and a cave-in if the flame created an explosion. Such an error caused the Peekskill Mine collapse that made Buster Roderick King the first Westonian Guardian.

TULL

His eyes beheld the flicker of shadows along the tunnel's roof, where the moon shone through crevices, and he avoided counting the number of the Fallen First who filled the tunnel. They were small, knee-high at best, like lizards creeping across a downed log, and moved in the direction opposite his destination. The oily-husked creatures squealed and gnashed in their fright, and he stared into the blackened eye sockets of a handful that dismissed them.

As he furthered his exploration, he recited lines and verses from the Scriptures. Yah's irreproachable Word provoked the Fallen First and made them clamor for escape from the Truth. Their lament-filled pitch failed to drown out his voice, though. He who upheld belief tormented those who betrayed the Truth, and he noticed the shadows growing taller and increasing in breadth as he maneuvered them.

This time, he counted thirty-eight head. None taller than him, most walking on malformed hands and feet. A few held their heads high; though they had clawed away their features ages earlier. Even they, with their eyes extinguished and their jaws dislodged, kept *courts* of their own. Those who moved on stumped extremities, with cleaved hips and buckled backs, served by clearing away those who slowed the paths of the standing.

Some had oily husks, others bore limbs and bodies matted in hair. One sported charred wings that billowed like loose canopies with every step. Another resembled a feminine shape down to her cloven hoofs. None reacted to his presence; not even a snap of the jaw. They moved with their heads down, eager to flee provocation.

"Not one attempts to *heckle*. What have you freed, Anya?"

His lantern light danced as the winds fluttered like soft laughter. The activity earned a flick of his brow, then he stepped against the breath of creation. He brushed through a collective swarm of the fallen firstkind as if passing through a thicket of tall grass. A few stalks towered over him, swatting him with limbs. His eyes never stopped roaming for one familiar face in the crowd till that crowd diminished and he stood alone again.

"No. Not alone."

He accepted the internal voice that spoke to his heart, pushed further from the spot where he landed, and heard the snap of wood—actual wood this time. From the slip of his heel, lacquered and polished. He followed a trail of similar planks and discovered a shredded swath of silken fabric. His eyes twitched with a hint of identifying their purpose, but he kept his lips pressed.

Solemnness nudged a stride that stayed pointed toward what drove away the Fallen First. Where the air turned thick with the scent of mire and exhausted his lantern, the Jacobian tossed the iron rail spike into the vane that pooled along his left. When the mire ignited the core burned violet in color. Then putrid, green flame spread and lit a path whilst oily grit from ribbon-like smoke collected along the tunnel roof and bracing timbers.

The colors of the tunnel darkened as the reflective light of the pool captured the fire's soot. His eyes adapted, and he took the makeshift lantern from his hip. He overturned the jar onto the perforated lid and let the mire run out as he moved ahead. The terrane softened, like crushed chalk, and absorbed the mire to cut the pool down to a stream.

He crossed a burning fork in the course and ducked the slippery roots of trees that grew into the tunnel from overhead. The roots bore the same brass flecks he discovered in the brook, and he marveled at the way they twinkled like stars against the unnatural light. He tucked his head down when he passed under the nesting place of bats, the only creatures of *all* creatures immune to Fallen First influence. Even so, he found them ornery.

On the other side of the roots and bats, Tull discovered the skeletal remains of another thirty-three adults—plus the thirteen he landed upon. There, skulls sat plucked clean and broken like shells. He inspected the fabric of a shredded coat, caked with dust, and too pale in hue to determine the color in a flame's light.

A note of frankincense beneath the stagnant mire and old death teased his nostrils. The sweet resin served as a rub, a defense, versus the infestation of wandering spirits. He wore the same oils at Gutefiel. The resin harbored other purposes, but even the seediest of Partakers knew the might of a frankincense shield.

Tull continued, guided by the flames. One shadow moved under another power, not driven by fire or air. He watched this the longest, letting the soft edges find a form. In that time, he pieced together the discovery and mingled those facts with his knowledge of Judge Cyril Adair Mumus, whom he called *the Colonel* over voicing the monster's name. He exhaled a portion of his peace and shook his head.

TULL

"This is a tomb. The lacquered wood and the fabric a coffin. The remains are those who dug this grave. The Colonel's troops? Then there's the letter." He dared not speak Anya's name so near to the shadows.

"The church floor covered this place, like a guard on the gate. The Fallen First brought mire but the frankincense was for"—he turned toward the figure that created the well-formed shadow on the wall and craned his neck—"*you.*"

A sleek crown of rich, black hair and a deteriorated gothic veil offered the only concealment of a powdery-white figure; not pale by gene, rather from long-lasting absence from light. Still, she took Tull's breath. With a cinched waist *trained* by outside force, the feminine figure sauntered in the darkness of the tunnel like a prowling lioness. The veil slipped from her shoulders when she moved, and the embers flickered off patches of brass on her skin.

Not *on* her skin. *Part of* her skin. Where pressure on the body or pockets of sweat and moisture gathered, the skin turned not oily but hard like brass. Unlike *other* brass creatures in the land, she had borne the traits of growth via childbirth and the ability to conceive and suckle a child of her own. Enke'loi and the other female Ministers lacked those traits, for the hand of the Creator formed them above.

"Seko'tae."

The giantess stopped at the name of her kind and Tull shook his head at the slowest discernable pace. His disappointment toward Anya, his anger toward the Colonel, and his own pridefulness, led him straight into the nest of a Seko'tae. She confirmed as much when she echoed a guttural growl and snapped her teeth at him. The secondkind were punished for every advantage they held over *them.*

Letting pass the allure of her splendid build, her features proved her *difference* from the secondkind. Her upper lip bore a cleft that allowed her mouth to open wide. Her mouth required that room for the large, curved teeth that let her feast and war—like her father. Somewhere in time, a Minister drawn away from their purpose impregnated a daughter of the secondkind. Tull *again* stood with their fruit.

The pools of her amber-hued eyes fixed on him, but she hid her nose and mouth behind a tendril of her veil. Not her breasts, which rested above his head, nor the rest of her body. She proved ancient in her ways, for he had learned his ancestors believed a *dark sorrow* awaited those who looked upon the face of accursed fruit. Tull added dimness to his list of faults and looked her in the eye.

TULL

"You aren't The First and you aren't the red-haired one." His gaze proved as sharp as hers. He then sighed and realized by the paleness of her, "You are she who enraged The Last. He stomped out hordes to find you."

She looked upon him with no memory of those events.

"Another land."

Upon relaxation of the jaw and learning the shape of her mouth again, she responded in a dry, raspy timbre, "You speak of *lands* to me, gatherer?"

"I am the soul whom Enke'loi and Si'an-drosa'ahn keep from eternity. Your brother, Tai'bu Kaas, called me *I'ekuann*."

Her eyes flared, first with fear, then with wonder. She swiped her hand, solid brass and tipped to fatal points, along the scarred side of his face without damaging a cell. Her ribcage protruded from beneath the skin of her, less forgiving than bone. When she breathed out, she cast the bats from their rest and set the pollen of ancient bouquets upon him like snowfall. "Your kind served me well. Even when they grew feeble, they never asked that I free them from their servitude."

"They feared you. Fear isn't respect. Fear isn't gratitude."

She dropped to one knee, rested her forearm upon the other, and leaned in till she faced him. "And, do you not fear me? I am Si'el Uaen Söi'eä!"

His reflection showed in the brass of her chin and the ball of her nose. She possessed a feline's eyes, brilliant and startling. He saw his likeness there, too. He never adjusted in stance or batted a single lash, even when pecked a brass talon against his chest. His heart rate produced a soft ping, steady and smooth, and proved he was at peace.

"You will serve me as *conscript*."

"No."

She stomped her foot and extinguished the flames. Mire turned to fog-like smoke and formed a new veil around her head. In a show of strength, she took up another ancient skull and sank the tips of her brass fingers through bone as though an eggshell. He found the end distasteful and let their Creator know through silent protest.

"Remember that fear knows this child by name too."

TULL

In that same moment, *she* stopped. Tull watched her shadow-laden feet, her gleaming eyes, and the way the mire clustered in her absent breath.

"You hear, too?"

The Seko'tae roared and vaulted sideways, shoulder-first. She ran headlong at the tunnel wall nearest the Guardian. With might in her swing, she sank her fingers into the glebe and ripped away pieces he alone could not carry. To her credit, she never lashed out at Tull or let one fragment touch him afore she vanished into the darkness.

"If this is a bad idea, Patient and Mighty Creator, please be gentle toward this less-wise-than-humble *burden* You created."

Without delay, he charged into the escape tunnel forged by the Seko'tae. However fast she worked, the Guardian sprinted to match her pace, expectant that he might collide with her. Her roaring never ceased, nor did her bombardment of the glebe. His feet entangled with her spent veil, and he fell near where the tunnel disappeared from underfoot.

After he untangled his boots, he stood at the mouth and peered out into the darkness. He witnessed the collapsed village of the southern crest, nowhere near the divided falls. The rubble of elaborate homes mingled with the iron of overturned ships that surrendered to the Forbidden Sea. He saw a sliver of Si'el Uaen Söi'eä's color, then heard the splash she made as she pierced the waters.

"Pursuit is your purpose."

Tull leapt. He feared swimming. He disliked falling; but not worse than he feared drowning. Again. Fear took no true hold of him, for fire-light, purer than the sky-fires that kept the eve alit, hurled toward him. That great light flickered across the surface of the sea and filled him with calming breath.

Fire covered but never burned him. From the heart of the flame, two pristine brass hands extended and held him at the wrists. Gravity-fueled descent turned into an effortless, vaulting ascent and withheld from the sea one more fool. The terrane met the Guardian's feet and he bowed as the fire fell away from him.

"I thank y—"

The smile on the face of a Squire bled into a tremendous laugh that disturbed all that settled. The creature measured one head smaller than the Guardian, and the fire of his train fluttered like blossoms beneath a gentle rain. "Do not be afraid, Son of Mighty Maidens! I am a Squire of the one who kept you from falling afore and afore!"

TULL

"What shall I call you?"

"I am your cousin, friend, and your friend, cousin! Like you, I watched over the daughter of Elgaeus in her time of slumber. Elgaeus, brother of the one you call Enke'loi." The fire in his eyes burned hotter and Tull turned from him. The Squire spat onto the ground, then flame arose and warmed the Guardian. "The fire will not burn you, cousin!"

"I thank you for your intervention and your kindness." He observed the creature's smile. "Si'el Uaen Söi'eä, Si'el Uve Si'ellä, Vi'Epár Ducát, and Vi'emane. That's four of the Seko'tae I've seen. Four who've seen me. And Tai'bu Kaas makes five—though I have only heard him."

"A *sixth* hides in your shadows and a *seventh* keeps his true face from our Creator's second! He crouches among you in fear for his fruit and upholds his covenant with Mechh'täva to see her through her fragility lest he bloodies his hands."

The Squire looked toward the east. "Voices say of him, '*he is dead*' and weep! They do not know the truth of him. For however long his fruit lives, he will rise. A father honors his purpose when he comforts his child, when he fights for his child, as our Creator fights for us."

"Do you have a child for whom you fight, friend?"

"I am but a child!"

Tull recalled what he saw of the creature in the tunnel, through her riddled veil.

"Let not her beauty sway you, dear cousin. She is poisoned by the enchantress's spirit! And, she is tempted by the winds that brush against your kind. The winds tell her what fruit has spoiled."

"Is she wicked?"

"She is *Seko'tae*!" Friend's smile glimmered but remorse burned in his eyes. "Let me fulfill my purpose, cousin. Better you prepare for he whom you will see again."

Tull sensed the presence of faint souls upon them and pivoted till he faced the same uncounted soul who flustered Jules. Though not with them in true form, the disguised soul stood in tangible form but with the opacity of a specter. The Jacobian stared into the form's eyes and saw pools of blackness that drown glints of light.

"You will meet again where the snow falls upward."

"I remember . . . so many reunions."

Judge Gwynne's attacker hid beneath scarves of nondescript pattern and muted color. He wore common gloves of two colors; one black, and one charcoal gray. Plain gray trousers, rolled at the cuffs, rested upon boots salted by the sea and shrunken to fit another soul's feet. That contradicted how he walked and impacted how well the Guardians tracked him. Tull imagined he cobbled together a disguise from what he found discarded or fashioned a look that confused the descriptions of any witnesses.

"Let us end this deceit!"

He clutched a scarf and unfurled the bindings, one after another, and the uncounted soul never challenged. The *faces* that awaited surprised Tull. Rather, the *faces*. The blunt countenances of Wanderers pressed outward from within the body, and Tull observed that in the presence of the Squire one face smirked. Their horrid shapes deformed the flesh and made identifiable their jagged teeth and flared nostrils. The sockets of their eyes formed craters in the flesh and bile seeped from open sores in the skin.

The vessel's tones were not fair like Tull or Olley, not rich like George or Ingram, nor varied like Jules and Nita. His color bore the emptiness of necrotic blacks, anguish-riddled plums, and gaunt, abusive yellows—like Lucy. Wanderers ripped tissue, shattered bone, and burst cartilage when they fled the Infested. In this creature's case, the Wanderers tore apart his nose and mouth. Tull doubted he possessed the complete gift of smell or hearing any longer. Depending on the violence invited in, the ability to speak might have withered, too.

When Tull observed enough, the scarves he held disintegrated. Jules's uncounted soul remained. As the Guardian circled, he saw a scar on the aggressor's neck where a subtle light belonged, then the breeze cast the apparition away. He whom the Ministers kept from eternity looked upon the Squire.

"Our judges defended the Infested vessel who scarred my face. They gave her a purpose she would not have earned. They are vile corruptors! They stand on the necks of the pure while they compose more laws to cover their corruption."

"Your judges are not my judges. My purpose is not to know their sins or yours.

That humbled him.

"All belong in the design of the Creator, who desires that all be saved."

"I believe you are called to work for our Creator's glory, cousin. Though you may not understand His reasons, you may trust Him."

The terrane darkened and he lifted his head to find the Squire gone from sight. A flock of spirits scattered in the creature's wake, and the vanishing of their shrill cries improved the stillness that settled back into place. Those spirits—cowards without form—stayed away. Such was the mark that the Ministers and Squires impressed upon those that turned from the Triune.

"Your plan is for the best. I suspect I'll struggle against a creature that resembles Edurne; as Si'el Uaen Söi'eä does resemble her!"

Edurne, a beloved character Thesp Danele Gertie Zuriñe portrayed in the film *Atlantida*, was the aspiration of uncounted souls. The thesp, who too portrayed Maia Espe Zeck in a film that stung the heart of Tull's first love, was not. Still, he considered her copper statue outside the old Eidolon Pictures lot in Bel Geddes, of the Gierigian remnant. As he turned toward the remnant, the wind billowed across the plain and brought to mind the winds along the Jacobian bluffs.

"Where the snow falls upward, you say."

One for Me . . .

An Interim

THE 25TH MORN BENEATH THE MOON OF THE OLD EMBERS
THE 114TH GATHERING SEASON OF THE ACCESSION
IN THE BLESSING OF I'ESH, WHO TENDS THE HARVEST.

BEACON 085.16.989 RECOGNIZED NEAR 1219 REFORMATION WAY . . .
IDENTIFIER CONFIRMED—NITA NAOMI OZUL.
PURPOSED TO SERVE THE SECOND CREATION AS 23RD GUARDIAN.

On a narrow road, near the line where the Perlinese desert met the Westonian foothills, ill-will raced to construct a roadblock on the forgotten route to the Larson Territory. The trees, near petrification, took modest root in the eroded surface and cracked the dusty glebe each time the wind teetered the branches. Aquifers once fed the region, but the waters passed with the era that remembered them. So, Guardian Nita Naomi Ozul worked with what little faith remained.

She whom Tull replaced in the offering was an absolute tactician. Where others saw no way, she saw traps, lures, and the like. Three trees divided by neglected road, lit by the sky-fires, void of copper posts and gliders, presented a pinch-point to snare a rig. That rig was her first step at countershock against Olley's suffering.

Nita wanted a certain rig, with a unique measure between the road and the rickety headlamps, oft seen traveling that path beneath the veil of fog and sleep. So, she gauged oncoming rigs through a calibrated scope all eve. Ticks of the clock passed with brutality, spent on her belly or straining her back. Between gauging rig measurements, she set manacles around two poplar trees. That he whom she sought designed the manacles paid cruel homage.

TULL

At the first tick of the fourth watch, a set of flickering headlamps appeared in the darkness but the reel that played within the cab revealed the driver. Nita sprang the third manacle hinge and hurried to complete her trap. She bolted the cable and sought the *crook* of her web against the middle poplar. When the fixing bolt slipped in her hand, though, she cursed.

Then, a tug on the cable drew her eye across the road. There she found a soul, whose identity she could not confirm, working to secure the wicked end, completing the snare's V-formation. As if he shared her mind, he helped her construct her trap and crouched in wait from the other side of the road. She did the same, but neither lent voice to the intended outcome.

The engine's throaty rattle permeated the eve like the smoke that billowed from the stained, upright stacks near the cab. The beast looked and sounded as misshapen as the twisted soul at the wheel. Judge Marvin Elam Katch busied his hands with lever-style controls, shifting gears and injecting fuel, but focused on the feminine shapes that crawled against the glass. In this, he failed to see Nita's snare.

The driver's side headlamp burst then the cable whined and entangled the fender. Then a groan of ailing timber wheezed with the sputter of the engine. A chorus of muddled profanities from the unkempt judge thrashed at the eve. The tires spun and the body atop the frame creaked on aged rivets and brittle weld.

Nita covered her head as the manacle nearest her position snapped an iron jaw and devoured the tree. The cable sliced the air and cast down a screaming wind over her, uprooting the tree's blessed side. The slip of tires worsened, but never reached the pangs like those from the trees. Even the rig sounded *respectable* once an airy rattle announced a full stop.

The rig's squatty, elevated build survived the cable, but the driver's *hindered* build forced him off the road. The hands of the newcomer bawled into fists, expectant for a fight that his face, hidden beneath layers of scarfs, never conveyed. Nita dismissed his posturing and turned her attention toward the hull of the rig's enclosed rear. While she moved around to investigate, her *helper* preceded to handle Katch. Who crossed unto who's plot, however, remained uncertain.

The Guardian from the Shelby Territory set a fire, and the line that snared the rig burned from the core outward, undoing her labor, and leaving no discernable mess. The design rendered impossible any investigation into the events she caused.

No judge, no Guardian, not even a chief could track her hand, and she never lived in fear of the beacon in her neck. Still, she withheld her smile.

She brushed away the fiery ash with her boot, preserved the fuel tank, and spent another moment inspecting every tire. Gone by the time she reached the driver's side were her helper and Katch, and the setting remained hers to control. With or without the latter's wheelchair, the pair offered little challenge for her to track. Not that she cared over another's plot or the perverted judge's fate.

In her devotion toward Olley, she forgot the needs of the territories. She evaded word of the attacks on the judges. This was not carelessness. Till that moment, she had no hand in the wrongdoing. She acted as one so in love with another that her beloved's ache turned her hostile.

Rather than delay her plans with regret, she reached behind the right rear tires, deactivated the beacon on the side of the vault, then tested the lever-style handles that pressurized the chamber. The creature trapped within roared enough that the rig shook from side to side. *Who* she would set the thing upon remained her best-kept secret, though most would doubt her brilliance.

One passenger for her, one passenger for her unexpected helper. Still *one* unchosen soul remained. Vernard Voler flopped from the rig and onto his belly in a lump. His left leg turned outward and he leapt upward and onto his feet. He hobbled toward the tree furthest from Nita and dove headlong into the shadows along the trunk. Neither his feet, nor the rest of his bulbous frame, ever touched down or alerted the scheming Guardian.

In the silence of his wake, Nita started the rig and made a rowdy U-turn. The headlamps shone on the same tree but revealed nothing of the toad-like nuisance. He meant nothing in her scheme, less than Katch, so she made a getaway of her own. Three parties divided in three directions, each in the direction of a tree.

JULES BAKER SHANNON

A stammer and amethyst irises are not the traits that matter in this character. Jules personifies the Second Creation's purpose of living beyond self—a word oft used as a negative descriptor herein. There are few souls who are called to be sacrificial in all that they do. To be sure, they are heroic, and, in their way, they are godly. Though she does not bear the title of Guardian, Jules has a resolute intention to protect others—even her Guardians. She who was once a victim will not rest whilst another suffers.

Exposition

Thirteen

The 25th Peak beneath the Moon of the Old Embers
The 114th Gathering Season of the Accession
In the Blessing of I'Esh, who tends the harvest.

20 Sevier
A site of tremendous wonder and proof of Yah's intricacy.
Counted amid Tull's least favorite locales.

As they abstained from the air, the Second Creation kept too from the sea. The firstkind claimed the sky-fires and all that stood higher than eight storeys—even the forests. From the bluffs to the coastal shore of the Archibald Territory, the lands provided a margin of existence. The sea offered a reminder of that existence's fragility.

The Fallen First and the creatures that scavenged beneath the surface overtook the waterways and kept isolated the new isles. None learned if other isles thrived or if they exceeded the advances and blessings of their own territories. No travelers arrived from afar; minus Tull. The waters barricaded land and the Fallen First ruled the waters—in this time.

As Guardian, Tull witnessed the sea's offering of thousands of the Fallen First. He stood in towns of bone, heard stones lament, and saw a witch cut her way from the belly of a tree. He buried creatures that few imagined. Those truths mystified him.

But, the side of Creation that exuded goodness truly shook him. There, a child once ran to him after his mother's belief brought his sweet soul back from the grave.

A devout soul who ordered a fallen tree lifted off his broken body shook the Guardian's hand and let him touch the obedient wood. His own resets stood as a testament of the greatness that *swam* through this land, too.

Boastfulness almost swelled in him, but again the wind swatted his back, as a parent nudged along a distracted child, and sent the Guardian into the northernmost settlement of the Archibald Territory. Where the Loy River flowed into the Forbidden Sea thrived the district that Judge Cyril Adair Mumus—alias the Colonel—built across two territories: Sevier. Here, Tull kept a home within sight of the Colonel's tower—set there by an overseer unlike Marvin Elam Katch.

The Jacobian followed the gaslights and beacon relays past the lantern room of the Bellflower Signal House to the copper dome of the Kinnaman Immemorial Cadre and the antenna for WAM Radio on the westernmost shore. He approached the Sevier Aquarium Exposition with less reverence than trust. South of Mumus Tower, he let his shoulders relax, smoothed his hair, and adjusted his vest.

"My Creator keeps me from appearing dismayed."

Half of the aquarium exposition's body dangled over the bluff, and the hind end stood on stilts that extended into the sea. Those stilts cradled clear tubes, broader than the three-lane avenue, and delivered filtered saltwater into the tanks. Great precautions and better engineering kept out the Fallen First. The security within the site assured no soul tampered with that engineering, lest the foe overrun them. In the event of a breach, like a tank's sudden failure, duty fell on the Guardians to stave off the awaiting infestation.

Without a fuss, the Guardian blended into the line of blameless souls and families who sought a chance to see creatures that existed to them in books alone. *Different* creatures than those he sought. Some smiled, some stared, and few stood on the shadow he cast. The latter learned of his abettor's misstep, but he towed no wisdom from that previous land that might let him find her.

A canopy tarp partitioned an entire wing from the rest of the facility and away from the failed tank. Workers and their tools hindered the ambiance and cast their oblong silhouettes against the tarp. Not even the crude distraction cheapened the majesty of the aquarium exposition's design. The entry once stood as a pre-Accession opera house, and the secondkind's builders reproduced ribbed columns for use throughout the additional three wings of double-encased glass.

TULL

The sky-fires shone down, uninhibited by rooftops or billboards. On long eves, the view rivaled that of Olley's beloved observatory. Tull wasted two valuable ticks fussing over the setting, gauging distress in the glass, or searching for runaway beads of water, till the guidewires of a directory drew him back onto his path. As he focused on what scrolled beneath the reflection of light across the glass-and-copper plate, a sterile greeting awaited him.

IN THE CARE OF DOCTOR PAMILA SOLLARS GOOD,
WHO JOINS HER STAFF IN RECEIVING YOU.

He felt unwelcome, doubted the doctor's character, and dodged both the doctor's staff and the map of the aquarium exposition's interwoven floors. The flow of the crowd absorbed him till he redirected down paths with the fewest onlookers. But, as he passed families and classroom tours, he acknowledged the wondrous, bright-blue tanks. The water, the settings, the elegance, and fright of those marvelous creations who found home there, reminded most to give thanks.

The care lavished upon the exposition's occupants never ceased, and the funding allowed for the rescue of families of the thirdkind, not single dwellers. Few among the secondkind's first era enjoyed such familial ties. He found first and stood still afore the one tank he could not pass lest he betray the blameless soul he had tricked into eating soured leeks and entrusted with Zeck's campaign medal. He felt Q. J.'s weight upon his shoulders and the calming sensation that followed.

A team of ice cap bears frolicked beneath the thawed blue waters of a pristine glass case. The bears made visitors laugh, which produced a smile from the weary Jacobian. He appreciated the graciousness and gave a little wink toward one of the creatures. The same bear rolled sideways and swam away.

A warm-souled admirer adorned in a crisp uniform let three blameless souls pass, then eased alongside Tull. She also admired the magnificence that played in two-storey, filtered chambers with childlike wonder that let the constant glow of her visage reflect against the tank wall. Though subtle, she checked for gliders along the atrium and eavesdroppers among the onlookers. Her success in gaining nearness to him scorned others and created a calm wake when they dispersed.

"This is my favorite getaway in all the territories."

"I remain unsettled here."

TULL

Jules prodded Tull's side with her elbow and revealed a patch on her jacket sleeve for the 22nd Responsive Battalion of the host territory. "You and Hazy."

"Not bad company, by my measure. Though company measures so high."

The remark made the rescue medic smile brighter than the coats of the ice cap bears. Still, she corrected the measure of his hand till he matched the child's actual height. She then slipped the opposite hand from her jacket pocket and handed him a waxed paper-wrapped candy.

He grinned—an all-out, not a care in this land, not a trouble on his heart, grin—and accepted her gift. Tull forgot how she shimmered in this time. In every land, she wore her mood on her brow, towed pride by her chin, but her eyes never ceased to claim his thoughtfulness. Her eyes, unchanged in seven spans, staked his attention over every creature under the glass roof. "I thank you, J. J."

Though she patted at his chest with a hint of uncertainty, she kissed near enough to his lips that the corner of his mouth twitched, then petted his jaw as if she thought him rare. "You smell of fire."

He responded first with a *shurg*. "Have you followed me here?"

"Who, me? A soul can't rest imagining all the trouble that *you* get into." Jules shared glances with a boy who stood on the other side of her. She blocked him from recognizing Tull, then stared deep into the tank as she passed along a morsel. "They say the old bear near the back, with the belly, has seen *thirty* spans."

Old? Tull side-eyed her. He and the bear had their age in common; though, Tull lacked a *belly*. He confirmed as much with a hollow pat.

"He's lazy!"

Tull exaggerated good posture while Jules defended the bear.

"He's earned his rest. In the former age, an old *bear* let his hair and his belly grow as a show of importance. Never mind that the added weight put stress on the heart and the lungs and shortened that important purpose."

The Guardian kept still when she offered him a little smirk, and noticed the way her rescue medic's uniform lent her an air of trust and credibility; her work as an abettor unneeded.

After the blameless soul's friend joined him, Jules returned her attention to the Guardian. "Who cleared you from mending? Who knit your scarf? All fawned over you to your satisfaction, did they not?"

TULL

Even after fourteen spans, by linear count, she blew through curiosities like a whirlwind that upended remnants of her blamelessness. His patient grin eased her, and she smoothed her blouse till her fingers found the loops on her trousers, then hooked her thumbs against her belt in wait. She calculated her gestures; a gradual turn of her hip toward him, a tilt of her head in the opposite plane, and just enough emphasis on her shoulder to hint at the strength she held. Her chest rose without exaggerating the pleasant slope of her breasts and, as a final adornment, she offered a soft, lopsided grin.

"Curiosity keeps me alert."

"Indeed." He watched over the decent soul from whom Hazy learned to be a wonder. "I can imagine how your dad would gripe over the clutter up front."

She breathed, but not with an even pace. The warmth of his voice almost drew her in, then she turned in disappointment. "You're stalling."

Tull followed her ear. "You've rubbed off on me, dove."

She lifted her chin with pride, but not without a gleam in her eye.

"You went with *that* look." He recalled every word. "Sister Lois cleared me. Sister Agatha knit my scarf. Sister Delores stitched my shirt. Sister Charlotte proved curious about Ministers, not Guardians. You needn't—"

"War with Hofnarr, or Mumus again, and *the creation* will worry over—"

"You've heard about Hofnarr, have you?"

"And the glider you crashed."

Few souls knew the workings of his mind better than she.

"Not two moons since you finished paying for the last one."

Another *shurg*. "Hofnarr seeps evil, and the Colonel crushes purpose-filled lives till the husks of them aren't fit for Wanderers. I would destroy every glide—"

"Cyril's crept around unseen since"—her eyes caught his and she recalculated—"a long while ago. I—I imagine."

"Yet he holds sway over the lot." He realized his embittered tone and shifted his gaze away in a clockwise path while she looked counterclockwise. His chest rose on agitated breath, and she drew nearer, then their gazes met again. "A remorseful judge tows their strenuous ache with dignity. The Colonel never slowed to observe the aftershock he's created except to envy how well he's deceived good souls."

Jules's steam faded and she let her crown keep him from seeing into her amethyst eyes. Tull turned clammy, not from rejection, but when he and the structure swayed. Even downturned, she took hold of his hand. "This is no different than standing on the terrace at the loft."

"I'm not imagining, though. This place–"

She silenced him with a glance afore she nodded toward the blameless within earshot of his meaningful voice.

He sneered. "I mean, we're *fine*. We're all fine."

Jules released his hand as if testing his interest. He followed her to an opaque glass bench but let her sit without him.

"I could take you for cotton candy. *Outside*."

Her brow arched away from his antsy feet.

"Say, you've not heard from–"

"Ernie doesn't trouble me. He has you for that. You've heard about Tim?"

He recalled Marvin's barb about the mere mention of McCrea's name and saw how Jules grated the soles of her boots together. "He skedaddled with some fool's alms in his pocket?"

"*Noooo*, he's the reason why they've draped the place in tarps. He played Guardian during the offering. Chief Hont has him locked down till he appears afore our judges."

"I wish him well in the meantime." At last, he sat.

"What did you see out there that you're keeping from me?"

He cocked his jaw and his lips paled when he withheld from her.

"You'll say." She grinned the same way the wind tussled him on his path. "Well, let us have the talk I–I've dreaded. You're the new headship, and your favorite abettor not only lets two judges get hurt, but she loses the one soul of our kind without a beacon. Every crime that follows is my fault."

Soberness washed over him like the light. "Pardon?"

"Samuel and Conliffe. Don't say you haven't heard."

"Heard what, J. J.?"

"Sister Lois withheld from you again, as oft she does." Her defined shoulders slouched. "I–I believe our judges are in danger from an *uncounted* soul. Seeable, of course, but he disguises his face with scarves and wears a hooded coat. And, his i-*identifiiiier* beacon doesn't work."

She described the soul Friend showed him at the divided falls.

TULL

"He's hurt two judges. I—I found Samuel. Not as a medic, as an abettor. Mia went up the mountains, near the settlement where Lee camps with Maryna and Kara *Grace*, so we—Hamer and I—I—sent two relays. Both fruitless."

"What's Lucy doing?"

Jules shook her head. "She mends. Scion Meeker dispatched Chief Gensch and his deputies collected a crashed glider, whilst the 4th Battalion cared for Samuel. He remains non-responsive. Conliffe's daughter found him . . . castrated."

Tull stirred in his seat. "The same aggressor?"

"The same disguise and no beacon. He even took the scarf from around Conliffe's neck. Both judges tied to a pike. Both beaten for, what looks to me, watches. Say this is the same soul we've tracked all these moons." Jules moved nearer in her excitement. "You and Olley oft said there was a practical way that he goes undetected. None of us considered a soul with no—"

"Beacon." He recalled the absence of light in the specter Friend showed him.

"Imagine! A soul has found ways to live unseen beneath our judges' tech."

"Every Reformer will be suspect."

"Sister Lois will impose on you now that you're in charge again; worse, if she fears another soul will harm how she keeps her outpost. And, since you're in charge, I—I believe you should never have abettors who can't uphold their purposes. I—I knew Tim got into trouble but—

He bumped her shoulder with his. "I talked to the soul who lasted ten eves at Gutefiel. He tells me you do your duties and those of others well, and he thanks you."

"Well, *he* is a long-spined, long-legged soul who sees nothing but low hurdles."

"Meaning?"

"Tell you when you tell me what you saw. Was your duty to her of interest?"

"Compared to what you've found?" He considered all he learned in this land. "A clever soul, like yours, ought to remember the bitterness of the Infested."

Her brow furrowed and she nodded. "Sure."

"How oft they conceal their faces." He set his eyes on hers.

"The Uncounted Soul is one of the Infested!"

More than one visitor looked upon Jules, who prodded the Guardian again.

"What made you consider that?"

"Am I not clever too?"

She chirped.

"He wears boots that bind his feet. I believe he knows how George can track."

"How do you—"

"Friend told me. Rest assured. Sister Lois will practice the patience she insists others so oft exude. I'll tell Pine our time for mending has ended."

"I—I don't want you to weary—"

"Saved you first. Remember?"

She bloomed and wilted with a single breath.

"Judge Conliffe went and got castrated?"

"Chief Guild shared his reels for a change. I—I didn't even have to barter. *Much.* He softens at a compliment of his son's artwork. The joy is that he is a talented soul and so, so cute." Her slouch progressed into a tired sigh, a rub of her brow, and a gradual lean against the Guardian's shoulder. "I—I told the chief I—I sought Marko, who keeps away still. If he doesn't stop running, he'll top the mountains in Carpenter and roll right down to drowned Damaris."

"Have you slept?"

"No one to keep my feet warm, and Hazy won't share her bear." When she grinned, her eyes disappeared behind heavy eyelids.

Tull sat with her undisturbed till her shoulder drifted and her head dipped. "Did you hear of Nita's purpose for traveling north?"

"The body?" Her eyes widened, and her grin held. "No. She abandoned her report once you found Olley. That was brave of you, going back for him."

"The Helper proved kind." He stared stone-faced at a security agent outfitted with a shock baton. Strange, except for the exposition's nearness to Mumus Tower.

"The lottery decided on D'Aramitz Abbey. I—I see our judges forgot to inform their most critical Jacobian Guardian."

"We're your Guardians, not theirs." He batted an eye toward a boy whom the security agent intimidated.

Jules laughed, either at his claim or at the way the boy rocketed in the opposite direction from Tull's attention.

"He'll circle back." His mind proved as antsy as his feet when his claim failed. "You're sure they've decided on D'Aramitz Abbey?"

"Lucy trotted whilst I—I confirmed the decision with the chief. Carl says you gave up too soon at the offering. He says you should've stayed till Hivi'ern."

TULL

"Two spans from now, when I return to the offering, I'll strive to please Chief Carl Alvin *Lily-Liver.*"

"I—I admit, that would've been how Phinn Derek Wade arranged an exit." She lit up at the way he grinned over her teasing, then saw that he reacted to the blameless soul who returned for another peek at him. Jules laughed and waved; still, her words revealed her heart. "I—I can't decide if you're really unsurpriseable or if you bribed that runt to let me believe."

"I imagine both ideas suit me. What soul does Lucy keep near as of late?"

Mention of her benefactor flustered the abettor. "We've not met."

"Recall that attendant she oft ran to when she first joined the outfit?"

"*Uhhh*, Monte? No. Montgomery? Maybe." She bumped his shoulder. "Why so interested in Lucy?"

Tull's boyish grin proved enough to attract her smile. The fact that Jules recalled names close to the name of victim Chester Roldan *Monteith*, and recalled with little prodding, also proved that his suspicion towed more than a hint of possibility.

"I—I believe *you* spooked *her* when you helped her from the offering."

"I brim with astonishments."

"*Indeed.*" She mocked him with a gruff voice. "I—I saw Hector during the offering. He seemed less grim. Still scary. Very scary, but less grim. He seeks a younger bride."

What her remark withheld attracted his curiosity.

"Honor stayed in the rig till he moved onward."

Hector Geirolf Picadura, second Guardian from the Creighton Territory, turned his back on his beliefs and his purpose. No soul in the outfit relied on him after he abandoned them, yet Jules kept a wispy tether with him. Tull forgot why her rig partner, Sister Honorine Nowak, avoided Hector, but he admired such discernment.

"Do you ever imagine moving from under the lights and the noise? Giving up on your purpose and letting Ingram boast how he's the fifth Guardian from the Jacoby Territory?"

"Each time I'm swatted." He savored Jules's smile, but only glanced into the depths of her amethyst eyes hidden by lashes so long that they made a whispering sound when she blinked. "You?"

"Who, me?" The land fell short of enough rope to save a soul lost in her eyes.

For his sake, he looked toward her bare hands. He knew the standard she towed, so he played their game. "No, never you."

TULL

"Hard to believe I—I was ever a runt."

A blameless soul who stood in awe of the ice cap bears provided a diversion, but kept within Jules's reach, and invited her softest smile. She reached toward her thigh pocket, as if reminded, and retrieved a handheld transparent display plate like those fitted upon the projection-glider and throughout the territories. She wiped the face across her sleeve and set the device upon the Guardian's thigh.

"Let my heart rest and carry this."

Tull squirmed beneath the burden of tech.

"The connector turns fussy, remember."

"I'm meant to have whatever I have." Just like the two cakes. He slipped the device into his pocket. "I too crossed paths with an old acquaintance. Anya Nora Rains. I believe she gutted a church for the Colonel."

Jules struck his chest with a backhand. "I—I told you she was trouble!"

"As you say." He then rubbed the spot she struck.

They had neared six spans without her *told you so*. Now that she delivered her remark, she slumped into the palm of her hand to watch the ice cap bears and sulk. In her blamelessness, unto her time as a novitiate, she practiced the same pose whenever she felt dejected and, in that previous land, Hazy mimicked her front. When one bear waggled his hind end at Jules's mood and swam away, she sulked deeper, but within reach of the soul who cherished her.

"Afore she wed, my grandma was something of a duelist."

Jules cracked a smile and softened till her body turned toward him.

"In her first sowing season as a judge, she jumped on the back of her horse, crossed the Loy, and challenged Iwan Rüdiger Steffen to face her, lest he had no spine."

"She did not!"

"I tell you, that *coward* believed her threat with enough sincerity that he hid behind four bolted doors."

"Well, what happened?"

"Her dearest friend, Bessie, cleaned Steffen's house and sought mercy for the no-good on account he owed her a moon's alms. She got her alms, too."

"What put our elder judge on the prowl, do you imagine?"

"Grandma tired of him running atop the necks of locals. She tired of him belittling those who relied on his provision. Most of all, she tired of how the judge of this territory allowed him every offense."

TULL

"She sounds like a good friend; a good judge."

"She was the soul I adored most. Judge Juanita Gene James. *My grandma.*"

The proud lilt in his voice made her sigh.

"Back then, those who admired and loved her called her 'J. J.'"

Jules's eyes pooled.

"I tell you, I'll never stop earning each tick Yah lets me spend with you." He brushed her hand with his bare ring finger, and she held his finger with her thumb. "We'll find this uncounted soul."

"Give me your word."

"My word is yours." He kept his grin and glanced around at visitors. "The soul that attacked Olley and Marko wore one of our copper pins. Mind who you follow and who follows you."

She nodded in the way he pledged his word and bumped him with her shoulder. "My break's almost up, and Honor sours when she has to push Clarabelle to reach the battalion house in time for peak inspection."

"Tell Hazy to come see me."

"I—I believe she would love that." She held back her hair and kissed his brow. "Soon, you'll see me."

Jules slipped away but offered a playful look over her shoulder and waved farewell. The females in this land were powerhouses, able to mesmerize with a glance in a land where the firstkind and thirdkind roamed. Tull settled in her absence, unwrapped the candy, and ate. Cocoa made him wince in every land.

While he pondered reasons not to make the stop that she suspected from him, the same rear-wriggling ice cap bear vied for his attention. Others took notice, but the Guardian's internal warring deprived him of a bond with the immaculate creature. The judge who kept to the shadows, who strong-armed the port, and who betrayed those he served, deprived the bears of Tull's appreciation. So, the Jacobian hardened his heart against the Colonel and let his familial instincts guide him in a direction *opposite* the rescue medic's path.

FOURTEEN

<u>With his back to the Sevier Aquarium Exposition</u>

Within earshot of the perceived creaking of the facility's structure.

Short of breath and appetite.

Sorting what a soul became versus who they were absorbed Tull's time, even without distractions. Across the previous lands, he learned how to pace—or out-pace—time, and not exhaust his sanity. The increase of tension across the territories in this time hastened the surfacing of true characters. Word of his actions traveled afore like a breeze, while he plotted direction by the step.

Phinn Derek Wade wanted other souls to validate his choices over the purpose he forsook. Anya wanted souls to blame for her mourning. Hofnarr wanted loyalty to bolster his vanity. Mumus wanted authority to increase his legacy. The secondkind proved easiest of all creatures to anticipate, and oft disappointed in their choices.

As to his purpose, he entrusted Olley to Nita, George to Violet, Sister Lois to those in her care, Si'el Uaen Söi'eä to Friend, the Fallen First to the Ministers, and Jules to Honorine. This earned him some time till he faced Hazy again after letting her down in that previous land. Letting pass time or travels, the child oft saw through his cleverest façade. She would care for Q. J., for he would have the same effect on this land as the shifting exposition: filled with wonder and seldom still. This made the Jacobian laugh out of character to his roots.

"This land dims without you, Li'l Ornery." The words surprised another who passed by him. "Pardon me."

They traded peculiar glances and the stranger side-stepped the Guardian.

"My luck; he decides who's set in the asylum."

TULL

On the idea of *committedness*, another soul who evaded him needled his mind. He brought Jules's antiquated display plate from his pocket. Though the device was new in this time, he had to recall *the old ways* to search for resources and contacts when he noticed the inventor's insignia. Eight ticks and one diversion later, he broadcast on a private frequency to a contact he had not yet made in this land.

"INVENTOR BUCKLER. THE SEKO'TAE ARE CAST UNTO MADNESS BY THE FREQUENCY OF THE SIGNAL HOUSES. SEEK HISTORIOGRAPHER PRISCA FOR HER IMMENSE INSIGHT."

"That will upend him for moons"—he smirked—"as J. J. will upend me."

Then, another four ticks fell away as he remembered a fellow's passcode.

"Well," Pine's drawl wafted with the breeze. "You evaded another end."

"I appreciate the confidence."

"O, you oft mend. I've learned you crashed another glider."

Tull cocked his jaw. "Did you mend well?"

"I mended on broth. Heard from Olley?" He sharpened a knife as they chatted.

"I haven't the expectation. I'm told Lucy awoke in one of her *moods*."

"Imagine!"

"I've not heard from George."

"No frequencies near the storage cities. S'pose Tim is going to be sniffing all our butts to fill any gap that he can find since Marko's run off."

"Not his first sniff."

"Nor his second."

"I'm told he's in trouble with Chief Hont."

"Played Guardian again, I imagine."

Tull kept his comments on the troublesome abettor who abandoned him in that previous land unspoken. "Any sighting of Marko?"

"Other than Nita, I doubt there's a soul who seeks him."

"Do you keep from trouble?"

The man who settled aggression with a knifepoint smiled. "In point of fact, yes."

"I might've stumbled onto another of the Colonel's schemes."

"Need talked into a bad choice?"

"Not yet. I thank you."

TULL

Pine shrugged gratitude. "Watch your back. Some souls turn odd as winter nears. Those soul-damned Shelbian inbreeds, most of all!"

"Jules may have laid eyes on the soul we've sought all these moons. She believes he's behind the attacks on Samuel and Conliffe. He's removed his identifier beacon and has the tech to crash gliders."

Pine tapped the knife against the back of his neck. "Roaming without a beacon. Can you imagine?"

"I didn't. Marvin planned to locate a harvester with Voler."

"When was this?"

"Afore I mended. You've not heard from Ernie?"

"Naw." Pine held up the knife and the glimmer he created disturbed the lens. "Hofnarr made his steward whittle off her fingers to get out from under that *keepsake* of yours. Ten alms to your one, he ate her fingers. I'm about to venture over to his place for a look-see. I'll visit Marvin on my way."

"Need support?"

"You slugged me hard enough the first time." He meant the barb as a discredit of his own behavior too. "I s'pose we remember our purpose. You behave around the civil."

"You keep from the desert."

"I'll work hard to not shame you. Soon, I'll see you."

The winds cut through the speaker as Pine severed the connection on what passed for an enjoyable conversation. Tull worried over Katch. Still, the Jacobian needed a poor-mannered eunuch counseling him as much as Pine needed a scar-faced Believer mothering him. He pocketed Jules's device and stepped away from the copper beacon that created a signal.

Even as he held to the sweetness of Jules's presence, he glowered at the reflective, fortress-like tower that bore the name of the territory's judge. Out of contempt for the firstkind, the Colonel built a tower that stood *thirteen* storeys, one for every moon; with the two highest shrouded in almost constant fog. There he lurked away from the rest of the land; a land that sat in the shadow of his tower. At the base, a sunken courtyard slowed visitors like an ancient moat.

Tull removed Anya's wadded letter and journeyed toward Mumus Tower, where not one projection-glider monitored. No fiery Minister, nor the pull of the Helper turned him back, either. He possessed the spine for direct confrontation, while his foe owned the wit for slow-burning cruelty. The Colonel went unchallenged too long, and Tull wanted to haunt him.

He stepped further onto the judge's plot as proof that he sought trouble. In the tower's shadow, another visage drew him near and dissuaded him from mindless wrath. Without a word, the treasured face reminded him of his responsibility to those he served. His hold on Anya's letter softened till he believed he stood only to look upon that face.

SONDREA EBBE CONLIFFE
BRIDE OF HONORABLE CYRIL ADAIR MUMUS
SCULPTED BY BORDEN VINCENT ROACH

The cherished likeness of the soul who proved her goodness to Tull kept him still and brought his best manners to the surface as though he remained blameless in her sight. He straightened the hem of his sleeves, too, lest she find him lax in her presence. Even adorned in bronze, the sculpture lacked her radiance. While the Colonel's bride *favored* the Ministers, she held another sort of power over the Guardian: *adoration*.

In her time, Sondrea's eyes shimmered like the bronze surface. Her irises brimmed with mystery, yet filled with an emotion unknown to a child. She possessed a smile outmatched by any in the land; though Jules, in her joy, neared the lead. He wanted only to glean wisdom from a rooted memory loosed by Sondrea's visage. No other soul in the territories believed in, guided, or cherished Tull more than her—at no dismissal toward Jules, again.

The sounds of foot-peddling bled from the doors of the tower. Two recognized the Guardian and stank of concern. Tull counted footsteps, anticipated nearness, and took a final look at the bronze likeness. He then maneuvered to change the course of those who follow him away from others he was purposed to guard.

"I didn't s'pose you had the balls!"

"You imagine your Larsonite Guardian." He then took a cue from his grandma. "Say, why not ask your benefactor to set foot outside?"

"That isn't about to happen."

He reached into his pocket. "Why not hold something for me then?"

"Nelson James Tull!"

The calmer of the pair kept his fellow from Tull's *snare* as a fourth soul arrived.

TULL

"What are you doing down this way?"

The most authoritative inspector of the Jacoby Territory stood in the *Archibald* Territory needling Tull over *his* whereabouts. Jurisdictional right or wrong, he made both goons smile.

"What are you two dollops of horse manure grinning about?" Chief Inspector Carl Alvin Grover—alias Lily-Liver—set his sights on them now. "Do you believe your benefactor would risk his reputation for the two of you? Now, get! Or, Tull can demonstrate the rubblework he made of Professor Caley Buchanan McDow. *Get!*"

"Wait!" Tull faced Carl. "Have you a pen?"

"A what?"

One Jacobian stared at the other and refused to repeat his request. A moment later, the inspector handed over a pen to his Guardian.

"I thank you."

Tull held the letter to the tower's face and Carl read over his shoulder.

Archivist Rains—

By my father's instruction, proceed as planned.

—KYM

With Carl's pen, he crafted a response:

Scion Mumus—

As headship of the Guardians, I am suspending all activity upon, within, and beneath the Church Amid the Shadows given my discovery of a potential nest. Take solace. I will observe the plot without fail for your devoted father's sake.

—NJT

The Guardian tucked the paper along the original folds and coerced the tower's goons with a wave of his wrist. "See that the Colonel's daughter receives this."

TULL

He who doubted Tull's snares grabbed the letter. "Now get!"

"You don't have authority over him."

Tull watched the pair cower beneath the chief's reminder and obey. The chiefs patrolled the secondkind, aided by projection-gliders, inspectors, and deputies. Above them were the Guardians and abettors. The judges sat over every territory, over every Guardian, abettor, chief, Believer, Partaker, and elsewise.

"You scarecrows have the fun!" The inspector sensed Tull's mien. "*What?*"

"Caley Buchanan McDow?"

"I've oft appreciated the moral of that story."

"You can't boast a story lest you tell the details right. I wasn't Guardian then."

"Was that Zeck or Perry? No, Zeck."

"Perry."

"Well, when will you do something that I can remember? Only ten eves in Gutefiel? All Jacobians howled! Tragic!"

"Next time I'll take you along."

"Did Marko truly take Olley's eye?"

"No."

Tull watched Carl step toward the panes to inspect the sculpted bust.

"Ernie sent you then?"

"No. If you're done here, let me give you a ride."

He let habit goad him. "Colleen Kerris Snow Dove's shop is—"

"Colleen Kerris *Paget* is a *Shelbian* shopkeeper now and you are not permitted in that territory. I tell you, you needn't worry over my home."

"In no way. Though, I tell you, I enjoy counting how oft you mention Barbara when you see Colleen."

The chief flustered, then made a beeline toward his rig. Tull smirked as the inspector's gait increased, then followed till he circled and redirected the barb. "You ought to get Jules some flowers, if you're interested in flowers."

Tull looked at him in silence. In point of fact, his mouth almost disappeared behind his beard. "What do you mean by that?"

"Who do you s'pose asked me to find you? Nelson James Tull within reach of Cyril Adair Mumus? Any time that happens, neither of you miss the chance to take a piss on the other's shoes."

Tull looked down at his dry boots.

"No. You *didn't* win. I spared you embarrassment. Now, let's get! I didn't seek Hont afore I entered the territory. Three moons since we've had an actual face-to-face talk. You'd s'pose we weren't still friends."

Tull followed, but the inspector pulled away with his friend's foot still planted. He shut the door and avoided a stack of apple crates plus the soul selling them. The Guardian double-checked the near-victim, pointed at the decal on his door, and settled in his seat. The inspector cursed beneath his breath and accelerated away from Mumus Tower and the route unto Tull's home even as he accessed files the way that Katch watched reels.

"Rescue Medic and Abettor Shannon, Jules Baker. *Jules Baker*. Says here she's the seventh of seventeen souls named in honor of Reformer Jules Carrion Baker."

"I believe the eleventh *Carl Alvin* speaks with envy." He looked through the rig's rear window as the inspector crossed Desard Bridge into the Jacoby Territory.

"At your pace, there won't be any souls named in *your* honor. They'll shed a few tears, then start weaving for Kemp." He savored the groan his jab produced. "In her last appearance afore our judges, the verdict fell in her favor; five votes to two. And I speak of Barbara lest you forget the error of your—"

"Barbara honors *me* with a new scarf and an invitation to celebrate the Feast of Gratitude with the rest of the Snow Doves each span since . . ." His brow furrowed as he lost count of the invitations since his father's end. "Archibald and Shelby seldom side with the outfit."

"Who riled the Shelbians?"

Tull shifted on his seat and looked toward rows of colorful homes and trimmed yards. Those along the Loy lived well and boasted their prosperity.

"A sweep for beacon 089.86.218 sets Jules in the field; 1982 Secord, to pinpoint. By this, she's responding to a single-victim combustion fire. Not her first visit to that plot either." He read further. "I see here a petition notice for remotion from the outfit; even with four moons still on her assignment. I doubt your promotion motivated her. She didn't say? How oft do *you* speak of Barbara?"

Tull shook his head, but applied the info to whatever troubled Jules.

The inspector browsed through four images of Jules, then back to one that he preferred as he eased back in his seat and drove easier. "Fourteen spans she has suffered you. Less time than I've suffered you."

Tull exhaled as others swore.

TULL

"Don't reach for your trick rocks now! I was going to say that, as your oldest friend, I believe you ought to bring her to dinner at the house."

"Is that why we're here?"

"A meal in the territory you guard! A bottle or two of homemade wine. Beauty on either side of us, not monsters. A chance for all to tell what thoughts they hold in too long. Such could be good for you!"

"Could be better for you not to press."

"I don't press! I'm a longtime accordion player." He wriggled his fingers.

"Have you received word on our judges?"

"Sure, let us speak of stiffer necks. Even when you're ordered for mending, you find ways to get into trouble."

"Then the chiefs prefer the Guardians abstain?"

"Fair point. Lousy delivery."

Tull looked through the open loading bay of a roadside cannery, which builders would demolish in the one hundred seventeenth span to allow for a hydro-powered sawmill. He never visited either. During the gathering seasons, he worked fields and maintained heat lanterns through the winter. The crews that gravitated toward the mills never interested him.

"I tell you, I thought the Partakers lost their fool heads, laying with monsters and spooking Believers. Then this loon crept into the open. I have no trouble with Partakers tying up their playthings or humiliating uptight Believers. But hanging a soul to choke the marrow from them?

"Strange rope, too; woven, not braided. How they worked the restraints kept the neck from breaking but deprived Conliffe of enough breath and blood that he might stay soporose." Carl pointed at a honey locust tree flayed open by lightning yet not barren. "Remember how Perry ran when that ripped open?"

Tull had more interest in present problems, so he let Carl's poor memory slide. His benefactor saved two souls from the tree's fall. The inspector's former superior ran and hid in his rig.

"The noose on Conliffe made a figure-eight impression, about the size of a copper alms, over and over. In each loop, they found punctures—bite marks—that paralyzed the muscles when he fought back. Gensch's report lists the same pattern on Gwynne."

"Same tactic, same tools, and the same aggressor. Conliffe, then Gwynne?"

"Conliffe on the eve Falk entered the offering. Gwynne on the eve you exited."

"And the victim in the north?"

"Monteith? He had the noose marks, too. He was knotted wrong and broke open."

"When?"

"Ozul claimed the reels but never turned them over afore she ran to Falk."

"Jules calls him the Uncounted Soul."

"He whom you've chased how many moons?"

"Time will tell."

"Not one of her better titles! Monteith interests you. Too random, right?"

Tull buried his opinion.

Carl made another turn and tapped his passenger's forearm with the back of his hand. "They oft called old Judge Gwynne a puppeteer. Jules's *Uncounted Soul* took Gwynne's fingers. And, he castrated Conliffe; whom most of our betters despised."

When they reached the turn-off toward a park that Tull favored, the rig turned the opposite direction. Had the cannery sat across from the home of Laurence Rodney Snow Dove, his warm-hearted bride, and their fiery daughters, Tull might have shown more interest in the sterilization process of glass jars and vacuum treatments. Though he held no complaint against imperishable food, at times he doubted their mutual preservation.

"The wounds look like eel's mouths. I s'pose that class field trip to the aquarium exposition stayed with me. Remember that? Say you remember afore I start believing we aren't friends. We were—"

"I remember."

"I remember you retched! You swore the place shifted."

"The place shifted."

"I was there. I never—"

"The place shifted."

The chief laughed. He turned too sharp, so he and his passenger leaned.

"When last I talked to Pine, he sought Marvin. Have you a word on him?"

"No, I haven't." Carl's face went solemn. "I'll make an inquiry. Ernie retreated once George entered the offering and you weren't in Gutefiel alone. I doubled patrols and a deputy commandeered his nephew's glider for additional surveillance over his cabin after I got the word about Conliffe."

"I thank you. When he proves cranky, tell him I ordered the patrols."

"I oft do. He says you live to rile him."

Tull debated who riled whom more.

"As I see this, he attacked whilst you'd all be preoccupied or mending."

"Why not sit in wait for Nita?"

"No reason to believe this is about the Guardians, is there? Lest he seeks to prove a point against the Guardians." He looked at Tull. "The blameless soul Jules tends—"

"Her name's—"

"Hazel-Sue."

"Why are you bringing this up?"

"Two attacks in Lucy's territory; one a judge." He fogged the glass with a sigh. "Gensch registered a disturbance citation at her plot the eve that followed your retreat from Gutefiel."

"*Retreat*?"

"Now Jules wants out."

"I didn't retreat." He clutched the dash as they twisted uphill again.

"Gensch has proved lenient for Hazel-Sue's sake afore. With our judges harmed, he cannot risk kindness on Bright Moon."

"Afore?"

"Talk to Jules." He slowed the rig as he looped downhill and lowered his voice. "Conliffe wrote the law that lets fathers and daughters . . . *know* each other . . . so he couldn't swing for laying with his fruit. Both he and Gwynne parade their daughters with lust-filled intentions."

Judges Conliffe, Gwynne, Hofnarr, and Elwell passed the law of Carl's allusion. Judge Katch, to the surprise of every soul, withheld his vote. Judges Bliss and Mumus sided against them. Rather than admit the Colonel upheld decency, Tull believed Mumus's scion—and niece to vile Conliffe—cast the vote in her father's stead.

Carl looked upon his friend. "I'm a father now, Nelson. I cannot bloody my hands in another fight against these families. I'm not you. The way your soul rages. A soul could go gray!"

"I am going gray."

"But you're earning character, and I've never seen you retreat. Bright Moon and Pine owe you for dragging them from the offering. As does Olley."

"Anya's involved this time. Somehow."

TULL

"I read. Odd turn, how I said not to let her close. She's Gierigian, as I warned. You ought not to have done to her what was done, or you ought to have done to her what was not done. Then she would not be so devoted to wearying you."

"Ty'mä!"

"I tell you, an idiot cannot be wrong every time!"

"Composed your next campaign slogan, have you?"

Carl pulled the rig into a recessed portion of the sidewalk. "Are dig sites a worthy complaint against the judge of our most advanced territory? Where you live? Where *Jules* lives? At this time? Why lend an undeserving soul sympathy?"

"I'll gather more facts." Whilst he led the outfit, defended the judges, patrolled three territories, named Monteith's murderer, learned of Anya's involvement, sought what troubled Jules, ensured Hazy's safety, corrected Lucy, kept an eye on Katch and Pine, sought Bliss, and dodged Carl's henpecking. How he wearied his spirit.

"Some of the chiefs suspect your outfit's up to no good. Worse, none of us know who we'll root for if suspicions prove true. Maybe we've lived beneath the rule of our judges too long. Maybe we need a change."

"Seek a king, serve a tyrant."

The lesson made Carl squint with confusion.

"Why are we in the Jacoby Territory?"

"I'm amazed you recognize your true home! Ozul petitioned every chief to bring you here once you stuck your head up. I'm duty-bound. I've called you a friend since we were blameless. You would say if the Guardians were plotting."

"I would *not*. But I would keep you from harm."

The chief inspector wiped his face from the slope of an unshaven chin back to the nape of his neck.

"I thank you for the ride."

"Wait!" He fished through his display for a string of numbers. "Here. You owe the territories four thousand, two-hundred twenty copper alms for glider number CTQ840429, which you destroyed."

Tull laughed at him.

Carl remained sober. "You're to appear afore our judges on the nineteenth morn, beneath the Moon of the Wandering Fog, with the full sum."

Tull waffled. "I accept the dinner invitation."

TULL

"That would be swell. My bride and I prepare our table to receive you—and Jules—any eve *after* the nineteenth moonset, and I'll not expect you to bring a dish." He nudged Tull toward the open door. "Don't make a grieving soul wait, now!"

Calmness benefitted the Guardian. Though he growled, he accepted his reprimand and leapt from the rig. The chief watched over the glutton, least till the next projection-glider patrolled the area. One hundred seven open investigations against the most powerful judge in the territories. While the chief inspector learned not to doubt Tull's bravery, a nervous soul challenged his sense.

FIFTEEN

<u>212 Danton Road</u>

The Silas Chamber House.

Kept hidden by the hem of Leander Jonathan Bromley's forest.

Due to the secondkind's creation of smaller structures, few properties stood three storeys or higher. Given the lesser count of the populace, they had access to greater plots of land and expansive floorplans. They built downward, beneath the surface, for the storage of remains and advanced recovery. The common names for the latter were *chamber houses.*

These facilities offered short-burst, rapid-recovery treatments that replaced the pre-Accession hospitals, withered dependence, and rid the secondkind of long-term pain rehabilitation. Reformers created healing agents from elements that let the firstkind live for thousands of centuries and cured patients in watches. Few raised concerns over their methods of experimentation and enjoyed augmented forms of mending and wellness.

Tull's notoriety expedited him through security at the Silas Chamber House and identified him as a permitted guest due to his purpose—letting pass his temperamental behavior at the Gyddingford Chamber House seven spans afore. That Olley mended at Silas surprised Tull. The Archibaldian strayed as far from sites named for Silas Hendrie Falk, Jr., as all his proven and suspected siblings strayed from their father.

Even so, panels lit from their undersides led Tull toward a dedicated recovery room, which let the facility discard signs and nametags in lieu of privacy. The gesture, while proper-hearted, made the visitor aware of the isolation. For their celebrity, as the secondkind measured celebrity, the outfit stayed isolated. When the panels led into an empty room, though, the newfound isolation clung to him.

"This feels a bit much." He directed his posture toward the display plates and microphones in the room. "Guardian Nelson James Tull, responding to an invitation from Guardian Nita Naomi Ozul."

The panel nearest the room's secondary door flickered and a direct path illuminated to guide him. He followed the panels and entered an interior chamber subjected to gauged temperature, pressure, and light settings. All in the room appeared washed in false light. The air proved so cold that frost appeared around the furthest recesses of the chamber. Tull shivered and yawned at the same time as his ears adjusted to the staged atmosphere.

Twelve doors, twelve rehabilitation and renewal chambers, three souls in mending, and not one sign of Nita. Another soul sat between the two rows of chambers, his feet almost trampling one of the slender reflections that poured from the center-most chamber. He read from the same newspaper that Anya's grandfather started, which made Tull suspicious. An elder of the previous era's forearms trembled enough that the Guardian turned woozy as he watched the corner of the paper flutter, so he turned his sight elsewhere till a soul addressed him.

A team of three hovered around a soul who flowed with child at the furthest chamber. Her uncovered belly revealed a proud scar, created during the injection process in which all members of the secondkind received their identification beacon. A medical tech turned a smooth cap in a counterclockwise direction and pulled a copper disc the size of two adult hands from an opaque gelatin satchel. The disc concealed seven points of anchor for the mechanical umbilical cord, which pierced around the navel of the soul already adorned with one disc, the size of a child's hands. Four of the anchoring needles infused the body with restorative cells and synthetic nutrients while two removed refuse.

A tech coupled the umbilical and made her patient twitch and whimper. When the anchoring needles set, they stole the breath, till her kneecaps *clanked* against one another. Though her body trembled and her preparation table swayed, she brushed her belly with a tender hand that soothed even the Guardian. Her way proved all that the outfit defended and eased some of the abandonment he suffered.

Two techs helped her, as she alone staggered to steady her feet with closed eyes and shortened breath. Tull stepped toward, and even the elder let the newspaper

TULL

pages fall till her steadiness held. She acknowledged the seated reader with a smile, then met Tull with a direct stare. As he looked away, he believed he saw a polite grin on her face.

He visited chamber houses enough times to recall the process as the techs ushered her onto a raised, disc-shaped pedestal. A hollow glass tube shot upward and sealed overhead against a canopy of polished copper and a head of cables. The soul within stepped sideways, turned her attention toward her midsection, and continued to soothe the child within her. The glass fogged as her body heat rose, anxious over the transition from breath to the breathable gels that invaded the tube.

Air funneled from above the tank as recuperative gel bled up from below. This broke down the gel into a thinner liquid that occupants took in through their nostrils and mouth. Elsewise, the density of the gel let them drift in the tank, as if weightless. Complete muscle relaxation let a patient slumber, though vivid synthetic dream-states toyed with that rest.

Some theorized that the dreams reflected traces of the method that the First Creation communicated unto one another and their Creator. In the eras of old, words like *visions* and *prophecies* defined the effect. Physicians called them *vapors*; forgotten memories and moments never shared. The debate raged without rest.

Science never told what that seventh needle contained. If withheld, the mind convinced the body of drowning and a violent end followed. Patients broke their bodies in desperation because their minds told them not to breathe. Though all *could* survive in the chambers, the dreams, the mishaps, and the tedium invited struggle. That fact, and ailments he towed, made Tull dislike the tanks.

Mindful of his invitation, he stepped deeper into the chamber, and discovered a eunuch with necrotic limbs who underwent spinal cord reconstruction from the mid-thoracic vertebrae upward. He faced a ginger-haired nymph whose body developed at a pace slower than the size of her wide eyes. The glare of light from Tull's position reduced her to a pale sliver with a plume of flowing hair, like persimmon-colored ink in milk. She smiled at Tull, as though a friend, and touched her tube to welcome him.

He then caught the rage-intense stare of the occupant afloat in the tank nearest to him. His arm, cleaved in two, sported puncture marks not unlike those caused by the bolts of Nita's crossbow. The patient battered the tube with his blunt brow as the color of his tank ran from lurid red to carnal black. Had he his front teeth, he might have seethed, but a surgeon deprived them—due to violent gnashing—long afore the visit of he who reacted with no more than a flat stare.

"Eight moons pass like the eve." A rustle of newspaper led to a clearer voice in Tull's ear. "You and Arthur George Green followed that coven from the Church of the Fallen Star down the face of the northern bluffs then, whilst your fellows sought those who cut the Bikiak twins into scraps for their accursed feast. Chief Inspector Katch observed how Nita Naomi Ozul unloaded a brimming quiver into that wretch afore her husband played intercessor and took his arm. Clubbed him with that limb halfway to a fractured skull."

"Why is he here?"

A technician's voice trembled as she stepped nearer with outstretched hands. "His mother owns this facility."

Tull glanced toward the soul with child and reflected on the tenderness that a mother applied to her child regardless of what they became once born. The peace that settled him mingled with the fiery amber hues of the double-occupied chamber and let the tech retreat into her work. Still, the newspaper-wielder set aside his distraction and stood to face the newest visitor.

"Guardian Nelson James Tull. You might not remember me. I am Leander Jonathan Bromley."

The casualness belied the fact that Tull's greeter owned a fruit and timber enterprise that hired hundreds of souls across the northern territories. He served the Jacoby Territory as Bliss's Advocate Scion. Riddled with age and hidden behind a wooly beard, Scion Bromley's clear, blue eyes spoke to his fear that Tull would, in point of fact, remember him beyond his title unto a morn when he visited the Guardian in his time of blamelessness with a meager gift and horrid news. A mechanized voice kept back that confirmation and issued an alert:

BEACON 114.82.416 RECOGNIZED . . .
IDENTIFIER CONFIRMED—BLAMELESS BABE KIND HAND
BEACON 082.72.902 RECOGNIZED . . .
IDENTIFIER CONFIRMED—ELSIE ILONA KIND HAND
RECUPERATIVE PROCESS STARTED.
MENDING TIME: 3 WATCHES, 18 TICKS.

TULL

Tull honored the Creighton Territory's intended judge when he averted his eyes by turning away from her in her nakedness. He remembered the portion of the tale that Sister Lois Westmore shared with him about Scion Kind Hand, and checked the display plate attuned to the unborn babe. The blameless heart rate moved with the same intense anxiousness that Tull felt near the chambers. Most souls with such a heart troubled their mothers.

"Elsie is Damari by her birth . . . and Creightonian by our judges' law. Her heart will abide." Leander batted an eye at the persimmon-haired chamber sprite, who watched Tull's every move, then waved a finger in her direction. "My granddaughter, Lindy; Sean's firstborn."

All from the Jacoby Territory knew the logger-and-scion's family tree. Because Tull served him, Leander spoke with a familiarity that hinted at acquaintance. He nodded, with respect, but dodged another glance toward the Silas House mermaid. What he remembered of Lindy's case—which Jules studied in wonder—made certain that the scion's granddaughter could not live outside the chamber. What the family spent on her care strained their empire and their souls.

As two techs hissed over authority, they agitated Tull's ear. "See now! Scion Kind Hand and her babe, and Scion Bromley's granddaughter, rest in your care, but they rest beneath the full protection of the Guardians. Regard them well. Mishandle them, or berate them, and dare not doubt we'll find you."

Protection from a Guardian took ever-changing forms. As the headship, a simple *hint* of undefined punishment changed a cynical will and made souls tremble. Leander held a tickled gleam in his eye when he looked upon Tull's stern face, unable to gauge his sincerity beneath his scarring. Mingled with a gentle regard for the dominant gender and recent accomplishments, his word towed a credible scope.

"Scion Bromley, might you point me toward Guardian Ozul, please?"

"This way." The logger offered a wink toward his granddaughter and led Tull to a portion of the chamber house that stood behind her. He even waggled his finger afore she teased him. Lindy drifted in a clockwise direction as they passed and watched with winsome curiosity.

The chill Tull suffered fell to near-hypothermic temperatures. He kept his head down and paced his gait to the staccato tap of wooden boot heels as they crossed the circulation chambers that percolated with color and harsh light. The power units of each chamber offered a flirtation of warmth but faded with equal whimsy.

TULL

"Nearly every soul in this room stems from a family who helped grow these territories. The doctor and her staff. The bodies in these chambers. Perhaps I've done my fair share. I find those in your purpose have let our kind realize *more* possibilities. As my imaginative fellow scions oft remind me."

Tull smirked and imagined that *fellow*'s name. "How is Otto?"

Leander chuckled. "Does he change?"

"Not once in my time."

"There'll be no peace near him if Elwell falls." In a low hush, rooted with earnestness, Leander spoke with a regard for his own well-being. "I have not learned where your fellows have gone. They were here, but Falk's bride squabbled with the director for the same reason that you objected to finding her son mending. She threatened to pull him from the tank, in point of fact. We reasoned that we stood a better chance of you responding to a hail from your fellows and baited you to preserve our own hides; to which, I must now apologize to you."

In place of that apology, he stepped aside and let Tull see two octagon-shaped tanks that sat low to the floor. Each contained male patients kept under dim light in a state of suspension. Rigid, rear armatures immobilized the backs of their heads, their spines, and their limbs. From their front, which angled toward the floor, equal-sized armatures kept the pressure points of the body from irritation and rid their joints of tension. Then, with a tap of Leander's fingers to the glass, single-unit lights revealed tortured faces.

In the secluded nook, Judges Conliffe and Gwynne underwent recovery. They looked as Carl described them, though even he omitted details. The figure-eight pattern marred their bodies with tar-black lesions deep into the muscle from their wrists, to their throats, and down to their midsections. Just the sight of them produced an ache in Tull's ribcage.

Rather than cloy on their suffering, he focused upon digital likenesses of their frames and the rework to their systems. While one device restored broken bones in Samuel Herbert Gwynne's arm and shoulder, another repaired knife-damaged muscles. Likewise for Dale Marius Conliffe, whose large intestine underwent reconstruction along with a collapsed lung. Their failing bodies mended, regardless of when failures or ruptures occurred.

Tull remained wary, though. The care lavished upon the judges bolstered the darkened heart that imagined the assault. He feared the rampage that followed in the wake of *when* the Uncounted Soul learned this secret. All the while, hope seemed brave. Neither judge offered a response by measure of brain activity, which turned the effort as sour as decayed fruit.

"They celebrated all through the Shelby Territory when word of Conliffe's attack rose." Leander's head wobbled till he uttered a rebuke. "Savages!"

The judge's deeds once brought him a public beating when whilom Guardian Hector Geirolf Picadura kicked the despised judge down to the banks of the waterway that contained the town that bore the family name, Conliffe's Landing. Even cruel Hector let the judge suffer his shame with less brutality.

"He made a fit leader. His heart rotted long afore they turned."

The Guardian redirected his attention to Samuel, whose facial wounds kept him unrecognizable apart from his bushy mustache. Tull ignored the transparent gelatinous sacks that concealed wounded hands and feet. Treatment boasted many abilities, and the judge would again have workable digits; provided he woke again. Movement behind his eyelids hinted that he might.

"I'm told this *gel* targets the fluids and the spine and regenerates damage even unto the mind. There's slight expectation of recovery, but you can imagine how this hurts our numbers as a populace. The old wolf, our judge, ordered them moved here after the broadcast your Abettor Shannon sent to Gensch and Meeker."

Tull's heart for Jules swelled; still, he twisted at the waist and observed the rest of the room. "Is Ernie here?"

"Among more than two souls?" Leander's eyes flashed with color and he fluttered with anxiety. "I sit in his stead. No one will bat an eye at the idea of a grandfather visiting his granddaughter."

Tull observed the mermaid who watched over Leander with adoration for a soul she had never touched or embraced.

"As the headship, you're privileged to certain details that no other soul needs to learn. Not even the chiefs. That includes your outfit."

"What makes you imagine you can trust me?"

"Can we not?" He shared a grin with Tull.

"Nita and Olley?"

"They departed afore either tank arrived. You won't like this next part, but Ernie promised you'd keep safe the two monsters kept here in exchange for the silence of the crew and their benefactor."

"You might have them warm a third tank."

The old logger squinted and took a step back. "Is that a sort of joke?"

"I fear Judge Katch will prove the next occupant. Pine seeks him now."

"Alone? You trust him?"

"Above most."

"And the Infested one? Bright Moon."

"When you find a tree filled with worms, do you sell off the wood?"

"No. I watch till such a time when I have to cut roots and all to preserve the neighboring trees." The logger then understood Tull's analogy.

"You last spoke with Ernie when?"

"This morn."

"He's well?"

"He's what he oft seems. Bristled, cantankerous, long-winded. All the traits we adore in him."

"Abettor Shannon keeps close to Otto. If Elwell fell, Otto would tell her."

The logger watched as the Guardian patrolled the tanks.

"Hofnarr had me brought to that derelict farm he keeps and sought my show of servitude on behalf of the outfit. That leaves one judge uncounted."

"We do this in secret; even from *him*. No one will look for them in a place that doesn't meet the protocol requirements for housing such high-minded wineskins."

Tull valued how the scion joked now, and better understood Leander's presence, but weighed the dangers he placed on his granddaughter. "The portraits and names ought to be removed from every display plate and the chamber walls shielded."

"This is a low-security station."

"All chambers are designed at the same shop. The security is in place, regardless of what house they're set in." Scion Kind Hand's agitated legs drew his eye, and he watched her cradle her stomach as her heartrate struggled. Sadness washed over him like the reflections of the gel, and he turned away as though caught when the medical staff enacted his suggestions. "Ernie calls every soul in this care his beloved child."

"What more can we do?"

"Our judges withhold their reels and add to the difficulties my outfit faces in keeping safe all they hold dear."

"A born negotiator." Leander stepped nearer, as if they spoke the same language. "I can't grant permission, but I'll take your request to our judge. Scions Madár and

Meeker are coarse, but I've oft found them cautious. Now that they're judges, they'll henpeck every petition."

Tull remembered Madár, whose family farmed the way that Leander owned a few trees. He recalled visiting the scion's Shelby Territory in his blamelessness. The smell of the air, the deep-green crops, and the sight of workers fishing stayed with him long after the territory withered. His mind's eye directed his focus onto Samuel's arm lesions and connected two times. "Back in the Era of the Falling Lands, a soul who fished the northern bluffs developed a tethering net to withstand how the winds dragged their hauls against the bluffs."

"They used expandable mesh, not braided strands."

"When the material stretches, the *mouths* open and a team of spiny, copper teeth curl out and sink into the meat."

Leander's brow arched, and he compared the wounds on the two judges. "How in Ki'eoppa did you recollect that? That was afore you were born!"

"I read my way unto slumber." He rested his arm on the beveled ledge of Samuel's tank and leaned nearer for a look at the wound. "The idea was to bleed the meat of spirits back afore the firstkind ran us from the water."

"That's when Holston Lucius Buckler designed new irrigation systems and fish hatcheries and made his fortune." He chuckled. "Old circles. You believe he, or someone in his camp, is involved?"

"I imagine his supply stores in the territories of Carpenter, Weston, or Larson suffered a recent loss of inventory."

"You say *imagine* but you sound *certain*."

The Guardian righted his posture. "Once the Partakers swarmed into Shelby, those who despised their ways abandoned the territory. I doubt a business-minded soul risks losing alms to lawlessness when another territory can protect wares. Creighton favors hunting over fishing, and Mumus's need for controlling Archibald would've produced conflict in a proud soul like Buckler."

"Why not this territory?"

"Bromley Timbers & Fruits brokered a protective arrangement to preserve seventeen thousand trees along the northern hem. No way the design of the nets works without mussing up a few trees."

TULL

Leander suppressed his grin and cocked his jaw. "Ernie told me you were sharp. Satisfactory. I'll voice my interest, so you don't have to ask your friend Grover or appease the upper crust."

"I'm wrong to speak of such matters to lesser ranks without invitation."

"That's good of you."

"That's the law of our judges."

"I'm not sure they're as rational or as sensible as you."

"I'm called to obey, lest they turn against the Triune. Then my purpose to them changes."

"You're a Reformer?"

"I'm not cultured enough."

Leander gauged Tull from his mannerisms to his words to his handmade clothes. "If you aren't, then I'm not sure they'd have me, either. I'm not one for watching reels, so most of what I learn comes from writings and conversation. You're the soul who doesn't end his foes. You offer repentance to all.

"When I was a new father, I reasoned with an absoluteness. A soul commits a crime, you make that soul pay more than they owe. Then, I became a grandfather and towed regrets of my own. From that moment on, I've realized the preciousness—the value—in each soul. Why the Triune lets us behave any other way puzzles me!"

"Don't blame the Triune. We war because the first of *our* creation chose."

"How do you mean?"

"You're a logger, you've heard the tale. There's a tree in a garden. On one branch sat a Liar who offered enticement. One simple choice. Now we've surrounded our souls with choices. We've let in every upsetting thing. This is the result."

"Every upsetting thing."

Though both towed greater regrets, neither threatened further disturbance of well-kept secrets. Leander oversaw his granddaughter's care and the child within Scion Kind Hand, with the occasional offer to assist Tull. The Guardian patrolled the facility, made an adjustment here or there, and watched over the room of workers, patients, scions, and judges till the eve dimmed the peak without incident.

SIXTEEN

<u>SQUIRES LEAP</u>

AT THE HIGHEST HEM OF BROMLEY'S FOREST OVERLOOKING THE SILAS CHAMBER HOUSE. WHERE THE TERRANE DROPS UNTO THE LOY RIVER.

The view from the Jacoby Territory changed little in Tull's time. He liked how the altitude changed the colors and shapes of the other territories and how the pylon's song changed on this side of the Loy. Time never dulled the sting he felt toward the old bridge or the void that stood in homage. He looked further south, toward the sweeping lantern at the Bellflower Signal House, then further still in the direction of the Shelley Signal House where his travels began. From where he stood, he guarded over all he loved, be they in one land or another.

He turned toward the sound of the No. 9 Steam Tram, soon to reach Holly Landing, then counted souls who rushed across Cheswell Path in hopes of attaining passage afore the moonrise. His gaze evaded Mumus Tower for the WAM radio antenna; larger than the rows of copper beacons that let travelers use their handheld devices. Tramcars skirted the same path where Guardians fell in that previous land, and those he guarded moved about; too busy for a *scarecrow*. The offering ended, and the return to normalcy settled within two moonrises.

He missed how Olley's laugh softened Nita's resolve *there*. The chill tucked in the breeze faded when he considered the bloom of energy that followed Hazy like a Minister's shield. She mimicked Jules in that way; and how the medic exuded a spell-like air when she lingered for a moment away from every soul in the territories but him. He could only crave the season when they all delighted together and basked in the scope of Hazy's gentle wisdom and Q. J.'s brilliant imagination.

TULL

The instant he pushed back against his heart's ache, the sound of whimsical laughter showered down on him. Two warm hands scooped him off his feet and arms of brass held him secure. The Squire Friend glowed with a pureness of light that radiated with his laugh. "Let fall your troubles, *cousin*! I will not drop you!"

With an uproar of laughter, Friend and Tull rose across the Loy River. They vaulted through the air like an arrow that no breeze restrained. The Guardian suffered no fear, and experienced a heightened sense of the elements and the richness of color. What he disregarded as dimming a moment ago now gleamed beneath the Squire's flight.

He saw the waves of radio frequency from the WAM antenna and the fire-like shimmer of light on every soul. The aquarium exposition burned with a light not unlike the Squire's eyes, and the sea revealed to him the portions of neighborhoods the tides cradled. He heard the song of the pylons; no longer haunted, but prayer-filled. They ascended higher than the Somers Roundabout he taught Hazy to love, then his feet touched down without impact or tottering.

1721 FRESNEL PARK

BACK IN THE ARCHIBALD TERRITORY.
HIGH ENOUGH THAT A SOUL REMAINED SHORT OF BREATH.

An anthracite-fueled fire erupted in four copper bowls atop a decorative iron rail and cast visible heat through the durable, transparent plates that formed the terrace. Tull remembered every detail about the terrace of his loft-home. Once he agreed to sit, he found his worn boots removed from his feet and no memory, nor time, spent on their removal. Friend drifted and let Tull's vision recalibrate and focus on his perch six storeys above the Loy River.

"See! My brother has gathered preparations for your retreat, cousin! Our Creator desires that your soul align with your purpose and your stillness with His wonder."

Near the base of an anthracite kettle, Tull discovered his worn pack, surrendered at the time of the offering. Though Tull's heart was so well-known by the Squires and Ministers, Friend delighted in the smile that formed on the Jacobian's face as he inspected the pack.

"One canteen, filled. One blanket. Two pieces of flint." He held a glass tube fitted with a cork. "And incense."

TULL

"Packed on the side *opposite* your journal! My brother tells me you must add *salt*."

Tull chuckled as if blameless. "I thank you both."

A vaporous shape, like a round body, formed around the Squire and fretted with a delicateness that betrayed his build. Though not tactile, the Comforting Minister who looked after the Guardian declared his heart for the one whom he called *slow to learn*. "You have your warm coat?"

"Si'an-dro Sa'ähn! I'll wear two coats, if only to please you."

The Comforting Minister, called Si'an-dro Sa'ähn, delighted and furthered what details he shared through the Squire. "You'll need bundling if you're to go toward the bluffs near the grove of myrtle trees. You'll hear the song of the spirits on the wind and *know* the place where your willingness delights our Creator."

Tull shut his eyes and the path, down to the precise grove, filled his thoughts. "I'll be back afore you know."

"How can you say this? How can *we* know?"

"I didn't want you to worry over me."

"My purpose sets me to worry. You would stifle my purpose? You would have me tell our Creator your knowledge exceeds His? I believe not!"

Silence. The *need* to speak troubled the Ministers who dealt with the Second Creation. Tull's heart—and tongue—rested. Then the Minister calmed too. The heart Tull bore and kept shielded drew his caretakers closer, even though the secondkind's anxiousness agitated the comforters.

They were caretakers, but their capacity for compassion opened them to the fears of those they watched over. Like a mother fretted over a sick child, a Comforting Minister worried over every trial the secondkind faced. Even so, Si'an-dro Sa'ähn cast hope upon him as light shone with a giddy flicker because Tull's faith increased.

"When next I see you, O Son of Mighty Maidens, I will sing with great joy!"

"And," Friend's voice rose, "I will sing over you this eve, cousin!"

An involuntary blink of Tull's eye let both creatures vanish from his sight. In the void, another of the Colonel's gliders patrolled. Tull accepted the laws of citizenship, the surrender of privacy, and a loss of modesty via unceasing voyeurism in the name of *monitoring*. Gone were moments of true privacy by the law of the judges.

He secured his pack and stood where the eve's chill collided with the heat from the nearest anthracite kettle. The terrace drifted like the rise and fall of a body at rest and offered him the effect of riding upon the forbidden sea. As the veins of sky-fires bled unto eve, clouds unfurled feather-soft ash upon the territories. Such conditions infused solemnness and drove most of the secondkind indoors till morn. Gliders kept closed the bridges, and even the steam trolleys stopped till the morn.

He claimed a seat while Friend fulfilled his promise and sang over his cousin till another who adored the Guardian called upon him. The Squire let his melody fade into the breeze and spirited away as Jules stepped onto the terrace. She looked back into the undisturbed loft, then admired the coziness around Tull. He kept still till she set two chilly fingers against the lobe of his ear and squeezed.

"*Nel-l-l-son.*"

His gaze drifted as he inhaled, and a grin lined his face the moment her eyes captivated him. Even under the soft flicker of burning anthracite, they sparkled like gemstones; rich black with purple ledges. She fanned back her hair while she kissed between the scars on his brow but sacrificed her effort for the chance to hug his neck. He breathed in the aroma of peach blossoms and stroked the tips of her hair as she cradled the back of his crown.

"I said, 'Ten eves in Gutefiel and you didn't find time to write me a poem?'"

He could see the reflection of lashes in her irises; a feat that made him grin. When he realized she waited twice for his answer, he swallowed and shook his head. "I'm sorry to say, no."

"I miss those. How did you—" She stopped and shook her head. "How are you?"

"I find I'm short on complaints." He rose halfway from his seat, but she patted his shoulder. "How are you?"

She half-nodded and half-sighed. "No souls in the shadows, covering their faces with scarves, but Honorine wanted to hear of your rotorcraft trip."

He grinned rather than admit how the rotorcraft ride dimmed after his *flight* with Friend. Tull then claimed the seat furthest from her, despite her gentle protest. She grinned over the gesture and sat; though she offered a deliberate sigh over the way he missed an opportunity for closeness. The ashen snow still fell along the rail, but the warmth of embers made the setting bearable. Something about a fire on a brisk eve consoled the heart.

"How she once kept an oath of silence amazes me!" She caught his sympathetic grin and redirected. "I—I heard on the radio how Judge Hofnarr says you frightened two of his brides. He expects a public apology from you."

"I wish him well in the meantime."

TULL

"You remember writing me poems, though, do you not?"

"I maintain my recollections."

She grinned over his sarcasm. "Oh! Lest my mind slips, *Monteith*. Lucy ran with Monteith."

"You manage your recollections well."

She laughed when the terrace shifted, not unlike the aquarium exposition, and nudged her seat a hand's breadth nearer.

"Clumsy ice cap bears." He inhaled as the tether around Lucy and a victim tightened. While he dwelled, he slipped from the chair to one knee and removed the first of her boots till he found bare feet. The burning anthracite heated the terrace plates and comforted him, but not his oft chilly-footed visitor.

She tucked her feet onto the seat with her and curled her toes around the ledge. "Well, we're far from hot wine and a cold bath but, I—I thank you."

"You're welcome."

"You hadn't forgotten his name. You wanted me to confirm as much, right? And, now I—I have. Lucy was in Gutefiel with you, though." Her voice lowered till the Guardian tilted toward her to hear. "Is the same soul who ended Lucy's friend attacking our judges?"

"You're the smartest soul in my time. What's your theory?"

"Victor Simon Shannon's worst bugbear: *Only the lazy s'pose.*" She puffed out her cheeks as she pondered her father's wisdom. "He also says if you're going to keep roaming with no abettor, you should get a dog again."

"I spoke to Pine earlier."

Jules laughed. She knew he missed her remark, but loved his unintended humor. "I—I say dog and you say Pine."

"Marvin hasn't checked in." He watched her brow change and blinked. "Hazy's afraid of dogs."

"Hazy's afraid. I've learned nothing of Marvin this eve."

His inhalation of pain for the blameless soul sounded like the roar of fire and consumed his worry over a third judge's harm.

As if Jules distinguished his breaths, she combined both concerns with a somber wringer. "Did something happen to Lucy in Gutefiel?"

"What did she do?"

TULL

"She's turned *scary*. Chief Gensch came to the house after another complaint about her agitation. Who can predict her from breath to breath? The constant tiptoeing and whispering affect Hazy." She kneaded between her eyebrows. "She's getting to me, too."

Tull withheld an offer to interfere and waited for elaboration.

"I—I heeded your *advice*, followed the protocols, and went to Olley, who asked why you didn't help me. He endorsed remotion. Then his number came up in the lottery and he entered Gutefiel."

Tull awaited a horrible tale about Lucy's behavior at home.

"The reels showed how powerful she gets. She's sworn for spans that she doesn't have that side still. I refuse to believe her again. Leaving Hazy with her turns me sick."

Jules's stammer vanished when she focused, which proved to him how she set her mind on the matter. "I'd hoped she blew out her wick after she cleared the way in Gutefiel. Pine wanted to leave her. That's why you struck him.

"The radio polled to learn who we s'pose are after our judges. Lucy and Phinn Derek Wade; though, the doves who named your favorite thesp sounded jaded. Mediary Gesicht made third, and I—I forget which Berserker was fourth."

The way he breathed calmed her. "Maybe they aren't off? George and Violet are too kind and too superstitious. Hamer brims with loathing toward his father, not our judges. Nita's too smart to be that cruel. Then there's Pine, who's mean. And short-tempered. And—"

"Why not Tim?"

"Tim's got a glass jaw and he's not a good sneak. You should suspect me above Tim." She noted how the color flowed through his cheeks. "What? I—I can get riled!"

"J. J., you can't curse without blushing. You used to drape blankets over your head to keep from the embarrassment the projection-gliders caused you. You'll walk halfway across the territory for your favorite cotton candy, and you've saved more lives than . . ." His voice trailed off and he shook his head. "If you're a suspect, then this whole Creation is ended."

She sat up and grinned. "Well, at least you pay attention. If the attacks stop all of a sudden, I—I *imagine* more souls might suspect Tim."

"Do you have as many reasons to dismiss Lucy?"

"No."

"And, what's my excuse?"

TULL

"Uhm, *me*. Nelson, when did you last *wake*?" She gauged his expression with delight-filled eyes. "How far back did you come? A watch? A moonset?"

Tull shifted. "Seven spans."

"*Seven*?! I—I tell you, the fact that you lasted that long amazes me. Ha! I—I knew you came back! You spoke too slyly about Monteith and the Infested; plus, you don't behave like you did afore the offering."

"How did I behave?"

Her mouth pulled tight at one corner and she shrugged in fear of clarifying her remark.

"If I upset you in some way *then*, I hope you'll forgive me *now*. But, I tell you, lest you believe I withhold, that none targeted our judges in that previous land, and . . . I cannot tell you much more."

"That makes my toes colder." She leaned toward him and mumbled, "I—I truly want to know if you remember standing with me in the glen where your parents wed. Do you remember how souls we didn't know stood along the hilltops to get a look at us? After that, you took six moons till you stopped picking those little blue flowers and packing them in my gear."

"Forgive me that I ever stopped."

"I—I never wear *my* ring during a shift, and you asked me to hold *yours* till the offering ended." She plucked a chain from the zippered neck of her blouse and let two bands sway. "If we were Partakers, none could keep me from taking your name; not that I—I mind 'the bride of Nelson James Tull' hemmed to my already odd name and double titles. I've confused you?"

"The eighth eve beneath the Moon of the Falling Stars," he cited when they wed; in the final moon of the winter, three spans ago. "Your mom worried we might see snow."

"We saw snow and Momma laughed."

"You worried Honorine might drink too much pear wine."

"I—I told her that dress made her *jiggle*. Otto blushed each time she moved."

Tull sighed with a contented spirit as he found again his home with her.

"Remembering her jiggle?"

He shook his head and considered all Jules let pass to be his bride as she unfastened the necklace and placed their bands upon their fingers again. Like the brides of his maternal grandfather, Jules was not designed as Tull or the Nelson lineage back to the Jacobian's first era kin. The hearts of Bonnie Jo Arjeta and Ida Georgette Hobson failed whilst giving birth to his uncle, first, and then his mother. Otto, Gloria Bea Greer, and a host of Reformers warned Jules of the same end should she attempt to bear his fruit. She loved him too much to abandon him, but the aftershock of failed hopes seldom passed.

"You've never traveled so far afore. How bad was that land if you needed to get seven spans away?"

"You chose an old bear. I never needed such a running start when I was younger." He abandoned her in too many lands. "How oft have I told you my 'J. J.' story?"

"You asked me not to count anymore. I—I love that you love me enough to give me your grandma's nickname and that you never change your mind when you come back." She kissed the back of his hand. "I love my old bear and he loves me."

"He knows your scent and no other satisfies him."

Her focus sharpened. "Carl says he caught you at the door of Mumus Tower."

"I never reached further than Sondrea's bust."

"Why, you sly devil!" Her tone teased enough. "When you told me about your grandma, you were telling me you planned to start something to finish something with Mumus."

He grinned in recognition of the way she cited Harlan Bottin Vosburg.

"So, did you start something?"

"Who, me?" He matched her flicked brow. "Maybe no soul's seen the Colonel, but his hand's in this. He's corrupted all he's set his sights on. He's angling others evermore and—"

"Even Anya? I—I thought time might end afore we gave her another chance." Jules shrugged off the remark without an explanation. "Is she why you came back?"

He stilled her with his loving gaze. "Forgive me that I disrespected you by speaking of her."

"*One* land where you fail to wed me, and now you seek amends with Anya Nora Rains. She goes by *archivist* here. More like pain in the—"

The arch of his right brow stalled her barb.

"*Annalist.*"

His breathing hinted at his disinterest, but she kept his mind from wandering when she held his hand out of her way and slid onto his lap.

TULL

"The organ between your lungs gets you into more trouble than any other." She slipped his hand beneath her blouse and traced her body with his coarse fingers till his pulse mingled with her beating heart. "Every time."

He listened to her purr as she covered her breast and held his hand in place.

"Don't trust every soul; if you trust me."

"Evermore and evermore again." He smoothed the cuff of her trousers and stroked the arch of her foot. "I've missed you since I woke."

"And, you love me beyond words."

"Far beyond words do I love you, Jules."

His admission drew a sparkle from her eye, and she let loose of his hand to caress his shoulders. "Honor talked me into paying to see the film about you down on the old Eidolon Pictures lot. Imagine! Me, Momma, Honorine, and two of her sisters."

"Which two?" He brushed her abdomen with the back of his hand.

"Feisty Patience and stubborn Charity." She sighed with a gust that changed the direction of a few ashen flakes. "Charity, who wonders why you don't fight with your shirt off as much as Phinn Derek Wade did. Dad was right. A waste of alms! Nice to get Momma away from the inn for an eve, but the worst possible substitute."

His fingers pecked at her belt buckle. "Few souls see what that place did to ours."

"They believe and still deny. Some look the most obvious thing and refuse to see."

He drew an inquisitive breath, like the wind needed to power a sail across the sea, and she drifted closer.

"Imagine if they told a tale about *my* rescue!"

He traced her chin. "Truly, my heart pounded."

"Then who's to say how you kept your mind in Gutefiel!"

"Gutefiel proved me terrified of Yah's abandonment." His honesty stirred Jules. "Lefty found his madness, and Lucy's rage paled. Pine and Nita lost their hearts, but what weakened dear George's nerve burnished Olley. Animals hunted their fellows with menace whilst our own kind cut away pieces of their bodies and flung their parts into the burning pits."

Smoothing his beard, Tull remembered the place as if the heat of the fire remained upon his face. "Fathers bred their daughters, and still those daughters lusted. Mothers castrated and cut out the tongues of their sons. The once innocent burned their elders. Their hearts cried out for absence and the Triune proved what that absence *invited*. And, I've repented for what I observed each moonrise since."

TULL

"You know, this is why we never let you tell Hazy beddy-bye stories." She returned to her feet as the mood drifted. "Do you not?"

Tull looked at his bride with mouth agape, which she closed for him.

"I—I worked on her Hivi'ern gown between shifts and reels. She's going to look so rare and so blameless! She's excited for every soul to see."

Tull smiled in anticipation and the way she towed him from dark regrets.

"*Have* you seen her in her gown afore?"

"I'll never say."

She prodded his side with her toes. "Gutefiel is a bad memory for us. You're home now . . . and I can rest and breathe again."

He nodded. "I've not taken time and let my mind or heart settle with this soul. Which is not to say I want to leave your side."

"You need to retreat. Not like the last time, though. The last time here, not the—"

"I won't be away long."

"Give me your word."

"Two eves at most."

She held her breath in discomfort.

"I must visit Ernie." He massaged Jules's sides till she took a breath. "Then I will return to you. My word, and the rest of me, is yours. Still and evermore."

"I—I picked up our aged chops, and Perry sent over an attractive bounty in your honor for Hivi'ern. He thanked you for the saw and claims the bottle of mead he included to you survived the Last War. Do they still eat colcannon in the hundred twenty-second span?"

"We do."

"Then say you give your bride a kiss, take her indoors so we can make dinner, and stay in together this eve afore you go."

Tull stood and lifted Jules. She squeezed his waist with her thighs, and he wrapped his arms around her. As the door responded to their beacons, his bride nuzzled at his neck and he kissed her face till their lips met. The lights of the loft reacted to their entrance, but no comforts surpassed her tenderness.

Deliberate Ends

An Interim

The 26th Eve beneath the Moon of the Old Embers

The 114th Gathering Season of the Accession

In the Blessing of I'Esh, who tends the harvest.

Beacon 087.68.013 recognized at 9 Pierce Trail . . .

Identifier confirmed—Robbie Rudat Pine.

Purposed to serve the Second Creation as 24th Guardian.

The search for Judge Marvin Elam Katch, the fourth *known* victim of the Uncounted Soul, proved less nerve-wracking than the discovery of Samuel Herbert Gwynne. No tearful mourners gathered around Katch the way that Lizzie Dale Conliffe mourned her father. Strays circled him and nipped at his swaying hand till Pine chased away the creatures and cut him down from a barren tree branch. There ended fanfare.

Now, the Larson Territory awaited the naming of their new judge, as Marvin never named his scion aloud. The Katch oligarchy ended with no heirs or spouses to claim his judgeship. For the first time beneath the rule of judges, a Larsonite stood a chance to prosper. They might even esteem Robbie Rudat Pine.

The irritable Guardian tore off another bite of pan-seared fish, raised in pristine waters on a special farm that catered to the judges. He slumped on the judge's dusty kitchen table as he chewed the meal that he prepared from the food supply in a home that never held an invitation for him. So, he made his own meal. Spilled yolk traced his chin as he sucked the white of a fried egg into his mouth across oil-slickened lips.

While he digested, he turned his attention onto the handheld device that shared his table. Since early that morn, a new relay gathered viewings at a stomach-dizzying pace. As for Pine, he watched the reel for the fourth time since he arrived at Katch's home and knew the chronicled setting well, though some time passed since he last visited Tull's loft too.

As the projection lens shifted from the distant horizon and onto the Guardian's face, the outfit's current headship offered a nod to all who watched him. "I am Nelson James Tull, the fourth Guardian from the Jacoby Territory. I am the grandson of Judge Juanita Gene James, and the proud son of Departed Patrick James Tull and Kara Doe Nelson. Some consider me the soul who lasted ten eves in the place where good fell. I've served as Guardian since the one hundredth sowing season of the Accession.

"When the blameless of the era that warred formed the Guardians, they meant us to keep safe all Yah's creation. We began as rescuers, as defenders. Then, the judges of the Era of the Reformers invited us to war against the Fallen First. Now our era of judges are targeted, just as we targeted the firstkind.

"I tell you, we have failed them. Each of us who are not blameless. We've become so entitled that we no longer keep safe what is *right*. We no longer keep safe the honesty of our judges."

He stirred, even grumbled, but nevertheless proved his obedience. "As of this tick, till a time when I cannot, I offer to keep safe every judge in these seven territories, their families, their scions, and the families of those scions. We cannot rest in safety whilst harm rises against these souls.

"To those who fear harm due to the laws declared by our judges, to those who live in fear, seek your Reformers. Return to your churches. A Guardian, chief, abettor, medic, Believer, or Reformer will find you there and keep safe your soul. I say this on behalf of all *recognized* Guardians."

The projection lens focused upon the streams of blinding light that vaulted across the sky-fires behind him. Once the view sharpened, the lens caught Tull admiring the same sight. His eyes drifted, as though a solemn thought reached him. He then proved

TULL

> able to comfort with little more than a warm gaze and a soothing voice.
>
> "We reside in a time when every soul of the secondkind must guard the other. Let not *one* monster dwell among you—or in you. Protect the blameless, and we will protect you. Harm them or any feeble soul, and no law will keep you."

Pine set aside the device as the endless loop of Tull's reel played again. His eyes crept upward in curious submission and nodded in a manner worthy of any Guardian. He learned that agreement with his purpose seldom cast his displeasure away. While he lacked the proper words, he chewed on another egg and let his curiosity over the scuff marks against a pantry door uproot him from his meal. He wiped the yolk across his thumb and opened the door without touching his bare hand to the surface.

A pulley-and-cable system, fitted with a wooden lever, raised a false floor and revealed a ramp access to rooms beneath the old house. No creatures charged toward an escape, not that he offered thanks to the Triune. He heard tales about the judge's secret purpose but feared the truth too much to investigate. Now, ignoring those tales felt lax.

As he descended into a cave-like substructure, he discovered the true heart of his judge. The longest, constant wall of the basement supported anchors which housed display plate after display plate without gap. Each plate showcased reels—some live, some relived—of those throughout the territories who turned the judge's eye. Fifty-eight reels showcased those souls in ways that made the Guardian squeamish.

"I imagine this is how Tim's house feels, thirty moons from now."

Judge Katch wasted too much of his purpose on the behaviors of others. Pine, who served him, harbored no inclination toward such behavior. He felt only the shame of bowing to a soul who weighed the value of others in flesh and pleasure. He detested that his judge clawed for more power through the appetites of others.

Pine turned his whole body away from the wall, uncovered his eyes, and opened toward the sight of shelves lined with dusty and discolored jars. No one who observed the trinkets kept in those jars denied Katch's sickness. The Guardians oft claimed that they would hunt him, were he not a judge. Katch made Pine's skin crawl, so he harbored no repentance for eating his food or snooping through every room.

TULL

Behind a trough where the judge performed *experiments* and *surgeries*, he found another wall lined with smooth cabinetry and embedded display plates. Each plate, one atop another, sported a hardwire connection to a glass recess fitted with an identifier beacon. When Pine stepped closer, he noticed that each beacon appeared stained with blood and matted in tissue. Each beacon remained active, and generated whereabouts for the creature to whom the device belonged.

BEACON DESIGNATE: 079.64.227
ROBERT JEFFREY MCCLOSKEY.
LOCATION: 93 HUTTER TRAIL.

"Across the Loy, is he? Let us see . . ."

He pulled the beacon from the receptacle and both plates faded to a transparent surface. A chirping alarm pierced the confined space in response. With a slight push, the beacon reinitialized, and both plates flickered with color. The same designate and name appeared, though the location leapt between the judge's homestead to the false location along the Carpenterian foothills.

"How sly."

BEACON DESIGNATE: 079.64.227
ROBERT JEFFREY MCCLOSKEY.
MAPPING . . .

"So, you worked both sides and deceived us for Partakers!"

Pine identified McCloskey by the markings on his arms. He bore the implanted shapes of metal and bone beneath the tissue and boasted his number of lovers with tattooed strings of identical symbols along his forearms. Pine ignored McCloskey's reel for another that belonged to a soul eighteen spans younger; by the first three digits of the designate code and, by the second grouping, the eleventh soul born unto the secondkind in the ninety-seventh span of the Accession.

BEACON DESIGNATE: 097.11.730
CORA LILY SÓWKA.
LOCATION: 307 AYA HILL ROAD.

"Another Shelbian!" He heard the wind-down of an engine, which he blamed on a reel from the other room, and again set his attention onto the wall of sham beacons.

BEACON DESIGNATE: 078.01.063
BERWIN GILBERT FORGNEY.
LOCATION: 1254 VILLÁM FORK ROAD.

"Never will I trust a Forgney! Deceivers!"

He yanked the beacon from the reader, as a fuse fit into an electrical box, and ended the false relay of Berwin Gilbert Forgney's whereabouts to the chief inspectors across all seven territories. One dishonest soul meant nothing to him. His attention landed elsewhere, and made him reach toward a cobweb-lined shelf. In his efforts, Forgney's beacon fell to the floor and rolled underfoot.

Pine pulled from the shelf another tin case, this one's lid embossed with a commemorative alms from the territories' first hundred spans. The beacon he dropped pressed into the cleat of his boot, tucked away as though his own. He took the foremost beacon from the tin case and plugged the leads into the empty recess in the table. Heat produced an odor as the dust burned from the contacts and the display plate flickered till the recognition sequence started.

BEACON DESIGNATE: 072.32.993
SISTER PATIENCE MILLER
MAPPING . . .

"Why, you old cuss! Oft have I wondered what became of her soul."

Though cleaved from temple to jawbone, the graceful build and flaxen hair shielded the hideous contempt seared in her soulless black irises. Fragility and beauty hid her true *form*. As for Marvin, he appeared as a young man, still bandaged and sore from his new confinements in a wheelchair—a choice Pine never understood. His grin never once relaxed, and he delighted in peeling away layers of Patience's body.

"How a small token changes much." He rifled through the tin, for he lacked the stomach for gore, and swapped beacons with the glass reader.

TULL

BEACON DESIGNATE: 065.52.115

KARA DOE NELSON.

MAPPING . . .

"Sister Patience and Mother Tull?"

She looked as fragile as a bloom in snow, and Katch treated her with similar care. The judge, who stood on both legs then, held a compress to the wound he caused her pale flesh and offered another for the tear that discolored her cheek. Katch's tenderness never diminished the hurt that Pine observed in her pale eyes; eyes that matched his friend's. The calmness she displayed lured him in, and he remembered the love and comfort he found in his own mother's care.

"When he sees this, Marvin, he'll end you over and over as long as he breathes."

Pine cursed, then a pool of rich, black blood slathered the tabletop. His posture swayed and the room turned cold; still, except for the adrenalized beat of his heart. He wheezed for breath and wanted to scream, but his voice failed him. Then he caught the glint of a blade that cut his throat from behind.

For the way that he spoke of her at Gutefiel, after seasons of agitation, Lucy Bright Moon tossed his breakfast knife upon Pine's chest and took the last breath from his lips. She never sought an apology, nor another soul to deal with her offense. As circumstance arranged, she found herself alone in a house where neither belonged and no soul would suspect her hand against the territory's Guardian.

Though she *enjoyed* the warmth of his spillage between her toes, other necessities drew her feet and attention from the basement. As she pivoted away, she plucked each beacon that Pine viewed. Light-headedness slowed her ascent up the ramp, though, so she tottered and impressed a spotted handprint upon the wall.

Tull's voice lured her into the kitchen, where she mopped handfuls of water from glass jars upon her face and neck. Upon the base of her neck, the tattoo of her true face now appeared segregated by an incision mark. Though she would never touch the judge, like Pine, she borrowed the comforts of his home when she slept in his bed, bathed in his tub, and read from his many journals.

Her soiled feet moistened the dried trail of spillage from the abducted judge and followed her out of doors. There, dust and blades of grass muddied the stains, but she paid greater attention to the feel of the breeze on her skin. Droplets of water mingled with beads of unexpected sweat turned her skin waxy and kept strands of hair against her face. As she prepared her handheld device, she stumbled and drifted, and let the weathered face of a post press between her ribs to keep her upright.

"Guardian Lucy Bright Moon seeks contact with Guardian Nelson James Tull. Passcode: Enoch Two-Six, Two-One Fetter."

"INTERFACING. SEEKING AUTHORIZATION . . .
AUTHORIZATION GRANTED.
FREQUENCY: INACTIVE.
ALTERNATE ACTION?"

She groaned through her nostrils. "Relay a reel."

"INTERFACING. RELAYING . . ."

"Well, *handsome*, this is your sharpest arrow, and, if that doesn't cost you your sleep, hold on, for I must say this to you."

The remnants of what once filled her wailed with laughter and strained the perpetual hoarseness of her voice.

"I thank you. You made my exit from Gutefiel less . . . profane. Better I make use of my purpose; lest you believe I avoid your headship. As you sought the Devourer, I seek a monster, too."

She used a creature from blamelessness to dampen her odd smile. The fragrance of sweet grass and sage rose with her body temperature as she imagined Tull's suspicion against her. If her temper rose too, she might reduce every glass in Katch's home to powder. In those tales that the blameless told to frighten one another, her soul made a mouth-watering dish for the Devourer.

"I seek your territory's new *husk*." She gnashed her teeth and kept her heavy head from jittering and opening the wound on her neck. "Monteith has kin, and kin have expectations."

In truth, she sought a soul at D'Aramitz Abbey who shared her proclivities with the soulless body of Chester Roldan Monteith.

"As to *your* expectations, I said I would ruin *her*. So, what you'll do if I frighten her again—*when* I frighten her again—interests me." She raked trembling fingers through her locks. "Soon, I'll see *youuuu*."

TULL

She ended her relay to Tull, then authorized contact with another recipient in fear the device might force her to reenter her authorization. Given the nature of her request, and the shrill voice of her contact, she switched functions to non-verbal messaging and chose a contact from a lengthy list of souls.

"THERE IS ANOTHER FOR YOU AT 9 PIERCE TRAIL."

While she waited for the device to relay her message, she considered the threat Tull made toward her via a private reel. He proved willing to defend the judges, Hazel-Sue, and her abettor. She received only a vague threat.

"I deserve better than they."

For Tull's slight, she created a blinding fire in the pit of her hand and cast his mother's beacon into the white-hot heart of an unnatural flame. Her fingertips and palm remained unblistered as the plume hovered and never touched the flesh. This ability separated, even from other Partakers and Infested, yet Tull still issued his warning. The marvel who took the primality of her infestation replaced their void with *gifts* that let her cast tendrils of energy through the territories and down giants in that previous land.

In her heart, she felt no hint of remorse for ruining a definitive lead to the mysterious end of Tull's mother. Kara Doe Nelson was no more of a mother to Tull than Lucy was a mother toward Hazy. That selfishness resided in her since her first step. Never one for *favorites* of any sort, she burned the other beacons she swiped from Katch's basement and held no regard for the souls who shared her deceit or what trouble she created for them.

III. | Cabin Pressure

Seventeen

The 27th Morn beneath the Moon of the Old Embers
The 114th Gathering Season of the Accession
In the Blessing of I'Esh, who tends the harvest.

Taft Bluffs
The most isolated portion of the Jacoby Territory.
A place where few souls treaded and fewer rested.

A time of retreat let Tull *align* his heart with his purpose and ensured he followed his Creator's will for him. He fasted since his meal with Jules; now two moonsets ago. Since his declaration to the territories, he traveled without one glider alerting him of a judge's request for protection. In the same way, he learned nothing of the attacks on Judge Katch or Pine.

The Jacobian followed the coastal bluffs north, beyond the Archer Signal House, past the first homestead of Lea Christine Fabray, but short of reaching the territorial storage cities. There the secondkind maintained volumes of seeds, grains, cryo-frozen crops, and meat, in the event of a doomed crop. He disapproved of the smell of those cities the way that Hazy disapproved of the smell of Arthur George Green's herds. They shared the same wrinkled-nose response even at the mere thought of a whiff.

So, he gave thanks that the winds blew harder north and further cast away the scent. When his stomach growled over the missed aroma, he gauged the allure of letting his belly grow fat like a certain ice cap bear who shared his age. "If you wanted fatness, you might've shown more care in that previous land."

TULL

His ornery smile turned into a gleam of praise when, a few paces ahead of him, he spotted a grove of crepe myrtle trees. He never knew the tree in all his time, yet this morn he knew with certainty their type.

"Why, Si'an-dro Sa'ähn," he laughed with an air of joy, "you brass-bellied rascal! You've earned this song at my expense. Well-deserved, indeed."

Their branches produced a gate-like fence along a rocky clearing and held back the wind. The ash found a cradle amongst those branches and let some of the grass along the path remain lush green. There fed a rabbit who mocked Tull's grumbling stomach.

"Have a good laugh at me, sure. Laugh all the way to the stewpot, chubs."

The rabbit craned his head and listened as the Guardian stepped nearer.

"You know what awaits past these trees, do you not?"

As the gathering season dwindled with the abrupt return of winter, the winds that raced up the bluffs doubled the conditions. Tull's heart raced toward that season on aching bones. Till the sowing season brought the rains and the thaw, what fell downward rose back upward and over the clearing and blanketed the rim up to the trees. He watched the path of falling snow and then realized he stood where Friend warned he would face the soul who turned judges soporose and troubled his bride.

"The snow does fall upward, Friend."

At last, the Guardians held an advantage over a betrayer, and Tull believed the firstkind nudged him onto the proper path.

"Of all places . . ,"

While not his usual path of travel, Tull recognized the peculiar setting. He breathed well as one worry lifted and stared across the clearing where technology's reign plummeted like the bluffs. Judge Ernie Purcell Bliss built a small cabin there, void of electricity or frills, minus two lattice windows. One such window faced the grove on the path that Si'an-dro Sa'ähn instilled in Tull. What he intended for prayer proved a means for delivering him to the door of the judge who cared for and led the Jacobians since the passing away of Tull's grandmother.

"How you arrange us and move our feet, Creator. I thank You that You guide me."

Unarmed and unsupported, he trusted in a Creator that surrounded him with Ministers and kept him from his end. He observed the heelprints of small boots in the snow; no more than one watch old, if the winds over the bluff held steady. Unsure right step, crooked left step. The judge bore a crisp, direct gait. The difference made him alert for *two* souls.

To test them, he entered the open glebe and stopped for a three-count after every completed stride. No response. Not even a glimmer in the picture window. He then listened for the hollow steps across floorboards and the motion of a trespasser out of doors with him.

What he heard turned him from the absent sounds of breathing and toward the cabin's peak. Load-bearing timber creaked at him, like a wheeze for breath beneath constant strain. The sound repeated, and he heard a strained breath, then another of brittle pain. He imagined those boot prints circled around the back of the cabin, nearer to the ledge, and Tull walked as Bliss walked.

The lone step onto the porch, which he crossed in one and one-half strides, delivered him to a single plank that formed the hand-carved door. In his rush, he paid no mind to the copper posts tucked behind two potted trees on either side of the step. Those posts, like the posts fitted along the roadways throughout the territories, read the beacon in Tull's exaggerated spinal column. The security system for the cabin, far more elaborate than the furnishings, reacted at a slower rate than the Guardian's gait, but unlocked the door.

As an authorized *entrant* of the judge's cabin, Tull observed how a pneumatic cylinder pulled open the door for him. Firelight flickered off the copper cannister of that cylinder but lost his eye. His focus shifted toward two figures inked in silhouette from the window that looked unto the sea. One belonged to the restrained judge, suspended by the wrists from the cabin beam, and the other to his attacker.

No time of interrogation arose and no challenges of the tongue stalled reaction. The Guardian who swore off the violence of his calling capitalized on his advantage of surprise and charged. He who held the advantage of weaponry stood behind a shield: Judge Ernie Purcell Bliss. Tull proved worthy of a rebuke, and struck Bliss with enough velocity that his body swung and struck their mutual foe.

The force of their collision wrung the tether between the load-bearing beam and the judge. Tull clutched a splitting maul from the fireplace and thrust the blade into the beam. The forged metal's sharpened edge cut through the weaponized mesh and the pulp of the wood, but the Guardian's momentum tore the axe loose. Bliss fell to the floor, bound in his own home.

TULL

Tull then used the weight of the anvil head to turn the axe end over end as he pivoted and struck Bliss's attacker with the breadth of the axe handle. He batted him toward the open fireplace and made no attempt to keep him from the flame. Satisfied with the distance gained, he swung the axe against pressure points of the binds and loosed Bliss's arms and chest.

The Uncounted Soul—known neither by his face nor his beacon—leapt off the stone composition of the fireplace as his own weapon. With boots too small for his feet, he struck Tull on the lowest ribs and hip bone. The Guardian buckled while the attacker fell flat on his back. He then drove an elbow against Bliss's kidneys and vaulted onto his heels from a prone position.

He proved an agility equal to his mean streak and dove headlong at the Guardian. With his shoulder against the same ribs he had battered with his feet, he rolled Tull, toppling a handmade set of wooden dining chairs. Still, the move weakened his shoulder and turned the arm slack for three-fifths of the next tick.

Tull lowered his center of gravity with one knee against the floorboards. He leveraged one foot beneath him, in line with his shoulder, and reacted. As he rose, he grabbed his foe's shoulders, drove a knee into his midsection, and flung his body toward the plank that formed the working surface of Bliss's dining table. In his hands, and to his surprise, he held three of the four scarves that obstructed a tormented face.

Unlike the way he appeared when Friend presented him, he looked afraid first, then proud. His irises floated on blood-shot red, irritated eyes. His tear ducts, nostrils, and even the corners of his mouth wept scars. The tissue, ripped outward from the casting out of wandering spirits, healed in loose patches that changed the lay of the face and shape of features. Then Tull stared again into those ruined eyes and the mouth of broken teeth that marred and bloodied lips from constant biting.

"*Lefty.*"

"How a small token changes much."

With that, the fight ceased. Guardian Asham Benjamin Gera, who the outfit called Lefty, missing from his purpose for three spans, stood to his feet and set the chairs and the table upright again. He offered one seat to Tull and checked the pulse of the judge. Then, he took the second seat and let out a settled breath.

Segments of Asham's face remained dull and jaundiced whilst other parts turned ripe with color. The scars on his face uncoiled in pallid shades of white that set his irritated eyes in crimson pits. His face contorted in pockets of trembling, but contempt worked against his portions and made him horrific in form. Gone were the features that made him handsome in the eyes of those souls who adored him.

"I oft told myself that you would find me first, brother."

The Creightonian consumed portions of each of the territory's beliefs and oft gravitated toward the path of the most influential soul in his presence. Tull heard plenty of the Fallen First recite scriptures. Still, he appeared less surprised than the prodigal hoped.

"You, who knows such vast wonder! I cannot imagine the terrors you observed." He bowed his head with earnest respect for Tull. "I kept myself ready for you. I wanted us to feel the thrill as once we did!"

Asham's claim towed hints of truth and kept Tull silent. None believed in resets with greater or more rapid fullness than Asham.

"I stood over you in Gutefiel with a saber in my hand. But time proves dull without you. You—and our fellows—deserved to know who you've chased these many moons." He laughed, and multiple voices flowed from his lips.

"I find no shame in confessing that you've come close to catching me more than once! You gave me what I wanted. You've chased me as hard as any target we ever chased together. I believe I've made you all better. Our kind is better because of me."

Tull cast aside the scarf. "You've frightened souls, not changed them"

"All I've victimized have victimized *us* first. Conliffe, who raped souls throughout his territory; including Nita's aunts. Including Nita's mother. Gwynne, whose supremacy broke George's father's will. Katch, whose mother ordered Pine and every male in the Larson Territory turned into a eunuch, replaced love with carving open bodies. Does a soul truly weep for their twisted stature?

"I chose vile souls and made them so that they might never have a chance to right their paths. Better I confine them to the rubble of their ideas. Let *that* be their legacy, and not the *broken* souls they've spawned. On their ends, all the territories may celebrate that they are no more; just as you might celebrate Anya's end."

He dangled proof afore Tull's eyes in the form of a shattered yellow sapphire pendant that Anya cherished.

"What she suffered was for the wrong she committed against you, brother. Her choice demanded my hand."

"Will I find her on a hook as you set Monteith out for Nita? At last, you divided her from Olley's side so you could get an advantage."

TULL

"Monteith was an overdue end!" He picked at the unevenness of his brow and made a circular gesture with his hand as he constructed within his darkened mind. "Not that *I* ended him! Chief Hont keeps that soul under his roof already. My abettor proved over-eager, did he not? If you've passed your bride's favorite site in all of Sevier, you have every reason to believe me."

"We swore to keep him from this."

"Noble, but needless; like the idea of Guardians. You should have warred in my honor, not fattened the vultures. These judges, who rot with power, cannot see what they trample any more than they've seen the scope of what we've seen, brother. Our era shall end starved and broken, lest these judges suffer."

"That isn't the eve I've seen. That isn't the eve that Hazy will see."

Asham soured at the mention of his fruit's name.

"She wept for you, coward. Her heart breaks on the hope of your return. What creature makes their name great at the cost of their child's blamelessness? You never were a father to her and you're no Guardian. You're a husk for other cowards."

Criticism weakened him. "I'd forgotten how you cut. Imagine how I feared you. You caused me that time I spent apart. I had to be sure you knew nothing of my plan, lest you die and reawaken, then stop me a breath earlier than the moment you failed afore."

Tull shut his eyes in lament. He preferred the many endings he imagined his long-absent fellow suffered versus the husk that sat with him now. With a slow hand, he felt the copper pin that Olley kept in his hand at Gutefiel and observed the torn lapel on Asham's coat. His constant state of prayerfulness struggled as anger blistered his heart and took away his words.

"Suffer no shame, brother. Our mothers bore and nursed us whilst apart, but we were sired by the same purposeful Creator. We both believe each soul carries His intention. Just as you found yours in the fiery train of your Minister, I found mine in the cold grip of that mountain."

The disgraced Guardian took hold of the unfilled seat, and swung with a might that broke the grain against Tull's shoulder. He swung a second time, connected the back of Tull's head with the backrest of the chair, and hammered his forehead against the floorboards.

Asham then wrapped Tull's crown and jaw with an arm's length of braided net like he used against the judges. He deprived his so-called brother of his voice and flooded his senses with enough pain that his heart could not cry out for a Minister. Even though Asham's hands wept blood, he forced the copper teeth into the Jacobian's face and scalp.

"I'll not end you. I know by the give of the breast, the retreat of color in the eye, and the fade of struggle when to stop. I have—"

A shallow ping resounded like the mightiest thunder when the scoop of an ash shovel connected against the aggressor's skull. Asham fell sideways, bloodied at the temple, and Tull found release. Gutefiel's victor plucked the copper teeth from his flesh and cast the mesh cord away from *his* rescuer. Less forgiving than Tull and more *durable* than his fellow judges, Ernie Purcell Bliss held up the shovel, now bent to reflect how well he struck Asham.

"That boy with all his chatter could rile me like no other."

Bliss looked dapper with the scarf Tull flung aside tied around his throat for protection. He gathered another, steadied his balance when he knelt, and blotted Tull's wounds with a gentle hand. Though his voice lacked booming resonance and his swagger wilted, he let his razor-fine smile project his imagined triumph.

The two offered separate prayers, and once Judge Bliss stood away, Tull fastened the copper pin that he took from Olley's hand in Gutefiel back onto the collar of Asham's coat. This time, the symbol of the Guardians' protection worked against their former member. The weight of the small pin proved mighty and kept him face-down on the floor.

"Come!" Bliss invited him. "Let us cleanse afore we celebrate your belief!"

EIGHTEEN

Bliss's call for celebration went the way of the smoke through the chimney after a guttural roar shook the panes of glass in both windows and rattled the doors set in their jambs. Tull turned toward Asham, who remained as still as double-vision allowed. He then tried to usher the judge toward the empty seat, but his host stopped him with a pat to his shoulder. Even then, the sound of vibration continued.

"I've taken worse nips from a cocklebur. How's your head?"

Tull nodded and swayed.

"Alleluia anyway!"

Tull removed his pack. "I must check *that* out."

"Your advocate urges you not to. Best you convict Gera with tales of how you searched for him all this time for he proves slow to suffer pain in his flesh now."

Another roar shook the panes and reminded Tull of his last battle in that previous land. Twice he kept from letting Jules know what a bride should hear after she claimed his heart. He intended better this time, yet counted excuses as his faults. With a restricted breath, he nursed his jaw and turned toward the door.

"Guardian." The judge enticed him to carry a knife with him in his disobedience.

Tull took his eyes off the horizon line and looked upon his elder. A third roar shook the ash off the limbs of the grove and decided whether he chose or refused the offering. He accepted the weapon rather than invite more harm on the judge due to a lack of preparedness. Keeper Victor Simon Shannon called such choices the law of "best to have and not need."

The cool air soothed and stung the Guardian's throat in equal measure just as a sound of ringing in his ears lessened how well he perceived the threat by sound. By sight, twin scarlet oak trees fell, north of where Tull arrived, and seemed the most obvious of destinations, and led him back into the grove, far from any rabbits or crepe myrtles, along a ravine, and provided a bridge that spanned his height times seventeen. When the ravine deepened, he leapt into the empty pocket.

The way the route turned, he lost his view of Bliss's cabin without traveling more than two ticks from the front step. The splay of needles and the silver hues of ash-laced ice proved lesser details than the tart odor of scalded metal and burned wires. A mist of smoke rose and vanished as the breezes above the ravine swept away the discernable vapor. He destroyed enough property in his time that he imagined the cause his sight confirmed.

He sifted wreaths of broken branches and greens till he found a twisted glider. Contrastive to those designs that Mumus's investments produced, the flimsy shell buckled under the weight of the fuel cartridge; a crude, ether-based formula from the dizzying stench. The Guardian disengaged the cylindrical projector and snapped the relay disc to preserve Judge Bliss's sanctity as much as the craft-owner's privacy.

"They'll withhold my alms for this, too." He tossed aside the broken piece as he pivoted, then that same piece struck him on the rebound. The Guardian paused with an exasperated sigh as the ground rumbled underfoot. "Can't say I wasn't warned."

Tull turned in time, or at the wrong time, and the snow-covered soil of a tapered ravine burst outward with a wave of energy that knocked the Guardian off his feet. A sinewy-limbed creature composed of necrotic, black tissue and an infection-stained exoskeleton punched through soil, rock, ice, and snow; not unlike how Si'el Uaen Söi'eä carved her escape. Eras of vines and roots slowed, but the creature's tendrils cut through the trappings.

At eleven heads high, the shadow of Marvin Elam Katch's missing soul harvester made Tull curse the blood on his face. *Whose* blood the creature sought remained unsure, though he knew whose land they stood upon. Once a harvester tasted the blood of the secondkind, no pursuit and no passage of time kept the creature from feeding upon the victim till only bones remained. That the harvester showed little interest in Tull cleared him as a potential meal and, in some way, relieved the blood-soiled Guardian.

As prone as any faced with overbearing odds, he took hold of a bad decision with both hands. He stayed his ground and, as a symbol of his calling, resisted the creature's advance for the sake of guarding Bliss *and* Asham. A Believer who remembered his sins could not reject another soul as *unsalvageable*. So, armed with one knife, a reasonable skill, and debatable wit, he lunged.

Tull pinned the borrowed blade through the fallen creature's forearm and into a sapling. The beast squealed and turned a lone eye onto the Guardian, who drove a broken root between his foe's exposed footbones like a weighted tether. The beast uprooted the sapling without removing the knife and snapped at the Guardian. Jagged, stout teeth cast a breeze that rippled Tull's beard and cast upon him the most apprehensive expression to take form in uncounted spans.

The harvester then swatted at him with the sapling and the Guardian rolled away. He considered his certainty over the creature's disinterest till a backhanded swing shattered the sapling and cast him in nature's detritus. As the debris settled and the wind shifted, the harvester's snout lifted toward the sky-fires in recognition of nearby prey. When the beast leapt, Tull gauged the amount of land the harvester's feet covered in one stride and pursued at a harder pace.

The harvester struggled as the wind produced a lull through his hollow frame like a billowing sail and the rocky glebe proved too slick for proper footing. Tull minded his two feet whilst he hoped the creature slipped on all fours. As he gained on his foe, he looked ahead toward the cabin. Judge Bliss, who stood in the open doorway, threw down a relit cigar, took a fiery breath, and vanished indoors. When he returned, he held his splitting maul, and broke apart the threshold of his cabin.

The wooden faces splintered on the blade and divided Tull's glances between the harvester's nearness and the hidden contents of Bliss's hollowed doorposts. The harvester snapped at Tull when their paths crisscrossed, and the air from another missed bite propelled him a half-step further. Hind hooves broke a patch of ice and glebe into dust and trampled harder to regain the lead and keep the Guardian from his purpose.

Tull reached the porch, seized the weapons from the post, then visualized the harvester's projected path. Like the weapon he held at the end of that previous land, he held the longbow and accompanying goatskin quiver of another guardian. He shook the dust from the quiver and restrung the bow. He then brushed the residue of wax down the shaft of two bolts, loaded, and took aim with a keen eye and overextended limbs.

"You'll separate your shoulder using Zeck's arm."

TULL

Tull released the bolts, but not his tongue. The low-pitched percussion of each iron-tipped arrow produced a haunted echo that drew a shark-like smile from the old judge. When the first tip struck less than a hand's breadth from the harvester's location and the second struck the creature's thigh, Bliss gathered two more bolts and slipped indoors.

"Should've stuck to your prayers, boy."

Tull flicked his brow, rather pleased with his efforts, and rubbed the immediate soreness in his shoulder. The dual strings of the longbow relied on extra cantilevers designed for an additional pull length that accommodated bolts longer than Tull's arm. He reasoned, from tip to nock, that a single bolt stood as tall as Hazy; at least by Jules's measurement of her. Such was the reach of mighty Beau Itzal Zeck that required an overhand pull from his third successor.

"Try these with more than your usual swiftness." Bliss, who held two burning, high-tensile bolts, possessed a knack for fiery darts as well. Verbal barbs. He pressed the nock to the string and spoke to the Guardian like a soul who never learned. "That tip's an alloy mix, not pure ore. You want to make that thing remember fear—use fire."

Tull heard his judge as well as the pangs of the harvester and held his opinion the way he held the glowing tips at bay. He drew back, fired, and bit through the pain. The third bolt hammered into the harvester's forearm. The fourth veered and struck the glebe.

"You're off with that outer line evermore. Just like Perry." The judge sighed. "Hotter now, though!"

The harvester roared as the dripping alloy struck bone, then galloped toward the cabin on two wounded limbs. That the creature bore wounds on the same side proved favor toward those limbs. In reliance on the opposite side, the harvester overextended and fell face-first against the slick glebe. The beast wailed in frustration and pain, heightened when the bolts sank deeper into rotted marrow.

"What did I tell you?!" Bliss conditioned his arms via back-patting, oft his own, and opened his lighter.

"The beast doesn't step nearer."

"I have eyes that see too, beloved."

Tull said nothing of who else watched them; as if a specter.

"Knew more about this land when I was half your age. Knew more about these beasts, too." The judge broke a lantern, mingled the fuel with a small horn of cobalt-blue granules, then doused the ground and the outer edges of the boards that composed the porch under their feet.

"Your plan sets our position on fire?" His contrary tone needled when his might could have swatted his elder and judge with ease.

"Yes."

"And, given all you know, you remember the bluff behind us?"

The one who built the cabin smiled in such a way that only his molars showed. The ridge of his brow darkened his eyes, and the fire he set shimmered in his buckeye-hued irises. Bliss laughed against the breeze, which Tull considered warmer once the sound reached his ear. Even the harvester groaned.

"What a remarkable idea."

The Guardian's eyes lifted toward the sky-fires. Thirty ticks with the judge challenged thirty watches of prayer and fasting. Still, the frustration that made him inhale also let him detect notes of cacao and chicory root. Tull forgave curious souls but hesitated lest he judged friend as foe.

"Enjoy the libation."

"Pardon?" Bliss swept his arm. "We'll make a line around us and the cusp, then we protect what rests between."

"And," he shouldered the longbow, "when the cabin's burned to ash, how will I defend you?"

"Haven't you a way out by now? Why, I built this cabin from the slowest-burning wood along this bluff. We can last till the eve if you need the time."

Tull sneered in uneasy silence. Anxious feet spun him, which he played off as checking on Asham. After he watched the fruitless struggle and understood his current plight, he looked toward the harvester. The way the creature behaved, with a hand that swiped at the wind and hammered a detached-looking skull, made the Guardian imagine Asham's blood-scent had vanished.

"Only ten eves in Gutefiel?"

He sought respectfulness, but proved he knew how to peck another's resolve as he pocketed one bolt. "Does Nita hold some grudge against you?"

"Who doesn't that uppity child hold a grudge against?"

Tull added a second bolt to his stash. "I get along with her."

"Bless your heart. Why are you asking me about her?"

TULL

"Katch used Vernard Voler to lure a harvester and, if my sense of smell is true, I'm about to lure Nita from the trees."

Tull stepped over the crackling flame that lined the edge of the porch. As he approached the second, arching fire, he set his intentions on the accuracy of two thoughts. The first, that he and Nita remained on respectful terms and that she cast no blame onto him for Olley's condition. The second, and more immediate—that a harvester who ingested the *wrong* blood suffered remorse.

The Fallen First dragged the weight of their sins. Few took that into account. Tull knew they delighted over their victories because they feared the aftershock of eternity's worst motivator: *shame*. He also knew they fell upon their faces every time a Believer worked a miracle in Yah's name.

Tull crossed the second fire and stepped close enough that he tasted the granules of bitter ash the wind scrubbed from the harvester's husk. "Hear me! You, who failed to bring glory to Yah, our Creator."

The harvester whined at the Truth and Tull struck with the force to drive one end of the longbow between the same foot he punished with the sapling.

"You who helped scourge I'Esh."

The harvester buckled and swayed away from Tull, who bent the stock till he rammed the bow's other end between the sinewy lines of the creature's neck.

"You who have turned deaf to the still voice of the Helper."

The harvester howled; worse when Tull drew back the interior bowstring and pinned one rancid arm at the wrist. While the creature's own weight provided leverage, the Guardian loaded the exterior bowstring and fired two bolts into the creature's shoulder sockets. The roar that followed echoed and Tull offered Bliss a smug grin, as he had not missed *that* time.

He pressed with awareness of his exertion. Nothing proved that as much as the creature's backhand that spun the Guardian four times, then set him on his back. The harvester's howl reached the fiery sky, aided by the elevation of the bluffs. Still, not one Minister swooped down and dealt with the creature—or Tull's arrogance.

"Bei'stei'ele!"

A voice as warm as the glebe warned the harvester into stillness. Three hisses of a pneumatic cylinder and the hammering of high-tensile bolts into rock sent a vibration down Tull's spine. The creature roared with an additional song of humiliation; trapped, alone, and forsaken. Such noise made even the judge look away in disagreement.

The airy chime of tousled ice grew nearer to the Guardian's ear, and the breeze deposited another veil of crystals and ash upon him. Two tanned boots drew to a halt the slender figure of Nita Naomi Ozul. Adorned in a long, white coat and copper-rimmed goggles, she stared down her frame at her fellow.

"My, my! Do I see the soul who lasted ten eves at Gutefiel?" She laughed with only slight inference to his condition. "Worry not; I'll never tell how I saw you turn your back on a harvester and get bested. And, I thank you. I enjoyed my chicory tea as much as the show!"

Tull strained to hear her over the vile rumblings from Bliss's lips.

"You were not meant to be in this. You did right by me and my Olley, and I'll not have a hair on your head harmed *lest* you keep me from making my point."

"Your point?"

"They made a spectacle of us. Danced us about like marionettes. I want that pious misborn to stare down a harvester knowing neither I nor my Olley care enough to save him. You saw him. He gave his pound of flesh for their amusement! I expect the same of at least one of them!"

"Bliss didn't design the offering."

"*Bliss*?" Her teeth shone with her eruption of laughter. "This hasn't a thing to do with him. No! My *hammer* seeks Lefty's head. Where is yours?"

"I've pondered that all the morn!" the judge squawked from his perch.

Tull sat upright. "You knew . . ."

Nita crouched and dusted Tull's beard. "He helped me swipe his own end. Odd turn, though. I swore at the time that Pine was my helper."

"You! You let him take Marvin?" Bliss's voice splintered. "He never—"

Nita stood with a swiftness that replenished Tull's beard with ice crystals. "That honorable soul, honorable in title, spied on and manipulated all he could! Ever ask how a fool of such magnificence went unseen all this time? Katch took the beacon from his neck! I went into his home afore I found him roaming! I saw the jars in his collection. I'd say he made a nice earning off removing the very beacons he—you—order us to bear! Can't let a soul so twisted live with such valuable secrets, can we?"

Tull rose to one knee. "The soul you're working with—"

"I work with you, Nelson." She took his forearm and helped him stand. "I work with my Olley, with George, and with Pine. I have no hand in letting that betrayer do well. In the past thirteen moons, how many battles did I compose a safe way through for all Guardians? Do you doubt I've imagined every possible end this time?"

"Where did you get his blood?"

"How soon you forget that I am resourceful!"

Because of how much she loved *her* Olley, and because Tull still felt the weight of her in his arms from that previous land, he extended the Shelbian the chance to retain the authority she surrendered to him at Gutefiel and faced their host. "We'll all talk with him now, Judge."

NINETEEN

After Tull freed Asham from the burden he pinned upon him, Nita and Bliss took their turn. They used his scarves and bound his arms to one of the judge's dining chairs. Nita's cruel streak and Bliss's authoritative scolding made Asham yawn. Then started the assault.

For her lithe build, Nita threw a tremendous punch. Bliss preferred a backhand, much like the harvester, and *tools* of punishment. Tull never relished interrogation. He preferred hemming together clues and unveiling motives. He observed and listened, but never interrupted. All the while, Asham held eye contact with him.

"I asked *why* you lied! Each of us combed these territories in search of you. Why did you hide? Why did you abandon us? Your family?"

"How did you survive unseen all this while?!"

When he had listened long enough, the bound aggressor interrupted his chatty captors and spoke to Tull. "Have you decided, then?"

Nita followed his gaze toward Tull, who offered nothing in return. "Decided what?"

Asham laughed that same irresponsible laugh that used to ease tension and now worsened the mood. Nita struck him across the face with a closed fist.

"Decided what?"

He ingested a tooth fragment, fractured from his time as an Infested, lest he provoke the harvester's *taste* for him. "He knows. Don't you, brother?"

"Do you? Tell us."

Still, the Guardian held his tongue.

"He knows your choices. You can't swear off your purpose this time." He made a point to swallow his blood again. "This won't end me; no, that would disappoint Olley when he found out you had Nita arrested. So, you have to end that beast out there and keep me safe."

Nita and Bliss scoffed, bickered, and challenged him.

"Elsewise, elsewise!" He gained their stern eyes. "What's to stop the beast from an easier prey than me?"

"You dull and—"

"Say, my fruit. Half my blood fills her tender veins."

Nita, who had *less* maternal instinct than Lucy, waylaid Hazel-Sue's father with a kick that splintered a leg of the chair and split the skin beneath his scarred jaw for his mention of an unimaginable end that preserved him. She never instructed a blameless soul. Never even spoke a sweet nickname. Even so, she drove her foot against Asham's groin hard enough to stamp out any future attempts at producing another heir, and sank her nails deep into the twisted flesh of his face till they tore from their beds.

Bliss hoisted her away, with pieces of the traitor's face still on her fingers, as Tull moved in. He mopped away the blood with a scarf, even as the harvester squawked, and burned the fabric. In his heart, he and Asham agreed on standing against the bad laws and the need for a change of the secondkind's judges. They even agreed on the possible outcomes of this moment, minus one more result.

"Three spans of letting us believe you'd met your end—hurt, alone, suffering. You destroyed our hearts. None more than Hazy's. Hers you wrecked long afore. You've treated her with more cruelty than any of these whom you've attacked have shown."

Tull removed the incense Si'an-dro Sa'ähn prepared for him and spread the loose powder across the stone ledge of the fireplace. Once he nourished a fragrant smolder, he crossed the cabin floor and righted Asham's seat.

"Is this a time when you need more foes? Tim proves more unreliable with age. You've lost Lucy. You can't even show—"

"What do you mean, I lost her? How did I lose her?"

Tull shrugged as though the gravity meant little to him. "She's fallen into a backslide. She's living again as she lived with *him*; with *Monteith*."

Asham scoffed and blew blood from his nostrils. "She would never!"

"She went to him at D'Aramitz Abbey. She went to a soulless body in your stead."

"And, you let her?"

TULL

Tull grinned at the double standard. Asham impregnated another woman but imagined Lucy as loyal to his desires.

"I deserved that, did I not?"

Nita's bootheel hammered the floorboards. "You deserve—"

"If each of us got what we *deserved*," Tull calmed Nita with a gentle pat of the air between them, "we might all feel the teeth of a harvester."

"Were our lives without *cleansing* blood!" Bliss rejoiced and clapped his hands with the impact of thunder that cast a ribbon of incense smoke through the cabin.

Tull squeezed Nita's shoulder as she swayed from the judge's enthusiasm. "We're not Shelbians. Your way hardened you. If you don't wish—"

"I stay." She tucked her arms against her body and let the weight of her fists drape. "Olley would never forgive me."

Tull slipped the knife from Nita's boot without disturbing her stance and looked toward his judge. "We're all going to walk out that door. And our returned fellow will lead us out."

"He's practiced at such feats."

Tull made his point against the belly of restraints and cut loose the Creightonian who let spirits infest him rather than serving as provider and foremost mentor to the blameless soul he fathered. Asham scratched at a pocket of fatty tissue that healed askew to the lay of his face, but none who knew him believed he took release with such disregard. He manipulated his way into too many beds and from harm too oft to fool them. As proof, Nita held a position between him and the judge he targeted.

"Say, should you let me beat him some more afore you cut that last—" The glint of light flashed across the blade as Tull freed Asham. "Right, then."

"I thank you, brother."

Tull scraped at the same fatty pocket on Asham's face with the tip of Nita's knife. "If I ever hear you leverage Hazy again, believe that I will turn you inside out—and I'll not seek a weapon."

Asham proved his heart when he leaned into the blade and cut his own flesh. Tull reacted with a pivot of his heel, which Asham used to drive the dining chair against the Jacobian's hip. He then lunged toward Nita, grabbed the pockets of her snug coat, and thrust her at the judge. The two butted heads and, whilst Tull shook off his pain, Asham fled. He created the deliberate sound of metal scraping metal as he raced out the door but failed to discourage his fellows.

TULL

Both Guardians chased him and never sought the source of that agitating sound. Even Judge Bliss, deemed a brilliant wit and flawless observer, failed to give proper inspection. In long-suffering's stead, he wasted his voice on name-calling those who let his attacker loose. His saltiness made even the incense smoke turn bitter.

Out of doors, Asham never bothered to leap over Bliss's defensive fires. He let the frayed cuffs of his trousers smolder like Tull's incense and fell face-first toward the shadow of the harvester. How he managed to stay clear of the creature's swipe spoke to the knack that kept his soul unscathed through many battles. He then lifted his hands skyward and grieved the harvester with a lament.

"O Mighty Creator! Forgive me . . ."

Mire dripped from the harvester's mouth in place of saliva and singed Asham's heavy coat. Though the beast roared for a taste of the blood on his face, one bite of a repentant soul meant a fate *worse* than damnation. Every Guardian learned and believed this law. Only one proved deranged enough to test the truth.

Tull stopped in his path, extended his arm to the side, and kept Nita from passing. "Keep from feeding him to the monster."

"Which one?"

"I lost my way. I've wandered so long!"

Nita set her hand across Tull's shoulder and rested her chin. "Notice how well he slips into the skin of a penitent soul? Downright sickening!"

The Jacobian agreed with a coarse breath but held onto hope.

"You knew the incense would drive mad whatever spirits rest in him."

"I like incense." Within, he thanked Si'an-dro Sa'ähn, but the sound of Asham's *feigned* weeping drew his attention.

"I tried to be like my brother! The spirits wanted more!"

As Asham sought to free one of the bolts that Nita fired, the blood that dripped from beneath his nail beds enticed the creature. The harvester roared and stomped one loose foot.

"Even then . . . even then . . . I wished that he might find me and join me!"

Nita squeezed Tull's shoulder. "Not oft do you hear how you're another's inspiration! Certain you don't want me to end him now?"

"The Guardians keep safe the secondkind. End him, and under law of the territories, you'll force me to hand you over to the chiefs."

TULL

Asham leaned from a side position and watched the harvester's bones chip with every thrust against the bolts. "Remember me! O Mighty Creator, remember me!"

"You love my Olley too much to see me punished."

"We go back a long while, all of us," Tull agreed. "And you more than any soul know what I'll do to keep safe a friend."

"I'm your friend, too, Nelson."

"You are. So, I'm asking for your help to end this. We can take him in and prove to the territories that we reside beneath the same laws we impose."

Nita trembled and dug in her heels. "They hurt my Olley! While I was away, checking on Monteith. I've watched the reels. He was there, in Gutefiel, with Lucy. They turned on us. As certain as that monster's bones are blistered by the flames of Ki'eoppa, I tell you, they turned on us."

The thumbnail of Asham's left hand snapped away, but he pulled loose the bolt. Even as he groaned in pain, he played innocent. "I s'pose the Triune heard me, brother. I *believe* They want me to start anew."

Tull stepped through the second fire toward the *two* monsters. Asham dragged his pinky finger along the exterior bowstring as he rose and latched the nock then pivoted. He used the weight of the harvester to his advantage, pried back on the cantilevers, and shot into the trio that stood behind him. Like Tull—and Perry Wallace Rudat—Asham proved a wide shot. The bolt missed both Guardians but scratched the cheek of the judge and broke through the picture window.

"Can not *one* of you shoot straight!?"

"I told you to let me end him!"

Asham reshaped the longbow into another weapon. He pulled down on the same bowstring snared around the creature's arm and tugged the levered spooling pulley that let an archer gain extra arm span on the bow. The pulley hurtled upward and hammered the elbow joint of the harvester's arm. His efforts proved successful when a sharp, wailing noise amplified the pitch of the harvester's voice.

"Will you say something?"

"The bluffs suit your gait."

"Not to me!" She jabbed the air with two fingers and pointed out the beast.

Tull huffed and tromped toward the creature that *bested* him once. He reached out and tugged the harvester's face downward, not letting the bow loose. The harvester's cold, gelatinous eye found him and from the beast's nostrils, blood and mire went up like a mist. A flowing ribbon of incense smoke that drove Asham from the cabin turned the creature anxiety-ridden. Now, the theatrical aggressor watched through the exposed ribs of the harvester while the solemn Jacobian proved his belief and his regard for Yah's Creation.

"Forgive us, *cousin*, for not showing you peace."

"Are you mad?"

Tull kept the harvester's snout pointed toward him. "He Who Sees has an eye fixed on you. Show mercy, and may mercy be shown to you."

The creature understood Tull's words but snapped at him; as oft the firstkind rejected the secondkind's view of courts unseen; courts that the befallen rejected.

"Refuse and you'll know *only* torment and hunger."

Si'an-dro Sa'ähn's incense cleansed a soul and invited in the Helper. Tull's nemeses proved less contemptuous now versus their arrivals. The coldness of air and richness of smoke tickled the Guardian's throat as he watched over the two creatures who sought the blood of other souls. While others might strike down a foe, he obeyed the law of the Creator.

"How long have you strayed from your home, lost unto your purpose? Call out for peace. Let us help you."

Asham's breath changed as he heard the genuineness in Tull's voice. He goaded the creature between them, rather than lash out. "There is no hope."

"There's still time."

"You know what's true."

Nita rushed toward them in anticipation, and the harvester's chest spread wide. The twisted bones of the beast crackled, and the head atop reared with the force that plucked the longbow and shattered the wooden frame. The bowstrings snapped and sliced as the freed prowler's fingers cracked with a clapping motion. Tull plunged to one knee and avoided the bowstring whilst Asham leapt from the heel and Nita dove from the hands.

She drove her doubled fists against the creature's breastbone with enough force that the riveted foot cracked both mire-blackened bones of the lower leg. Tull drove his shoulder against the knee joint and clasped the harvester's worm-ridden thigh. When the creature buckled, Asham twisted his pursuer's shoulders in a clockwise fashion while the weight of him bore down on the exposed neck. Whether one

TULL

affected more than the other or if the trio remembered their better efforts as a team, the judge remained undecided.

Asham sensed the harvester's next action and gouged out the beast's sole eye with his thumb. Putrid, green fire burst from the socket and scalded his hand. Both roared in pain, but the deceitful Creightonian held on when the harvester reeled. Enraged, the creature swung hard toward Tull; hard enough that a full strike might crack the neck and end him.

Nita spared Tull and seized the arm, brought her legs off the ground, then spun in a corkscrew motion till gravity reclaimed her feet. With this, she snapped the beast's arm and proved her word to protect Tull. As thanks, he cradled Olley's bride at neck and waist, then vaulted her over his shoulder. She flipped and landed on both feet and a hand that stabilized her. Now behind Asham, she charged and drove her fists into his lower back.

Asham seized at the harvester till the creature stomped, and a spark formed against the frozen glebe that Bliss built upon. Nita anticipated. She stepped upon Tull's thigh as he circled, then his shoulder. As she took to the air once more, she twisted at the waist and drove a solid kick against the harvester's face, which drove the crown against Asham's scarred face. She also swiped his hand with enough force to draw blood from flesh, lest her aerial attack only dizzy him.

The harvester bucked when a single droplet of Asham's blood touched the uncovered bones he abused. The beast's anguish increased tenfold when lust for blood oppressed eternal shame. While Asham worked on destroying one foe's ears, Tull appealed for mercy on the creature. Neither saw Nita's elegant landing or the way she vaulted onto Asham's back and sought to topple both foes.

Leander Jonathan Bromley's forebearer charged Asham, and sparked an identical reaction from Tull. The younger Jacobian proved less compassionate toward his former fellow, for good reason. Asham leapt and used his leverage against their elder. He swung with all his might, and Bliss toppled over the bluff. No last words, no grace; but a violent plunge to his end that proved Asham unsympathetic.

"Better I sacrifice one judge than risk another of your resets, brother!"

All that spared Asham from his due pummeling unfolded with a percussive blast that shook the bluff as Bliss's cabin exploded. The concussive force extinguished the defensive fires set by the judge. The same blast rendered both Jacobian and Creightonian unconscious and flung them across the terrane like two sleds that crisscrossed on opposite sides of Nita. A plank careened toward the Shelbian, who raised her arms in defense of her head and chest. When struck, both arms and wrists fractured, and she fell with a howl of pain.

A severed pane of glass launched outward and took the head from the soul harvester's neck, as the might of incense claimed the eye, rotted flesh, and innards of the creature till an empty skeleton remained. Bits of the cabin and all that Yah provided the judge rained down. In the confusion *sparked* by Asham's rapid departure and a well-aimed bolt, none of them took the time to challenge him about his antics. Now, the trio smoldered from prostrate positions.

Nita trembled in excruciating pain that brought her onto her knees. Tull bled from the ears and nose, and cast his breath at a steady, shallow pace. Nita sought to end Asham, but the pain stole her ability to hold a weapon. She could not see to her own needs, let alone check the vitals of the other souls, so she abandoned both as Squires plummeted and collected the head and arm of the harvester.

One Squire looked upon Nita with disappointment, and, as Tull had done at her husband's side, she did also for her husband's best friend. "Creator, *please*, hear my voice and remember me. Protect this good soul. Save him from my choices and forgive us in this watch."

She who spurned Anya Nora Rains out of friendship with Tull fled from the soul she once defended. Fire erupted from the belly of the cabin floor and burned hot enough to warm the abandoned souls, even as the wind sang through the ribs of the harvester. Over the next watches, as the air proved cold and violent, snow and ash blanketed the fallen and hid Nita's footsteps. Still, the bundle of incense Si'an-dro Sa'ähn prepared for Tull burned and filled the heavy air with sweet fragrance.

Myrrh spiced the wind, but neither this nor the salt of fire produced the dominant aroma. A spirited song *breathed* into the flame by the winds along the bluff cast a sound upward toward the sky-fires. That song mingled with the bouquet gathered by a hand of the First Creation and praised the Triune for Their compassion and warrior-like love for the Second Creation. The first note had not dissolved when Squires numbering more than the trees in the grove circled the wounded and staved off harm.

TWENTY

The heavy coverage of clouds introduced a false dusk along the bluff. Flame still burned from the remnants of Bliss's cabin, and snow covered two-thirds of every soul on the ground, both from above, and blown back by the winds. Through those same clouds, five projection-gliders crashed against the rocky glebe and cast their parts over the brim. The scene fell under the shadow of the unknown; a rare sensation in this era of constant watchfulness.

A plume of red phosphorous-like light announced the arrival of one trained to chase vanishing footprints and wounded do-gooders. The light appeared in the grove, thick with shadows, and paced with calculated hesitance. Not one needle bent and not one fleck of ash fell from the branches overhead. The light waited till the final glider piece stopped skipping across the terrane.

Then Lucy Bright Moon tromped out onto the clearing and held her closed fist above the flicker of light. She opened that fist and dropped into the red plume a trigger that crashed gliders via remote impulse. The device burst into flame and burned so fast that the awaiting palm received the ash. Like that, she erased proof of her guilt in downing the surveillance crafts.

In the harsh light, *ribbons* of blackness flowed through her skin and eyes, but never lessened her focus. Those remnants benefitted from her whole body as she benefitted from the slightest traces of their spirits. She dropped her hands to her sides and observed the aftershock. The flame in her hand went tart and uneven when she clasped her fingers, and she ran toward her husband without spotting Tull. Not even the harvester's bones drew her eye.

She loved Asham with a blindness he had not earned. His bride's hands trembled with violence as she checked every limb, patted every bone, and checked his heart, neck, and eyes. Her breath conspired till her oft raspy voice roared and her inability to swallow choked her. With the same fury she had turned against Marko, she shook her husband's body.

"Asham! You must wake. Please!" Lucy buried her face into the mop of chocolatey licorice-hued strands of his wavy hair and pleaded into his ear, as if the sound of her voice might stir another Squire. "Please. I need you to wake."

"You were to stay away."

She gasped and tried to hold him as he drifted from unconsciousness. "I've spent enough time without! You can't stay here. The chief—his deputies and medics—are on their way. I raced, but they are near."

He shook her off and sat upright, as if another soul untethered the back of him and a spring pulled him upright. She patted along his torso and kissed his scarred face. He responded with a squeeze of her forearm, then plucked away her hand. His attention turned him to one side with bone-crackling abruptness as he observed the aftershock of a great reunion.

"What happened here?"

"Nita." He laughed colder than the winds on his bride's skin. "Devotion—*true* devotion—invites the strength to cleave away one's own limb if that sacrifice sheds a foe. A mighty, mighty example!"

"Nita saw you? Where is she?"

He shook his head. "Has Nelson risen?"

"*Nelson*? I didn't—"

"Check him! Get!"

She obeyed with haste once she heard his snarl. Though she fell to her knees, she kept from touching Tull and let her body shield her disobedience from Asham's sight. "He breathes. He saw you too?"

Asham raced away on foot, no more than a smudge of charcoal hues against the snowy backdrop. He never spoke toward her and never looked back. His bride waited with no idea when or where she might see him again. Such was the pain she towed for three spans behind the backs of her allies.

In his absence, a team of artificial lights on the hips of six deputy inspectors and rescue medics subordinate to Chief Inspector Carl Alvin Grover sifted from the maze of trees that fenced the bluff. That they abandoned their rigs on the opposite side of the trees pleased Lucy. Every rig offered Asham his getaway. Her heart lightened faster than her stomach, and she pretended not to notice their approach.

That proved difficult when the responders passed through the gathering of Squires; for every creature of the firstkind departed at once. Their flight created a gust of wind that overturned snow and debris. Even the fires of the cabin stoked and burned brighter in their wake. That flame forced Lucy back—away from Tull—and away from any implement she might turn against him.

"Set a perimeter! Keep an eye out for stragglers. Get!"

Two responders took to the woods and two others rushed toward the cabin. Each, of leaner build than their order-giver, reached their destinations ahead of the unsure-footed chief, who stopped a few strides shy of the harvester's bones. He marveled over the size and build but shook his head rather than learn from another in Tull's stead. With a sigh, he set his sight on Lucy and no other.

"Guardian Bright Moon. I called out for you, say, ten times. I s'pose you never heard me."

"Well, the forests are filled with coaxing sounds, are they not?"

He sized her up, then he looked over his friend.

"His hand?"

The rescue medic that traveled in his shadow opened Tull's palm and found the tissue blackened. He used a swab to take a sample, but Lucy informed them.

"That's transfer from the beast. He sets his hands on these things and they *seep* out onto him."

Her audience grimaced. She half-expected an interrogation. How did she get there? Who told her where to find them? In duty's stead, she waited for one soul to notice her husband's tracks.

"We're lucky you were up this way too."

She shrugged off his regard, but light-headedness stole her snide remark.

"He went too silent too soon after his gabby relay, so I tracked his beacon. I s'pose Jules nudged you to do the same."

Lucy smiled under feigned innocence. "She's a worrier."

"I wed a soul like hers." Carl studied the ledge from afar. "They say a body that falls from these bluffs suffocates afore the water swallows them. I imagined Judge Bliss might outlive us all. How's our Guardian, Brackett?"

Tull's rescue medic shrugged. "If he met his end, I wouldn't be freezing."

TULL

Lucy made Brackett flinch when flame burst in the palm of her open hand.

Carl teased the medic's ear. "Consider that your work light and be grateful that my friend still breathes."

Lucy watched the nervous flutter in the medic's jaw, then peered around at the others who intruded upon the bluff as her heart raced. Carl, who observed the harvester once more, proved a simple soul. Those whose purpose involved answering to him impressed her less than the chief. She watched a rescue medic, not unlike her abettor, who tiptoed around the fallen glider. No one suspected her hand.

"*Hmmm.*" Brackett purred like a well-fed kitten.

Carl's voice raced over the top of Lucy's head. "Concerns?"

"No, no. Nothing that time in the mending chambers can't cure."

"How much *time*?"

The rescue medic fluttered away from her with a wave of hands and a rattling voice. "He *might* miss Hivi'ern."

"Guardian Bright Moon, what're your orders?" Carl held rank over the medic, but even he answered to the Guardians. "Can he be moved?"

As their only *functioning* agent, Lucy held authority over the fate of every soul on the bluff. The law of the judges she helped strike down allowed her to protect Asham. "The Mannering Chamber House is nearby. Move him there."

"He gets nervy around that much water," Carl reminded her. "We could take him over to the Scurlock Chamber House. The haul's longer, but the woods ease him."

"No. The Mannering Chamber House is more secure." One loose end remained. "What about Nita?"

The responders looked at one another.

"Has no one *found* Nita?"

Carl cleared his throat. "We followed Tull's beacon."

"I, myself, saw Nita Naomi Ozul and Robbie Rudat Pine run from this place. Search for a narrow boot print with a pointed toe; that's Nita. She was here. If they've gone missing, the territories deserve to know why!"

Carl followed up with a muddled, "Get!"

Nita made the ideal scapegoat, and Lucy kept secret that Pine could not defend her abuse of his name. She tossed all shreds of guilt and wrongdoing onto her fellows; the one whose territory detested judges and Guardians, and the Guardian whose penchant for agitation startled many Believers. If her efforts failed, she could spin a better yarn whilst Tull remained unconscious in a mending chamber.

"You imagine Nita's behind this? In Olley's name?"

Lucy reacted with a concerned wrinkle in her brow and a hesitant nod fueled by a gasp of uncertainty. "Could be, Chief!"

"I s'pose we won't know till the hardhead wakes." He waved an arm outward, across the carnage. "She probably took out the gliders, too."

"She does love to tinker. She's our resident inventor, you know?"

"No, I didn't know."

She almost laughed at the way puzzlement contorted his face.

"I'll make the call."

While Carl directed a dispatcher to task new gliders on a search path for Nita and Pine, the responders bustled on foot. The female medic stayed behind and helped Brackett. Neither she nor Lucy feigned commonality. In truth, the two begrudged one another. One believed in science, the other in Nature. The former admired the harvester, though.

"What becomes of the ugly one?"

"He turns handsome again once you stop seeing the scars."

"I meant the *monster*."

"The Fallen First will pick the beast clean by morn."

"Some brave soul sure gave that monster a fight!"

Lucy's smugness trickled from the corners of her mouth as a lewd smile changed the shape of her face. Her cheeks collapsed in pockets, and the scars on her chin formed distinct wedges in the tissue. The pools of shadow around her eyes flowed through the old breaks in her eye sockets and ascended upward toward a spade-shaped peak above her nose.

The more she relied on facial expression and less on rest and a replacement dose, the faster her true face bled through her falseness. Still, she loved to hear speak of her husband's bravery. In point of fact, she struggled to silence the laughter of many voices that wished to ridicule those she duped. She blasphemed the names of the Triune in her mother's tongue, which brought trouble in the form of four Squires upon her.

TULL

They looked like lions of fire, and their wrath burned her shape upon the frozen terrane. The brilliance singed the tips of her hair, burned away tags of her skin, and turned to ash the outer threads of clothing she wore.

She challenged them with a spite-filled glance, even as Carl covered Tull, but her eyes pooled with hemorrhaging afore she found their faces. When she failed, she fell prostrate and shielded her face.

"Repent, *cousin*! Lest the gravity of your choice condemn you! Lest the serpents who coil your soul bury you in eternity's flame. Repent!"

She mustered only a scream of anguish over her blasphemy; an *ample* lament. Three Squires ascended like lightning, but the one who spoke proved unmovable. His lower canines protruded over his upper lip while the fire in his eyes burned with judgment.

"Were you more valuable than the spirits that fill you, I would ask our Creator whom you have blasphemed to end you; that you be spared from what seeks you."

When the creature roared over Lucy, she tumbled toward the fallen Jacobian and the inspector who covered him. The Squire looked upon the harvester with compassion, then rose and created a whine that dispersed the falling ash in his wake. For the next few moments, all remained still. Then, while Carl and his deputies recovered, Lucy sprinted away in shame over her correction.

Rotted 'n' Sweet

An Interim

The 28th Eve beneath the Moon of the Old Embers

The 114th Gathering Season of the Accession

In the Blessing of I'Esh, who tends the harvest.

Beacon 109.64.435 recognized at 51 Riverpath . . .

Identifier confirmed—Hazel-Sue Lael.

Between Fresnel Park and Sevier.

Imagination, wonder, and the thrill of a moment long desired thrived as gifts of blamelessness. The realization, though sometimes paled, stirred the heart and drove a soul faster through space than time passed. On the last moonrise of the gathering season, while adults stood leg-locked on every curb and in every doorway along the Riverpath, two slender feet fitted with shoes shined to a gleam bustled through the crowd. Unaware of another priority beyond celebrating the Feast of Hivi'ern, those little steps propelled a soul adorned in purple velvet and a flowing pearl ribbon toward the Page Battalion House.

"Stoke the—O, I do beg your pardon, blameless soul!" A drunkard with a bushy mustache tipped the rim of his stiff new hat toward she who never slowed, and cleared his throat at her dismissal. "I say, stoke the fires!"

Hazy walked a full, defiant stride ahead of Lucy, who ignored the drunkard's repetitive call but minded the display plates built into the river barriers on the opposite footpath. She held to the small hand that strained with all might to pull her one step closer to the glow of false light that stretched from the destination. A grunt emphasized the plight and the slip of each knuckle symbolized freedom from that torturous hold. The urge to reach the battalion house worsened to the point that Hazel-Sue teetered with all her might to reach the next cobblestone.

"*Momma!*" The frustrated growl sounded like a dozen others from blameless souls trapped in similar holds. "Momma! We have to go in there! This is Hivi'ern. You said we couldn't go in there till Hivi'ern. Don't you remember?"

"*Shhhh!* Let me . . ." Her voice tapered off as the imagery on the display plates swam in her eyes.

Hazy's frustrated huff rose into a wheeze of dismay. She needed longer legs or increased leverage for if she could break free, she might soar.

"Take one more step in that direction and we will go back home now."

Preposterous, unbearable cruelty! What proved more important than the fun—fun that evaded specifics or names—that Lucy kept her from? "*Please*, Momma!"

Lucy ignored Hazy's plea and indulged her own whims. As she hardened her position, a small sparrow leapt from the roost atop the battalion house. The path of the bird's flight intersected the gap between the two. With sudden ascent, the air cast by the wings covered Hazy with stillness and upset the smugness of the Guardian. As the false-faced teetered, the blameless soul gained a step on her path.

The advantage satisfied the blameless soul. Her challenger struggled against blasphemy but took the embarrassment in silence. She awaited a gift for her own selfishness, and let her cheeks collapse beneath a misshapen scowl as a new reel overtook the display plates. In a response tailored to the arrogance demonstrated by elitists who believed their souls *better* than the Guardians, he who abandoned bride and blameless fruit reappeared with a message for all to witness.

> This time, Asham masked his eyes behind goggles issued to field workers in and around the Larson Territory. Less advanced than those worn by their Guardians, these shielded the eyes from the abrasive dusts and mining grit that never settled. While the new accessory further disguised the Uncounted Soul, the lenses reflected the sky-fires as seen in the most desolate of the territories.
>
> He limped about, then faced—through goggles, hood, and scarves—the gaunt face of Judge Charles Kurtz Elwell from the neighboring Weston Territory. Elwell served longer than *three* judges of the Creighton Territory combined. His snowy hair and

weathered face *hinted* at wisdom most profound, but his beady, dank irises proved the coldness of his heart. The piercing white lights affixed to the goggles of Asham's disguise stung the judge's vision and haunted his view.

"Did you not hear of the offer to keep safe your soul?"

Elwell kept his mouth stretched through a tight clench of his teeth and responded with an uneven bob of his head.

"Did you not call to him?"

This time, the judge's worn body swayed as he confessed his rejection of the Guardian's offer.

"Why?"

The smallest of all the judges let out a fierce breath and trembled. "That misborn trickster—that orphan—never merited his purpose! These territories belong to your judges! Not to Guardians! Not to Yah! They are ours! You—"

Asham swatted Judge Elwell in the mouth with a light-duty hammer, that they might both suffer broken teeth. The old judge inhaled like a kettle and lifted his tear-bloated eyes toward the sky-fires as if he sought rescue from those who punished blasphemy. He wheezed teeth, blood, and a ratcheted breath as the vastness above remained empty. Asham struck his mouth again, for losing his attention.

"The time for saving your soul has passed."

Lucy ignored how every squeamish soul turned from the example her husband made of the judge. She kept a proud eye on the display plates and a firm grip on Hazy. She who shared Asham's plan watched every strike he landed with approval.

The mutterings attributed to Elwell flowed from the lips of another soul. Asham dusted red grit from the arm of his additional victim as he circled. The lights from the projection-gliders followed. He slapped and flung ruby-hued blood from a deep puncture wound that overlapped an old scar on the exposed, vein-strewn belly of Judge Hansel Ornlam Hofnarr.

TULL

The judge's face showed his aggressor's disapproval till only his false incisor and glib, flat eyes served as identifiers. Pairing the two judges hinted at brilliance for those who appreciated humiliation. Hofnarr and Elwell served as absolute and unrepentant foils. The younger judge broke bodies through excess and pleasure, while the older judge broke lives through unyielding harshness.

Both shared in an intense beating, dire humiliation, and cruel bindings. Asham wove some added meaning into his work and set his intended victims with their backs turned on the territories they ruled. He tormented their souls the same way that he stung their flesh. They had offered no mercy and, at their end, received none.

He remained silent beneath the muttered ramblings that betrayed Hofnarr's dust-chapped mouth and offered one final taunt. As the soul who had stabbed him in the gut spans afore, he unfurled enough of his disguise that his foe—and only his foe—saw him. "Now you see."

"You?" A perverse smile arose on Hofnarr's face, either from respect for Asham's commitment or amusement for his new face.

Whatever the inspiration, the expression provoked Asham. He plucked Olley's saber from the dust and shook his head at an accusation the judge never cast. "No, this is not for me. This is for Nelson James Tull. You ought to have heeded him."

The crowd erupted in a shriek that startled Hazy and turned her rigid from experience. She faced the opposite direction, so she never witnessed how the judge of gluttonous cruelties convulsed so hard that his spasms erased any recollection of his once-idolized beauty. Fear-filled over Lucy's temper, she surrendered the gained step and stopped struggling as the sympathetic sounds heightened to a level where joyousness felt wrong. The frightened little soul stood in utter stillness and held to the only hand that felt familiar to her as onlookers fled from the display plates.

Hansel Ornlam Hofnarr, the film star who purchased his honor, shed his dignity, and spilled bowel and bladder in his last performance. A vile humiliation of a soul whose depravity matched his captor's. Asham flung the saber into the terrane and hid his face as a second projection-glider found them. The new craft showcased greater terror and broadcast his testament.

"Monsters shape their souls with cunning disguises. They dress as noble elders and trample the necks of those who bow to their whims. But their hands bear the claws that shred innocence and strip morals, just as their teeth sport the sharp edges that devoured those souls who oppose them. This ends their rule, and soon I rest."

The judge of judges stood in weakened solace as a third and fourth glider hovered. He let his victims writhe and strangle away the breath their minds needed. The dust and grit blew, but none stopped him till he finished his work. As he held out a device that would fry the circuitry of every watchful device near him, he uttered one final, playful remark.

"Stoke the fires!"

"Stoke the fires!" Another drunk called out and received the phrase back from souls along the avenue who cared nothing for the two judges.

Lucy swooned as though Asham spoke to her alone and surrendered a small step that the soft-cheeked soul by her side refused to claim. Hazy stayed still and kept her eyes averted from the coveted destination. When Lucy realized her advantage, she took one step backward. Her mischievous laughter signified the celebration of her husband's success, and she delighted in the chance to needle his frightened fruit and kept two other souls interested.

Hazy kept her gaze low and her sad expression hidden, whilst Lucy taunted through reclaimed cobblestone tiles as they withdrew from the battalion house. One of the two who watched the undeserving Guardian's antics approached at a casual pace; distant enough not to provoke a sense, close enough to provoke worry. He robbed the occasional scarf from the necks of the inattentive till he collected enough to satisfy a new disguise. No other soul noticed or counted him.

The other watchful soul stood static; a haven if the blameless soul broke free, and a threat if the lingering scarf-thief continued onward. While far from unspotted, yet also unseen, he hid beneath a leathery hood that drowned his monstrous form in shadows. From the left, he looked pale and unwell. From the right, freckled by the elements. A dark mole sat beneath his eye, which seemed ill-fitted with his drooping eyelid.

"Stoke the"—A cheerer then took sight of that mismatched face—"Almighty!"

The onlooker hushed him with a raised hand of misshapen fingers toward a face lined with copper *spiders*, medical-grade tensioners that conducted one's internal current and kept tight loose flesh. The implanted devices littered his face and formed a zipper-like effect that extended from his crown of wavy black hair, across a sharp brow and high cheek, then ended beneath his rugged, square jaw. In the falling temperatures, the copper instruments emitted the occasional spark. Even on this eve of joyousness, the look of him garnered reactions that his pride no longer savored.

His eyes misted for the taunted soul and, once focused on he who walked behind her, burned away that mist with anger. The freckled *side* of his face sagged when he bared his teeth, and the nearby sound of a child's laughter introduced a sharp note of pain through his ear. When he covered and turned, his body reminded him of his lacking sense of balance till he propped a muscular forearm against the iron column of an unlit building.

As he contended with equilibrium and closed his left eye, he set his focus on the one who concealed his face with stolen scarves. He focused, but the constant dance of light and the unpredictable chorus of sound sickened him till those who moved appeared as triplicate specters. Their chatter and squeals haunted his stomach, and he rested his brow upon his forearm while an untoward hand reached toward the precious soul's soft limb.

"*O, blameless soul, flee!*"

Even as Asham neared from between two passing souls, another pair of hands rescued Hazy and lifted her off her feet.

"No more eves till Hivi'ern!"

The relieved soul shivered and threw her arms around Jules with a thankful gasp. Those who observed them paid no mind to Asham, who stood close enough to breathe in the scent of peach blossoms. The attention of other souls preserved Hazy and forced her father's retreat into the shadows and an end to Lucy's taunts. Jules drew the child close, nuzzled her neck, and stood in a way that told she missed Asham's latest reel and present nearness. In response, Lucy added distance.

Jules stared at her benefactor but reassured the child. "I have you, love."

The Page Battalion House's well-recognized rescue medic dressed in a soft pearl-hued gown that matched the ribbon on Hazy's gown. Her tenderness elated that cherished soul, whose eyes sparkled with adoration. Her exhalation produced a ripple of joy as she rested her cheek upon the shoulder of she who treasured her above all others and watched the sparrow fly away. Jules drew her near for one more hug as the call for fire in preparation of the coming winter rang out again.

Lucy stood outnumbered and backed down whilst so near to the rescue medic's stomping grounds and the cacao scent oft emitted by a fellow's cigarette. Her abettor played mother to another's child better than she, anyway. Neither threatened as the scent lingered. Likewise, there were no concerns for either's wellness or the condition of the Guardian from whose side Jules seldom strayed since the ruckus at the cabin.

"I waited so you could take her inside." Lucy's body language claimed elsewise, as did the scrunched-faced reaction of her husband's fruit.

"I'm surprised Honor didn't run out and greet you." Jules whispered into Hazy's ear, "Should we go to her?"

The blameless soul she held offered an enthusiastic nod.

Jules pulled two foil-wrapped candies from the pocket sewn into the gown and waved them to attract her silver-green eyes. "Remember to give these to Honor?"

She snatched them away with a single, bold nod.

"Tell Momma bye."

In obedience's stead, Hazy pressed her mouth against Jules's shoulder.

"I'll wait out here."

Neither looked toward Lucy. The blameless soul who observed her fifth winter clung to Jules, who missed her every tick they spent apart. She chased the sweetness of her scent and peppered her small neck with kisses. In this, she uprooted the woundedness that stemmed from Lucy's mistreatment. Hope and anticipation returned as they neared all that the Archibald Territory's northernmost rescue responders prepared for those they served with contagious energy.

The moment they entered the Page Battalion House's gate of long silver, white, and powder blue ribbons, away from Lucy, the blameless soul erupted with a gasp that outsized her build. Some hundred-plus bundles of clean firewood intended as gifts to locals formed the perimeter and rested around fire rigs, responder cycles, and the medical rigs like Jules patrolled in. Cinnamon-laced incense smoldered in copper bowls and souls assigned to the house bore new suits and gowns in place of their uniforms.

Straw bales meant for the wintry comfort of horses and dogs partitioned the garage and provided seating, whilst blockading the doors to the battalion house supply stores. Music added ambiance, along with roasted foods and hot ciders served by those who volunteered on their eve off. Fellow rescue responders congregated around Jules; some to learn of her husband, some to dote over the blameless soul they oft heard so much about, and some to admire the medic-then-abettor in her new gown. Only she who admired from afar, Sister Honorine Nowak, received a spirited wave from she who snuggled against Jules.

Whilst of curvier build than her rig partner, but matched in height, tone, and wit, Honorine reacted with a pronounced, bellowing voice. "My goodness! What a fine gown you wear! Why, my eyes have never beheld such a magnificent color!"

Hazy reacted with a well-pitched kiss from the same hand that kept, till that tick, two candies intended for the proclaimer.

"A gift for me?"

Honorine was an innocent soul, the eldest and purist in Jules's time, and she never perceived the attention she collected when she bent over to collect sweet alms. Unlike Jules, her rig partner brimmed with accents, voices, and make-believe personalities and, in times of fright, Yah let this gentle soul create swift trust in the shyest and most frightened of His Creation. She proved those talents on an eve designed for festive imagination, afore the sorrow of a long winter's isolation began, and shed the bellowing voice of an aristocrat for the breathy swoon of an overwhelmed damsel as she held up the candy.

"I declare! I want to gobble you up and see if you taste like this candy!" She teased the child's cheeks with a brush of fingers. As Hazy fluttered on Jules's arm, Honorine supported half the weight of her. "Did you see the—"

"Yes."

"Did . . ." She tipped her crown toward Hazy.

"Truly, we hope not! I—I got here after the reel ended."

"You sat with your husband?"

"Till they dismantled the chairs." She ran her fingers along the child's ribbon. "Almost lost my chance to show off Snuggle Runt."

"We would've waited, and waited, and waited," Honorine insisted, if only to capture a smile from Hazy as she tested a croaking, slow-talking voice. With success, she grinned and softened her tone. "All to keep us from ending Hivi'ern without you. He improves?"

"His heart won't ease. I—I told them he hates to be immersed. They're *technicians* though. They know all."

Honorine hugged her partner and sandwiched Hazy between. "He will mend. Chet told me he would cover you if you wanted to sit longer in the morn."

"Chet Harold Ferrifelder? He is never what he seems."

"No. I agreed to that cordial sip of fortified wine he's offering me evermore."

"Truly! You are the best."

Honorine smirked and nodded in agreement. "The chief says he oft wants to dance and take off his clothes after he has too much of that wine."

"Chet won't complain then! I—I should tell you one of the techs said they might send Nelson home in the peak afore the third moonset of winter."

"See!"

Hazy laughed at Honorine's outburst, though the rest fell outside her interest. She then used her own silly voice on Jules. "*See-e-e-e*?"

Both medics claimed a side and teased her with kisses till she cackled. Jules whispered in Hazy's ear, and the child nodded hard enough to make the medic stagger. "Ask, then give her the other one no matter what she decides."

"May I push the siren?" Hazy held out her hand and offered the second of the candies to the rig driver.

"Two butterscotches! How can I refuse you?"

Hazy answered with a remarkable shrug; unsure of any refusal.

"And, just like that, your soul belongs to the runt." Jules wrinkled her nose when the child stared her down.

"We drift toward the souls we want to be." Honorine savored the first candy and gave Hazy a wink. "Let us go see our other girl."

In the only manner which she ever wished for Hazy to visit her rig, Jules approached the gleaming red-and-white work rig as her passenger leaned headlong as if to increase her gait. Honorine took a moment and wiped off a smudge. The rig driver then held open the door, transferred Hazy from arms to seat bench, and climbed in behind the controls.

TULL

Jules rounded the passenger side, admiring both souls, who kept eyes on her too. Hazy divided her curiosity on the array of dash gadgets and nodded whilst Honorine explained the purpose of every function. Jules stole another backward glance, in case Lucy followed, and stared into the absent location she wished for her husband to fill. Rather than taking from Hazy's fun, she rubbed at the ache that his absence created.

"That's correct! What a wit you have!." The driver's voice broke Jules from a stuck place and prompted her entry into their rig. "A little soul worries over you."

"She fusses."

"And this one?"

"Imagine the sound, Hazy."

"We both rely on having our Jules around when we need her. Which is evermore. No recklessness."

"I haven't planned any recklessness." She aided Hazy. "Kuh- *kuh-*."

"Recklessness seldom makes plans." Honorine spoke with sweetness and let her eyebrow carry the weight of a good scolding. "Kuh-*lair* . . ."

"Kuh-lair?"

"Two more sounds. Take your time, precious." Honorine grinned till her eyes met Jules's. "I know you grew up with them, and they make you brave, but I grew up with horses, and that doesn't make me fit to race and jump."

"Kuh-*lair* . . ."

"What makes a sound like *ding-dong*? Besides the name of the driver."

"A bell! Kuh-lair-*a-bell*?"

"*Clarabelle*. My grandma's name." Honorine beamed.

"Honor's grandma was a rig."

"She was?" The gleam in the child's eyes outshone the rig's gleam.

"Suuure!"

"If I saw that reel and wanted to stop what's happening, then I am certain you do too. I'm asking you not to try." Honorine then tapped another label. "Can you read this word for me?"

Hazy purred. "*Siren*. Siren! Siren!"

Honorine extended her shortest finger. "Push the siren button *one* time. Elsewise, we'll be mobbed by sticky-faced monsters who'll stain my Clarabelle with icky hands. Then Momma's going to have to stop all their wayward hearts."

"Well, they didn't name you *Kindness*." Jules brushed Hazy's forearm and kept her close. "Not Momma-your-momma. Honorine believes she's Clarabelle's momma. She's from Carpenter, which will make sense to you as you grow older. Can you give the button a push?"

Hazy leaned nearer to the dash and pushed as hard as her finger allowed. Every light on the rig—twenty-eight in all—illuminated, and cast a flood of swirling color through the battalion house. She obeyed Honorine's wishes and released the button, covering her mouth as she marveled over the proof of her effort. All the while, the child never let go of her hold on Jules's index finger.

The festivities emboldened monsters, and the man who watched Hazy from afar now lingered on the hem of artificial light that shone from the bay of the battalion house. He pressed his forearm against the girder that formed the outermost corner and shielded his face from Lucy Bright Moon's abettor. Each additional time Hazy jabbed the siren, he laughed with her and let their revolving lights catch in his eyes.

She who almost ended Asham at Bliss's cabin slipped her fingers around the hand that dangled behind the peering man's back. "We must return now, Olley."

"They've set their hearts against one another. Lucy and Jules."

"That's nothing to me."

"You never wanted for their friendship."

"I wanted for you, not sirens, or gowns, or friends."

"My bride lacks imagination."

His words, however true and innocent, nicked her pride.

"Only a child can make the painful precious. What's she call them?"

Aware of his lament, she filled the gap in his memory with an air of discomfort. "A *bumbler* bee. Her language skills leave much to be desired, but I confess she fosters a habit for preciousness."

"My bride's taken away her mask on this . . . the last eve my territory won't shrink away from me . . . appalled by what they see."

Nita shut her eyes and searched for the comfort of her husband's voice; a comfort that never reached her goose-pebbled skin. Her forearms showed no trace of the fractures she had endured the previous eve, and her fingers held to the soul whose hurt turned her unforgiving.

"I dreamt of surprising her with gifts. Now, I fear her reaction when next she sees what I am. What sway the beauty of innocence holds over the hideous."

"You are not hideous! Be glad we've kept back. Imagine all those clumsy feet fumbling across our path and those sticky hands pawing at us!"

"I imagine just that, and delight." His smile collapsed as he fretted over what the eve lacked. That he took so long to realize the absence produced a film of uneasy sweat upon his mangled brow. *"Where is Nelson? Jules would drag him on broken legs rather than let him miss this spectacle."*

"When has Nelson ever made the land aware of his time or travels?"

"He keeps his promises to her."

"We have to get you back anyway."

"Not till I find Nelson. Not till he learns who I saw. She's who we'll all fight to keep safe. Even you, my bride."

Nita inhaled with the same discretion that contained the movement of her frame. "Come. We'll walk toward his loft. No doubt we'll meet him along the way."

Olley considered her strategy and, letting pass her penchant for manipulation, limped away with her anyway. No other soul turned his head, though he held out his hand in a manner that let every jubilant, cheer-filled creature sweep his palm. Their zest inspired him. They gave him the might he needed as he sifted through his worries.

As they passed an adjacent route, Lucy turned from the breeze and lit a hand-rolled cigarette, which kept them from recognizing one another. She grated her temple with the nail of her thumb, even let the ash burn the skin, while she cast out the shrill sounds of laughter and sirens that dripped through the walls of the battalion house.

Lucy hated how the face, the nature, and the prestige of Lana Robin Lael needled her mind. She who gave Lucy's husband a child haunted well. She proved her soul lived on through Hazy's stubborn spells, fierce independence, and nerve-riling. That Lucy needed the remnants of Wanderers to drive back the ghost she found in blameless eyes further weakened the fearsome creature.

"One of us ought to have stayed in Ki'eoppa."

Asham arose from the pitch shadows close enough that the ribbon of smoke that draped over Lucy's shoulder attached to the fibers of his new disguise. He let his shadow consume her back and leaned in to smell her hair when the smoke proved too faint. His gloved hand traced her shoulder and arm till his fingers trembled over not caressing her. She took another drag and he let his hand hover along her hip, taunting fortune, lest she turn and face him.

"We've stayed too long."

"I keep hearing that."

She took her last drag from the spiced cigarette and flicked away her vice. Neither shamed Guardian watched the butt land, and both turned their backs on Hazy as they entered the eve's cloak.

HAZEL-SUE LAEL

Two drafts of this novel existed without Hazy, who turned the tale away from horror and invited the wondrous creatures in the fantastical land of the secondkind. Despite her fuzzy companion, her fascination rests on birds. What one soul sees as a bird might appear as a Squire to another. We can never know their cleverness or who they let see their true form, but we can believe that every creature has a purpose in Yah's plan. This little darling's purpose reaches beyond the gates of Tull's discernment.

Second Chance

TWENTY-ONE

THE 1ST MORN BENEATH THE MOON OF THE WANDERING FOG

THE 114TH WINTER OF THE ACCESSION

IN THE CARE OF THE HELPER, WHO KEEPS SOULS FROM FRUITLESS WANDERING.

1721 FRESNEL PARK

THE ARCHIBALDIAN HOME OF JULES BAKER SHANNON AND NELSON JAMES TULL.
A GIFT FOR THE GUARDIAN'S SERVICE TO THE SECOND CREATION.

The sky-fires shone a bit too bright, distracting music burst much too loud, and a conversation between off-balance voices drew Tull from slumber too soon. Each time he drifted, an absurd trumpet or a grating laugh drew him back. Another voice entered the plot's highest-standing loft. Judge Otto Meynell Chessy proved a familiar guest around the home Jules kept with her husband.

After eight spans of primary education, her blamelessness ended, and Jules was taken on as novitiate to Otto. She joined his household whilst he provided her medical internship. With him as her benefactor, she advanced beyond Tull's and her dad's level of learning; a gift she oft imparted to Hazy. The two—now seasoned rescue medic-then-abettor and scholar-now-judge—enjoyed a peculiar affinity. Jules upheld a keen, if not sportive, weakness toward her jovial elder.

"What you need, my dear Jules, is time away from your duties. Your learning, your purpose, your other purpose . . . take their toll." He chuckled as he straightened a pair of wire-rimmed eyeglasses. "That is, *t-o-l-l* and not the family name of your husband. He, like his bride, takes on too much."

"As you say, Otto."

TULL

The judge's cheeks turned rosy at her word. He needed a well-groomed mustache to round out his character. When last he tried, he found his upper lip sensitive and his nose prone to *fits*. After he sneezed upon the peevish chin of Marm Millie Esther Bellamy, he shaved and never again adorned his face.

She who revered Otto through *fits* and embarrassments then prodded a touchy topic amid the outfit. "Ingram lives like a Guardian and Hamer took a devaluation to *serve* as Nita's abettor. CeCe needs experience, but Dory—"

"A soul our Guardians will never trust, I remind you!"

"Well, she has behaved for three spans. With Nita *away*, Olley hurt, and who knows where Pine hides, the pact could stand some loosening."

"Their pact meant little if they loosen their word because they're weary."

"I—I know that's true in concept, but two souls cannot guard seven territories or what remains of Gierig."

"Six territories and what remains of Gierig, but you mustn't turn from Nita."

"I—I'm not."

"You are. You've let your mind convince your heart not to trust her. Would you handle her circumstance any different?"

"You tell me. *My* husband was hurt, and Nita hasn't got a runt who deserves at least one soul who cares more for her needs than their own."

Birds bickered with slapstick timing and no shortage of intrusive whistling. Rich, green leaves never fluttered, minus wobbling lines in the center. A brown tree with spiraling bark sprang up from a head adorned with two equal ribbons of rich, black hair. The light refracted through the pink glass cubes that kept each ribbon fastened and stung the eye and cast their shape across the floor.

Tull's heart leapt at the sound of blameless, delighted laughter, and he preserved her song in his memories along with Jules's concerns. He took one glance at her in this land and distrusted the reels that failed to capture the calming stillness she possessed and the small space she claimed. Another candy went missing, snatched from a pile by a small hand as a rather sensible dialogue between talking birds flowed. A slip of waxed paper rustled as the scent of cocoa wafted. Seven spans in reset now revealed their reward and he savored the moment like Hazy savored candy.

"Not with toffy?"

"Toffy is bad for little teeth, Otto."

TULL

From over the chocolate-devourer's shoulder, a worn teddy bear stared back at the nearest Jacobian with smug eyes. Lavender threads that matched the number and pattern of Tull's facial scars adorned the furry face. Small, candy-grabbing fingers now plucked at the keepsake's blunt wrist. In that time, the bear never stopped staring and never stopped sticking out a pink, fabric tongue at the drowsy Guardian.

A warm burst of anthracite heat blew a stack of empty candy wrappers across the sunken floor but failed to divide the bear's interests. Atop the footstool, a Hivi'ern bell sat upon one side and echoed the harmonics of Sevier. The scents of cocoa and sugar teased his nostrils again and he let out a soft sigh as he heard small teeth break the next piece of candy. He missed the sight of her in her purple Hivi'ern gown and begrudged Asham even more.

"Don't be late for your meeting, and don't go looking for trouble."

"No, no, I never would!" Otto chuckled. "Be well, my pet!"

"Soon, you'll see me." She purred and smacked her lips.

The strong-shouldered rescue medic with a dynamic waistline dressed in snug trousers and an undervest crossed her husband's field of vision and limited his view of the blameless birdwatcher. She clutched a display plate with white knuckles but bent at the hinges and kissed the top of the smallest crown in the room. Hazel-Sue strained her posture toward affection and giggled to the effect of *smooching* noises.

Tull smiled at their bond even as he admired the head-smoocher's full backside and sculpted thighs. He cast his gaze toward the perches, as far from her curves as the confines of the decorative iron ceiling beams allowed, and restrained his thoughts with gratitude's prayer. Even in his peripheral, though, he saw Jules brush back a pearl-hued crown of long hair, treated whilst he was away with an indigo-rose-based dye for Hivi'ern, as she set the display plate on a charging post. He shut his eyes, turned his face from his splendid bride, and asked Yah's blessings upon her.

"No staring. Remember?"

"I was far from staring." His voice sounded unused and distant. "*Admiring* the Creator's design, at most."

"Nelson? What did you say?"

He peeked and saw three faces staring at him. The wide-eyed child with swaying ribbons of dark hair drew his smile. The ever-watchful, mocking bear drew his raised brow. The apple-cheeked rescue medic drew his breath. His bride's sparkling eyes

TULL

proved a hard match for Hazy's curious timidity. In the end, he settled on the bear's tongue. "I forget."

His bride kissed him more times than he counted, hugged him till she risked smothering him, then kissed him again. With a twist of her waist, she made a plea of their guest. "*See*? He's awake. What silly soul thought he'd sleep evermore?"

Hazy betrayed her concern when she spun away and slouched sideways. Tull sneered at the bear, who cushioned her dignity, for she squished him well and drew emphasis upon his wrinkled, pink tongue.

"She's kept a close watch on you. In between reels." Jules claimed a seat and his hand but kept Hazy involved. "Have you not?"

The blameless soul pursed her lips into a twisted pucker and buried her confession by letting her head sink into her shoulders. Jules smiled, her same great smile, and Tull considered how his bride cared for Asham's daughter and for him.

"We had a long eve, and you an early morn." Her sigh turned her head and directed his attention toward a child's belongings. "Ingram and Carl met us at the Mannering House and helped us get situated. Chief *Lily-Liver* wanted me to tell you that the Jacoby Territory will not withhold your alms for the damages at Taft Bluffs."

Her husband sneered. "How is Ingram?"

His Carpenterian bride smiled. "Hearing your voice again makes me want to kiss you. Ingram seeks to make you proud and keeps George aware of his travels."

As fast as he winked, Hazy spun back toward the animated hijinks, and Jules raised Tull's shirt. She inspected the healed puncture marks along his abdomen, courtesy of time spent in the mending chambers. The pad of her thumb drifted along the definition of muscle and brushed the tender flesh along his hip. He squirmed and seized her elbow.

"Cold hands."

"Ticklish tummy." Her hand traced his pelvic bone, then roamed across his chest and soothed his heart. The way she sighed, their reconnection by touch soothed her, too. "You mended well. That and plenty of cocoa kisses have been my salve. Your heart did not want to be in that tank. Do you remember?"

"No."

"Good." She drummed her fingers on cue with his heartbeat and breathed out. "Most patients remember the full experience."

TULL

"I remember the swiftness of the blast, how loud the wind whistled just afore, how fast Ernie dropped, and how you soothed me when you put my hand to you that I might feel your heart."

Her teeth grazed her lip and she squirmed as the color of her eyes dazzled him.

"How bad was I?"

"Puncture wounds, abrasions, a cracked jawbone, a blown eardrum, a severe concussion, three fractured ribs, torn muscles, gelidity, and—"

"My shoulders? Zeck's bow *strained* them."

"Long spine, long bow. Your shoulders mended first, but you have a surprise iron deficiency; all of which cost less time than you spent on your hike to Ernie's cabin. Sending you to Mannering kept you here. I—I confess that time passed like the winter for me; which we entered as of the last eve."

"Ernie?"

Jules shook her head with remorse. "Your territory mourns for you both. Larnelle gave thanks and prayed for your recovery."

Tull considered his lost judge's esteemed sibling.

"I—I would've put you in bed, but Snuggle Runt walks when she slumbers. I—I draped the terrace doors to keep back the gliders till Chief Hont threatened me with a citation lest I—I clear them. Here's hoping that fine costs less than crashing a glider!"

He appreciated how she teased.

"Another glider relayed from the cabin. You showed your integrity to the territories again. Can you tell me why Inventor Holston Lucius Buckler seeks and seeks me through the display plate that I lent to you?"

"I cannot." He let his gaze soothe her curiosity.

She watched him with certainty that he withheld from her and sneered. "Our *new* judges mean to send up a glider to discuss your protection offer. And, one of Judge Hofnarr's husbands wants to know why you haven't—"

"Do I answer to the spouses of judges?"

"Sondrea and your grandpa excluded?"

Her smirk made him squirm. "All have watched, have they?"

"Imagine an identical flicker from every display plate, as far as a soul can see, whilst every eye in the territory watches the same reel." She marveled as she announced, "Ginger told how there's an increase of souls who wish to carry your seed; Olley's first downturn since he shaved his mustache.

TULL

"And, Judge *Bromley* called on you. He visited the Mannering and stayed and read the newspaper. Did you know he knew Juanita? He wanted you to know that Chief Fox raided a storehouse where a supply of *fishing nets* went missing."

Now that Tull knew of Asham's involvement, his interest in stolen nets disinterested him and, from rudeness, made him stop listening to Jules's rant about the use of those nets on him.

"Katerena told us—*the territory*—that Judge Mumus remains unharmed in reclusion." She hesitated for her husband's sake. "Pine and Nita have hurt Conliffe, Gwynne, Katch, Bliss, plus Elwell and Hofnarr at once. Nita probably returned to—"

"Pine?"

"When Lucy got to the cabin, he and Nita were gone."

"Pine wasn't at the cabin, J. J. Lucy was there?"

"Pine wasn't at the cabin?"

"I want to talk to Lucy."

"First Pine's beacon stopped relaying." She stretched across him to speak into the ear furthest from Hazy. "Then Lucy walked off during Hivi'ern. She won't accept my relays and her beacon isn't detectable."

"I won't need a beacon. She needs to tell why she's shielded Asham from us."

His tone made her shiver, still she admired the difference she saw in his heart since the reset, as she struggled to process his claim about Asham.

"I suspect that, with Katch's help removing the beacon, Asham has maneuvered as your Uncounted Soul all this while."

Silence settled upon his bride, though her eyes spoke of betrayal's sting. She twisted as if to shield her next words. "You saw *him*?"

"Nita, Ernie, and I saw how he hides his mangled face behind scarves."

Her gasp rolled through his ear like thunder and her crown rested upon him when she whispered one final warning. "Be gentle with your voice. Hazy's upset that you were hurt."

Tull looked upon the profile of their blameless guest and studied the way she tucked her bottom lip between her teeth; afraid to breathe or make a sound. She tried her hardest to hear their every word but the distance in her eyes as she stared *through* the animated reel told the Guardian the truth. He nodded to his bride's request and stayed mindful of their feelings. He then raised his voice only for the child's benefit.

TULL

"As for me, I've taken my long nap and am ready to greet the winter and the faces afore me. Maybe not the fuzzy one."

"I happen to love the fuzzy one." Jules raked his beard, then kissed him.

Hazy played coy, cowered toward one shoulder, then offered a curious peek.

"You can tell him what you want now." Jules nodded when she spoke to her. "She's waited the morn to speak to you."

Hazy pulled her bear into her lap, buckling the soft body as she picked a fluffy ear. The smallest voice crept out. "Hi."

"Hey, whirlybird."

The pet name made Jules laugh. "Now she's bashful."

"She's unflawed in all her ways, Jules."

"Yes. She has little use for me except to help her load Dad's old animated reel collection and to sort out the chocolates that have fruit in their bellies."

"Chocolate has a belly?"

"According to some!"

Jules lunged and pulled Hazy closer to them by her suspenders. Hazy crouched and giggled, but never sacrificed one candy. The rescue medic hugged soul and bear, then peppered the preferred nose with a kiss and wiped a trace of chocolate from her lip. They shared a penchant for bite-sized chocolates, but their bond proved deeper when Jules licked the smudge from the pad of her thumb.

"Nelson doesn't eat chocolate."

The aghast expression, heavy with fear and immediate assurance of his insanity, struck Tull in a way that he lowered a wall on lingering concerns to end her dread. "Till I lost my dad, I rivaled your fondness. Then a soul who meant well, but lacked the way, offered me comfort with chocolate doughnuts."

"I—I thought Sondrea told you."

"We sat in her mother's home. My unsuspecting soul, Sondrea"—he remembered the sympathetic kiss she set on his face—"and Judge Bromley."

"Judge Bromley?"

Hazy offered him the kindest grin. Then, as if the moment passed on the breeze, she reached for another candy.

"I—I believe you've had enough chocolate, whirlybird."

The blameless laughed with mischief when Jules used Tull's pet name. "*Noooo.*"

"Yessss."

TULL

Hazy shook her head till Tull reached and poked the bear's belly in her stead.

"I am told you helped make your Hivi'ern gown."

The eager response made her bangs fall in front of her eyes. She swept them away with the palm of her hand and surprised him with words. "I wore purple and ribbons and Jules colored my fingers?"

"I'm certain you and your *fingers* were the loveliest of all His creatures."

"Jules showed me the fire rigs! And we saw Clarabelle. And I got to push the siren three times, but Honorine said I could only push the button one time."

"Honorine is unreasonable." He found she already mimicked his ornery grin, which pleased him. "Sounds like some sweet soul took good care of you."

She nodded and squeezed her bear, but her fingers petted Jules's arm.

"The last time I saw you, you were taller." He caught her reaction and laughed with Jules. He then leaned toward her ear and whispered *something* that produced a smile and made her eyes swell.

"*Yesss!*"

"I believed you might. If you know in your heart that you must keep from inviting in wandering spirits"—he turned over his hand and revealed a wrapped candy—"then, you'll take this from my hand, and we'll go."

"Where did you—"

Hazy snatched the candy from his palm faster than Jules focused.

"Whoa!"

She then sought whether she could keep her gift with a single look.

"All yours."

Hazy scrunched her brow and turned from Jules lest the rules deprive her of one more treat. For the first time in fourteen spans, Jules witnessed Tull on the losing end of his own feat and her jaw went slack.

"*Well*, find your shoes and a jacket. I'll clean up, too. J. J.?"

"What's the adventure?"

"Trust me?"

She shook her head. "No."

Tull, Hazy, and the bear stared back at her with unblinking eyes.

"Yes."

The Guardian goosed her, which made her chirp and hop to her feet. Her reaction made Hazy cackle.

TULL

"Who's going to tell me where we're going, and who's getting tickled?"

Tull received Hazy's famous expression of *Well?* and shook his head. "We mustn't tell of surprises. We have to show them."

Jules raised her hands in an agitated manner and covered Hazy's ears. "Chelcie Ryan Lavoie surprised me once. I—I kicked him so hard that one of his testicles swelled like a pear. He fell, and he broke his ankle. And a finger."

Her husband batted his eyelids with pause. The child wriggled free from the hands that protected her hearing and waited for them to speak again. When they proved silent, she exhaled through her nostrils, and rushed to the bedroom with rigid, fast-swinging arms to prepare for travel.

On her way to join the child, Jules mussed her husband's hair. "Best to leave this land braver than you arrived."

Tull huffed at his least favorite of all her father's proverbs.

TWENTY-TWO

707 LITTLE OAK WAY

IN THE JACOBIAN SETTLEMENT OF MINDER.
WHERE NELSON JAMES TULL SPENT HIS BLAMELESSNESS.

Two ticks afore the next watch passed, pace disproved the ease imagined in one Guardian's plans and delivered his bride, the blameless soul in their care, and his mending pride to an old church that blocked the eye from a field of graves where monumental influences on Tull rested. Though Hazy basked beneath tenderness and brightness, he felt a chill from Jules that nudged him toward the porch steps of the entryway. Over the spans, he sent countless souls to this site when they had nowhere to turn, and buried bodies that had no other soul to see to their care. He seldom met another of the secondkind in this place, yet souls in need found help on every occasion.

Families buried their lost at no expense, on the condition that they volunteered there from moonset till the next moonrise once between each thaw and winter for each interred loved one. Such were the *laws* of the plot's owner. He balanced four pieces of luggage, a picnic basket, and a bear whilst he held open a door without locks and received a brisk pat to his scarred cheek as his bride entered with Hazy.

The trio lost seventy-four ticks from Tull teaching Hazy to tie a durable knot with her shoelaces, which hushed Jules's fussiness. Hushed her in a way that hinted at a need for considerate action and sparse orneriness. Since the reset, he had put her heart through more than he had planned. That this was all deliberate rekindled the hardened crust of her temperament that kept out those souls who promised too much, too fast; though fast felt like mockery at their present pace.

TULL

As he hurried and adjusted the lights over the sanctuary, he heard light footsteps race by on a path toward the elevated altar. The first time Tull brought Olley there, his fellow Guardian decided as much wood resided inside the church as in the forests that Judge Bromley owned. Hand-carved wooden spindles adorned every bench seat, two sets of staircases, a sanctuary platform that extended outward from the altar, and in small window boxes that draped every stained-glass window in the sanctuary.

The bench seats matched the open rafters, which matched the empty cross that swayed on the gentle disturbance of the trio. Even past his time, Beau Itzal Zeck held up the cross, which took three backs to carry into the church. Tull bought the place the winter after the territory interred their first Guardian. Zeck feared the fire and filled a casket that required the might of eight souls to carry. His last challenge to Tull bore similar weight that the fourth Guardian of the territory kept unshared.

Jules walked as if burdened, too, with crossed arms and a set jaw. She might have dusted the rafters with the arch of her brow, too, but her husband reasoned a glance might land him in another land. Because two Guardians, two judges, two grandfathers, and her father-by-law also rested on the plot in memoriam, his bride kept from grumbling. This site troubled her, for Carpenterians believed fire the safest and truest method of loosing the soul from the body, and she held memories of being buried in the glebe.

A solid plank of wood, like the face of the pulpit, provided a perch for the only visible locks in the sanctuary. Hazy knocked with a flat palm and knew the routine well enough to lift her arms toward the abettor. Jules rewarded her with a smile for her obedience, but the expression faded as they faced Tull. He took her spurning in stride, set aside the baggage he had convinced her to pack, and fished a set of keys that fit the locks.

The Comforter who oft met him there hid; a ploy he admired much in that moment, for he stood outnumbered and *trapped* if the surprise turned on him. Tull offered Jules a nervous smile at the doorway to the basement and received the sting of a small hand he believed meant to pat his cheek. He scolded his conceit for entering Minder without notice, and wielded the lunch basket and Hazy's bear like a shield for his back. The luggage he kept in front, should Jules put a boot to him and hurry along his descent into the basement.

Down thirty-eight steps, lands and appearances changed. Beneath the antiqued sanctuary they entered a furnished, modernized home, of sorts, complete with kitchen, living and sleeping areas, a full bath, and a supply of food, clothing, and gear; outside the four bags he towed for bride and blameless soul. Few creatures entered the lesser-known retreat for the soul who lasted ten eves in Gutefiel.

"Are we on an adventure yet?"

Jules laughed at Hazy's timing and sighed. She then toed her Jacobian's backside with a playful nudge. "Are we?"

He set aside luggage and lunch. His latitude with Hazy then narrowed when he tossed her bear alongside the basket.

"*Whoaaa!*" Hazy side-eyed the Guardian.

"We'll let him guard the place while we're away."

"That's how you want to leave this land? Keeping a girl from her bear?"

Tull shook his head and let curiosities peak while he swept the furniture, lamps, and bookcase from the living area. He cast a pleasant grin upon his audience and maneuvered around the room, setting scissor-gates across every doorway, including the exit into the yard of graves. When his activity caught Hazy's eye and set her into a series of sharp twists and pivots, lest she miss a single move he made, he fanned his palm against her lush cheek as an example of how the gesture ought to feel.

"Come, my loves. Come see my surprise."

The inseparable pair looked at one another, held hands, and obliged. He offered no further explanation, but approached the furthest wall of the nook and traced a strip of chair rail for a recessed latch. When the wall popped from the seam, the dismayed and impatient gasped and stepped back. Hazy even checked on her bear.

Their guide tugged on the false wall, made from local woods, and reinforced with scissor gates. The gate opened as the clock turns, and he fastened the frame with a rod that dropped into a copper anchor in the floor that a chair oft covered. He repeated the act with a twin wall, with an inverted finished side, which anchored near the opposite wall. Jules stepped closer this time, but Hazy stepped back again.

Once he set the anchoring rod, he retrieved a copper-shelled device he stowed in a drawer below his display plates. The shape resembled a kettle lantern. Such a device seemed handy when he vanished into the belly of darkness that lingered behind the two walls. Then, the basement fell still.

"Nelson?"

The whine of dry metal upon dry metal created a shrill sound and made Hazy shiver and bare her teeth. Then, as if knowing Jules worries over dark rooms, false light shone down on the Guardian. Not *just* the Guardian, though. Still, the way he grinned from ear to ear made him hard to look away from.

"You're cute, but this is a lousy surprise. A dirty tramcar?"

"This is no tramcar."

"No, this is the tinker-saurus that kept you and Dad away from your brides far too oft."

The wheels of his steam trolley looked more like pulleys, with a U-shaped groove around the circumference in place of shock-absorbing tubes. A rectangular, black cargo case, slender and deep, formed the rear. From under the case's canopy-style lid, he took a handmade duvet and shook loose the pressed folds. He tossed the covering to Jules and watched both members of the audience reach out to catch. Hazy cackled when one corner of the duvet wrapped over her head.

Tull removed two canteens, brushed passed them, and swapped them out for fresh water in glass jars that he kept in the refrigerator. Those he set in cushioned holders and buckled leather straps across the lids. By then, Jules and Hazy stood at the rear tire. Two seats with clamshell-style tufting and cushioned leather sported dangling belts for safety. Between them, a gear shifter extended into a vaulted casing beneath the trolley. No fuel tank, no gas.

"Does this heap still *get*?"

"Indeed."

Tull retrieved a steering wheel from a pull-down storage closet in the ceiling, and returned. He secured the steering wheel onto the opposite side of the steam trolley while Hazy climbed onto the passenger seat. She shared smiles with him as he shook the entire chassis whilst he tested the hold of the re-mounted steering wheel. She giggled again and watched his next move.

"Help me push this button?" He tapped his index finger against a sealed button, like the glass key of a typewriter.

She set her whole hand upon his finger and, together, they ignited the heating unit that boiled the water that produced the steam that provided the trolley's propulsion. The frame shimmied on all four wheels and Hazy's eyes grew large as her grin turned small and unsure. The gurgling and shimmying announced rejuvenation, like a drunkard waking from sleep, but the engine took some time reaching a steady, idle pace. Then, she set her attention toward identifying every portion of the dash area.

TULL

Tull watched over her and sifted through his set of keys. With one he unlocked a bolt and twisted a handle that released two flat bars of iron, each a hand's breadth, a finger's thickness, and seven heads in length. He gave the wall in front of the trolley a nudge, then shifted the iron frame sideways on a swinging cable-and-pulley system.

"Oh! That's ripe." Tull fanned the air but Hazy beat him in covering her button nose with both forearms. "*Shoo!*"

His abruptness made her laugh and drew the same response from Jules. She stepped closer but breathed through her mouth. He hurried around his bride, retrieved their lunch, and sealed them off from the basement lest the odor permeate the living areas. With one door set, he still shook off the air around him.

He buried his face in the crook of his arm and rushed into the adjacent tunnel. Stagnant water on the floor of the tunnel made him leap between two iron rails. Water dripped through one of the cobblestones overhead, like those stones that lined the walkway in the courtyard and the roads. As far as he could see, the tunnel appeared passable. Given the smell, the *eye* test sufficed.

On the furthest side of the nook, he pulled a sheet from a spoked handle fitted to an iron rod and bevel gears. As he cranked, a connective spur arose. With all his might, he raised the trolley off the crushed limestone floor till the two tracks held in place. Jules lunged, not certain of the parking brake that kept Hazy stationary.

"I wouldn't have let her sit there lest we sat secure, J. J."

"You used to let me help when you needed extra hands. Not even a brake to set."

He turned away, used a rag to dust a wall-mounted lantern, and tapped the copper case that affixed the jar to the outermost beam.

Jules tilted her head and read for Hazy. "Seven-zero-seven."

"The address; 707 Little Oak Way. This is our first stop. Imagine you can keep Hazy on your lap?"

"Imagine this *heap* can outrun whatever else lives down here?"

"I believe so."

Humorlessness settled on Jules's face as she scooped up Hazy.

He buckled them in, helped tuck the duvet around their legs, then stooped toward Hazy's ear and spoke with a hush. "We're about to take a ride through the dark and the shadows. Don't be fearful. I won't let harm find you. My word is yours, Hazy, and yours too, my bride."

TULL

This time, the child patted the side of his face with trusted gentleness. She then flicked her brow, as if tired of waiting for him, and he rushed to take his seat.

"Let us see if this heap can outrun my senses."

Once Tull released the brake, he directed the steam trolley onto the adjacent set of tracks. Hazy cooed; more once her driver activated a string of headlamps. With a hard-wired remote, he closed the outer door on the nook and focused on a ride more unique than any other he knew. He let the route convince his passengers of the promised adventure, though.

Given the lack of fortitude the trolley possessed, the trio stayed on the flattest route and one nearest the surface; no deeper than the church basement. The decline from the nook onto the tracks offered the sharpest angle, which the trolley handled well. If he planned other trips for them in the future, and he suspected he might, he needed to upgrade the wheels and the engine's output. Given the count of cobwebs Jules swatted, a windscreen addition seemed courteous, too.

Despite limitations, the ride offered both passengers alert gazes and softer countenances beyond their common gentility. Jules loved the view as much as the opportunity to hold Hazy in her arms. The child consumed all the details her wide eyes allowed. She pointed out curiosities, and even rested her hand upon Tull's forearm while he held the wheel and taught.

"When the firstkind arrived, storms arose and overturned the glebe. The winds peeled back entire farms, like blankets, and set fields atop houses, buildings, and *towns*. My grandmother's era discovered tunnels. They say survivors dug till their breath ran out. Few survived the force of the storm."

Mines and caves littered the route, void of all but recessed magnitude. The scope worried Jules for those houses—those souls—built atop mighty caverns. The miners scraped clean every portion that their eyes beheld. They abandoned trolleys and carts, some attached to cables and asway over murky pits with no mapped bottom.

When Tull pointed out an arrangement of exposed tree roots filled with bats, the rescue medic covered Hazy in the duvet and draped one corner over her crown. A staircase that extended into the next pit made the Guardian tilt from his seat to see the depth. He then stooped to see the mouth. The land beneath offered countless secrets; more than judges or duplicitous allies realized.

In one spot, after he coaxed them from beneath their covering, he showed them an entire house sunken beneath an overturned foundation. A tree grew through the windows and tipped the frame sideways into a fissure. An empty rig rested alongside, with mud-caked headlamps no longer seeable. Then, for eight ticks, all that surrounded them was the tunnel. Hazy yawned and the ride's fancy depleted.

With no warning, they came upon a buried horse-drawn carriage, intact down to the vine-entangled skeletons of four horses. That sight earned a poke in the ribs from Jules's thumb till he covered Hazy's eyes. His care impressed his bride, who grasped the kneaded ring of the steering wheel and learned the uselessness of the tool on tracks. After that, she expected her husband's arm around her and rested her head upon his shoulder.

He obliged, and scoured the shadows on the opposite side of the trolley. Beyond the cobwebs and roots, the vines that grew downward and those that feasted on them, he expected to find other travelers. Vernard Voler, for one, ruled kingdoms few souls of the secondkind visited. He also expected to find Si'el Uaen Söi'eä cutting a new path through the land.

When the sandstone turned to ruddy clay and tree roots overtook the old copper mine, the Guardian used his free hand to adjust down the throttle. The steam engine puttered, and the pistons eased to so few decibels that the two spoke without shouting. The decrease in speed annoyed Hazy, who took to rocking to make the trolley go faster. She stopped when her driver slipped his arm from around Jules and took hold of a helpful hand.

On a second hard-wired remote, he held the bottom of three buttons. The result lit an amber-hued bulb that made his thumbnail *glow* by her witness. When a distant amber beacon illuminated, he pointed her gaze in that direction. She found the signal as a string of amber lights in a square-shaped pattern lit the darkness. She showed Jules, then Tull taught them the next step without stopping.

"We have to slow down more. *See*?"

He squeezed her hand as they pulled the lever into the lowest cradle on the dash and expelled steam from beneath the runners on either side. The trolley shuddered and made Jules laugh.

"Brake."

He moved their hands onto the handbrake lever between the seats. With a swift tug upright and back, he reduced their speed to a crawl. He then let Hazy hold the steering wheel without him.

"We're turning *right*."

TULL

Hazy looked in the proper direction, but her arm stayed rigid. Tull repeated their direction and startled her. Jules kissed the crown of her head and helped her to steer. The pair, together, caught the spur of another stopping point and felt the adjoining rail take on their weight. A tile plate of numbers announced their location.

"One-eight-nine-five. Who might remember that number for me?"

"Eighteen ninety-five."

"*Nooo*, Jules, one-eight-nine-five."

Tull smirked and applied a choke lever that stifled the flow of steam. He activated a second spring-brake as the wheels grated ceramic buttons. They reached a full stop upon a spur fitted on hand-cut planks. Without an explanation, he slipped from the trolley, released two latches on the plank, and reeled the rotating base beneath them till they faced the opposing direction.

"Again!"

"We're going to get out for a little while."

Hazy groaned as Jules looked at Tull for support.

"Are we not?"

"Up we go!"

He uncovered them, rolled and slung the duvet over his shoulder, then gathered their lunch basket. Hazy jumped onto the revolving floor and hopped with excitement. The rescue medic caught her hand as she twirled toward the Guardian's palm and emitted a feisty little roar. She snagged his hand, too, and dipped ahead till they pulled her upright and onto her heels.

She whose fingernails shimmered held their hands in chain formation as their Guardian led them up a smooth dirt ramp to the threshold of a door. Jules took over the basket-hauling duties while he unlocked the final passageway. The door popped open with a shoulder nudge and age-faded straw fell from a broken bale that served as Hazy's hurdle. As she leapt from her hand, Jules shut the door, wiped blistered paint flecks from her palm, then held back to admire her travel companions. Her idea of an adventure differed from theirs, but she savored a glimpse that fueled hope.

TWENTY-THREE

1895 Appledash Road

80 PARASANG WEST OF MINDER ON A 14° SOUTHWARD ARCH.
TULL'S FAVORITE PLACE IN HIS BLAMELESSNESS.

Hazy kept her hand wrapped around Tull's ring finger and pinky and squinted as they neared the hem between neglected dirt and a vast field. When they stepped from beneath cover, a forest of trees bowed her back as she strained to see the tops and greeted them on an easy sway of branches. The same breeze tousled her bangs and she swept them from her eyes lest they keep even one detail from her.

"Do you remember what the river's named?"

She hopped and declared her answer in unison. "Loy!"

"Correct. And, on what side of the Loy do you live?"

"North!" Another hop.

"Good."

The Guardian led her across an old gravel drive, overcome by similar grass found in the field, and turned toward a looming, elevated home constructed of cedar pikes and glass panes. Dual cedar joists formed the structure's exo- and endoskeleton, sandwiching panes of thick, soot-covered glass. A full, wraparound porch cradled the modest charm, open from corner to corner except for the bathroom.

Tull knelt at the blameless soul's feet, inspected the tightness of her shoelaces, and snugged the fasteners of the Guardians' copper pins that lined her overalls. "I ask you to remember the places we visited together. The loft, at 1721 Fresnel Park, and the church at . . ."

"At 707 Little—Little Oak Way."

TULL

He grinned and pointed out the structure behind her, where Jules kept the watch. "This place is called a *stable*, and the plot is called 1895 Appledash Road."

Her face scrunched, and her upper lip curled. "Apple-dash?"

"One-eight-nine-five. Appledash Road."

"One. Eight. Nine. Five. Apple. Dash. Road." She nodded each time she pronounced the location.

He brushed away her bangs. "This is my Hivi'ern gift to you. You can run as fast as you can run, yell as loud as you can yell, but I want you to keep from the road and never wander unto the trees without me or Jules. Promise?"

Hazy nodded with a rush. "I promise."

He believed her tone and grinned. "Have fun then."

She took one big leap, then a second. When no one scolded her, she broke into skipping.

"Look at her go!" He cheered her on and folded his arms across his chest.

Jules admired them from the other side of the driveway, her shoes in one hand, their lunch basket draped over her shoulder. "Most terrane in the Carpenter Territory is for crops and horses. Not little feet that step on—and in—every imaginable thing."

"That's what little feet are made for."

She almost toppled them as she leapt onto his back. "My little feet learned their lessons long ago; not—*not*—so long ago. I—I was young still. You weren't."

"Come on, little feet." Tull rubbed his bride's toes and carried her onto the field where Hazy played.

Jules twisted away from her husband for a better look at the setting of their first home together. "I—I can't believe we lived in a *barn*."

"A *stable* made into a well-lit, well-heated, well-built elevated home, I thank you."

"For horses."

He exhaled and watched Hazy drift through grass that scraped her shoulders while Jules kept leaning in the opposite direction.

"The trees got tall!"

He agreed with a nod.

"She looks so small here."

Tull held his hand to her height, as he had done at the aquarium exposition, and Jules took hold. The whole trio looked dwarfed in an open field lined with trees that ascended as high as the bluffs stood above the sea. Two plots, tethered by their secret railway, meant more to the Guardian than the loft in Sevier, and bound him to a time when souls counted him as blameless.

He and his bride watched she who turned a sympathetic eye toward a cluster of abandoned flowers as a bluebird draped in gleaming light settled near her. What they saw soothed Tull more than familiar settings or the approving kisses from Jules. The return to this place coaxed gentleness he never experienced in that previous land and relaxed him till his knees turned soft. His bride's purr of satisfaction then reminded him of her place upon his back.

"She's not said a word about Lucy."

"She's thoughtful. Once she works out the new arrangement, she'll ask."

"I—I don't know what I—I'll tell her." She watched with him as Hazy rested alongside the flowers, where she sang a song to them. "All this time, he's pretended she has no father to care for her."

"Lana feared his selfishness."

"I—I should have learned more from her. She intimidated me." She bit his ear when he chuckled at her confession. "So, as an old soul who's seen and done so much, do *you* believe we can wear the sweet runt down with laughter and chasing?"

"Indeed."

"Good." She kissed his face, squeezed his sides, then gave chase to Hazy till they needed a rest from breathlessness.

He found a spot on the ground where no shadows or thorns lingered and unfurled the duvet. There, he sat and removed his boots and socks and stretched out beneath magnificent sky-fires. The wave of joy spread further than any creature's wail and settled him as best he hoped in this season.

He thanked a giving Creator for that, as well as the beauty that surrounded them. Repentance for betrayers, truth for deceivers, and peace lest he destroy abandoners rounded out his time of communion. To his requests, he also asked forgiveness. He failed the judges. Though not one reached out for protection, he believed he owed them *more*.

"Hey, old bear! You can't catch us!"

The Guardian sighed at the sound of Jules's taunt via Hazy's sweet voice. Even the way the medic bobbed behind the child enticed him to his feet. He rolled his sleeves as he waded into the field, catching more taunts for his delay. Then, when he broke into a sprint, both reacted like those madcap birds from Hazy's animated reel; knowing not which way to scramble.

Their voices grew near, carried far, and cascaded into bouts of hilarious laughter. Hazy proved most agile, able to stoop and run between Tull's legs. Jules proved fastest on her feet and hardest to catch. The Jacobian still put in an honest labor, till he ended up with one seated upon his right shoulder and the other held in his arms.

Each time he regained his breath, one of them slipped away and started the chase again. Hazy blamed Jules. She leveraged whoever shielded her from the fastest chaser and caused the abettor and Guardian sacrifices aplenty. As a result, they ran her till she toppled in exhaustion.

After sandwiches—one with cinnamon, one with mustard, and one without crusts—soured leeks, ginger-pickled carrots, cored apples, and one shortbread apiece, the three relaxed from bellies to toes beneath the expanse of sky-fires. Each claimed a spot on the duvet and two claimed a spot upon Tull's right side, where they rested their heads as birds roosted around the hem. His side proved less pillowy for Hazy's head, so she rolled and scooted till her crown found Jules's breast.

Her pleased sigh flowed into the rustle of treetops and her still admiration prompted the same from Jules. Through the simplest of activities, and a little adventure, husband and bride made the abandoned soul safe, cherished, and the heart of their home. Jules covered Hazy's heart with her hand and proved her happiness with a beautiful smile. She then reached backward and pinched her husband's ear.

"I believe you topped the Somers Roundabout, partner."

"I tell you, I fretted. The last soul I worked to impress was *yours*." He admired how she looked upon him and watched as she looked, with similar fondness, over the plot.

"We kept a cozy stable." She turned toward Hazy and drummed her breastbone. "Remember when Nelson and Jules used to live in a house for *horses*?"

"Noooo."

"We did."

The branches swayed on the next exhalation of the wind. A few leaves took flight, the past season's firmest holdouts. Tull shifted his weight, withdrew his hand from beneath his head, and reached along Jules's torso to touch her tummy. She held the same hand and let her head fall toward his heart.

"Did Anya come here, or would that have agitated Barbara?"

TULL

Tull turned her attention toward *other* feats with a cautious breath. "I threw a *lurker* over the southwest joist once for watching me sleep."

Jules teased more. "Or the historiographer you fascinated back when?"

"I've no memory of any soul by that name."

"What name?"

"Who?" He grinned. "The first time Hazy said *my* name, we were in the kitchen. She sat on the counter eating a jellied orange and she called me *Toe*. Or she meant the spider crawling on her foot."

"I'll bet you didn't care one bit." She buckled with a painful sharpness and held Hazy's head from bouncing. "Nelson. Nelson, what is that in the trees?"

He let her gaze direct him. His eyes roamed the treetops first, till he found branches alit in droplets of fire. The trail of smoldering embers looked like a comet's tail and cut a wide path against the branches of a cypress tree. Still, he searched.

On a branch some fifty heads above them, a red-hued creature with fiery, white eyes rested upon a drifting branch. One leg dangled with a cleft foot, while the other coiled around the bough. Narrow hands, shaped like pruning shears, picked at scorched ash and open wounds on that same leg. In all, the creature measured less in length than Hazy. Whatever the beast's purpose, presence meant nothing.

"Well?"

"That would be the Fallen First equivalent of the sweat bee. Irritating, but less scary than the family tree."

A spear of light skewered the creature as a Warring Minister seized the foe back toward the battlefield overhead. Even the Guardian flinched at the swiftness and took hold of both souls in arm's reach.

"And, *that* was startling!"

Another Minister swooped down and gathered every ember, lest their warring kindled the great forest. The cautious creature flew straight over the trio's position and covered them in a warmth like fire. A peace-filled expression lit her shimmering face and she acknowledged them by fluttering skyward in a massive loop. In her wake, flecks of brass as soft as petals fell upon the field. Jules laughed as flecks melted against her cheek, as harmless as vapor.

Tull waved, and a burst of light radiated through the sky. The Minister vaulted and forged a shimmering trail for their eyes to follow. A half-dozen rapid heartbeats drummed and, on the seventh, the trail vanished. Silvery creatures, shaped like doves, congregated in the field and feasted on the ash.

"I—I forgot how much activity we saw out here! Snuggle Runt missed out."

Tull saw how Hazy slept. "She slept through that?"

"The lamps are out and the stable door's wide open."

He chuckled and jostled his bride's head.

"This place agrees with me. Too bad you set fire to the floor."

"*Olley* set that fire."

"O, I—I remember." She sighed and composed a list. "Olley started you off on house fires, wolf-chasing, diving in the sea—"

"Gravedigging."

"Gravedigging?"

"I was twenty once." The arch of her brow concerned him. "*Twice*, now that you make mention."

"Well, afore the moonset of my twentieth span, I—I ran through the Carpenter freezer morgue as bare as I—I was at my birth. And, drink hadn't dizzied my blood yet. My medical internship was a poor influence."

"Arguable."

"But, lawful. Don't tell my dad!"

He watched as she stretched for the corner of the duvet, covered Hazy, and admired the sleeping child.

"Is time better for"—Jules pointed at Hazy—"*there?*"

His hand hovered near his breastbone. "She's about this high. She's thoughtful, but not a talker. Kind; she's kind. Give her a book and you won't see her face till she reads the last word. She got spectacles after too many souls caught her squinting to make sense of her lessons."

"Well, we need to take care of that!" Her brow softened, and she stared at Hazy's profile. "Bet she looked cute."

"She's a button. Funny, like Lana. Sly, like Lucy. Considerate, like Honorine. Bold, like Violet. Wise, like you. You're a giving influence. When you're both stubborn—"

"Who, me?"

"*Almighty*!" He felt the softness of her mane. "Your hair's dark there, like your mom's. You said to tell you to stop blaming her for what she never had time to teach you. And, to talk you out of a—"

"Asham shouldn't have a right to her." The words burst as she sat up. "Not after three spans. She wasn't his priority then or now. We can't leave her without a shield. I—I've got to offer a better way."

They had kept the same debate going over Hazy's upbringing across multiple lands. Letting pass the reset, that much stayed unchanged.

"Is Lucy a better mom there?"

"No."

"Does Lefty come back for his daughter?"

"No."

"Do you save Lana?"

He lost his breath. "No."

"But, Lucy raises her? Still?"

"She does." He watched as defeat pressed along Jules's shoulders.

"Mend her heart and peace shall bloom."

"She does due to foolish choices I made then. I disregarded my Helper. I disregarded my bride's heart, for I believed my way proved—"

"*Better*? And how'd that end, Nelson?"

"Here I am."

She scoffed and shook her head as the muscles of her back swelled. "Clearly you don't tow wisdom with that old soul! You see your end there, open your eyes here, and have warred since. Hofnarr, Mumus, and now Lefty and Lucy."

He withheld his encounter with Si'el Uaen Söi'eä and squirmed.

She reacted with a harsh brow. "When will you make the choice *here* that you should've made *there*? Why must *your bride* be kept waiting to see if you're the soul she loves or some stranger in love with a soul I—I haven't become yet?"

He considered how best to tend to the needs of her heart till she elbowed his side.

"Well?"

"Would you believe I came here to escape that loon?" His smirk faded as her shoulders sank deeper. "If I told you what I faced there, you—"

"You are my husband. There's nothing you could sacrifice your soul for that would ease my heart. Say you believe me."

"Yes."

"Then stop leaving me without you in other lands. I—I need you there, too."

"I'm trying, Jules."

"Well, get this time right. Learn to listen, will you? To the Helper and to me. I—I'm helpful to you, too!"

"I realize—"

"You had better!"

He nodded in solemn surrender.

"You could prove your word by putting your lips here." She tapped her bottom lip. "Lest you'd rather mope than *fiddle* around some with your young bride, old bear. But, there I—I go, playing hard to get again."

TWENTY-FOUR

The hum of overworked propellers received a mutual grumble from Tull and his bride. He squinted when he counted four propellers, four display plates, and enough projection lenses to relay every corner of the plot. Jules shielded blameless Hazy from every lens and laughed at miserable timing whilst her husband rose to meet the intrusion with obvious contempt. With nothing to hurl, his hands felt useless.

"Maybe we should've brought the bear."

"I—I don't imagine Nelly Belly would help you here."

"*Nelly Bell*—"

Jules goosed him in time that he jumped with surprise. She proved more refined than he toward the audience of faces who considered her husband without charm. She then stepped in front of him. "Honored Ones. Guardian Tull still mends, and—"

"What's this?" Judge Gary Lee Madár disapproved with harsh eyes. "Are you not assigned to another, Abettor Shannon? Where is the scarecrow you serve?"

"I'd remind my fellow that Abettor Shannon's time does not belong to us." Judge Otto Meynell Chessy smiled in a way that lifted his cheeks and buried his eyes but did not soften Tull's posture. "My brightest former novitiate is on her own time."

Jules tilted her head downward and concealed the well-pleased smirk her former benefactor, oft her judge, deserved. Her husband kept his stare fixed on Madár.

"You appear lavish with your time, Guardian, and uncaring toward your judges. Those you serve see your neglect and—"

"*How* he mends is not our concern." A second time Otto proved a defender. "How *are* you mending?"

"Sprawled on my back much of the time, Otto."

TULL

Three of the new judges shared curious expressions. Not sneering Madár. The Jacobian then winced when Jules prodded him.

"My apologies, *Judge Chessy*."

Otto fanned his soft face, as if the sound of his title off the Guardian's lips might make him lose consciousness. "Guardian Green reports all is well for him. We've proven fruitless in gleaning an audience with Guardians Ozul, Bright Moon, or Pine."

"Yet, we found you," Madár proved his disdain. "After you told them to scatter."

"Guardian Tull is not a judge and we are, by no means, his Guardians. Mightn't we learn from his fourteen spans of keeping safe our territories?"

"That count is debatable," Judge Harding Dwiazda Meeker weighed in, "but he is the grandson of one of our finest predecessors. Her name has earned him leeway in his efforts to challenge that misborn Pine and keep—"

"Do forgive me." Tull stomped on the first compliment Judge Meeker ever paid him. The way his elder huffed, he might never earn another. "I have kept no soul safe from Guardian Pine. I cannot name the fool who started the tale of his hand in this scheme, but—"

"Chief Inspector Grover is the fool"—now Madár interrupted—"and your oldest friend, is he not?"

"Yes, he is. I tell you, I faced Asham Benjamin Gera at my judge's cabin."

"You're certain of this, Nelson?"

"As sure as the Triune purposed me." He faced Otto's display plate, but noticed the attention of the Creighton Territory's new advocate and bowed his head. "I ask your forgiveness, Judge Kind Hand, I ought to have informed you of your Guardian's dereliction afore now."

He remained silent till the expectant soul he observed in a mending chamber, and ruler over Asham's territory, offered an appreciative nod.

"Guardian Ozul learned how Judge Katch bolstered his alms and removed beacons from the necks of any soul who met his fee. I suspect that's why none of your chiefs have tracked down my fellows. That would include Lucy, Asham, and perhaps his abettor, Timothy Todd McCrea."

Jules offered a bullish retort through both nostrils but held her tongue.

"If you can't find Nita and Olley, trust she's protecting him. If you can't find Pine, seek George. If he can't find him, then trust that the Larson Territory sits without

Guardian." He caught how Jules's hair drifted on the breeze. Soothed by her strands, his agitation dimmed.

"Judge Madár, the Guardians continue to abstain from your territory as ordered by Judge *Conliffe*. Judge Kind Hand, by the setting of the next moon, I'll resume my habits of patrolling your territory, along with the Archibald and the Jacoby Territories. As for the Larson Territory, the Carpenter Territory, and yours, Otto, there's no one better than George to oversee the souls there."

His reassurance settled the new judges, each limited in their dealings with him. Otto nodded in approval of Tull's *management* and offered Jules a wink when he caught her proud glance. "I would say he mends well indeed!"

"A benefit of the mending chamber!"

Tull held his tongue till Judge Kind Hand looked troubled by the remark. "Advocate Kind Hand, as you and your unborn babe suffer sleep terrors, might I suggest passionflower?"

The judges stirred at the reveal of their fellow's struggles and how well-informed the Jacobian proved. Judge Elsie Ilona Kind Hand stirred, but the projection-glider teetered to let her seem unaffected. "You have learned of this?"

"You seek appeasement for si'el uni'epotus."

Whilst Reformers eradicated the worst of diseases, some infirmities proved as ancient as the firstkind's warring. Loughery-Ruben Syndrome, which presented in mothers and those they bore, struck the harshest. The syndrome aroused the hearts, stole the sense of balance, and invited vibrant sleep terrors of undoing and grief. Blameless souls born to those who suffered oft towed a rarer struggle unto their end—a distinctiveness the firstkind called si'el uni'epotus—due to hereditary conflicts between mother and father.

"My mother suffered your woes when she bore me." This he seldom regarded, but for Jules's sake. "Even now, immersion goads my heart."

The judge laughed, as if decorum faded. "My son stirs, too, when we rest in the mending chambers. I liken this time to holding a hummingbird in my hands, he's so anxious! I must remember *passionflower*."

Tull exemplified distinctiveness. "Sister Lois Westmore and the souls in her care raise some of the finest, though a commune for Partakers in Judge Madár's territory has developed a heartier crop. I believe between the lot of us, a soul will arrange for you to receive a rooted bouquet."

"I thank you. I *do* thank you." Her warmth coaxed better characteristics from the judges and Guardian well beyond the attempts of others.

While the male judges kept silent, Tull asked something of she whose heart might fail whilst bringing her son unto them. "How may your Guardians serve you better, Judge Kind Hand?"

"O, yes, I recognize your concern. We've studied the laws, abided by them, but nothing mirrors the power to define them. Just this morn I've observed how my comprehension affects another in their purpose."

From her own words, Judge Kind Hand of the former Damaris Territory offered the Creighton Territory a judge far removed from Hansel Ornlam Hofnarr.

"Both of, I dare not say *sides*, but *causes*, our causes, have suffered. I presume our wise and gentle brothers, who sit on this bench with me, share my belief that the safe-keeping of every soul holds invaluable significance; not just my son's purpose. Our numbers have suffered too long. What, Guardian, do you require to let us believe that we *are* kept safe?"

Tull looked toward Jules first, then toward Hazy. "Allow the Guardians and abettors access to our judges' reels till those against us are caught."

"*Caught*? You mean to let them live?"

"The Guardians aren't executioners, Judge Meeker. If our former fellows face sentencing, you'll have chance to prove how you'll judge these territories." Though he withheld a hunch from Jules, he spoke with confidence. "Only they might name who set them against those you served."

"I see no fault in that logic." Judge Kind Hand smiled over them.

Judge Madár groaned as he leaned back in his seat on twisted limbs and challenged Tull's upright posture. "Provided you uphold your purpose and see that we cannot withhold what we never possessed."

"Give the Jacobian what he needs. All our access, minus what Mumus keeps even from us. Let us see what he does." Judge Meeker followed his remarks with a tickled laugh that made others smile.

"Then we are unanimous!" Otto half-cheered. "Leander offered his endorsement first . . . with his granddaughter's generous approval."

"I have the support of the Larson Territory?"

Otto put an end to that concern. "I believe you could tell us how well Sister Lois Westmore avoids our technologies. She and Katch wasted spans bickering over purpose and rightness, and all the while he plotted that she would succeed him. Though, I imagine he intended some spite for every soul; including his unrealized scion!"

"The Larson Territory *will* endorse you," Judge Kind Hand summarized.

Tull could tell tales of Katch's games and imagined the changes intended by the Reformer whilst he guarded Hazy. "To keep our judges informed, Abettor Shannon and I will see to the raising of the blameless soul abandoned by those we seek."

"I know you'll both look after her well. Lest my fellows object, I'll perform a homestead review and gauge the child's health and learning."

Not one judge protested Otto's plan.

"Spectacles."

"Abettor Shannon?" Judge Madár spoke up. "*Spectacles*?"

"I—I s'pose she needs her eyes checked," she glanced toward Tull, "is all."

Madár and Otto both adjusted their eyewear. The latter declared, "See to that."

"I—I thank you."

"Then we are adjourned. Keep us apprised, Guardian."

Jules shivered from the authority of Meeker's voice and Madár's cold stare but remained in a submissive posture as the projection-glider took flight.

"That wasn't too painful. Though, I heard the daughter of Victor Simon Shannon *s'pose* afore our judges."

Jules brushed his arm. "I—I thanked you for standing up for us. You wouldn't have done that *afore* you woke."

He offered no challenge; rather, he let her correct him.

"I—I *imagine* we have to regard Sister Lois as our authority now, but you can't blame me if I—I prefer Otto or Judge Kind Hand. Judge Kind Hand was nice."

"We do well to regard all mothers while we have them."

"Will she . . ." Jules touched her breast near the heart.

"She sees her end afore she holds her son."

His bride fixed her sloe eyes upon him. "You would help her if you could."

"Yes."

"You believe another turned Asham and Lucy against our old judges?"

"Brutes and fools require direction."

"I—I should tell you something."

"My attention is yours."

TULL

"Best I—I *show* you." From the interior pocket of her jacket, she removed her handheld. She activated the device and angled the glass plate till they shared the view. He kissed her crown afore the flowing color gathered all the attention. "Remember my friend Pez?"

"Has a soul ever forgotten Pez?"

"She oft claims so. When Carl told me that they took you to Mannering, and since Bluebird was full, I—I asked around all the other chamber houses to get you moved. She let slip that Anya mends at the Caidin Chamber House." She accessed a bay of still images. "This is her as of the past morn."

Suspended in a copper exoskeleton, clothed in bandages, and adorned in tubes, Anya Nora Rains looked two shades of awfulness *less* than Tull's worst fear for any soul. A clear mask held her face together, concealed her bold eyes, and almost convinced Tull that Jules presented the wrong patient. Equipment kept her heart beating, filled her lungs with air, and plotted the activity of her mind.

"She's received an experimental spine that her father designed. I—I saw one, well, saw a scale model of one at a medical exposition that Honor and I—I attended. Fine needles are inserted into the nerves, then this alloy-ceramic likeness is fitted in place of the damaged spine. The nerves are protected, the body retains mobility, but she'll never sleep on her back again. At this stage, no soul can say if she'll stand, walk, or move on her own either.

"The medical report logged her first trauma surgery on the fourteenth morn of the previous moon. When a soul falls from a point so high, their body *bounces*. Once she landed, she lost her ability to lift her own weight. They report she almost drowned in *salt*water. Pez says she jumped—"

"Jumped?"

"The security logs at her home show that she was alone, and the rails around her terrace would require a climb. As much as I—I dislike her, I—I'm one of the last souls who'll believe she jumped. Lest she was getting away from a worse end. *Worse*, like an *uncounted soul*."

"He claimed he went after her for what she did to me." Tull heard Jules's exasperation over his soft reveal but his focus led elsewhere. "The fourteenth morn of the previous moon?"

"Afore you were *you*."

"Sister Lois let me believe a soul spotted Anya at the church while I mended."

TULL

"*Judge Westmore* manipulates you because you believe all Reformers are noble."

The barb felt familiar.

"Pez told me every time they imagine Anya's on her last breath, she fights back." Jules tilted her head and observed, but never hindered Tull's view. "With my build, I—I would struggle against Lefty. She's at least one head shorter and tows little chance of overpowering him in a fair fight; letting pass how oft she's proved wrong her doubters in other ways. Why end Monteith or try to end Anya if another soul points him toward this victim or that?"

"Few would connect them, and not having a beacon permits much freedom."

"Does he seek to humble our Guardians?"

"Understanding his reasons isn't part of my purpose. He blames Monteith's end on Tim." He knelt and ensured the duvet kept Hazy warm. "Don't let Anya be the first sight she sees when she wakes."

Jules grinned and cradled the already-dimmed plate. "Why do I—I have an idea that you two made good partners in that last land?"

"Fret not. You remain our favorite of all the other souls in the land." He kissed Hazy's brow, then rose and offered Jules the same affection. The sting of all the times he withheld regard or encouragement from them made him wince in shame. "Could I ask if my bride still resents my request to stay here till our purpose against our fellows ends?"

"She doesn't resent you. She resents having to leave you for longer amounts of time so she can get to work on time. And she resents not learning what you will do here that you cannot do at the loft?"

He responded with the ornery grin she adored. "I'll show you."

Creatures & Creeps

An Interim

The 2nd Eve beneath the Moon of the Wandering Fog

The 114th Winter of the Accession

In the Care of the Helper, who keeps souls from fruitless wandering.

<u>9 Pierce Trail</u>

The Homestead of Alixus Elam Katch.

A place untouched by kindness.

Near an entanglement of buckthorn trees that grew on opposing hillsides, there sat a moss-eaten home that belonged now to no one. Vacated by the owner, yet undisturbed in the belief he could wake again, the place sat like an isolated tomb unknown by all mourners. The Larson Territory knew *mourning*, though. No judge, no Guardian, and no abettor represented them.

Their new judge, who never served a heart's beat as scion, embodied the *former* customs. Sister Lois Westmore strayed from the eye of neighbors, lived behind walls, and lived free from technology. If she accepted, she marked the first judge of another bloodline than Marvin Elam Katch, his elder brother, Sidney Elam, their mother, Alixus Elam, and her elder brother, Harry Newton Katch. Alixus took the authority and virility from her sibling, then put the knife to her sons. Not even Lois was so chaste.

By the time Alixius reached the height of her power, every masculine soul of the territory *proved* their purposes hers to reshape. Her hatred of uncleanness and sexuality bloodied every house for three of their four eras; Robbie Rudat Pine included. Judge Alixus Elam Katch survived eighteen chronicled attempts to distance her soul from her body. She met each attempt with brute retaliation and lived ninety-nine spans till a spider bite delivered her to her end.

Those who bore blameless souls, by her law, agreed to castration of the father afore the child's thirteenth moon, lest the father move from the territory and never return. The locals grew either without siblings or in homes with many fathers. Since most fathers abandoned their families for homes along the hem of the territory, they made new families. Now, in the fourth era, not one soul of age expected fruitfulness.

The Larson Territory, much like the homestead, existed beneath neglect. Though *Judge* Westmore's outpost thrived, the mass graves and declining repopulation kept the territory barren. Lest she changed the law, familial lines would end with this era. So few Larsonites knew the Reformer that none *hoped* for their futures.

The territory made the ideal hiding place within fields of barrenness and neglect. When the creature whom Tull discovered beneath the Church Amid the Shadows resurfaced, none noticed her. Washed in the sea and scrubbed by coral banks, Si'el Uaen Söi'eä hid her shimmer beneath the knotted branches of those trees that cast shadows upon Alixus Elam Katch's home. Not the welcome her *kind* oft met.

Wolves howled from the neighboring Creighton Territory; not to frighten, but from their own fright. All the eve's predators hid from *her*; still, she trembled in the newness of the age. With sparse covering and surrounded by the scraping branches of trees culled in the gathering season, she turned her gaze toward the brilliant and horrific sky-fires. Gone were the stars and the heavens of her blamelessness.

If *one* of her father's line discovered her, damnation awaited. She made her stature small; the way she remembered her mother, and her mother's line. Even then, she remained taller than any head in the land. So, she kept hidden in a frigid stream of slow-moving water and let her coal-black hair spread against her back like the branches of the trees.

The creatures that patrolled the secondkind frightened her, too. Their eyes blinded her, and their voices hurt her ears, whilst their bizarre shape spoke to a perversion her mother's line suffered; a fixation on the inner workings of the body. Like her own brass skeleton, the projection-gliders looked to her as birds composed of copper and nickel skeletons. She wanted to stay undiscovered, and likened them to the scavengers that awaited the fall of the beautiful beasts that once ran wild through the same field.

TULL

In low light, the brassiness of her skin appeared dull. This formation of brass was an oddity of her existence. Whereas the secondkind produced oils when they sweated, she produced brass. Her own pores ran rich with the armor that kept Warring Ministers safe in battle. In sleep, where pressure of the bed and fabric touched, more brass overtook the flesh.

The more she stood in the light, ate of the fields, and swam in the Forbidden Sea, the faster her form returned to a flesh-like complexion that resembled her mother. She grew in stature and build, put on weight, shed hair, and even towed the chance of bringing other forsaken souls into the land. Her siblings taught her how to make her teeth less of the celestial lion-like appearance that the firstkind took in battle. Their teeth and eyes, more than their height, startled the Second Creation.

She wanted peace; for her existence, for her siblings, her lineage, and the Second Creation. She loved her mother's line, and marveled over the purpose of such simple creatures. The war of the First Creation excluded her. They abhorred her, called her an abomination, and kept her from knowing their Creator.

Her brothers, Tai'bu Kaas and Vi'emane, warred too. The eldest wanted a serene rule, the youngest wanted turmoil and servitude from the second heirs. Both sheltered her, which ended all they agreed upon. She *sensed* that Vi'emane slept still and took hope in the idea. As for Tai'bu Kaas, she prayed he enjoyed peace, but sensed he suffered tremendous pain.

The scent of their pet, Otai'ele, lingered near the abandoned farm; frail, but unmistakable to her, and not known to the secondkind. She towed no expectation of seeing her siblings, but *part* of a familiar pet—one of Yah's Fallen First—rested in the house where Alixus Elam Katch ruled and where Marvin Elam Katch kept his wicked playthings. Her eyes, which at rest shimmered like the orange moon, flared in brilliant delight as another scent reached her. From the cracks in the stone skirt of the house, a scent that produced an ache in her belly lured her nearer.

"WAM Radio. All eve and into the morn. Stay tuned."

TULL

The obnoxious jingle of the territory's widest broadcast radio station hid the tremble associated with the movement of a creature like Si'el Uaen Söi'eä. Abysmal shades of green and yellow fell from the open entryway of the kitchen where Robbie Rudat Pine took his last meal, and uncovered patches of bubbled enamel and rust stains on the cabinetry. Other indescribable stains seeped from beneath the doors and coagulated in dust-blanketed shadows. Rodents crept along the seams of the rooms but evaded the home's new tenant.

Even the noise from the radio fell short of his ears, yet spilled into every empty room of the dingy house. A tongue split into three tail-like shapes raked across cracked teeth. Those teeth forever broke the skin of the lips and stained them with caked blood and infected scabs. Now, a face once known for mischievous smiles bore the look of genuine wickedness as he ran fork and knife through his next meal of boiled eel and beets.

"For all the memories of my awful blamelessness, a soul never knows true despair till the loneliness of an outcast's path steals all other choice. O, the joy from eating a meal other than another soul's spoiled refuse!"

> "You're listening to the arch address of Jacoby Territory Advocate Leander Jonathan Bromley on WAM Radio."

Asham turned his head toward the radio, as though a person sat in the room with him. He expected gratitude from the new judge, and listened with an intent ear as he stuffed his mouth with a full eel.

"Offer your gratitude as my footstool, lest I introduce you to Marvin's dungeon," he hammered the floor with his boot heel as he threatened the radio. "Then you best not blaspheme me at all!"

When his meal slipped free as he laughed, he prodded the tail back into his broken mouth. He swore the territories once regarded him as the most beautiful of all scarecrows. Now, rodents fled the sight of him. He still observed his reflection with conceit, yet he almost choked as he swallowed the eel without chewing. The flesh of his face turned multiple shades of red and yellow, and thick bile ran from his mouth as he coughed in a manner that spoiled his amusement.

TULL

> "I have served my beloved friend and worked hard to see us prosper, as I have prospered, beneath his rule and the rule of Mohr Dale Howarth, and Juanita Gene James afore him. I bear a tremendous weight as I now serve you. The tears that salve their absence too germinates an Era of the New Judges."

"Ingrate! All is well! All is well! So ends the rule of our foes."

Asham shut his eyes as he forced his side teeth into a beet with a sawing motion. Though the juice stung his sensitive mouth, he hammered a tin jar against the table. The scent, though tart like licorice, drew his ink-black iris threw a blood-red, irritated sclera and let him focus through the pain. As he reduced the root vegetable to mush, he tilted back his head, lest he spill onto his shirt in admitted defeat.

"There's nothing as contrary as finding one's soul worthless, but not without purpose."

> "Judge Bromley, have you chosen your scion?"
>
> "I have."

"Notice that he's calm only long enough to needle interest?" Asham pressed his tongue against a fractured tooth. "How admirable I find him."

> "When I've reached my end, I'll pass my burden to Nelson James Tull; the Guardian and rightful judge of this territory."
>
> "You would have a Guardian ascend—"
>
> "Guardian Tull, from his blamelessness, showed bravery and let belief guide him. I say he will serve all Jacobians as judge, and I believe he'll show our blameless in every territory a soul worth trusting, if others let him."

"'If others let him.'" He laughed from his belly. "Nelson will hate this! And yet, he cannot strike Bromley down lest he promotes his very will!"

> "Who *seconds* your motion? Truly! You have the approval of *two* sitting advocates, do you not?"

TULL

"In point of fact, I hold the approval of *four* seated judges: Otto Meynell Chessy, Elsie Ilona Kind Hand, Harding Dwiazda Meeker, and the esteemed Sister Lois Westmore."

"But Sister Lois Westmore hasn't—"

"*Judge* Westmore. You'll not make that mistake twice in my presence. Judge Westmore represents our new purpose. A purpose filled with hope, with dignity, and with grace. Who are we to contradict her wisdom?"

A swarm of voices challenged his announcement and nominated other souls in Tull's stead.

"Enough of this! My choice stands as these trees."

"Did Scion Katerena Yvette Mumus oppose your choice, Judge?"

"I have work to do; as do we all."

The reel reached an end and stillness bled into the room, till the familiar jingle of the radio station disrupted Asham's train of thought. He wiped the corner of his frayed mouth with the collar of his shirt and gauged how the judges of the Jacoby Territory upended his plan.

"I wanted to wait a tick and scare them well into winter. As our honored one says, 'I have work to do.' Why, if some rabble-rouser went about hindering judges, our sullen friend might step into a role of ruling over the territory that turned their collective back on him and cast him into this purpose he's led in the first place. All is well. All is well!"

A creeping noise settled and stilled the rats as he took another breath.

"You say something?"

The jarring racket of scraping against a wooden surface drew him into a hurried sprint toward a closed door. He fumbled with the skeleton keys, wrestled the rusted lock, and forced a swollen door from an uneven frame. As he burst into the spare room, he discovered the entire outer wall *torn* from the home's exterior.

Si'el Uaen Söi'eä looked beautiful, though caught, but her face changed as she sensed the spirits that entwined Asham's soul. She snapped her feline-like teeth and roared with an intensity that batted him from the room. Her flesh-and-brass figure raced from sight, hammering the ground beneath her tremendous proportions.

TULL

Debris fell from the torn house in her wake, and the eve swallowed her shape as the attacker of judges' vision failed.

She offered no warning, no reason for her intrusion, so the current trespasser searched for a cause. Dusty shelves, empty drawers, and undecorated walls offered little. One glass jar filled with five black relay discs—stolen from gliders—remained. A tin held more of the beacons that Katch took from the necks of those who shed their beliefs in the Triune.

From his time away in the mountains, Asham learned the ways of creatures like the Seko'tae. When he found a barren spot, where Katch kept the eye of the soul harvester—Otai'ele—who tasted Asham's blood and pursued him to Bliss's cabin, he perceived that she caught the scent of a creature familiar to Si'el Uaen Söi'eä. He then considered the traces of other souls on him and laughed. In the presence of a giantess, Asham Benjamin Gera laughed.

IV. | Still

Twenty-Five

The 4th Morn beneath the Moon of the Wandering Fog

The 114th Winter of the Accession

In the Care of the Helper, who keeps souls from fruitless wandering.

<u>1 cubit west of the Jacoby-Shelby border</u>
90 parasang from the Shelbian settlement of Kërcim
and the home of Edythe Frances Ozul.

The constant wail of creatures unsettled even the fog that drifted through the trees near the valley where the first Guardians ended Bärz'yim; a monstrous horde that endured the Accession. Most souls believed the place haunted, for not even the Kuusa Si'epä dwelled there. An occasional rustle in the trees, a loud thud in the darkness, and the indiscernible chatter of shrill voices added to suspicion. Tull sat idle, sans coat or gear, and without the slightest interest in disproving gossip. They were the tales of blamelessness, compiled upon pages chocked with brilliant illustrations.

He sat not far from D'Aramitz Abbey, though two hillsides obstructed path from perch. No trace of Hazy or Jules. No sighting of Asham or Lucy. Shy of his shadow's span reaching the Shelby Territory and provoking that unruly lot, he passed the time revisiting old reels and those he kept near in the current span.

Some of the names, relationships severed by conflict or death in later seasons, proved bothersome to witness now; where simple groanings created the first trickle of flowing shame and troubles to come. How he took others for granted! How little of

TULL

his compassion he gave! That soul needed *reset*, however much that previous land meant to who he became.

Then, there was Lucy. No warmth existed between them. In point of fact, till the moment he carried her from Gutefiel, no interaction existed since early in the one hundred thirteenth seasons. Now, he sat brooding over a reel sent from her while he mended in a chamber.

Tull stared at her true image with flat eyes, but shrill voices drew his attention toward figures that fled opposite his location. Five males, three females, and some breed of four-legged creature disturbed the air like branches scraping the sky. Had they run toward him, he had help to spare. By their own laws, though, the residents of the Shelby Territory kept the Guardians off their plots.

The distraction deprived him of re-watching Lucy's reel, and he slipped the device into his trouser pocket. He listened to the voices turn to whispers, then into stillness. His focus rose on the ash that fell like a winter's storm and snuffed out the sky-fires visible through treetops. The sight brought a smile to his face.

"How right you were, Leander. Mighty indeed."

A sudden clap corrected his posture and honed his nerves. Then, a sleek figure in a hooded coat ascended from a hillside set lower than the one the others ran from earlier. From the scent in the air, she of sleek build smoked another cacao-laced cigarette. Her feet stopped with a gradual, effortless glide and her voice fanned like the smoke she exhaled. "Come to swat me then, have you?"

He never afore paid mind to the ways that Nita Naomi Ozul favored Lizzie Dale Conliffe. Stern, angular faces, cool and contemptuous eyes, lean builds; predators' spirits in preys' disguise. Now, he realized the true slight she towed. She served her territory beneath the heel of a judge who never confessed to fathering her.

"In truth? I meant that harvester for Marko. I imagined how he might writhe as he met his end one bite at a time."

Tull looked as though he suspected her success.

"Relax, will you? I've not seen him!" She found no gain in a lie.

"When did Cam exit Gutefiel?"

The oddness of his mind took her by surprise and drew color from her cheeks till the hues of her eyes flared like the sky-fires. "You traveled here on the off-chance to ask that of me?"

"I once walked three moonsets to deliver my bride the first flower of the thaw."

TULL

"Tell me, what's the count of moonsets you've sat in wait for me? Truly!"

"I've watched the moonset from this perch two *unfruitful* morns now." He admired the sky-fires. "The approaching morn should bring a mist. Cam?"

Her poise swayed, and the train of her coat collected ash. "Cameron Lou Fenner entered the eighth eve and exited the ninth with nothing more to prove."

"Mick?"

She gasped a misty, smoke-filled breath at his bizarre line of thought. "Mick Curtis Whigham cracked the foot of his prosthetic leg the fourth morn and walked out *spewing* vulgarities. I'm told he stank of vermouth."

"Hector?"

"Nelson! Why are you here in the woods? *These* woods of all places?"

"As your successor, I must determine who hunts our judges; lest you enjoy that many believe you and Pine responsible. Even after the way you've kept us these last thirteen moons, most fear your broken heart."

"Asham and Lucy hunt our judges. How hard did you strike your head when Ernie's cabin—"

"Neither of us believe them capable of a well-crafted ruse. Hector?"

"Hector Geirolf Picadura returned his summons in a jar of, one trusts, *his* excrement. And, afore you ask, none have seen Alison Brackett Nance, Herb Atkins Benest, or Ember Willows Martel since last our judges sequestered us. Perry would not risk getting so near to his fruit."

Tull turned pensive. So deep, that he seemed rude as he ignored Nita.

"We must face that our fellows were not our allies, and you ought to reimagine the future of the outfit." She stepped toward the scorched line that marked the Shelby Territory's end. "Perhaps now we create new futures?"

"Lucy abandoned Hazy, as we warned our judges she would."

Nita exhaled a mouthful of smoke with a single huff. "Better that child has your bride, I say. She was purposed to keep a soul true."

"Why didn't you let us comfort you, Nita?"

"Am I who needed comfort?" She took a dizzying, chest-aching drag from her cigarette and pointed the burning end at him. "The one comfort you can claim was that I stood with you at Bliss's cabin!"

He let her laugh at his expense and watched the steps she took.

"Why you'd die for any of them horrifies me!"

TULL

"We've died for worse." He remembered her nobility in that previous land; where she and Olley rested together.

A bare leg slipped through the train of her coat as she leaned toward him. "Not another word of that!"

One entire foot crossed into the Jacoby Territory.

"We fend off *Their* monsters and suffer beneath the laws of our own."

He watched the calf muscle swell as she distributed her weight.

"I cannot believe you—of all of us—put your soul in harm's way to protect them. You're a pious, damned fool!"

"*Belief* didn't put me in a mending chamber."

Nita threw her cigarette aside and dragged her back foot nearer to the territorial line as she raised splayed hands. "I had both of my arms broken! I mended."

"How well do you believe Marvin will mend?"

The sudden turn of beauty to bitterness chilled him. Then, that *need* for Shelbian superiority took hold. Her hips and chest spread, her mid-section drew inward, and she lifted her head with a smile as slim as her belief. "That crippled misborn's vile deeds paid for his pain-filled end."

"Ki'eoppa is worse for those who believed but still turned." The moment Nita's heels touched Jacoby Territory foliage, Tull checked the skies for vengeful Ministers. "I've a friend who's seeks to have a conversation with you about our judges."

"What?"

The lights atop Chief Inspector Carl Alvin Grover's rig, and that of the Shelby Territory's chief's rig, blistered the trees and flared in Nita's eyes as the sirens agitated the forest's wails. Where others might have lunged or run, Nita stood surrounded and devoured Tull with cold approval. To his credit, he sat in stillness and never looked away. He proved stubborn in his purpose, well-prodded by the lawlessness of allies.

Carl moved toward the territorial line faster than Nita. On his way downhill, he pressed a device fastened to his belt near a shock baton. A row of seven small lights pulsated a numeric passcode. Larger bulbs on the belly of the projection-glider emulated that passcode, then the device emitted a radiating beacon not unlike the sirens on his rig. Like that, the privatized glider captured Nita's confession and arrest for review by the judges.

"Guardian Ozul, by the law—"

"All I've done is protect my Olley."

TULL

Carl stopped and looked toward his deep-rooted friend.

"I believe you. In his absence, I must stop you; lest the morn comes, and he no longer recognizes his bride, as I no longer recognize my friends."

"By the law of—"

"I am your fellow and friend. You could see to my purpose"—she swept her hand toward the shadow-blanketed forest behind her—"*there.*"

"Nelson?"

Tull ignored Carl and listened as his fellow kept her punishment from the judges' lips. No soul who grasped what existed within the shadows made a thoughtless offering to enter them.

"Send me after Voler. Truly, he has committed greater woes than I."

More rested there than Vernard Voler. Time compounded upon space and forged streams of darkness that carried away souls. Only souls trapped by immense despair sought hope in those streams. A *land* of Volers did not equal one soul like Nita. Even so, the shame of imprisonment paled against the rejection she faced from her husband when he learned how she acted in his name.

"Everything square, Grover?"

Both Guardians faced Carl, who addressed the voice that broke through the radio attached to a wire-free rig on his belt. "The problem's in hand, Guild."

Nita pulled back at the neck of her covering and revealed a dull key.

"This is in hand, no? You're letting me constrain her?"

Nita shook her head in the slightest way.

The inspector crowded his friend. "Almighty! Nelson, you recall the count of souls who've come back from the shadows. You recall none were—"

"*Guardians,*" Nita spoke over him with her smooth tongue. "None were *Shelbians.* Let me find Voler and atone there."

"You're down how many members? Look at the damage Asham's done. Do you really want to lose one more soul to the shadows?"

"Guardians do not submit to chiefs!"

"I speak to my friend!" Carl's authority grated Nita's velvet tone. "You have a better heart than this, Nelson. You must lead those who aren't well enough to lead."

Nita showed fear that the inspector reasoned in a way she could not.

"In thirteen moons, I'll surrender the headship. Return to this place, in this time, on the brightest eve beneath the Moon of the Falling Stars, and I'll find you here. All

TULL

will be forgiven, and I'll see to your recovery those seven moons afore the next offering." He paused, then unfurled another of her secrets. "I'll see to Olley and your father's protection in your stead."

The color drained from Nita's face.

"Chief, if you prefer not to see . . ."

"Almighty!" He exhaled and braced. "I stay."

Tull approached Nita, and she let the chained key fall into his hand.

"I wasn't yet Hazel-Sue's age when my mother put me in this." She shivered. "I await your hand, my trusted friend."

He proved his hand steady and aim keen as he offered a silent prayer over her. The key he held, bent rather than shaped, fit into a miniscule lock in the choker that Nita wore around her sleek neck. When the lock disengaged, three needles as fine as a strand of hair exited her throat and protruded from the surface of the neckpiece. The unfastened choker fell away and coiled on the ground like a snake, which Nita flung with her foot. As he pocketed the key, she slipped from her coat.

Carl looked away. "I don't believe you're doing this."

"Your ears work well enough, Chief." Nita crouched and gathered her coat, which she flung over his shoulder. "So, I speak with certainty when I remind you that you heard me request this path. I consider our headship's trust my great honor."

"My ears work as fine as my nose when I smell—"

"Nelson." Nita turned toward her friend. "The moment I saw Monteith, I suspected *her*. I raced toward Gutefiel, imagining how I might rile her while she remained inside.

"Then my *sister* called to me. As if, in my position, I knew nothing of our father? I bore too many secrets. I plotted too many revenges. Now, see the cost I pay."

He took her hand. "This is not your end."

Her smile gave Carl a chill and he turned away as tears filled her eyes. "A doctor in Sevier has a gift for non-traditionalism. She's *used* my Olley in ways I hadn't counted. Made him into a *creature* I struggle to recognize. You'll see.

"She keeps a site beneath the Sevier Aquarium Exposition. In the archway past where the octopi *bob*. She took a tentacle from one. S'pose that makes a septapus. Tells of her mind, I tell you. I watched my Olley till I couldn't bear the sight of him."

"And, you believe *he* will go into that place for you?" the chief huffed.

TULL

"Your dove visited every peak till you returned to the territory from the offering. She has an affinity for the ice cap bears; not that I've intruded, as she's never intruded upon me. I've oft respected the trueness of her heart for you and for Hazel-Sue. Keep near to her and don't stray."

Tull weighed the value of Nita's words and kept her account of Jules.

"If you find my word is true, set Olley loose for me."

"If your word to me is true, I'll do what I can for you both."

"Then we have an accord. George will watch over you in the absence of the rest of us. Be kind to whatever remains of me, and I will seek to remember that Nelson James Tull remains my trusted friend."

"Guardian Ozul, you—"

"My name is Nelson James Tull, fourth Guardian of the Jacoby Territory, and, in the name of I'Esh, I speak to all creatures that reside in these shadows!"

Rustling increased till even the fallen leaves sounded like chimes as they scraped at one another's skins. The temperature dropped while darkness swelled, but a single voice swatted back like the thunder.

"Oi, saa stune et jahy läti'it si'eli'ute, kuule mi'onun äi'äneni."

Carl deciphered none of his friend's words, but the tone proved that he threatened the dark the way a lone drop of rain threatened the desert sand. Nita radiated as she listened and tiptoed on slender legs, as aware of the nip in the air as the cold that awaited. She stopped at the hem of faint light, admired how a single soul fought for her, then looked toward Carl as if unsure he could protect Tull the same way. The inspector knew the language of a dismissal and corrected his posture.

Without further retort, the Guardian from the Shelby Territory dove with grace. She fell headlong into a pool of shadow that rested between two mighty cedar trees. Her overlapped hands never disturbed the terrane. The shadows pulled her from sight as she entered a place few braved with only a dust of her outer layer shed to remain as a tether in this land.

"Almighty!"

"Sii'llä oh'än on mi'nuen raako'as sesarei. She is my beloved sister."

"Almighty!" The inspector repeated and circled behind his friend.

The choker that kept back the infesting spirits let the wearer enter the shadows without obstruction. Freed of the unnatural, Nita increased her odds of surviving *the swim*. Those souls born in the Shelby Territory counted the shadows as a portion of the waterways and inlets that irrigated the territories and the trees that stretched high above head. Nita possessed countless books by theorists who never dared face what she stared down. In Tull's heart, he believed her the bravest soul of all, and withheld eulogy.

"Our judges won't abide this. You might say all is forgiven but I tell you, they won't feel the same. They'll nab her as soon as she gets back."

"Did you not hear? She's not coming back. I imagine she'll seek a version of Olley in the shadows and find a new purpose *there*."

The inspector kicked away leaves in search of Nita, as if he might uncover her. Tull respected his friend's need for wisdom and let him snoop till he dealt with the current Chief Inspector Guild, whilst he hurried up the opposite hillside. A lone quail ascended from the hood of Carl's rig as the Guardian reached the hilltop. His limbs caught up to his heart, and he pulled open the passenger door with a relieved smile.

Hazy raised a straight arm out from beneath his coat and pointed toward the console. "I pressed the siren! But only *one* time."

"You did well."

She crawled toward the edge of the seat and relied on gravity to pull her the rest of the way. Tull scooped her up as she plummeted and raised her till her cheek nestled his shoulder. He draped his coat over her head, fussing over an even hem that let her breathe without exposing her to the elements. Her fingers plucked his suspenders as she hummed a child's rhyme, but never troubled him. Letting pass how the setting disturbed, she let her feet swing as if on another adventure.

"Should we get you home now?"

"Back to Momma?"

"Jules and I seek to keep you a while longer if you let us."

She proved the gentlest creature in all the woods and kept her head nestled toward the Guardian till she unnerved him.

"Hey, whirlybird, can you tell me the address of the church?"

An eager breath raised the pitch of her voice. "Seven-zero-seven Little Oak Way."

"Correct." He then whispered, "Jules loves you."

Her eyes fixed on him and stopped drifting.

"Where else did we go?"

"One-eight-nine-five apple . . . Appledash Road. That's where we run!"

"You're precious to us in every way. Where do we stay when we cross the Loy?"

Her eyes rose, then drifted down. She caught the glimmer on his face, then stared straight into his eyes. "One-seven-two-one Fresnel Park."

He watched the sky-fires gather in her curious eyes and swore he *felt* her neck crane as she took notice of the vivid colors above them. Though he spent much time in a similar pose, on this morn, he watched only the way that she reacted to the firstkind's activity. "See how they fight over us?"

She nodded without sacrificing her view. Ministers and Squires concentrated above the Shelby Territory due to the rampant behavior of their siblings. The sky-fires burned with deeper luster there, and the sparks of battle fell like burning coals. Hazy never shivered in terror, and he savored how she pursed her lips in uncertain curiosity.

"There are lands where souls behave as though their Worthy Creator abandoned them; as though Yah's lavish affections for them ceased. They believe He turned away from them and bears no interest in how they carve out their purposes, but this is deceit. Once, we behaved the same."

Her chin dropped and her eyes found his with absolute, unwavering clarity.

"Then we learned that we are not alone but surrounded, and, in the moments onward and evermore, we've watched armies of might battle; lest our Creator lose even one soul. Me . . . Jules . . . you."

He let too much remain unspoken between them in that previous land and counted every soul that abandoned her there; even his. Even now, where the betrayals of friends bloomed like the thaw, he almost let distraction turn him one more time. Hazy reared back her head without breaking eye contact, pecked his face with a kiss, then rested her head upon his shoulder. Her sweetness took away the sting of those wasted lands and softened his fear of what mistakes he might commit if he declared responsibility over her soul.

"I'll undo every woe this time. *Watch*."

Carl shuffled his feet as he ascended the hilltop and perked up Hazy's ears till she searched for him. That her curiosity twisted the Guardian as she climbed his arms made the inspector chuckle.

"All is well?"

"I stopped seeking to learn as much as you a long time back. *This*"—Carl shook his head—"was a momentary lapse of my sense. How is she?"

"Soon to outsmart me."

TULL

"'In the absence of fathers, the blameless look to heroes to raise them.'" The Countess cited that from Zeck's journal at your dad's interment."

"As you say?"

"As I say." He shooed the fog from the blameless soul. "You keep a good eye on short stuff here. I might make her a deputy!"

"That I will."

Carl held up a lush sack fitted with a drawstring and copper button. "Nita kept this and a receipt for a thousand gold alms in one of her coat pockets. You know what's inside?"

"An offering to the Loy. We take nothing from the Shelby Territory."

Carl waited for Tull to smirk but turned impatient. He then hurled the sack toward the waters and heard the splash. "That sounded like a thousand alms to me."

"That was a big splash!"

"She agrees with me."

Hazy furrowed her brow, as if accused of choosing sides.

"Or not. As bad as those needles looked, ripping out a beacon must slow a soul! I watched them fit my sons' beacons. The way the babe takes that first shock then falls into deep slumber? Almighty! Bea can tell you that those next watches waiting on them to wake lasted evermore!

"Max did fine, but Will came back with the hiccups! Can you believe that? The whole thing made Bea groggy and dehydrated." He then shifted his weight downhill and nodded toward the rig, so they might leave. "Let's get!"

Tull offered him a smirk and a nod, then claimed a seat in the rig and buckled the child in the center seat. As Carl rounded the front end, his feet slipped, and he vanished for a moment. He arose with laughter then limped toward his door.

"Is he your friend?" She wondered as she stared at him.

"Till this moment, I never realized how early you mimicked Jules's bothered tone."

She mimicked his bride's displeased sigh, too, when he withheld his answer, reached across the rig. and opened the inspector's door for him.

TWENTY-SIX

707 Little Oak Way

In the frost-covered Jacobian settlement of Minder.
Where word of Nelson James Tull's homecoming spread.

As advocate scion and headship of the Guardians, Tull felt his reclusiveness fade like the departed warmth of the sowing season. By the thaw, lest he challenged his judges and let the territory believe him insubordinate, a permanent relocation awaited. The privacy that the church offered seemed suited for the protectiveness Hazy needed, though, his bride detested their nearness to the shed bodies of souls mourned and forgotten. For now, he carried his blameless sidekick from Carl's rig to the gate he re-installed on the courtyard fence and prayed the grave markers hid from curious eyes.

True to a reputation that unsettled, Katerena Yvette Mumus had already sent a proxy with a basket of gifts and an invitation to celebrate a new era of judges come the next moon. The gifts included a bottle of plum vermouth from Jules's favorite winery, an elegant handmade doll that resembled Hazy, and neat's-foot oil for boots. Jules teased Tull about that gift. All the reels of him, the tales and legends, even the film of his actions in Gutefiel, and the heiress learned nothing about him *except* his partiality toward old boots gifted to him by her mother.

Hazy proved more like the Guardian, put aside the doll with a complaint of the smell, and joined him on the morn's adventure. Jules smelled nothing; even after two fingers of vermouth opened her sinuses like the thaw opened for the bud in sowing season. Husband and bride perceived the veiled message and took turns checking the roadway for unwanted trespassers. Elsewise, the trio's first eves together in the Jacoby Territory passed without complaint.

TULL

"Remember to greet Jules with a hug and thank her for helping you from your shoes and coat. Will you do that for me?"

Hazy offered an enthusiastic nod, then hugged Tull's neck. He placed her on the interior side of the churchyard and stood the watch as she took the path toward the door of the church. The rigid sway of her arms amused him, but the way she opened the structure's heavy wooden door on her own impressed the inspector who waited on the Guardian. She offered a wave, then slipped into the sanctuary as if helped by an unseen creature.

The morn brought a hard frost that tempted souls to stay indoors and sent Tull back into the warmed rig. He and the chief watched the reel from the new judges, sent without a vote from Madár or either Mumus, that showed Asham and Lucy as they turned on Olley and Marko at the offering. The layout and presentation differed from what he knew of the reels and proved that the judges *spied* upon the secondkind beyond obvious intrusions.

"How a soul could let that child live with them . . ."

Even with the red grit that surrounded the scene, the judges' gliders collected discernible images of all involved. Lucy knew of Asham's return. Worse, she kept the secret from those who searched for him. *When* her heart turned against her fellows mattered less than his belief that she never truly counted them as friends. The truth turned his attention toward the church that kept safe Hazy and Jules; who suffered the most beneath she who scarred him.

"Watch this one now—from the morn you received your basket."

BEACON DESIGNATE: 090.01.302
ARCHIBALD TERRITORY ADVOCATE SCION
KATERENA YVETTE MUMUS.
LOCATION: THE SILAS CHAMBER HOUSE
212 DANTON ROAD

A sleek soul with silken, black hair took long, presumptuous steps through the chamber that housed the fallen judges of her father's era. She moved with a feline's awareness and implied nobility without invitation or a sense of belonging. Her heart never rose a tick and her respiration offered only what air she needed to cast off the fragility of the setting and those deemed *weak*.

She dressed in a fashion that haunted and enticed, letting all who saw her *share* in her endowment. For the amount of flesh that she showed, she bore no *color*. Alabaster white, with no hint of the veins beneath the surface, contrasted her mane and the fabric of her corseted gown. Other than an inlay of gold along the tips, even her nails shimmered like opal daggers.

Her eyes she kept from any lens or eavesdropper. In point of fact, she seemed to know the scope of every device without chasing their attention. She dragged her nails along the octagon chambers of the two most vile judges without regard and entered the space of her uncle as if accustomed to sharing his company. One hand brushed the smooth face of the chamber and another held back her hair while she imprinted a kiss upon the glass between them.

Her breast shifted as she took what looked like her first breath since the reel started. Her head tilted and her hair swayed as she rose and looked over the chambers of all the judges. Even Judge Hofnarr received a chamber. She then pressed a single, gold-tipped fingernail into one of the tubes that fed oxygen into her uncle's chamber.

"Wake, *honorable elders*, and see the plans I have."

She took away her finger, but her touch stayed on the glass. With one hand, she let the tips of nails scratch Marvin Elam Katch's chamber on her path toward an upright chamber and an occupant that captivated her. She kept her talon-like claws tucked behind her back and cast her breath upon Lindy Meren Bromley's tank.

"Soon, I'll enfold this house. Then your care will be mine to decide. Imagine! I could set you in my tower and see the sky-fires burn through the lens of your chamber. A mermaid of my own!"

Katerena flashed a toothy smile and Lindy sank into her recuperative gel as far as she might flee. The scion drew a heart with a mermaid's tail in the condensation, then departed. None stopped her, for they proved concerned in keeping stable the Silas House Mermaid's heart.

Carl ejected the black relay disc. "While the Mumus on this reel is not the soul you've so oft turned contrary, and I near-admire her creeping beneath your nose—"

"Not just my nose, *Chief*."

"*That*—is another's scion threatening a soul you've sworn to defend."

"Judge Bromley's granddaughter?"

"Settled. Our judge isn't so calm."

"I imagine not."

"She is like you? His granddaughter. The way she—"

Tull took a raspy breath as he braced his joints.

"As you say. You will challenge Katerena, will you not? I ask because she makes a habit of invading the lives of souls she frightens. Beneath this moon alone, she's set her eye on Judge Bromley's granddaughter, his scion, his scion's bride, and my future deputy. Why not wrap up this purpose of yours? I no longer crave a winter's chase, and there are other troubles to consider."

Tull wondered if he ought to count them as the same trouble.

"Judges, then Guardians. Then he might go for the scions afore the chiefs."

"He might."

"Well"—the inspector held up the two discs—"*get*. Find him afore he decides."

"Be still." Tull's smirk changed into a wince when he plucked a disc of his own from the pocket of his vest. "I need an authority to see this."

Carl remained tight-lipped and exchanged Tull's disc for the second disc he intended to show. The Guardian sat almost ashamed and grieved.

REVIEWING 1 REEL FROM
CARPENTER TERRITORY GUARDIAN
LUCY BRIGHT MOON.

The first frame showed Tull in a mending chamber. His body twitched, and his head turned in sharp, agitated bursts of energy as turbulent as the pewter hues that radiated from the chamber tube. Whatever he perceived whilst kept beneath provoked violence

TULL

within him; enough that he hammered the glass with a closed fist. His body bled into the restorative gels and from the large-bore needles in his abdomen.

Mechanical alarms and barking voices prompted a view change. The display rotated with the flick of a wrist as Lucy skulked. From over her shoulder, Tull convulsed inside his tank while techs worked to soothe him. A perverse smile formed on Lucy's face without breaking the blunt ledges of her teeth.

"When Harlan reintroduced us, I told you that no souls go without *breaking*. Oft I wondered how you—"

"Open a ninth line afore his heart stops!" a tech shouted loud enough to cancel the betrayer's voice.

Lucy rotated away and her eyes roamed an unshared horizon. "Turns out, the easiest way to beat you is to shove you into water."

"Rebalancing! Almighty! He's near to tearing his umbilical."

"When Asham told me his plan, I worried you would be our biggest obstacle. Then, I watched my abettor and I—I—I knew how to control you."

She glanced over her shoulder like a coward, then spoke as if fearless. "I'll *let* you have what you've wanted but can't do on your own. I'll let Jules have her happiness. I'll do that, and you won't come after me or Asham. In this, you repay me, since I could've ended you at Bliss's cabin."

"Nelson!"

The focus turned again, this time onto the mocked abettor. Dressed in full uniform, she barreled into the Mannering Chamber House. Her stoicism surrendered to helplessness and her face bore the same level of fear she displayed in her voice as she read her husband's display plates.

"You set him in full immersion?"

"We're rebalancing him due to his Loughery—"

"He suffers Loughery-Ruben Syndrome due to si'el uni'epotus or did you not notice his structure!"

TULL

> While a tech challenged Jules, Lucy hid from sight. "Come after us—seek to take *my* happiness—and I'll see you go through this land with nothing but ashes."

Tull let the reel fade. His forearms trembled from elbow to clenched fists, but he never lashed out. He kept his head bowed and prayed to the Creator for restraint. Then, as he repeated his heart's need, the edges of a pair of disc cases cracked in his hand.

"Does she steer Asham or does he steer her?"

"One fool feeds the other."

"You imagine them the puppets on another's string?"

"I cannot prove my certainty."

"Well, I tell you, I inspected the frequency times betwixt Monteith's ransack and McCrea's crime on the aquarium exposition. Hont's deputies seized McCrea the morn afore the last eve Monteith breathed. From what I remember of him, he lacks the wit to cause two tragedies on opposite ends of these territories."

Tull absorbed the information that cleared Tim of Asham's accusation but offered no response.

"What will you do?"

"What a wiser soul ought to have done spans afore."

"Row for the next isle? What's Jules say?"

"She tows the blame over not seeing what she could not see."

"I'll post an extra pass along this route and see which deputies need to impress me and the territory's new scion. Whoever that may be will watch the moon rise and set from this location till I say elsewise."

"I thank you."

"I don't want to be Kemp's subordinate, Nelson. I just got you trained!"

Tull accepted the barb. "Could I ask you to gather a petition of embracement in my name, subordinate?"

The inspector's smile beamed, and he reached across the cab and patted Tull's leg. "I can do that! Yes, I can do that. You'll need a recognized signatory to stand for you."

"If you would."

"I'll make the arrangements and track you down."

"I thank you."

TULL

"Nelson, you don't have to thank me! Look at you! Almighty! You've gone and done something I'll be sure to remember well. Truly!" He breathed in his satisfaction, then settled. "Well. *Get.*"

Tull entrusted the disc to his friend and obeyed, while the chief let the momentum of driving away shut the passenger door. He offered a playful tune on the horn and Tull offered a wave of his hand. But, he bypassed the path toward the church doors, bore no doubt that Hazy completed the tasks he gave her, and roamed the field of graves for a time of meditation and prayer. The territories mourned Ernie Purcell Bliss, which meant that any action from Lucy and Asham attracted objection.

He remembered how Asham made Lana present Hazy to the territories alone, and how Lucy made all around her miserable to further punish Asham for his straying. By the time he observed the next offering, the territories would celebrate the arrival of Hazy's greatest sidekick and tormentor. The mere thought offered Tull a hope-filled breath, and he used that spark of joy to ease the heart of the territories through another relay.

"Beloved!" An easy smile lit his face and tears filled his eyes. "*Beloved.* Our departed judge spoke that word more than any soul in my time. In our time of mourning and remembrance, I ask that we not forget that Ernie Purcell Bliss loved even those who riled him. This I tell you from immense experience!

"Ernie was the steady judge over three Guardians. I never learned his way of letting in other souls with such ease; with no mind for their flaws when their hearts needed an intercessor. I tell you, that's a flaw of my character: my inadequate way of assuring other souls that I regard them with favor."

He winced from the weight of his titles. "As your Guardian, I must not fail you. If my path pleases our Creator, believe that I will follow Those who guide my feet and grant me a purpose. As headship, I tow the blame for the fear my fellows have caused you.

"Soon, and very soon, all will rest with the peace of a Reformer. Till such time, I must ask that you continue to display the resolve of a Guardian. Defend those who belong to your line, care for those who are abandoned, and give honor to your new judges and our Worthy Creator. Believe that I thank you for your patience.

"In this field, we remember the souls of this territory's bravest and those who made a path for us. Souls who cut a path for me." He patted the top of his father's wooden grave marker and let Zeck's copper statue reflect the gleam of the sky-fires.

TULL

"Now, I follow a path that isn't mine alone. I must keep a path that eases the steps of every blameless soul in this land and those babes we've yet to celebrate.

"On this morn, with the backing of the chiefs from the Jacoby and Shelby Territories, and one adored soul, I oversaw the constrainment of Guardian Nita Naomi Ozul—my friend—for her hand in events that enabled the loss of Judges Marvin Elam Katch and Ernie Purcell Bliss. While Nita fought against a common foe, she confessed her mistakes, and offered her own punishment. She maintained the bravery by which she led and entered the shadows where she will guard us against further terrors. Keep our sister in your hearts.

"As to those souls responsible for the injuries inflicted upon Guardian Olley Hendrie Falk, which drove Nita to wrath, I name Lucy Bright Moon and Asham Benjamin Gera—who evermore forfeit their purposes as foes of the secondkind. I tell all authorities to retaliate against them unto their surrender. Further, I ask those who live in territories who refuse the services of the Guardians to also refuse shelter to our aggressors or be counted with them.

"I have given my word to our new judges—and now to you—that these two souls should answer for their hand in the attacks on Judges Ernie Purcell Bliss, Dale Marius Conliffe, Charles Kurtz Elwell, Samuel Herbert Gwynne, Hansel Ornlam Hofnarr, and Marvin Elam Katch. My additional accusation is made against Lucy Bright Moon for the unwanted infestation of Abettor Marko Glenn Stran, who has served these territories yet never known our affection.

"I ask the chief inspectors of all territories and our included remnants to oversee swift and thorough investigation of our betrayers' conduct and renew the outfit's protection of Abettor Timothy Todd McCrea; though he stands accused of crimes that he must explain to our judges. That much I will not cover. I ask that any soul who sees Guardian Robbie Rudat Pine contact me." His smile softened him. "Don't let my scars frighten you."

He breathed for those who watched the resting places of his heroes, the horizon where the sea and the sky-fires met, and his most peaceable expression. "This is not a time for fear, beloved. Be still and be joy-filled in all you can. Hear our new judges and trust that your Guardians, our abettors, and the scions defend you still. I thank you."

Tull ended the relay on the device that Jules lent him and fussed over his father's grave marker. Memories he kept of Patrick James Tull's interment mingled with the reel that Carl shared with him. "I believe they mourned the wrong loss in the Colonel's house. Katerena is a soul with no heart to guide her."

"You know how I dislike those *gadgets.* I cannot see them as you see!"

Tull pocketed the handheld device and faced another Minister, this one with a grandfather's build. "My apologies to you, *Si'an-dro Sa'ähn.*"

He tipped his head. "Remember! Tell me nothing of the land that was, cousin."

"I would only tell you I'm glad to see you *again.*"

"Why? I am but a *clumsy ice cap bear.*"

He who nudged Jules's chair nearer to the Guardian's when they sat on the terrace together, who prepared incense and guidance for the Guardian's retreat to Bliss's cabin, and who kept watch over the church and the surrounding graves, proved temperamental versus the sense of humor of the soul he oft comforted.

"And, you blame me when your siblings catch you talking to no other."

"I called you a clumsy ice cap bear only to remind my bride of our time together at the exposition."

"She needn't any reminder! She's thought of your visit many—"

"I thought we agreed you wouldn't tell me." He paused. "*Many?*"

The Comforting Minister flicked his brow and pursed his lips even as the Guardian smirked over the newfound knowledge.

"I shared your grief over your friend. My brothers and my sisters are no longer welcome near his soul. That is how far from the Creator *your* sibling has turned. To cast away every Minister and every righteous chance! All that remains in the heart is *despair.*"

Tull doubted Asham lost his heart by a single pitiful choice.

"I once heard an expression that tickled me; yes, tickled me to my center. 'How do you eat an elephant?'"

"I've seen an elephant only in photographs."

"'One bite at a time!'"

"Did we eat elephants afore the Accession?"

"I tell you, in this manner, a heart casts out the Helper. One poor choice devolves into a law that takes away the guilt. Then, that law lets in the next choice. Alas! There is still time to mend!

"Your heart worries over many souls: the daughter of the *Straw Worker*, the daughter of *Legalis*, the son of *Ancients*, the daughter of *Valjeta*, the son of *Ragin*, the son of *Valke*, *Bucca*, the daughter of *Ciarain*, and even the daughter of *Ruine*. How I fill scrolls with your worries!"

"You know why I was returned?"

"O, yes. I thank you. Yes."

A breath failed to settle him. "Wherever I've gone—all this—sets me on a course to *do* what's expected of me."

"Not expected. *Asked*."

"Your sister had a definite tone, and that tone veered far from *asking*."

"The warring leaves her *sharp*. She forgets not every soul wars. Try to remember her profound love for you. Every soul on high sings over you!"

"Would you watch over the judges, Si'an-dro Sa'ähn?"

"I *do* watch over them, cousin."

Tull hesitated, forgot his woes, and marveled over the Minister's humming and the gracefulness he emitted. How brawny Si'an-dro Sa'ähn swelled with *delight*, yet refined Enke'loi fought with *barbarity* struck his interest. Tull's kind perverted the two *builds*.

After the Minister draped an arm across his shoulder, Tull confessed, "I feared the influence I'd have on Hazy and Q. J., so I shunned Jules each time she spoke of being their home. Now I see the wrong parent's influence causes a worse effect. The Colonel led Katerena to rot. Asham and Lucy have given me all the anger I need to want to keep them from Hazy, but do I honor her or spite them?"

Si'an-dro Sa'ähn grinned and patted his belly like a kettle drum. "I ask you, why have you limited your purpose by your boasting?"

"I boast?"

"O, how you dull your wit! Some boast with arrogance, some with joy. Your heart boasts through grief, but pain lies to you, cousin. You are closer to our Creator's design for your soul than all your steps afore and afore."

Tull considered the Minister's wisdom and feared all he wanted might crumble come his next mistake.

"Fear created pain's tale and the Liar whispered in every ear of every soul. Our foe seeks to keep us from bringing our Creator joy. If we grieve, our Creator grieves. Even our foe—even *in* those victories—grieves." Si'an-dro Sa'ähn leaned nearer toward Tull. "I tell you, we know who wins in the end!"

"We do indeed."

TULL

"And you!" The Minister prodded Tull's shoulder. "You pulled your friends from a place of wickedness and showed your heart for the son of Valke and his aberrant friend. You faced a brother you despised but did not let him take you from our Creator's plan. You even proved obedient when you went to a church that, you imagined, had no purpose in your return.

"You soothed your bride's heart and satisfied the curiosities of the soul you now call judge. Your siblings' sins only nudged you. The blameless soul keeps you rooted and true. Now, I tell you that you must let all that's started mingle. *Prepare*, cousin, for the time looms nearer."

"So soon?" Tull's voice fell beneath the heaviness in his chest. "Do you think she'll set me much further from seeing Q. J.? All I've lost, I never realized how much I could miss one soul."

"Think no more on such concerns. Those who are with you now await."

"You'll stay with them, won't you? *After*."

"As you say."

"You already do."

The Comforting Minister set his hand upon Tull's shoulder and took away the Guardian's worry. In the same manner, the creature surrounded the soul he watched over with warmth that blocked out the wind. Where they passed, alongside every grave marker, a single tulip bloomed. Hazy would love the flowers, and her desire to count each one would nudge Jules to step out of doors while she fretted over what awaited them.

TWENTY-SEVEN

When he crossed the threshold into the basement, Tull felt Si'an-dro Sa'ähn drift around him into an unseen, calming, and warming breeze that flowed unto every room. The same coat and shoes that Hazy wore that morn rested now alongside Jules's cold weather coat and a muddy pair of slippers. He hung his coat with theirs but kept on his boots. A light shone from Hazy's room, but the light of his display plates offered Jules all the light she wanted and played against the steam that wafted from a kettle of tea that rested between husband and bride.

"Need a warm-up?"

"No." Jules slouched toward the left-hand plate in displeasure.

"Hazy returned?"

"Yep."

"She behaved well, and only pushed the siren one time."

"She's a learner."

"You watched my relay?"

Jules nodded, then turned from the display plate. "Can Nita outswim Valery?"

"I'll believe whichever soul returns to us first."

Jules turned back toward the plate and let silence move through the room like Si'an-dro Sa'ähn's warmth. Many souls believed the shadows flowed like water. One led into another and connected a hidden place that thrived beyond the eyes of the secondkind. Souls from the Shelby Territory proved obsessed with the possibility. Tull observed enough in the light that the darkness disinterested him.

He towed the kettle and refilled his bride's mug anyway. "Is there a septapus at the aquarium?"

She laughed in an uproar. "That isn't what they're called."

TULL

"What would you call an octopus with one amputated tentacle?"

Her mouth shrank in consideration and she noticed his efforts.

"Is there?"

She hid her confirmation behind the steaming mug and a glance at his backside as he returned the kettle.

"And, you visited there each peak while I was away?"

"Yes." She glanced for a sighting of Hazy. "My former benefactor and her stray are far from competent schemers. I—I've observed how she gets cornered in a room by the remnants she keeps in her, and Lefty told of his every idea and deed to any soul he passed."

Tull sensed his bride's distressed stare as he raked a tea leaf from her mug. "I cannot disagree with you any more than I can explain away the feeling that another gained more by our judges' removal than the two of them."

"Judge Mumus?"

Her husband shrugged and let her take away the mug.

Jules lowered her hands and rested the mug, but remained pensive. "Of all the *monsters* you've stood up to—most of which have me needing a glass of hot wine and a good cry—Nelson, why are you so certain that Mumus is sinister?"

"There are civilizations beneath our feet. There are bodies in our backyard whose names we don't know. I blame him for their sakes."

She reached for his hand, lest she push him away with her words. "Maybe you aren't meant to guard them. All these trials cannot be *yours*. There are thousands upon thousands of souls in these territories."

"Five hundred eighty thousand—"

"Six hundred eight souls," His bride shared his knowledge and then some. "As of the first eve beneath our present moon."

"My fear is that we've already buried that one soul who imagined a better way than me. What do I do now?"

"Two more babes are due to arrive afore the next horned moon." She released her hold and grinned when he stayed within her reach.

"Each peak?"

Her grin lightened him. "When the judges sent me to the Page Battalion House, so far from Momma and Dad, from Otto . . . and the inn . . . all I—I wanted was—"

"Family."

TULL

"I—I wandered into the exposition, and sat on a bench all alone. I—I felt certain I—I'd made a mistake serving in the Twenty-Second."

"Till?"

"My love of these past fourteen spans silenced Kí'séi'ortő. I—I was seated there, full of woe, when two cheer-filled novitiates caused a commotion as they raced afore the ice cap bears. The word came from the radio that the tempter who ended Mylon Joel Kerry's camp of Reformers cornered the Guardians, but you took all seven of the monster's tongues and shut the Liar's mouth that eve. You fired only three arrows."

"Two arrows and a bolt." He shrugged off boasting.

"All wanted to learn of your deeds! There I—I found souls who listened to me as long as I—I needed to talk my way from lonesomeness."

"And that made you love the *aquarium* more?"

"There are no Ministers who swoop down and realign me. When I—I am most afraid, most unsure, the Triune has sent *you* again and again." She brushed his ring finger as proof of her belief. "I—I decided that lost or alone, a soul that I—I loved, who loved me, would find me there."

"Well, I believe the ice cap bears will feel jealous from now on."

She giggled and pulled him close enough that she could kiss him. "Don't forget who walked into a place they claim to hate looking for me when they could've come to the battalion house or waited at our loft. You craved your bride!"

His face stretched to one side as he bore his embarrassment and afforded him time to preserve her heart. He wanted her to remain in awe of the exposition and, against a promise to his own heart, withheld what Nita told him about Olley. Still, he nudged for more knowledge. "Then you spent the morn reviewing local reels?"

"No. I also broke the steam hamper. You need to fix that."

"So much for letting my hair and belly grow." His brow furrowed when she patted his abdomen, and he spoke with the fear of a husband who had lost the love of his bride. "Nita sounded relieved by her choice; as though she's grown afraid of Olley."

"Nita afraid of Olley? Never!"

"Whatever she feels toward him, she made the shadows her escape."

"From humiliation. From the shame of the territories knowing—" She cut short her own argument. "You heard her, not me. When our judges learn—"

"Better we answer for our own choices than be any of them when they answer for theirs."

TULL

"I s'pose Leander does know what he's doing!"

"There you go s'posing again." He set the two relay discs on the table so his bride learned what he learned. "As for our new judges, I imagine you can find a way to set these discs on displays around the territories; like that reel of me at Ernie's cabin."

"Do I have to call on Phinn Derek Wade for his help?"

"I can't tell you how I hope not." He kissed his bride and felt her rake his beard.

She swiped two kisses. "I'm glad you're home. I—I'm sorry about Nita."

"I'm sorry I'm so slow."

"In what land?"

"Thirty, twenty-nine, twenty-eight . . . you can imagine." He passed the kitchen space and proved he still knew his bride's ways. "How's your mom?"

"She's fine." Jules met him with a sheepish grin. "Do I ever surprise you?"

"Indeed."

She groaned.

"You *brim*."

Her brow arched. "Momma asked if we were taking care of Snuggle Runt and when we're going to bring her to Parantua so she and Dad can see her."

"Afore the winter settles."

"O, afore the winter settles, really? Do I—I have a say?"

"If you've a grievance to present to our judges, I know a scion who—"

Jules flung and struck her husband's backside with her slipper. "I—I know a medic who can bandage you if you don't get."

Both then laughed at the other and went about their commitments. Still, more urgent to her than either disc was a need to bow her head and offer thanks. Though she lacked the familiarity her husband kept with the Ministers, she spoke to their Creator as he went to check on his littlest sidekick. Such was their new arrangement.

The first object that caught Tull's eye as he neared the room kept for Hazy was the doll sent to her by Scion Mumus. The recipient propped the toy face-first against the corner of the wall joints furthest from the doorway. Her choice reflected the child's grasp of humor, sarcasm, and lessons learned. Jules shared a similar way, but he appreciated the idea more that the response came from the blameless soul.

He found Hazy seated on an old, elevated bed, slumped over a book the way that he remembered his bride reading from countless other books. His weary bones creaked as he sat on the unforgiving floor and rested against the side of the bedframe.

TULL

Then, warm air drifted into the room with the Minister's fragrance. Tull sat in satisfied stillness and listened to the next two pages turn. As a delay for the third page lingered, a small finger pecked his shoulder.

"Yes?"

The book scooted across the bedding and the corner prodded his shoulder. He reached over his shoulder and took hold of the hard cover and heard her grunt as she lunged and pointed at the word that confused her.

"*Astonishment*. Astonishment means wonder. I wonder why they didn't just use the word *wonder*."

"I wonder why, too. Grr–uhh–eye–fuh."

"Grief."

"Good grief!"

"Good grief!" he mimicked. "I'm astonished by the way talking birds lure you."

"But I like birds! They're funny!"

"Come on, whirly-twirly."

He brushed aside the book, scooped her up by one ankle, and towed her from the bedroom she kept to the bedroom that he and Jules kept on the opposite side of the kitchen area. As she climbed his arm and torso, Hazy hushed him with a pat of her hand against his mouth; lest they distract Jules. She then set that same hand on his shoulder, her cheek upon her hand, and watched him wrestle a key into the lock on a glass-encased bookshelf as she obscured his vision with a ribbon of hair.

"I believe *this* might interest you more." His low voice hummed and made her rub at her tummy where she leaned against him. "Let us see."

They left the glass door ajar, the key in the lock, then took a seat on the chair where Jules kept her lone attempt at a knit blanket. Hazy nestled against Tull, away from the coarse blanket, and waited on him in curious silence. He brushed his hand over the red face of the hardcover journal, then thumbed through the pages, stopping to admire, every now and again, the photographs secured to the dyed paper with adhesive foil discs.

"Here she is."

Tull forced back the binding, that the page might rest flat, and kept the weight of the journal away from his bright-eyed sidekick. The photograph captured a warm gaze, and a smooth jaw bore an expression that hinted that she liked the company of

TULL

the photo-taker. Her teeth showed in a graceful smile; not intense or practiced, rather eased. Whoever looked upon the photo swore she delighted in them.

He brushed Hazy's hand when she pushed down the edge of the foil disc. "This is your mother, Lana Robin Lael. I believe she loved you more than one soul could love another. All who knew her, and every soul who lived in the Creighton Territory, knew *grief* when we lost her."

Hazy rested her elbow on the page, far from the photograph, and covered her mouth with her hand. She sat and stared at the face. Tull found more of Lana in her than even he remembered, but plenty of Asham, too. Like her daughter, Lana oft struck a similar pose when she faced what seemed an unknowable, unconquerable mystery. He pulled the photo loose and slipped the corner toward her resting hand.

"You keep this, so you can see your momma whenever you want."

As a display of affection toward him, Hazy turned her foot at the ankle and rested her toes against his leg.

"Your momma loved to sing." He followed Hazy's glance toward the side of the bed where Jules slept. "Not like Jules sings; Lana had a *beautiful* singing voice. When she read, she would read to whomever sat near; books, scriptures, laws, even remedies. She loved growing vegetables, breaking kettle lanterns, and taking naps at the base of the walnut tree in her front yard. Right where every soul could see her.

"We went mad when we lost her. That's what she meant to us. You can thank Jules for showing us how to mend." He covered her mouth with his hand as she oft obeyed in innocence.

Hazy laughed, and every time she blew into his hand, her belly jostled the journal and the photograph of Lana. Tull uncovered her face, held up the photograph, and sat with her as they admired how Lana's eyes followed them. Then, the blameless mimic squinted hard and took a deeper breath than her size required. "Where is your momma?"

"That I've never learned. Now, others will tell you that you can't miss a soul you never knew or that you can't remember knowing. I tell you, that's not so. You can miss them every morn and every eve if you choose. But, don't grieve for those who rejected you, and never give your energy to those who won't fight for you."

When he looked upon her, he relied upon the maturity and wisdom she attained in that previous land. Ever-perceptive, he found no sense in spelling out words or speaking in a simple manner. "Do you love Jules?"

Hazy's eyes flared and her head nodded till the swish of her bangs tangled with her lashes.

"She loves you without fail. You're her astonishment."

Hazy looked at him and grinned.

"The first time you saw her, you ran right into her arms afore you even knew her name. You were so eager to hug her that she could barely keep hold of you. From that moment, she never stopped looking out for you, or worrying over you, or hoping for you. That's the truth about my bride. You have to charge with all your might to get into her heart, but she won't let you out once you get there."

Hazy prodded at her own chest. "In here?"

He tapped the soft knuckles and grinned. "In there. You'll learn how she loved you, how she mothered you, more than any soul. Till my end, you never stopped running to her or looking to her for trust. There you'll keep your love for Lana, and for Jules, and for Lucy."

Her fingers reached toward his face and traced along the scars that Lucy and his stubbornness put upon him. In this time, the pads of each finger touched the depth of the heaviest scar. One of her caretakers oft kept her from such *intrusion* though he never complained. He believed the act showed an awareness that she never risked hurting him.

"Why not find a place in your room to set Lana's photograph, find another pair of socks for these tiny feet, and I'll look in on Jules?"

Hazy offered one swift nod and slipped from his lap onto her feet without upsetting the journal. She cradled her mother's image close to her heart with both hands and took gentle steps; ever mindful of Jules.

For the first time, so early in her time, he stopped withholding his heart from she who was neglected by many. "I love you, whirlybird."

She spun on her heel, lips pressed tight, and stretched her face into a pleased grin. Then, without returning the words, she went about the task he presented her. Her obedience guilted him, and he rose to carry out his end of the arrangement. On the way, he returned the journal and locked the case.

From there, he roamed till he sat on the lowest step that served as both a curb for the wall and a threshold for the closed and bolted door. With the troubles that loomed out of doors and the potential hostility that awaited now that Jules knew he kept the judges' whereabouts from her, he reached and tested the bolt on the door.

"Worried I—I might corner you?"

He scoffed and offered a loose, nerve-wracked smile. "Who, me?"

"*Heh*. If this is the worst secret that you keep from me."

He held his tongue.

"They—Lucy and Katerena—have such . . . *sway* was the word you used. They are vile and selfish. I—I hate them for having their hands in Hazy's purpose." Jules looked away from him and toward the concealed tunnel. "Part of me keeps wondering if they're not waiting on the other side of that wall, breathing as the wind howls."

"I could set your mind on better possibilities."

"Better possibilities?" She pivoted with a smile. "As you say then."

"Judge Kind Hand will not let trespass stand . . . if she is the judge of other lands."

"She was at the Silas House when you visited. When you saw our judges."

He acknowledged her claim with a nod.

"She makes you imagine Sondrea."

"She makes me imagine my mom. I would want a soul who shares my home with me to watch over the judge and her son-to-be."

"Hazy can spell her name, but passcodes undo her." She continued in her duties. "Who is Q. J.?"

"The boy who tramples shadows! He who brings joy and mayhem to every watch. He who makes me work for every approval." The Jacobian breathed in a manner that satisfied and proved his ache.

"I'll tell you, he vies for Hazy's approval, then pretends he never needed support once she surrenders; which oft sends her billowing away. Still, she fusses over him like a mini-maw. She protects and bullies him! And, she is golden in his eyes."

"My hero!"

"And mine."

"He must be remarkable."

"Soon I will tell you of our tethered purposes and of Vi'emane." He beamed as his heart reminded him of the blameless boy's antics lest his bride worry.

"And, he's named Q. J.? The secondkind has never formed names with a symbol claimed by the firstkind afore. What—" She sprang upright, covered her mouth with her fingers, and tucked her leg beneath her afore she sat. "What does the Q stand for?"

"Ornery."

Jules's eyes lost their radiance. "You don't spell *ornery* that way."

"The Q is silent." He chuckled over his own amusement, but considered his bride's heart for a family. "I'll tell you, you'll have a closeness with him that I haven't seen among many. He has all in his path wrapped around his finger, but with the other hand, he holds to my bride."

Her smile rose in warmth and deepened her husband's admiration.

"You read books on all that interests him, just so you can see his eyes light up as you teach him."

Jules brushed an anticipatory tear from her face. Of all the mysteries and tragedies, though, one curiosity spoke to her heart more than any other. "What happens if the changes keep Q. J. from being born?"

"If a single speck of sand is removed, does the sea lose the shore?"

"No."

"There's a purpose on that boy"—a smile spread over him—"beyond aggravating our favorite girl."

"You believe this?"

"I believe as Zeck believed. I toiled span upon span learning his last challenge to me. 'Keep safe my brother . . . from the Last . . . from my father.'" He inhaled her curiosity. "I imagine there are countless ways he's brought into this land, letting pass the ways I've counted. I believe his soul was designed long afore his body takes form."

Jules's breathing proved she took comfort in his word.

"As to the way that you're feeling in this moment; imagine that's how Judge Kind Hand has felt beneath the moons of her gravidity."

"I—I'll monitor her travels. The perimeter around her home, too, and ask Chief Katch to add a patrol to her travels."

"I thank you."

"Come nearer, husband."

TWENTY-EIGHT

From the doorway that led into the open room, Hazy set her attention on Jules's request and watched in careful silence as Tull obeyed. All the while, she wrestled her feet into a second pair of socks. She stopped midway through the task and leaned onto one arm as Jules held out her hand toward her husband. What she said next never reached Hazy's ear, but the child knew her caretaker was not afraid.

Jules spoke with excitement, but not with that hoarse sigh her voice towed after a nap. The difference in sound filled Hazy with wonder; not *astonishment* levels, though. She perceived the joy that Jules found from the Guardian and the way she laughed without fear of getting into trouble for making too much noise. Jules's laughter presented proof that they could behave another way than when at home with Lucy.

"Eight-seven-one-one Mornside." She whispered the address to her bear.

"These rooms are too calm."

Hazy heard Jules's remark and remained observant.

"A little bit."

"A *lotta* bit."

Hazy took the bear into her arms, let him *help* her with the sock, and reassured her sidekick. "We're going to like staying here more, Nelly Belly. He's not scary when we're slow or noisy."

"Hey, you two! Whirlybird and Nelly Belly!" Jules extended her arms and wiggled her fingers. "Come nearer."

Hazy turned wide-eyed, rushed to fulfill Tull's appeal for socks, then clutched her bear and hurried toward the pair. She kept her lip pinched between her teeth and her arms braced for resistance, even as Jules took them in her arms and pulled her onto her lap. The child pushed her feet down between Jules's thighs, lest Tull see that she chose a bad color of sock and turn angry like Lucy, proving her belief in him wrong.

"I missed you all the morn, Snuggle Runt!" Jules declared with a squeeze. She then set the softest of kisses on Hazy's cheek. "I love you so much. Breathe. You can let all the sounds out. *We* love you. *We* love hearing you and seeing you."

The pair spoke of things that exceeded a child's insight, so she focused on what made sense to her. She counted the times Jules smiled, how she held his hand, and how both shielded her. Even when she scooted on purpose, to test them, they adjusted and drew her back onto Jules's lap. Jules patted her calf and Tull brushed her arm. Neither scolded or hurt with their touch.

"She'll take some convincing." Jules's voice tickled Hazy's back.

The dark soul who visited the house on Mornside when Jules went to work never smiled and stared when Lucy got angry with her. Their attention frightened her. So, her eye kept watch on Tull's fingers as his hand rested on her forearm.

"That isn't a shelter she's *ever* had." Jules spoke and tempted the child to squirm. "She's never learned how to trust in a father's headship."

Here, Tull looked at her three times and Jules looked at her five times. They let her breathe. She looked at Nelly Belly and, for only her eye, the bear winked at her. This surprise reassured her as much as Jules's thumb brushing against her.

"I—I will."

Then, the Guardian sank to eye level with the child and offered her his full attention. "Could I ask that you and your bear keep an eye on Jules till my return?"

Hazy responded with a nod that obligated her sidekick too.

"I thought as much, and I thank you."

"You're welcome."

A grin changed how the light settled on his face and brightened his pewter irises. "Do you remember who gave you that bear?"

She faced Nelly Belly as if he might add *speaking* to his repertoire. When the bear failed, she shook her head.

"Nita."

Hazy searched Jules's face for confirmation.

"As I recall, she believed you and the bear an even match at the time."

"He out-measured her by an ear!"

TULL

"Did Nita make *Nnnn*"—she covered her lips afore she spoke the bear's name and pointed at the keepsake—"look like your face?"

Tull's posture changed and she nestled her shoulder beneath Jules's breast. "Who's to say I didn't match my face to the bear's?"

She remained still and silent till the moment he laughed. "Jules sewed those marks on him."

"Did Jules sew your marks onto you?"

For Lucy's sake, he lied to Hazy. "I can't remember who sewed mine on. They tickled for a long time, though. Do you imagine your bear's ticklish?"

"No."

"No?"

Jules whispered with intended hoarseness, "Nelson is ticklish."

"That—That's nothing she needs to learn yet. Lest I show her where you hide your stash of—"

"Say no more!" Her hand covered his mouth till Hazy intervened for him and tickled Jules.

"Should we take another ride through the tunnel soon?" He winced and isolated her crown. "Don't nod too hard."

"We need to wash that duvet afore we go again."

"As you say, my bride." He rose as if to leave. He kissed Jules's face, then her lips, and put another atop Hazy's head. "Time that I work, then."

Hazy cast aside her bear and twisted to slide from Jules's lap, lest Tull journey without her, till he set his hand upon her crown and hindered her.

"You have to stay with Jules this time, partner."

She squirmed in rejection and Jules offered him no reinforcement. Without a memory of the verse that Carl cited from his father's interment, he knelt afore her. The way Hazy looked at him proved Beau Itzal Zeck's remark true and reminded him of his farewell to her in that previous land. Lana, Lucy, Jules, Honorine, Violet, and even Nita, had a hand in raising this blameless soul, but no father figure kept a place for her. Across all the lands where she existed, he offered her only a fraction of devotion. Now, he sought a *better* portion to offer her.

"You won't be without me long. Do not be fear-filled. I tell you . . . 'Yah, our perfect Creator, makes war in *our* name.'"

TULL

Jules had learned his stories long ago and proved breathless when he shared this with the frail soul in his arms. She set her hand upon the blameless soul and taught her the other line of a comforting verse. "'So *we* must keep still.'"

"I go to be still, but soon I'll see you."

Hazy trusted his word and surrendered. Jules held her close and let her husband kiss her own neck. Both knew of his calling, though Jules's way of holding the child soothed her more than wit or promises. He treasured them with one more glance, then paused at the isolated stairwell.

"I love you both."

A flicker of light shone bright enough to tease the Guardian's vision and draw him into the sanctuary, where he found Si'an-dro Sa'ähn at the furthest door. The wondrous creature rested his hands over his belly and bore a smile as Tull approached. The Guardian believed without reassurance that Comforting Ministers protected Hazy and Jules just as Si'an-dro Sa'ähn watched over him. Still, he wavered in his step.

"If I weary you with doubts, I am sorry, but my soul needs to hear you say," he paused. "I s'pose you already know—"

"I knew afore you knew, dear. Their hearts will be kept well."

"Your generosity abounds."

"Why, yes! As does our Creator's!" He delighted both in the work and the gratitude, but also recognized the weight Tull bore. "After many seasons of warring, now you see the path clear afore your feet. They're *cumbersome* feet, aren't they? O, how you should let me shine those boots!"

Tull considered but did not speak the creature's name.

"I worry over you as I'm purposed! This much of me you know."

He kept silent and followed Si'an-dro Sa'ähn out of doors.

"Bei'stei'ele!"

The winds backed away, and the leaves in the yard settled unto stillness. No other disturbance loomed, and Tull held to the hem of Si'an-dro Sa'ähn's coat as the terrane beneath him glowed with flame. His true countenance burned with intensity till the Jacobian closed his eyes and turned away. Silence surrendered to a sound of glass chimes that created a voice only the firstkind perceived.

TULL

The creature who brought comfort turned his head toward the sky-fires and winced as if scolded. "I'll not arm him. This much you know. But, yes, yes. That I can do for you, sister."

Si'an-dro Sa'ähn's brilliance dimmed, and Tull searched the void for a trace of Enke'loi. Two petals fell against the stone walk and the wind rustled the leaves again. Branches swayed above head, but the Guardian never saw the one who kept him from his end. When he looked back, he met Si'an-dro Sa'ähn's sparkling gaze and modest smile.

"If warring comes, cousin, you are to survive—and do not sacrifice for the sake of the child. This is our Creator's will. Say that you hear me."

"I need—"

"Up you go!" Si'an-dro Sa'ähn touched his hand to the Guardian's chest.

The chimes that produced a voice in Si'an-dro Sa'ähn's ear created a tremor that shook the remaining leaves from their branches. In the same manner that Enke'loi drew a soul into her hand, Si'an-dro Sa'ähn cast Tull airborne. The watch gleamed with greater brilliance than the mightiest star, then space rippled. Caught in the wake, the Guardian skirred backward the way a hawk darted.

In his ascent, light fell like a single, striking bolt. Enke'loi pierced the sky-fires and never slowed. She caught Tull without disturbing a hair upon his head and whisked him away. As the ripple calmed, Si'an-dro Sa'ähn took one step across the courtyard then ascended over the church in a ribbon of flame and cast his warmth upon the place and those inside whom Tull loved.

Whispers & Wrecker

An Interim

The 5th Eve beneath the Moon of the Wandering Fog

The 114th Winter of the Accession

In the Care of the Helper, who keeps souls from fruitless wandering.

<u>Beacon 089.86.218 recognized at 707 Little Oak Way . . .</u>

Identifier confirmed—Jules Baker Shannon

Not serving the Second Creation in her capacity as Rescue Medic.

A moonrise ended and another started without word or sighting of Tull. His beacon lingered at the doors of the church, but he was not there. The Jacobian's bride committed her purpose toward those mysteries that he could not solve whilst he sought devious former fellows. This meant, too, that some of her duties passed on to her helper—the daughter of the soul her husband sought. Hazel-Sue's most cherished responsibility involved a leg-straining climb up thirty-nine steps to greet Sister Honorine Nowak.

Of the trusted cradles in Hazel-Sue's time, Honorine's was both sweetest and softest. She who turned from the ways of a Reformer to offer rescue as a medic had become neglectful toward her hopes of mothership; still, she gleamed when she held onto blameless souls and retained such innocence that her rig partner could not keep from marveling over the light in her. Even Hazel-Sue responded with a satisfaction that tamed her fidgeting and curiosities. The medic-then-abettor understood Honorine's chastity—and why she strayed from the duties of a nursemaid—but lamented for the fulfilment from other purposes that evaded her truest friend, letting pass her strength of character.

TULL

"You've recovered from your *nip* of fortified wine?"

"There will never be another." She patted Hazy's arm. "Nine is my fill."

Jules responded with a smirk that led to a breathy rebuttal, which led to praise for surroundings unfamiliar to her guest.

"You never told me that Nelson's church is the former Church of the One True Shepherd. This was a refuge! My grandfather's uncle helped to build this church. And when the earliest Partakers tried to set fire to her, he stood in defense."

Jules shrugged. "I cannot tell you what I've never learned, dearest."

"There is such reverence and treasure here, Jules. Nelson's great-grandparents and grandmother fed Jacobians and Shelbians and sheltered them through the long winter of the fifty-second span. Our judge was fourteen, then. Imagine!"

"Nelson hasn't those memories." She tapped at the ledge of a mounted display plate even as she faced her rig partner. "The histories of the Jameses, the Tulls, the Nelsons, the Hobsons, and the Ellises ended with Patrick. He has one journal from his uncle. He never even learned he shared the tree of Camp till after we wed. All he has is Lee's journal, some writings from Sondrea, and the annals of his grandmother's judgeship."

"I could—I *will*—talk to Papa about this. Truly! He keeps writings from every moon in his eighty-nine spans."

"Nelson says he cannot change the ways of the past lest Yah lets him."

Honorine sharpened her focus and nodded. Then, an unsettled breath flowed from deep within her.

"What?"

She who oft hid in the rig from *objectionable* characters looked stern, yet the words burst from her lips with minimal coaxing. "Syd. Jules, I don't believe he, or Tim, or Hector, or those you owe favors, consider your reputation."

"Who said I—I owe Syd? He has *one* reel to show me."

Honorine's brow arched with a disciplinarian's prowess.

"*Two.* Two reels. Two reels and a prelusion. He misses me, which ought to prove how seldom I see him and not that I owe him—or Hector and Tim—favors."

"Your vow is to Nelson; of course, you remember."

"Better than you, tippler."

"Yet"—Honorine twisted to keep Hazy's feet from striking Jules as she covered her friend's mouth—"you stay close to souls who do not call you their bride."

TULL

Jules kissed the palm of her friend's hand, then pushed her chair away from the work-worn covering. "Nelson hasn't a reason to fret, and he doesn't fret."

"Does he not?" She spoke of the soul she had not met since his return to this time. "I believe, rather, that he keeps other souls from learning of his troubles."

That soul was no more. Jules grinned in gentle denial and improved the lay of Hazy's sock with memories afresh of a side of her husband that few enjoyed.

"As his bride, will you consider how this might look to others?"

"I—I use resources to do my work as an abettor."

"You owe favors to souls you should never spend time alone with."

"To help *him*? To protect *her*? Yes. Evermore yes. I—I would make reckless choices for their safety. That's how I love them."

Now Honorine looked sickened with worry.

"I—I won't shame you, partner prude. You'll still take Hazy to the loft for me, will you not? The doors will accept your beacons. No other soul can disturb you, minus me or Nelson, lest you let them in."

"You don't want me to wait? Now, don't sulk!"

"I—I don't sulk. My way, you're both kept safe."

The remark softened Honorine, who offered ever-watchful Hazy her gentlest grin. "As you say, dearest."

"As I—I what?!" Jules's smile softened her ornery lilt and her appreciation showed as she stood to hug the necks and kiss the faces of her most cherished doves. Yet, she would not be the daughter of Victor Simon Shannon lest she teased one more time. "Soon, you'll see me."

"How we cannot wait!" Honorine mimicked her with perfection.

Hazy smacked her lips and mimicked her kisses. "Shoo!"

Jules's rig partner laughed without context.

"Nelson taught her a new expression. Mind Honorine for me, will you not?"

This time, the blameless soul chirped and offered a one-shouldered shrug.

Jules goosed her and followed till they reached the stairwell. In her duties as an abettor, she ensured they were safe as Honorine took all thirty-nine upward steps. Her rig partner locked the upper door behind her, and Jules locked the door at the base of the stairwell. She then counted footsteps across the floor above as the pace of her heart proved intense and confused her ear as the sounds grew distant.

TULL

She lost count and stripped off her hooded shawl, then fanned her undervest as sweat formed. Honorine convicted her, as a sister ought, but failed to realize the depths of Jules's commitment to her husband. Some wept for his soul, and whispered hope that he was unharmed this time, but absence encouraged his bride to not be still. Her beloved Jacobian endured ten eves in Gutefiel, forty eves alone in the mountains, and six eves in the desert beyond the mountains. That the secondkind showed cracks after a mere *two* eves proved their need for Guardians.

Not unlike her husband, Jules too entered situations that risked wellness and name for her title. Every abettor and scion who upheld their purpose took on more than their fair share. Some souls, like Jules, gravitated toward an overextension of their share. Honorine's concern stemmed from witnessing how her rig partner, like Timothy Todd McCrea, leapt unto recklessness afore the judges allowed her to uphold an abettor's purpose. Such tendencies attracted souls who sought to further her recklessness unto corruption.

"INTERFACING. AUTHORIZATION REQUESTED. . .
OBSERVER SYDNY GUNTHER BURZYCIEL—BEACON IDENTIFIED.
ACTIVE AT 12-6 CALEDONIA REPOSITORY."

Jules responded to one such soul with an anxious huff. "Abettor Jules Baker Shannon accepts contact with Observer Sydny Gunther Burzyciel. Passcode: Gypsum Two-Five, One-One Fog."

A soul with sunken cheeks and bulging eyes inhaled at the sight of the abettor and offered a smile that foretold the ideas he kept of her. Such words made their way from his lips, but filters on all the devices within Hazy's earshot prohibited much of what the observer had to say.

"Wait, Syd." She laughed at the muted sputtering of his mouth. "Wait!"

She leaned over the display plates and plucked free the delay filter that let a soul, not unlike Jules, clean the relays to preserve ears and keep souls blameless. This filter was a requirement on all the devices in Honorine's care, too.

"As you say?" She noticed a new reel on her device from him.

"Well, I was talking so fast that I'll have to send over a reel of this just to keep from depriving you!"

Her smile radiated till her warm cheeks blushed. "You look well!"

"I thank you, pearl-dove. My moon is set upon you!" He sighed like a soul struck by love but laughed like a spirit perverted by lust. "How I want your mark on my chest! How I want your chest on my—"

"Syd!" She wriggled her ring finger as a reminder to him. He might not believe in keeping a lone bride, but he understood the fear he would suffer if he crossed the soul whom she called hers. "You learned about Anya for me?"

"I did." He cursed till he neared blasphemy. "Truly! I did! And, what I found, I cannot expect a favor for. I must not! You recall my last passcode?"

"Yes."

"Add your spans to the postfix but . . . pray . . . pray for us all."

Jules had never heard the absence of orneriness or playfulness in his voice afore those words. He who partook like a glutton never spoke of reverence for the weapons of belief. This frightened and excited her, though she struggled to identify which sensation was the victor over her. "Dare I ask how you obtained this reel?"

"A soul like me turns restless beneath the urge to see what goes on in certain settings, even after the judges' projection gliders drift to the next beacon. Say that I manipulated the beacons and lenses so they believe my display plates belong to those in a particular locale. Say I can stay . . . longer . . . than expected."

"Any particular locale or just the one? And how much longer?"

Syd giggled in a way that made Jules stir. "You know me well, Whispers!"

The ideas in her mind turned her weary as she sulked till her chin sank into the palm of her hand and her fingertips skewed the shape of her nose and left eyelid.

"I have to patrol. Wait, letting pass the answers. Wait for me to return."

"I—I will, Syd."

With that, plus a flick of his eyebrows, he departed from her field of vision but left her with a view of his workspace. She did the same, as a courtesy to a friend, but listened to the silence around her long after the relay ceased from detecting his footsteps. Her hand slipped beneath the hem of her undervest and settled against the drumming of her heart but failed to comfort her. A labored breath followed as she entered the proper passcode, and then she watched.

<u>Beacon 088.60.325 recognized at 2 Ardent Peaks . . .</u>

Identifier confirmed—Anya Nora Rains

Intended to appear afore her Advocates in 18 ticks.

TULL

The Gierig Territory remnant affixed to the southwestern coast of the Archibald Territory played host to Bel Geddes, Eidolon Pictures, copper statues of thesps Danele Gertie Zuriñe and Silas Hendrie Falk Sr., the newspaper press that Philip Clapham Tarry started, and Ardent Peaks. There sat the glass-and-jade home of Anya Nora Rains atop a vast bluff that flowed unto a sweeping field. Every portion of the house responded to a combination of the annalist's identifier beacon and breaths to maintain a constant, focused atmosphere that ensured she offered her best to Yah. Each of the twelve rooms boasted comforts that had not yet reached the rest of the Second Creation, and that included her Guardians.

Her honey-hued, golden tresses had grown since Jules last saw a reel of her and her beauty increased in all the ways that invited devotion from some and jealousy from others. Her slight stature made the walls loom till the false light cast pools of shadow across her eyes—which shared the home's jade foundations. She turned away from a vertical desk toward the Forbidden Sea, visible through the oblong glass exterior, to focus on the projection glider. Unlike Jules, she wasted no time on a stare-down, but spun again once a dull, thumping noise created a chime across the walls.

"Jonas?"

From behind her, the projection glider departed. Then Syd's ability to seize the lenses within the home proved more than a boast. The angle and volume improved, along with the clarity, as the relay changed points of view. Another thump caused Anya's posture to turn as rigid as Hazy's arms when Jules's husband taught her to steer his rickety steam tram.

"Jonas"—now Anya spoke with a hush, then in another tongue—"Hori zu zara, Ion?"

Her heart beat fast enough to end the circulation of anthracite heat through the house. Then her wide eyes reflected her fear. A shadow blocked out the false lights and spread over the annalist, the polished jade floor, and—her upward gaze directed her audience—across the ceiling too. She who riled Guardians then shook.

"Seko'tae . . ."

"Get, Anya!" Jules provoked her own fright. "Don't stand and talk like a loon."

As if she heard the abettor, Anya pivoted, and never slipped. Even on bare feet, she sprinted as hard as Jules ever observed a member of their kind run. Still, what startled her also outmatched her, for what stood as a man pursued as a lion. A creature comprised of two-thirds flesh and one-third brass roared and made glass and jade fracture—the lens included.

"Almighty!"

Breaking glass the sum of a wall made brief, soon forgotten music as the creature roared a second time. Then, Anya vaulted. Unto the Forbidden Sea and bluffs beneath Ardent Peaks, she flung her body. Still, her pursuer leapt after her. Anya's falling scream proved unforgettable.

Jules twisted in her seat and vomited on the floor till her entire body shook with fear and suffocating emotion. Still that scream endured. Letting pass all that she had done to and against Jules's husband, no soul deserved—*that.* What Jules discovered afore, by way of her fellow Pez and the images of recovery, made her weep for a soul she had never felt kindness toward.

"On this eve . . . I felt fear for the first time in thirty spans."

Jules nodded in response to Syd's admission, as if he might see her.

"I cannot turn from my ways. Nor do I seek to."

She mopped her face with her shawl as she returned to her seat. Her friend of other ways let her drink from her mug and watched over her without goading. He who remembered her fresh from her time as a novitiate offered a smile that settled her stomach.

"I thought I learned all the beasts on this isle long afore—" He huffed and swallowed the foulness that she tolerated from him.

True to the ways of an old Partaker, Syd played the role of lecher and agitator with delight that bristled her belief. Merchant Clifford Miles Boromir, who stared too long at Jules's breasts and made her stand amid his pack of agitated dogs, at least served her hot tea while he offended her. Even Hector proved protective. These three souls were the coarsest of whom Jules spent time without her husband, a parent, Honorine, or Otto, near. She felt fear with each of three, but she never once felt what Anya suffered in their care, or when a wandering spirit infested Donald Elwin Longshadow, who buried her in the silica pits at Kanarek.

"Get your breath back, Whispers?"

She nodded at Syd, but still lacked her voice.

"I saw those images you stowed of her." He shrugged in expectation of her wrath, then scratched at his matted and bristled facial hair. But she kept her head downturned and her eyes hidden behind her pearl-hued locks. "After all the times I've seen you, I believed you would show me in your own time. I tell you, I felt grateful . . . to *Him* . . . that she missed her end."

Jules counted on Syd for at least one vile act each time they shared time together and he proved himself consistent, afore now. What frightened him away from misdeeds uprooted her from the peace she clung to in her purpose and from being the bride of a soul whose purpose proved most unsettling. A flow of nervous sweat fell over her body and her vision pooled with shadows as she wondered if such creatures cast him back to this time from seven spans yet to be experienced by her.

"Whispers?"

She suspected she might lose the light as she intertwined Anya's suffering with memories of her past and fears for her husband and Hazel-Sue if such creatures found them. Still, Syd proved loyal and patient. Many a moon had set since she last counted him an upright soul. He taught her much about the getting in and the staying out of trouble, about shame and humiliation, and about a wicked temperament. None of those lessons ended in kindness but she kept him as a friend.

"Lest my count's off, Green defends us alone now. Can a scarecrow swim?"

Jules heard the taunt in Syd's laughter, true to his character, but preferred that to the sound of Anya's last scream. His penchant for vulgarity took hold of him at last,

TULL

but her senses had a filter of their own. By the time his spew ended, she felt able to take a breath without trembling.

"See? You found your feet again."

She exhaled the fear she no longer wanted and hoped to make the Liar drift from her ear.

"Now, afore you count me weak, say I show you this other reel for one favor owed to me by you—a *steep* favor—for an old soul who's kept some of your deeds to himself. My word is yours... this reel will change your heart toward your favorite getaway in all the territories... but might just see that we still have territories come the morn."

Jules relied on a steadying breath to correct her posture and turned her head till she looked upon her bartering friend with an inclined gaze.

ASHAM BENJAMIN GERA

The original purpose of this character was to show the arc of belief, from Asham never considering his soul worthy of goodness to leading others unto profound faith. That changed with the addition of Ministers and Squires. Imagine having the sight of these creatures all around and still rejecting the existence of the Creator. Which is more interesting: The broken-heartedness of a hero turned into a villain or the letting go of anger as a wicked soul is forgiven and allowed to heal?

16:18

TWENTY-NINE

THE 6TH MORN BENEATH THE MOON OF THE WANDERING FOG

THE 114TH WINTER OF THE ACCESSION

IN THE CARE OF THE HELPER, WHO KEEPS SOULS FROM FRUITLESS WANDERING.

20 SEVIER

THE SEVIER AQUARIUM EXPOSITION.

A SITE THAT CLAIMED TULL'S BREATH FOR REASONS OTHER THAN AWE.

When Tull's heel touched the terrane, he saw a rectangular, antiqued bronze sidewalk alit in coral-green light. In his right hand, he held a canvas pouch of loose stones. On his back, he bore the axe that Keeper Victor Simon Shannon gifted him after he saved Jules; the same axe that failed him in that previous land. The heaviness of salted air stung his nostrils and, like the axe, reminded him of his most recent end.

The wind proved kind for winter, and he sensed Si'an-dro Sa'ähn's warning against sacrifice in his ears. Darkness crept below the pylons' song, and he felt the burden of the axe. Enke'loi prepared him for a battle that Si'an-dro Sa'ähn expected him to survive. Then, when all grew still, a chorus of applause erupted and created vibration in the pouch of small stones. He took less into Gutefiel and endured ten eves, so the presence of weapons excited the crowd that gathered.

Ten reflections surrounded him, courtesy of the multi-faced glass that formed the eastern entryway to the Sevier Aquarium Exposition. High-wattage lights indicated a swarm of projection-gliders; some operated by law agents, some by chroniclers, some for entertainment. The screen inside, oft used as a display plate for better-seeing creatures, now offered feedback of him and the backdrop of spectators whose presence confused him.

He lacked knowledge of Jules's findings by way of Syd or the influence his bride had on the local chief's decision-making. The public display plates broadcast an infinite loop of Lucy's threat mingled with close-up images of her and her husband. That success he credited to his bride, and enjoyed humble satisfaction over her ability to warn the territories. As a habit, he searched the crowd for her face.

The gathering of onlookers roared, as though he posed for them, and relayed his arrival as though part of a thrilling show. The soul who lasted ten eves at Gutefiel, who defended judges and traveled in a Minister's blanket of fire, signified their best hope for that thrill. Deputies of the Archibald Territory held to the barricades that created a valley of isolation around the structure's hem; though even they watched the Guardian and his shimmering *transportation*.

"I confess, I imagined you might set me elsewhere." He believed for certain that the Silas Chamber House deserved his attention.

Enke'loi looked upon him in absolute silence.

"*Here*, though?"

"You needn't fear the waters. I have stilled your heart."

"O, I hope you mean calmed—*calmed* my heart. *Still* would not please Jules."

Her eyes radiated and she rose in patience as he checked his heartbeat.

"Say I want to please my bride a season or two without fear of reset."

When he looked upon her face, his reflection changed beneath the subtle grin that she offered him. Her amusement made him smile, and her pleasure warmed him.

"And she tells me I'm ornery. I will miss you; lest you visit from time to time."

When he sighed and blinked, he felt the chill from the Warring Minister's immediate departure. The time when he stood outside the church versus the time displayed on the clock inside the exposition spoke to his time away from his bride. Worse, he held no recollection of those lapsed moonrises.

"Then again, Jules may see that I face you sooner than I grasped."

"Tull! Tull, I'm warning you!" Chief Inspector Lodi Steven Hont shouted at the Guardian from one-half block away and drew the attention of many souls. "Do not go in there! You do not have cause to provoke an incident in this territory!"

Tull responded with a smirk that once made Jules blush and now elevated the roar of the crowd. He doubted he had smirked that way since Gutefiel. Chief Hont maintained a public persona that sheltered him from the Colonel and another that fed sensitive information to the outfit. Even so, the Guardian tipped his head as a show of respect for Hont's authority.

"All you seek rests within, child."

"My obedience requires disobedience. Forgive me, Chief."

Tull liked Hont, and appreciated the circumstance he faced. Even so, he reached outward and pressed his hand against the glass door. The chief stomped and cursed as the crowd cheered the inevitable. As Guardian, his clearance bypassed the security measures that kept others locked out. The trespasser offered a sly glance to the wearied chief—who held back enough energy to cuss him one more time.

The sensors in the door produced his photo identification and name in the optic layer within the dual-paned glass. The locked door slid away, and he entered the exposition. Chief Hont, defeated by the lawful whims of the old judges, directed his anger onto his deputies and motioned for additional barricades. When souls sought Tull again, only a plume of silhouette appeared beyond the reflection of spectators who relayed his show of authority across the territories.

The array of gliders accessed the exposition's internal security, and every display plate in the vicinity turned into a viewing station. From the lull of creatures in tanks to Tull's steady swagger, down to the sleek figure who passed above the tanks, all showed to the territories and one another. The creatures who swam moved at their own pace. The figure in the shadows, however, awaited Tull's next move.

On a maze of utility walkways, Guardian Arthur George Green waved to his fellow and friend. He offered an all-clear signal, and Tull responded with a signal that set their course according to the map Nita relayed to him. Three steps across the floor, and he realized Si'an-dro Sa'ähn's concern over his boots. The soles squeaked against the opaque tiles, so he removed them and proceeded on bare feet.

He remembered Nita's account of the tank of octopi—plus one septapus—and recalled Jules's past remarks about a beloved site within the facility: an underwater walkway. Two corridors of arched glass let guests travel beneath the tanks and watch a variety of creatures who moved above. Where they met, a beveled archway that reflected the waters of multiple tanks produced a gem-like gleam that let the exposition lower the lights and create a romantic ambiance for first kisses and longtime loves to marvel.

The Jacobian shut his eyes and blew out a disruptive breath when the facility swayed. An elegant stingray fluttered with the grace of the breeze, as divine as the creatures who warred in the sky. When he caught the glimmer of brass-like colors on the creature's body, he took the next step and let sweaty handprints mar the glass. He set aside his anxiousness, though he had never reached the furthest end of the walkway in any previous visit.

The creature drifted at an accommodating pace toward the heart of the intersecting pathways. Tull followed his guide on slippery feet, without another glimpse of George, toward a tank filled with octopi. His obedience produced an almost *well-pleased* ripple in the creature's motion as his guide fluttered away. As the creature ascended, Tull pivoted and knelt toward the octopi exhibit on the first sublevel.

One hundred *three* tentacles swam through the waters. Only the misshapen body of a creature with seven tentacles sat camouflaged with the glass stones on the floor. That creature fixed sad eyes upon him, and the Guardian ached for the beast severed by a crueler creature's surgical tool. Tull pressed his hand to the glass, tilted till his scarred face showed beneath the light, and grinned at the kindred beast.

"Hey, sightseer." An agent of Mumus's security operation, allowed to roam the exposition by law of the judge, awaited him with a shock baton.

The light behind that agent changed to darkness, then brightened to the accompaniment of a gentle drum. Two beats, then stillness. When Tull smirked, the hired hand scowled and lunged by another's force. George ran him face-first against a heavy pane and dropped him to his fellow Guardian's bare feet.

Then, at ease, George smiled and held up the shock baton. Tull stepped over the downed agent, patted George's shoulder, then ran the face of one stone along his friend's sweat-tinged jaw. He set that stone on the breastbone of the one who rested at their feet. George, in that time, dismantled the baton with his bare hands.

"When the time comes, only you may move him toward safety."

George looked for other troubles. "I believed you would turn from this path. So much water."

"I've missed you too, George. Surprised as I am. I cannot remember when last you traveled so far from home."

TULL

The Guardian from the Weston Territory emitted a low, teasing laugh.

"Nita tells me"—he grunted and put on his boots—"Olley waits below our feet."

"Jules told me the same when she asked for my help."

"Did she?"

"She's here as well, my friend."

He nodded through his agitation. "This much I believe."

"I imagine she will not let you rush into trouble alone anymore."

"Mind that smile, or I'll tell Violet what truly wilted her tomato crop." Tull admired how fast George's expression turned blank. "Did my bride say where you might find her?"

"She asked that I find you and remind you of our time in Kanarek."

Kanarek hosted Tull in his debut as fourth Guardian of the Jacoby Territory, and marked where his path first intersected with his bride's. He first believed she meant to soften his heart toward her chasing harm. He then remembered the setting. Unlike the exposition, where all gleamed, Kanarek hid beneath a layer of grit that dulled every surface and color.

"Her words make sense to you, do they not?"

"When she breathed, silica dust blew upward."

"A puzzle!"

"That's how I found her."

Tull broke and gathered into his hand some of the mud from his cleats, then crushed till he made a powder. He sifted the powder in a trail along the corridor's opaque panels. When that covered two panels, he used the mud from the other boot. George patted at his arsenal, then plucked a weighted leather pouch filled with sand and held with a cord. He untied the pouch and poured the contents over the next three panels.

"Here!" A puff of air blew the granules away from the seam of the seventh panel and caught George's eye.

Both recalled how the menacing spirit they hunted in Kanarek took souls in a veil of granules. George squatted till he hugged the floor panel and fitted the edge of a knife into the seam. More air hissed and a cloud of debris rose, one-one hundredth scale of what they faced in Jules's hometown.

"She is too clever for you, I believe." He pressed against the rim.

"Who thought to put down the trail of dirt in the first place?"

TULL

"I would not be surprised if you've been here afore."

"Wouldn't I have just walked up to the panel and pried? Olley would never forgive me if I failed to feed your superstitions, George."

Both Guardians pried, and the opaque panel turned dim. A spring-loaded hinge buckled, then the panel rose from a recessed mount. They lifted and opened an access point into a room that went undiscovered beneath all the other panels. They saw a head of gleaming hair, then identified Jules when she peeked up at them.

"Nelson!"

The Jacobian winked at her.

"You make me proud, *runt*."

George chuckled over Tull's fleeting smugness.

"I—I never doubted you, George."

"My *clever* friend."

Jules smirked, complete with a single-shoulder *shurg*, then looked toward the other side of the hidden room. She tilted her head toward a sight neither Guardian observed and waved them down. "You need to see what I—I see."

"After you."

"I believe I will find the *other* way in."

George disappeared so well that Tull turned still. "I believe he seeks to turn me superstitious."

"Nelson!"

Her tone encouraged his haste and, though she paced the grate floor, she charged and almost toppled the late arrival with an enthused hug when he leapt down. He kept his axe from her reach and admired his lover for the same fearlessness that turned him gray. Out of his desire for her, he sought a kiss, but she slugged him on the shoulder and nudged his chin upward till he halted.

"Where have you spent the past two eves, husband?"

"Enke'loi took me—"

She cupped her hand across his mouth and shook her head.

He gave her finger a playful nip. "How did you find this place?"

Rather than tell her secrets, she bunched his shirt and pulled him closer for a thorough kiss. If Honorine's opinion proved true, and she caused him to fret over her heart, then the kiss offered evidence of who occupied that heart.

He tasted a tinge of bitter and sweet flavors on her lips. "Shelbian vermouth."

TULL

"Tell you later. After we talk about Anya?"

He agreed with a nod. "What soul keeps Hazy?"

"My prudish partner. We need to mind her time out of doors now that winter sets." She then prodded Tull's side. "Don't you ask if I—I mean Honor."

"Hazy suffers chest colds." He endured as she patted his chest with both hands. "Surprised I'm still me?"

"A little bit." She slipped her hands into the rear pockets of her trousers.

"Seems like a *lotta* bit."

"Who, me?"

He let her test the pace of his heart to see if he had experienced a reset in her absence and trusted her to make sense of his hurried rhythm. As he surveyed the surgical steel bins, glass tubes, upright mending chambers, and unsettling medical devices, little of what he saw comforted him. Even as a critic of the exposition designed to invite innocence, what he saw made him tense. Then, he saw the forms of bodies in those chambers that went without recognition due to harsh glares.

"Can't keep you from trouble, can I—I?" She slapped his backside.

"J. J., you arrived afore me."

"Better that I—I did! *Look*."

He followed her finger toward a dissection chamber; like the design of the mending chamber, minus one primary function. This chamber facilitated the removal—not the mending—of the body's every part. Whoever drafted the machine cobbled together the best devices of other inventor's creations. A brilliant, if not cruel, mind tinkered well.

The body kept within the machine appeared mutilated far beyond research and even curiosity—and brought to mind tales of Marvin Elam Katch. Each limb suffered amputation at the sockets, and the torso held a sadist's collection of incisions. A sheath of abdominal muscle hanged from a jutted pelvis and reminded the Guardian how Olley's face appeared when he found him. The *lacking* between the body's legs, though, drew Tull's eye back toward an absent throat.

"He's missing a face."

"I also noticed as much." He then inspected the exposed ribs.

"Believe me now that monster's hide in both of my purposes?"

A healed break in the second and third false ribs caught his eye.

TULL

Jules bent at the waist and leaned on an oblong display plate, larger than a soul towed alone, and started sifting. "He avoided cryo-suspension, and there's no log of heart or brain function."

Tull turned toward the sound of her frustrated breath with full faith that she would make sense of what she saw.

"No beacon. There's an unhealed incision and a catalog number for a stimuli inhibitor." Jules held up a ceramic strip laced with copper wires. "*This.*"

"Why do I imagine that had little to do with stopping his pain"—he looked upon an absent face—"and all to do with preserving the secret of this lab?"

"Can't have the runts scared away by another's screams of terror."

Tull slid his hand along her jaw and calmed her so she looked away from the display and into his eyes. "You've found Pine."

Her voice went still, and her breathing proved rigid. Even so, she squirmed when his fingers defined two specific ribs on her body.

"He broke these against a wrought fence." Tull's hands fell away from his bride as he faced the remains. "I held his arms whilst Harlan reset the bones."

Her breathing matched his sympathy as her hand slipped around his.

"Forgive us, our brother." His next breath changed his posture and tone. "Find a way to open these chambers for me."

"We need proper equipment afore we remove—"

"I'm not interested in removing the scrap. My friend is gone. I can do nothing for him. I want to know how this chamber opens so I can find who did this and shove them inside their own device. What they've left of him can haunt them."

Her mouth shrank in silence till she only nodded and averted her eyes.

"What keeps George away?"

His bride listened to the agitated *stomp* of his bootheels against the floor as he approached the lab's secure door. She kept a watchful eye over him and devoted glances between functions on the display plate and her husband's axe. Though she said nothing, the weapon *changed* how he approached a threat. The weight agitated him as much as the helplessness he towed over a fallen friend.

"He must have found trouble."

"Have you seen George pass by a closed door? There are thirty of them between here and the exit. Or, the sea cucumber exposition distracted him."

TULL

Her search for the chamber's design proved fruitless, though brooding stillness needled her.

"Look who else I—I found." She twisted him by his shoulders and nudged him till his feet caught up to his shoulders. "His brain activity looks great! The heart of an ox. Remember?"

In a tank designed for restoration floated Olley Hendrie Falk. His face rested beneath a fibrous hood, but Tull recognized the shape of his friend's nose and chin. The sight of him adrift haunted. More when the Guardian in the tank grinned back at his wed spectators from beneath his covering. Tears filled Tull's eyes, then rage coursed through his expression.

"The simulated mapping shows one hundred and forty activated copper spiders used in vast reconstruction. They're like the pellets we use in the field. They let a current pass into the tissue to maintain muscle activity and accelerate healing. There's no telling how extensive his wounds—"

"Jules! Once we're clear of this place, I'll hear the complete, breathtaking history of copper spiders and pellets. They're not keeping our friend another watch. How do we get him out?"

"I—I tried opening the tank. I—I don't know the access procedure." She arched her brow. "Do *not* reach for your axe. That's a pressurized tank, and we're standing in a glass jar."

Tull showed limited discouragement.

"Remember that time Chief Stanley cooked the pheasant at the battalion house? Sands *had* to touch the levers on the pressure kettle! Kimsey ended up with a concussion, Casper bruised her tailbone, and every soul ate corn for the main course. Never tamper with the pressure!"

He absorbed her story, then glanced at her in wait of her next barb.

"I—I checked Tim's reels. He kept monitoring traffic in and out of the fish tanks after watches."

"A healing—"

"You watched the same reels, then?"

He took a patient breath and exhaled his agitation.

"He's called this place the fish tanks since I—I've known him. He followed Asham here, but Lucy caught him. They set the device that wrecked the entryway; not Tim."

"By his word?"

"Syd collects the feeds and he showed me what happened. Tim tried to diffuse the charge. When he couldn't, he started running for the door. He tripped, fell, and the charge got away from him and went off. I—I tried to reach you and tell you. Wherever your Minister took—"

The blast of hardened iron cutting through weaker, more sensitive materials turned her complaint into all-out cursing. While she clutched her breast to restrain her heart, she watched her husband pull his axe free from a series of pipes and cables.

"I—I thought we agreed: No axe!"

"I didn't strike the pressurized chamber; only the tubes that supply the pressure. You visited Sydny Gunther Burzyciel in my absence?"

She softened her posture and held up two fingers.

"Twice." Tull sighed and changed his grip on the axe handle. With a second strike, he severed the fittings that remained intact on the back of Olley's chamber that created hissing, sparking, and an imbalance in gel-filled tubes.

Nervous and chatty Jules turned noiseless, but a grin overtook the Guardian, who catalogued all her tells across thirty lands.

"Back in my twenty-"—he squinted as he recounted—"*sixth* reset, you loved to tell all your secrets. Almost seems unfair now."

"I—I'll say!" Her face turned to putty as she contorted expressions in search of the right words. "They don't uphold their purpose well, do they?"

"Mumus's security?"

"Mm-hmmm."

"Imagine learning your purpose in the territories is to guard fish for the Colonel."

"Don't be proud, husband. We all pay alms to our judge. Even *you*."

"I thank you for the cruel reminder."

He took one last swing and trimmed a non-conductive veil from a recessed enclosure filled with wires and tiny glass bulbs. With a bare hand, he clutched every wire and tore loose their connections. The bulbs drained in color, and the gel that supported Olley flowed from the chamber.

"You can do all you care with electricity except pay the provider."

"Remind me to tell you how oft the wise soul who told you that got electrocuted by his own hand. Or how oft Momma put out fires at the inn."

"I count not one fire here." He snuffed a smoldering wire with his heel.

TULL

A flicker of light and color drew the eyes of husband and bride toward another display plate mounted in the upper corner of the lab. There, a sculpted face with flushed cheeks and large eyes focused on Tull's intentions. She climbed through a covered stairwell from yet *another* hidden laboratory. Beneath her, water ran across the opaque tiles.

Jules bowed nearer and whisper-shouted, "*That*'s Pamila Sollars Good."

"The body in that chamber doesn't belong to you." She spoke with the same lofty, well-educated voice that Nita and Ingram possessed. "And, I promise, he'll never be as you remember him."

"An elitist?" Tull's unenthused sarcasm turned him toward other means of destruction. He gathered his axe, which he hurled at the display plate, and fractured the ethereal countenance of their hostess. "If I can't see what you're up to . . ."

"Gliders, chambers, and display plates. Better you keep those destructive tendencies from Snuggle Runt." Jules recognized a portable defibrillator unit stowed in a bin near the ruined display plate and prepared a shock baton of her own. "Dad raised me to stay prepared."

"He taught me another lesson that might prove useful." Tull removed his axe, set the blade away from harm, then stretched and rubbed his shoulders. "'When the tech outsmarts you, don't waste time on thinking.'"

Jules turned away as her husband charged the chamber that held Olley. The new headship vaulted his body toward the door and used his weight and momentum to jar the seal. The entire chamber teetered, but the seal held. So, the Guardian stepped back further, tucked his stance, and growled as he charged a second time. He bared his teeth over the impact, so a smile formed with ease when the chamber door gasped and released the seal.

Olley slithered out headlong and into a puddle of recuperative gel on the floor. Jules, ever the rescue medic, clipped her husband's tender shoulder as she rushed to tend to their friend. While Jules announced her method of treatment, Tull walked the room in search of towels or clothing, and rethought the proverbs of Keeper Victor Simon Shannon. Then, some of his bride's last words to him in that previous land borrowed his voice.

"Far and slow till morn."

THIRTY

Jules swept her fingers through Olley's wavy, black hair and whispered in his ear; that is, the ear created as a part of him. The wounded Archibaldian took a vacuum-like breath and tore off the veil that protected his new face. Too big for Jules's arms, he fell sideways onto his shoulder and vomited the breathable gel. Her sympathetic hands drew his eyes, which flittered beneath mismatched eyelids, then he traced from fingers to knuckles, wrist to elbows, shoulders to throat, lips to eyes. Her brow furrowed at the sight of his pearl-hued irises with bead-like pupils.

"Well done, Jules."

The presence of his voice sounded ghost-like, as though carried upon a breeze. Not polluted nor overrun with Wanderers. More like he haunted his own body and struggled to settle his soul. She looked from his eyes onto his lips, then waved a hand back and forth. "Can you see?"

"I see the glint of light against the rims of your teeth. I see the perspiration that seeps from your pores; so small! I hear the beat of your heart and the way your tongue searches for saliva in your mouth. The taste of the gel, so bitter! The air smells of peach blossoms and iron."

"Yes, then?"

"Yes. What eve is this?"

"The sixth morn of winter. Nelson pulled you from Gutefiel on the twenty-third morn of—"

"The offering? I remember. I remember a time when the skies bled with the deepest shades of blue. No fire. No warring. You should have seen that sky!"

Jules's focus drifted; if not due to Olley's eyes, then by his haunted reciting of peculiar recollections. "Nelson's with me."

TULL

"*Is he? How I've missed him!*" Olley sat upright with uncomfortable rigidness. He chased the change in air temperature and faced the one who found him in Gutefiel. "*Not the friend I watched enter Gutefiel, this one. No. Thirty-one!*"

The glimmer in Tull's eyes delighted in and confirmed Olley's accuracy. "Do you remember seeing Lefty there?"

"*The devil appears to you too then, does he? I found him with Lucy.*" His fingers traced the absent wounds across his chest. "*He marked me with my saber as she marked you, Nelson.*"

"O, he marked Nelson, too."

"*You withstood the chambers, did you? Yes, you do appear less gray.*"

"See?" Jules prodded her husband only in word. "He's rid the territories of all our judges except Judge Mumus."

"*My friend Wilfred Doppelt Gesicht?*"

"Unharmed . . . as are those souls whose paths we've claimed."

"*He would keep from those who might swat him, would he not?*"

"Lefty's the uncounted soul we've tracked since the hangings along Conliffe's Landing!" Jules declared her discovery with victory that made the Guardians smile. "He cut out his beacon. But, Nelson doesn't believe he and Lucy could conspire with any success."

"*I oft marveled how two halfwits together made the other more of an imbecile and not less.*"

Tull shrugged with simple agreement when Jules sought his response.

"*Our allies conspire beneath us now.*"

"I—I haven't seen them." Same childlike tone; this time, apologetic.

"*Fret not, Jules, for the faces I've seen from within my chamber might surprise even your impassive husband.*" He faced Tull with two distinct smiles across one set of teeth. "*Say the doctor who remade me has the support of many souls whom we've appeared afore, defended, and even mourned.*"

"He's never heard of Pamila Sollars Good afore."

"*Nor had I. She approached my bride and swore to make me new. She led the imbeciles beneath. 'Timber fork and weaving loom. Ten pretty raindrops, four verbs.'*"

Husband and bride never seemed more alike than when their furrowed brows and blank lips reached a loss.

TULL

"I read Lefty's lips as best I could from beneath my shroud. I may have misread a word or two."

"I—I believe that's a safe bet."

"What is that?" Olley motioned toward the scarred and refabricated portions of his face. *"My hearing seems amiss on this side. That's what I get for letting that hack fit me with Pine's ear and cheek."*

Those who knew Robbie Rudat Pine tilted in the same direction to observe the mingled faces. As Jules predicted, Good hemmed Olley together with a string of four-prong copper medical spiders that kept alive the grafted tissue. The subject of her labor obliged his friends and turned his head to accommodate. From his left side, he resembled the defaced Guardian in full, but with a different profile.

"You remain less frightening to the eye than Noeu."

"Yah is not cruel."

Jules purred, and waggled her finger at the added portion of his face. "Too bad about the chin, though."

"Still weak, I gather?"

The rescue medic shrugged with a soft chirp.

"Appreciate my fright over having mismatched feet now. You remember my shoe collection! The way fortune taunts, I should give thanks that Good saved me from a time spent with two left feet." When his gaze shifted downward, he jumped as though terrified. *"Well, thank the Triune! She kept from making me a Larsonite eunuch!"*

Both looked toward his uncovered groin. Jules teetered, and Tull flung a sopping mesh hood at him. Olley laughed and looked over the outfit's best abettor. He then stood and tested the sureness of his new calf and foot; gifts also supplied from Pine's stock. He passed between his rescuers, pulled open and shut another bin, then one after another.

"How is Marko?"

"Unaccounted for."

"I thank you." Olley scavenged a fourth bin while Jules admired his bare backside and massive shoulders. *"I feared my bride might act in haste and make all watch his end."*

Jules laughed with an uncomfortable pitch and eyed her husband. "She's a handful! What are you trying to find, Olley?"

"Pants! Cloth as soft as my bride's hair."

"Here!" Jules gathered some laboratory-rated trousers and tossed them.

Olley caught them and brushed the fabric with his thumb. His head then tilted back, and he peered down his long nose at her. "*How do you know the softness of my bride's hair?*"

She stammered till his spectral laughter filled the air.

"*Alas! Say fare thee well to my bare—*" He cleared his throat and withdrew the wardrobe he wore when he trekked out of doors on Hivi'ern. Jules's lips smacked with disappointment as he covered his muscular frame.

"About Nita." Tull's voice towed no comfort. "In her grief, she made choices that invited harm. Some might rule that her actions *helped* those who wounded you."

"*What do you say, Nelson?*"

"Her love for you is a rampage. Less never suited her."

"*Her prison?*"

"She hunts Voler in the shadows." Though he and Nita arranged for her return, his tone spoke to the likelihood.

"*Such a drastic sentence speaks to her way more than her love for me.*"

Jules distracted Tull from Olley's claim when she started reading the labels upon pipes and tubes that passed through the hidden room.

"*I lose one offering and you let traitors come into my territory?*"

Tull shook his head and spoke toward the rescue medic. "Thoughts?"

"You had no control over them."

"I meant what are you—"

She flung her hand sideways and struck his torso. "These tubes supply the tanks with seawater. They shouldn't be open. See? The tubes on this side of the room handle overflow. They should be open."

When his bride huffed and shook her head but kept a worried eye on the tubes, Tull set his hand upon her shoulder. "Tell us anyway."

"When Syd worked here, he was responsible for water pressures, filtration, and circulation. He told me that they bleed the tanks each eve to reduce the strain on the facility."

"*Letting stubborn souls believe the place sways?*"

Jules covered Tull's mouth. "At moonrise, they release water to let the bones of the place settle, but the creatures sense the change. That's why I—I never visit in the morn. They bring new water in at moonset and, by the peak, every soul in the place is balanced again."

TULL

Olley stared at his boots, one sized smaller than the other. "*Imagine we believe Sydny Gunther Burzyciel and tell us why you fret.*"

"If they flood the tanks, we stand in the territory's biggest water balloon. What about the tanks?" She pointed above with short thrusts of her arm. "The *tanks.* We can't leave them unprotected lest you want a Wanderer-possessed ice cap bear hunting you. Then there are the six thousand, one hundred forty-four *fish*, octopi, seals, dolphins, crabs, wolf-fish, sea snakes, squid—"

"*Sweet mackerel! The lady knows her local attractions.*"

"No mackerel. One septapus." She offered both Guardians a hesitant grin.

"*But how do we control the intake from here, Jules? Once we stop Lefty, do we even need worry over the spectacles above? Septapus?*"

Jules's concern for a friend spoke through her posture and expression.

"*Whatever else has happened, you needn't fear me. My heart is mine.*"

"We don't fear you, friend, but I must ensure you're safe till Jules finds a trustworthy doctor to see what's been done to you."

"*Say we lock them in till they tell of every deceit they've towed. The snakes beneath, not those above, Jules!*" He cleared his throat and shouted toward the facility's audio system. "*My name is Olley Hendrie Falk, third Guardian from the Archibald Territory. Passcode: Charade Zero-Five, Zero-Five Bond. To all—*"

AUTHENTICATION FAILED.

VOCAL PATTERN NOT RECOGNIZED.

"*She cut me off!*"

A sly noise stole from Olley's contempt for tech and captured Jules's curiosity. He then retrieved Tull's axe and tested an unfamiliar new stature when others needed his support. When his fellow took the axe that he offered, he pointed in the direction of the hatch. Tull motioned for Olley to stand behind and stepped toward the floor-based opening. Olley and Jules wrestled over who blocked whom, yet none looked for George.

Olley seized a copper-jacketed tube the length of his arm from between two threaded fittings while Jules wiped her palms and gripped the defibrillator. Tull held his axe, but released a tense breath. The sound of footsteps in the throat of the hatch then reached a halt. Stillness crept till a flow of water trickled through the clear tubes and drew Jules's frustration.

The trio reacted with silence as Asham emerged, sans disguise. He stood as tall as Jules and as broad as Tull; nowhere near as muscular as Olley. His girth came from false layers, made obvious when he opened his arms as if offering to embrace them. He held no weapons; still, his presence attracted caution.

"Well, I'm not El'āzār! Come nearer, give us hugs." When none budged, he looked toward Lucy, who joined him next. "I tell you, when I was in this outfit, we laughed!"

Jules set her eyes on Lucy alone. Her husband's shoulders rose closer toward his earlobes and his knuckles whitened as he clenched his axe.

"Let evermore come what may!" Asham mopped his chin. "Brother, I am pleased you've mended. Once you warned me, 'What we make our god becomes our demon.' Remember?"

"You are no god."

"No, no, I am no god. I'm aware of such, slow wit. But I've looked a god in the eyes as sure as I've looked you boys in the eye how many times in our pasts?" Remnants of his former smile faltered beneath the mass of tissue damage through his face. "I learned much when I sought my solace in the mountains; as you did!"

"Like me?!" The comparison offended Tull. "My retreat lasted—"

"A moon and a half," his bride interrupted.

Tull nodded as his held breath allowed.

"Two moonrises shy of a moon and a half."

"As you say, my beloved, a moon and a half."

"Minus two moonsets."

"My point"—the outfit's headship raised his voice above the distractors—"is that I told all why and where I traveled."

A hand with mismatched skin tones prodded Asham. *"Whilst you fled us like the cowards we chase."*

"We believed you met your end at odds with us." Tull stabbed Lucy with an accusatory barb and felt Jules's nearness as she convicted Asham.

"You abandoned Hazy."

Tull shielded his bride. "You had Marvin remove your beacon."

TULL

"Two fathers chose selfishness over their blameless fruit in this era!" Jules growled and tugged at Tull's shoulder. "At least the other was in pieces when we found him!"

"Do I appear *whole* to you, J. J.?"

Hearing the pet name riled Tull, and he responded hard with a backhanded cross that knocked Asham to his knees. "You followed your own way in selfishness, so do not compare your way to mine."

Olley whispered toward Jules's ear, "*Thirty-one and he's still sensitive on that topic, is he not?*"

Her husband's side-eyed impatience kept her silent, though she snuck in a nod when he looked on their betrayers.

"Truly!" Asham spat blood and teeth onto the tile. "You owed me that."

"*You're owed worse.*" Olley's hand seized Asham's throat the same way he claimed the pipe, which he tossed aside. The copper pipe stopped beneath a frail hand when Pamila Sollars Good appeared through the hatch in time to see Olley squeeze his biceps hard enough that he pulled Asham from one foot. "*You exhausted our mood for you moons ago.*"

Tull watched Lucy and the doctor tug at Asham's hands while Jules's hands released her husband's waist as she stepped back from harm.

"Let him go, Olley. I—I want to see how he talks his way from this." Jules's bravery met with a soft touch, as George patted her shoulder as a way of letting her learn he stood behind the outfit.

"*Only because she would rake the smile from your bones if you fought fair.*"

Olley offered a nod to George, which told Tull their numbers swelled. Asham, all the while, lost his balance once released. He choked on a gut-turning heave for air and wiped spittle as he sought composure.

"*You never could stand on your own. Could he, George?*"

"As you say."

"Almighty! George takes a side against me at long last! You boys'll have to forgive my weak balance. Not one flaxen-shelled beast ever swooped down to heal me, brothers. Not even when the spirits that made me their hive *punched* their way out."

Lucy helped her husband to stand.

"The Creator spited me." He turned and held out his hand till his fingers teased the cleft of Pamila Sollars Good's chin. "Then a new creator found me."

TULL

The doctor looked more like an undeveloped vine in a forest than a shade tree.

"Meet your Guardians, Pamila. Save *one*. Robbie Rudat Pine, you have met, and Nita's incomplete other *half*," he laughed at the barb, then proved vicious when he clutched Olley's jaw. "Turn your head now, Olley, and stop being rude.

"He who guards the back is Arthur George Green, whom I suspect your agent misjudged despite my warning. The sloe-eyed tart with the surly mindset toward me is Jules Baker *Shannon*; the most fearsome abettor since Valery Leta Koslowski. And, last but not least, my brother in arms, a destroyer of tech, plus the most hen-pecked soul in the territories these next thirteen moons: Nelson James Tull."

The introduction elated the scientist and she offered a bony-fingered wave toward the name she recognized and teetered without misstep.

"She's a bit overwhelmed. In one of my many moments of weakness, I spoke of your feat of outliving your end, see?"

"I marvel over your ability and your build!" Pamila pressed Tull's chest and giggled as though short of breath. "Truly!"

"You're prime stock, brother. A Soul of Endless Futures!"

The sound of Pamila's yelping chased the electronic shock and chime associated with the use of a handheld defibrillator. Her slight build lowered her resistance and sent her flailing backward between Asham and Lucy. As the scent of charring worsened, a ribbon of smoke drifted from where she landed. Every Guardian—traitors included—then looked to the rescue medic whose demeanor seemed inspired by and protective toward her husband.

"*Clear*." Jules checked the amplified power cell on the portable defibrillator while all others increased the space between their positions and hers; none more than Lucy. "Next soul who touches him gets *two*."

Olley whispered in Tull's ear, "*Pray you never make her so angry*."

"Indeed." He glanced toward the lay of his friend's hand on his shoulder.

Olley retreated. "*Oft and evermore*."

Tull set his attention onto the outfit's truest deceiver. "I trusted you to look after Jules. To look after Hazy. Knowing there was never good in you. I should have ended you when Harlan fell."

Asham toed Pamila. "I paddled her good for fibbing to you, brother."

"You're my fellow. He's my husband."

"*Still he strayed toward Lana. She who refused him for his wretchedness*."

TULL

"She who gave him a brilliant, beautiful, kind child!"

Asham squirmed away from Jules's praise of his fruit. "I've never *connected* with that kid."

Lucy boasted, "He chose *me*!"

Jules glowered at Asham. "You've lost your mind."

"Lana warned him to keep from her."

"Better you show regard, Jules. This wretch has looked a god in the eye."

Olley drove his fist against the side of Asham's face. The impact resonated with thunder and the crackle of joints served as echoing. Blood pooled, foul and spoiled, and Asham appeared genuine in his fear as he covered the wound his former ally caused him. "*Where are your imagined gods now?*"

Tull slid the broken edge of his axe along Asham's chin and drew stares. "Consider your next words, lorn soul. Blasphemy bears worse than you've suffered."

"Ask your bride." Jules, who viewed the reels from Bliss's cabin, also witnessed and cherished Lucy's swatting by Squires.

"I found Ninnian, brother."

"Truly, you are insane."

"Let Olley control his mouth again, Pine!" Lucy hissed and pointed at Jules. "And you keep yours closed too."

Asham attempted but failed to push away Tull's axe. He then drummed his fingers against the steady blade and boasted a portion of his missing time. "She sits in the mountains, beneath a tomb of ice. They buried their god on a throne of jade. Ten heads taller than I stand! Face of a lion. Covered in brass. Born as we are."

Jules gasped her husband's name for what she recognized in the soul who pursued Anya.

Tull withdrew his weapon, which drew the interest of his fellows and lit a flicker of delight in Asham's pain-ruined eyes. The storyteller dawdled. What tweaks he might make to agitate the gathering he performed twice. He preened with a twisted smirk of delight that made gracious George breathe like wrath-filled Olley.

"When first I looked into his sapphire eyes, I found purpose. *He* offers freedom from the rule of judges, their corrupt laws, and their bizarre technologies. We belong in a land with no beacons, no display plates, and no gliders. Just *flesh* amongst the *teeth* of this wilderness. Such were the intentions of Yah."

TULL

The remnants of infested spirits made him contort with violence as he spoke of their rejected Creator and flung him downward upon his knees till he struggled to control his functions.

"Now that I enjoyed. Declare His name oft!"

Lucy hissed at Olley.

"My god turned on me. He commanded I serve and filled me with spirits that hated him worse than they hated me. Two spans I served him, while my spirits informed me of his deeds since afore the flood."

"Who's flood?" Olley leaned that he might hear Asham speak Yah's name again. He swallowed his laughter and one side of his countenance wrinkled with agitation. *"This lost fool we once tolerated betrays again!"*

Tull watched Asham squirm, then set a patient eye on the accuser.

"Two spans ago, the battles of the firstkind bathed those mountains in fire! You expect us to believe you found a village of ice?"

"While you paraded through these territories! While George buried much of his herd from that fire you tell of. And while you, Nelson, while you lamented for another soul—not mine." Asham stroked the pulpy mess of his face and chastised Olley for his new appearance. "I will not tell of the comings and goings of Pine so long as he refuses to look me in the eye. Oft was he too haughty for a eunuch!"

"Then you ended him for his unkindness?"

Another voice deepened with wrath. "Pine needed suffering, so he suffered."

"*You* ended him?"

A leer stretched Asham's bride's face. "Yes."

Olley looked on Tull. *"I oft warned him."*

"As for me, I'm allowed my recollection of time for all I've suffered! O, my god proved his power! He did not withhold from me! When I displeased him in my grumbling, he spoke words that cast the spirits from me. He let me remember *suffering* and *abandonment*, brothers.

"Each of you mended the space I once occupied. Without need for me, I turned toward my well-being. I sold the *spoils* of my god to Scion Katerena Yvette Mumus, who turned to my new creator for richer insight."

Tull laughed in a way that made his bride and fellows shiver. "Your false god who hides in the ice will feel the blade of a fiery minister who answers to the Creator who made you both. You turned from your purpose out of selfishness and cowardice. Do not speak of finding a better way. Your choices made you into . . . this."

Jules charged so hard that her clenched fist startled Tull when she struck near his backside. "You lied to Hazy all this time! I—I pity the spirits that filled you both. They're no match for the monsters *you* are."

"Monsters?!" Lucy howled.

Jules elbowed her husband. "Worried I—I'd zap you, were you not?"

"Better to be a monster in this era of cowards!" Lucy hissed. "Take away their light, their hope, and they'll scatter like the souls who proved too weak for Gutefiel."

"All we buried while the pair of you caroused for spoils."

"The weight of these fools—that wear the *burden* of believing their souls capable of making gods tremble—will crush them," the outfit's first Infested member seethed. "Let every vein split and see the befallen swarm upon them.

"I remember when the Number Four Vein opened. How the fools and Believers alike lamented! How Reformers stared deep into their own bellies; condemned by their shame. I won't suffer for them again! Better their time ends."

"My bride's rage burns like her devotion for me. Truly! If I see my end, all is well. All is well. My intent will survive unto the next era."

Tull lamented. "Totu'is'esti, iul'istan, että tämä sai'asta'inen si'elu tarvetsaa si'ödä ia tehdä uutta. Totu'is'esti. Totu'is'esti."

Jules asked with a hush, "What?"

THIRTY-ONE

How the mind cataloged a store of emotions! Glances that let inner sadness flare, ways hindered by the aches of the heart, an abundance of silence gripped by defeat and disappointment, and the tears of hurt that found no physical wound to salve, filled Tull's mind, and yet none belonged to him. He felt shame in his character over the times he observed Hazy tow such emotions and how he relied on Lucy to mend her. Now he turned his disappointed gaze upon she who failed to love a blameless soul the same way she failed to regard those who fought and bled by her side. She learned nothing of keeping or giving love, yet stood as though a conqueror over Tull's bride and Asham's child—over her fellows—for the lies she kept.

"You would turn every soul into what you were. You thought he would let you, but he set his mark on you," Tull fitted the pieces of this land together to see her plot. He compared the fist-shaped bruise on Olley's jaw to their foe's hand. He then looked at the masked flesh of Lucy's jaw. "In Gutefiel, afore your dose took hold, I observed how you bore the same bruise on your jaw."

Lucy turned a half-step further from her husband.

"You arose with anger. Not at me or Pine; you've no regard for us. You were angry because Asham forsook you again," Tull accused. "All that way into Gutefiel, hemmed in by the Guardians of two eras, the gliders; still, you abandoned her *again*. Why?"

"*Marko interrupted.*"

"He didn't know about you and Marko and you needed to prove your loyalty to him—by letting him escape from Ernie's cabin—so he then returned for you. All you lacked was—"

"Me."

The Guardians looked to the sole abettor.

TULL

"Jules carried Hazel-Sue in to see her rig, and these loons took their leave."

"Olley, how do you—"

"I dared not miss seeing Hazel-Sue in her purple gown and pearl ribbons."

Jules glowed with admiration.

"I concerned my heart with your whereabouts, Nelson. My bride told me of Bliss's fate, though not her hand, when we walked toward your loft to see you."

"Your dove set a harvester on me and my offspring."

Again, Olley leveled Asham with one punch. *"Consider reminders of Hazel-Sue's kinship vulgar to we who cherish her. Further, lest we give you permission, dare not speak of our brides to us. If your parents taught you manners over coition and mouth-breathing, you might observe how we detest hearing their names soiled by your voice."*

Asham scoffed. "Coition. You amuse!"

"Yes, well, mouth-breathing was the greater insult. You were remembered better in absence than you deserved."

"Olley." Tull turned and tossed his axe to George, then motioned toward the chamber that held Pine's oddment with a nod. When he turned back, he found Jules and Olley working to corner Asham and his bride. "Olley."

"I ought to let you suffer the gnawing of flesh from your skull."

She who cleared paths through ashen fields with a scream stood cornered by the rescue medic who would soon cling to a bridge rail above the Loy with two souls in her other hand. Lucy relied on the remnants of spirits to move her. Jules's immense capacity for protectiveness proved relentless.

"I haven't the time for this from you."

"When is the time?"

Lucy cringed, not from Jules's nearness but from Olley's grip on Asham.

"After you let us mourn for you? After you manipulated us?"

Jules slammed her hand upon a medical trolley and made the defibrillator whine. "My heart's broken for you for three spans! For Hazy!"

"Stop. Do not rile me!" Lucy threatened, but stepped back when Jules persisted.

"Do you believe our friends can pry me off afore you lose the light, you coward?"

"Hazy ran to my arms when she wept for her father! When she hid from you!"

"Stop me, coward. Pry my hand from your collapsing throat."

"Stop this!" Tull barked. He tried his best to make Olley stop and fretted over Jules's anger toward short-tempered Lucy.

TULL

"I tell you," the spirit of rage turned Lucy's eyes blood red, "stop!"

The pitch of the cornered Guardian's scream thrust Jules off her feet. She struck Tull, who proved his reflexes when he seized his bride's wrist. Still, the force knocked him over and, though he protected his bride's head and neck, they slid across the floor. Lucy's scream cast laboratory devices at her foes but she exhausted her breath too soon to burst eardrums as she had in that previous land.

From the rafters above the exposition, a miscreated scream rolled back into the hidden lab. The structure grumbled, and the shifting of water drew a groan of pain from the supports. As the site stood on the verge of collapse or settlement, the sounds of water-dwelling creatures turned timid. Jules's ache for them showed on her face, but a sound of twisted laughter provoked her empathy toward anger.

"This is where we put to rest your tales and your prophecies, brother!"

Tull watched only Jules, and inspected her for injuries with hands that caressed her form and softened her half-angered, half-terrified gaze.

"Let the place fall!" Asham roared with laughter and raced toward the Jacobian. "Let the waters rush down on those who forsook my bride's power. I feel no fear toward my end! I rest safe in Nelson James Tull's shadow! Not one Minister might risk him to sacrifice me! I need only outlast him!"

He then took a dagger-like glass piece from the remnants of Olley's chamber door. "Will the Ministers be so kind to the souls that go afore my brother's end? Will they delay my hand? I wonder!"

Asham reached out, as if toward Jules. A smile spread across Lucy's face and dizzied Pamila Sollars Good over a chance to witness a reset. None feared the reflexes Tull demonstrated, nor considered the displaced axe that George lost in Lucy's display of rage. In this, he taught them a lesson.

The sound of Asham's lifted scream collided with the patter of water droplets that struck the blade from above. Most saw the glimmer of false light across the face of the axe but missed the ribbon of blood that lined the edge. They reacted to the scream of pain brought on by the embedded glass dagger that shattered in his clenched hand.

Then, Asham fell to his knees and gripped his forearm. His breath hastened, and sweat gathered around those discolored pockets of flesh that remained colorless even as he reddened in pain. The flesh of his forearm opened and blood, spoiled by the remnants that once filled him, seeped with a slow, muddied trickle. With one swipe,

TULL

Tull's blade segregated the wrist and forearm flexor muscles from his foe's dominant left limb. He then pressed his foot to Asham's chest and cast him to the belly of the room.

"*Let us see, indeed.*" Olley winked at the axe-wielder. "*I tell you, from now on, I'll only refer to him as Lefty.*"

Tull seized the soul who earned his nickname after he gored Hansel Ornlam Hofnarr. "Reach for my bride again and I'll take your whole arm."

The axe-bearer shielded Jules and wiped his blade across his bootheel while Pamila sought to restrain the loss of Asham's blood. The roar from above proved louder than his cry of pain, and Jules held to her husband as if she believed they might all suffer their end. George protected Pine's oddment, and Olley settled for a spot between friends and foes. Lucy, all the while, never budged or reached for Asham.

Even as the sound of roaring filled the room like a fog, Tull calmed Jules with his voice more than his words. "The time nears . . ."

He set his hands against his bride's ribs and thrust her backward with all his might. George caught her, then a tremendous thunder echoed, and fragments of the panels above cascaded like granules of sand. The roar mingled with the sound of breath from a creature that sought another. Lighting flickered and sparks showered, but the peace-filled eyes of the soul who lasted ten eves in Gutefiel never wavered.

Arms of brass broke through the panels and the face of Si'el Uaen Söi'eä took the brunt of every shard. Brass showed beneath every cut, and the teeth of a lion preceded a roar of victory as she discovered her prey. The heels of her feet kissed the framework of illuminated floor panels and every loose object fell away in response to her immense power. As she crouched, her hands took hold of Lucy's calves and her nose smelled wickedness.

Her roar turned into an anticipatory groan, and saliva dripped around her jutted incisors. She offered Tull a grateful smile, less than a direct glance, and claimed Lucy as *hers*. With a backward somersault, she sought an exit without regard for her destruction or the souls she blanketed in aftershock. But the Jacobian, who called on the creature with a request in the language of the First Creation, seized Lucy by her wrists and halted the creature's plans.

"I saw the First beheaded, watched Ministers battle giants, and let those I loved most slip through my fingers that I might chase a monster among us."

TULL

Lucy buckled and resisted. She attempted to ignite unnatural flame, like the one that destroyed Tull's best lead toward his mother, or the one that lit her way to aid her husband after he ended Judge Bliss. Spilled water drenched her limbs and pooled in the palm of her open hand. Each flick of her fingers produced less than grit, till she resembled dull flint.

Tull pressed his thumb against her moist palm. "My heart has not yet stopped weeping for that land!"

While Si'el Uaen Söi'eä roared over his hindrance, she kept from pulling apart Lucy. She, too, savored the fallen Guardian's punishment and prolonged her torment and that of the remnants that hid within her next meal.

"I walked a trail littered with the bodies of friends whose sacrifice broke my heart and filled my soul with hope in brighter morns. I stood in the wake of terror so loud that the wail of the heartsick shattered my eardrums. With my last breath, and Nita's favorite bow, I set two arrows into a blinding storm of snow and salted ash."

Lucy cried out in anguish as the remnants twisted her body from within but could not free her from Si'el Uaen Söi'eä's or Tull's grip. Water crested over her and she alone witnessed the tears of truth on their storyteller's face. He used both hands and the full strength of his arms, but saw the unrecognizable pools of color in Lucy's eyes; blackened as the perceived depths of the sea. Nothing of his fellow stared back at him. Still, he spoke to the soul he faced in that previous land.

"All I sacrificed to end you."

When the remnants squirmed, Si'el Uaen Söi'eä roared as if to threaten them. Even those remnants that dwelled within Asham responded. He screamed out as he writhed, and his wound foamed. Blood flowed toward Lucy's face, pooled in the true pockets of a face she disguised, but not one tear fell from her eyes for Asham or her own fate.

Olley, who bowed and took a handful of Asham's hair, taunted, "*Be sure you watch your bride, brother.*"

Every soul in the territory heard tales of the creature. Few observed her.

"In the name of I'Esh, if you meant no deception, if you meant no harm to us, you'll slip from this creature's hand and I'll end her with all that is in me." As proof of his word, Tull released one of Lucy's wrists and gathered his axe.

Asham kicked and clawed; as fear-filled by Tull's axe as the remnants of wandering spirits feared Si'el Uaen Söi'eä—*the Devourer*.

TULL

"But, if my belief of you proves true, no Guardian will keep you from the feast you'll provide her."

His hand slipped from her wrist and over her palm till Lucy held to Tull only by three of her fingers. Globs of mire trickled from her mouth and opened the corners of her lips, but the remnants consumed her voice till only her deeds spoke for her.

"Believe I'll say a prayer for you each morn and each eve." His head trembled, and his eyes pooled with tears. "I'll ask that every Minister carry you to Ki'eoppa for breaking Hazy's heart these past one thousand ninety-five eves."

Every Guardian—plus Jules—kept the number of eves that passed since Asham abandoned them. Now, neither traitor looked upon the other's shame.

"I'll ask that your descent creeps like the winter, that you claw your way free morn upon morn and relive the terror of falling into the pit again; once for every lie she heard from your lips."

He remained still, but another of Lucy's fingers slipped away.

"Believe I curse the eve when the Count spared you and believe that *this* fate is *that* punishment which he kept you from."

The last any soul in the room saw of her, Lucy demonstrated none of the traits that defined her. None even recognized her true face. The spirits that manipulated her invitation screamed out as Si'el Uaen Söi'eä's hold proved righteous. Lucy faced an excruciating punishment but would live; a truth that Tull believed Si'an-dro Sa'ähn would agree upon.

"Impossible!" Asham declared amid his failure and loss.

"'*Impossible is an idea designed by the fear-filled to keep us from proving our dominance over them.*'"

Tull smirked, given the way that Olley here cited Asham's verse that made him cringe in that previous land. He watched the sea that flowed through the hatch between lower levels reach his boots and remembered the end he suffered between those lands. "George, lest my bride objects, I believe our time to go has come. Would you take our fallen brother?"

As George and Jules prepared Pine, Olley eulogized the fellow whose face he wore in part. "*May he know we broke those who betrayed us.*"

"Olley, I'll ask you to see the doctor from this place."

"Would this land not be better if we let them suffer their end? Would this land not be better if I stayed with them?"

TULL

Tull set a hand upon his shoulder.

"Come nearer, Doctor!" Olley pulled she who remade him to her feet and from Asham's touch. "You may delight in learning how I dreamt of you whilst put away in my chamber. O, what I plotted for you!"

Too overcome to resist, Pamila too abandoned Asham. Tull glanced upon the wound he caused and showed no remorse when the betrayer cast a hurt-filled glance upon him. "Leave me to my end!"

What Tull muttered in response never reached the ears of Jules, George, or Olley; but, Pamila used her weight to attempt to break free from her former patient's hold. The other souls, who gauged the door, watched her attempt fail.

Then, Olley called to his dearest friend, "Best to keep up, old bear! This exit looks more like a swim."

Fallen firstkind creatures of small shape and muted pattern swam through the saltwater-filled tubes. Some appeared transparent, except for rows of eyes and teeth. A vent burst from the tube on the opposite side of the lab, and an alarm then sounded upward, from the place where Asham and Lucy entered the lab.

When the exposition trembled a second time, the setting drifted toward sea, as evidenced by the spill of water from the tanks to the east. "*This place truly does shift! Imagine!*"

"Nelson!" Jules groaned, then gasped, for she saw what her husband held in his hand. He spoke in a hush and dangled the pouch of smooth stones like a hypnotic trinket. Then, he dropped them into the open hand he rested against Asham's midsection.

"*Why does the sight of this make me weary? Nelson?*"

"He stopped a security patrol with a stone from that bag."

"*What's to protect him from Jules?*" Olley turned from smugness when George patted his shoulder and seized hold of their prisoner.

Jules marched toward Tull and Asham with a stiff-armed gait that proved whom Hazy mimicked in a rush. "Nelson!"

"There are enough stones to cover every soul you harmed: Pine, Marko, Monteith, Tim, your judge, Nita's father, Samuel, Elwell, Marvin, and honorable Ernie Purcell Bliss."

"Nelson, please, we have to go. Hazy is waiting. She expects us."

Tull blinked and looked on her. "I've not forgotten."

TULL

"Well, then what does he have to say to release—" She furrowed her brow when Asham burst with laughter.

"Tell her!"

"He set the lock on his own head!" Asham laughed through each syllable. "His soul is the key."

Olley wrapped his arms around Tull. Though he tried till the original portion of his face turned red and his eyes dripped with tears, their new headship never budged. Jules shouted, then slapped at the bag and her lover's hand but cringed as she cracked the knuckles in her hand.

"Why would you do this?! I—I will not leave you here."

"Now, now, Jules. Nelson believes in every soul's right to redemption. This time, he hemmed your souls to that belief. What was that you said afore you set your rocks upon me? I dare not—"

"What did you say?"

Tull's smile failed to soften Jules, so he repeated the words as though he made a second plea. "Jos halu'un pelaestaa tämän si'elun, ru'koi'len, että pi'dätte kai'kki, jotka ovat mi'nu'n kanssani."

"'If I—I am to ransom—'"

"'Save.'" George backed away when Jules arched her brow in his direction. "I believe the word is save."

"'If I—I am to save this soul . . .'" Tull's bride looked upon him.

"'I pray you please spare all who are with me.'"

Olley roared loud enough to create an echo that paled against his regard for a stubborn friend.

"All is well."

"No, husband." Jules checked his pulse rate. "Your heart is racing."

"Toward what end?"

"If the water level reaches his heart, he'll go into convulsions. Once they top his shoulders, he'll go into arrest."

"Nothing brings them down like blasphemy. Or, one of you might cut off his hand. Lest you swing too deep."

The trio looked down on Asham.

"Forget I spoke!"

TULL

"*His idea might spare you till Jules got her hands on you.*" Olley nudged Tull with his hip. "*Truly! I will pay to have all your shirts tailored for two opposing arm-lengths lest my butcher can reattach your hand after I cut—*"

"You wouldn't hurt him, Olley!" Jules stilled him. "You couldn't."

"*Do not risk her soul for his. I tell you, he cannot be saved.*"

Tull drew a proud breath that gave away his struggle.

"Feeling winded, brother?"

"Racing heart, labored breathing"—Jules fanned her hand and tracked his eyes—"and limited vision . . ."

In the same manner he swept tears from Hazy's cheek in that previous land, Tull felt his bride wipe beads of sweat from his face. His breathing sounded like a roar in his ears, and he felt his extended posture give as light-headedness swayed him. His tongue adhered to the dry roof of his mouth, and high-pitched ringing overtook the sounds around him.

"Nelson?"

"*Why would you sacrifice for this misborn fool?*"

"A span comes . . . when Hazy wants to know her father. Will we . . . deprive her that?"

His thoughtfulness surprised Jules and made Olley laugh through tears till he turned away and retrieved the axe.

"The water on the other side keeps the door from opening. I'm sorry, my friends!"

Olley waved off George and steadied Tull as he sheathed the weapon. "*You've a plan through all this then?*"

Tull's keenness struggled against the waking conditions of Loughery-Ruben Syndrome, but he trusted the distinctiveness Yah created in him and remembered the Helper's words, which had run through his thoughts since he entered the facility.

"Let falling waters rise around you and pour back into the sea."

"I do."

Jules forced his eyes open and held him steady. "Give me your word."

"My word is yours." He rested his crown on her shoulder, wheezed, then rapped his knuckles against Asham. "And his."

"*I would stay and watch him drown in your stead.*"

TULL

"We won't drown, Olley."

"Lest you make the Ministers as frazzled as you make us!"

A tank above burst and created a wave fierce enough to rip open the mouth that Si'el Uaen Söi'eä formed from the sole panel that Tull and George removed. While the opening offered unrestricted views of the tanks above, George checked the seal of the door while Pamila wrapped a hand around one of the chamber latches. Despite Si'andro Sa'ähn's plea, Tull risked sacrifice for the unrepentant soul, and now the others, on his ability to discern the Helper's voice.

Olley scooped Jules off her feet with one arm and bounced her with two flexes of his shoulders. *"Let us keep you from floating away."*

"Olley! I—I don't want to be near your rear when the next tank goes!"

He chose a vertical support beam as an anchor. *"What's in that tank?"*

A voice as small as Hazy's crept from the abettor's lips. "Put me down first."

Asham repeated Olley's concern. "What's in that tank?"

She climbed from Olley's shoulder onto the same beam and rested her arches on the perpendicular rails used for hanging and storage. "Sea serpents."

As Olley cursed, Asham decided, "I might get my reset after all!"

"Friends!" Tull breathed with a soothing tone. "I believe you should all gather near and hold on."

Jules responded first, though she used Olley's arm as a slide, and nestled close to her husband's racing heart, beneath the arm that held the bag of stones upon Asham. Olley circled but hesitated when he saw his new face reflected on the blade of Tull's axe. Tull sensed the proud soul wither, and linked arms with his friend.

"George!" His voice weakened. "The time nears."

"I—I really despise that phrase."

Tull kissed his bride's crown between jagged breaths.

"I bolster Jules's claim, but ask that you keep your lips from me."

Jules reached to hold Olley's forearm too.

"George!"

Pamila Sollars Good screamed in refusal of Tull's plan and George's attempts to coerce her. She crawled into the belly of the chamber where she kept Pine and locked the chamber door like a vault. Her panting for air soon fogged over the glass; though, by then, George joined his friends and kept his arms around Olley and Jules.

TULL

Tull proved well-informed of his bride's favorite getaway and spoke to calm his friends. "The architect of this glass heap patterned her design on the boats of old, though inverted. The center supports rest higher, letting all water run toward the outer ledges in the event of a leak. As the tanks fail, the heart will rise."

"In my *design*"—Asham craned his neck to keep above the rising waters—"my bride and I ran out the front door."

"Your plan involved casting spirits and creatures across my territory."

When the disgraced former Guardian struggled to hold his head from the water's surface, Jules pulled on his crown. "You revile us so much that you'll let us meet our ends here? That's the way you want the next era to remember you? My husband's hurt. But I—I tell you, there isn't a more forgiving soul in all the territories than him except for Hazy. He protects her in your stead. Tell us the truth and I—I believe he'll try to forgive you and help you. Please, Lefty . . ."

"You speak to a soul that remains in the mountains, Jules."

A grumble louder than the echo of a handclap shook the whole facility. Jules arched her back and stared upward. The pressure-sensitive tubes that controlled the *soft* flow of water into the tanks now gushed unfiltered seawater into the whole facility.

Accursed creatures of all shapes and deformities plunged into the tanks, intent on freedom and havoc. Those elegant creatures that resided at the aquarium exposition panicked, further stirring their waters in retreat. Copper screws with heads larger than a Jacobian's hand turned out of position as the glass walls bulged in their setting.

"If we're to see our end, I'm with the best lot."

"Nita would've hated this!" Jules spoke above the water's roar.

Asham took his last breath as the water covered him.

"I—I could use that tube so he could—"

Olley cursed and pulled Asham's head above water, even at risk of breaking his sternum and ribs. "*Rile me and I will drown you. Then let us see who the Ministers save once—*"

"Be still. I know a creature who never gives up on fools."

THIRTY-TWO

Patience held, however well-tested, but the falling water rose and covered Asham's face a second time. While he struggled to breathe through a copper pipe, the increase covered Jules's belt. Still, none debated Tull's plan. Even when the bulk of spillage filled the corridor outside the lab, and still bled around the seal along the high side of the doorjamb.

What few creatures entered kept their distance, minus some spine-tingling sweeps of fins and tails against the Guardians' backs. A test of wills needled even more. Tull's belief proved as well-rooted as Asham's vainglory. The former proved his determination to *frighten* a friend into repentance, and the latter refused to surrender his scheme. Both exhibited a calmness that suggested fearlessness so near the end.

As the water teased Jules's breastbone, great light washed over them; as though her husband pled for her safe-keeping above his own. The sight of flames pierced the waters above. None moved with greater purpose than Enke'loi, who led a battalion of Ministers in response to the Son of Mighty Maidens' *call* for rescue. Siblings of the firstkind detached and warred against their befallen counterparts, while a drove of Squires raced behind Enke'loi.

She cut through the cascading waters with radiant elegance and drew a mace from the palm of her hand. As she sliced through the approaching wave, she reared back her weapon and focused on the traitorous soul. Tull held Jules with his thigh and tugged his fellows closer with one arm. Olley set his hands across the backs of their heads as George used his arms as shields.

Asham's irises pooled with color but paled amid other senses. Enke'loi wailed, and her voice drove back the water and scattered the pouch of smooth stones that pinned the Jacobian she protected. Her fire-forged mace passed through the once-infested body but did not wound Asham. In his flesh's stead, she pulled from him every wicked trace of the Fallen First that set him on a vile path.

Fire, like the eruption of a star, burst around them as the Fallen First burned. Squires gathered their ash and swooped toward the atrium. They passed through the falling waters as another Minister spread his mighty arms and vaulted down around Asham. Though he resisted at first, the once-infested aggressor found keeping in the Minister's hold just as Enke'loi's hold kept Tull calm.

The copper screws that reinforced the tanks darted through the air, burrowing holes through multiple glass walls. Seams pulled apart, and walls teetered till their weight fractured every face. Creatures that weighed more than the combined Guardians broke free while the Fallen First scurried to incite as much dread as possible. In eighteen heightened heartbeats, the facility interior fell upon the outfit.

While the waters crashed over them, not one succumbed. Figures of brass and fire shielded them while Squires who served Enke'loi towed the aquatic creatures through waves that crushed glass and shook the foundation. Two tiny plumes of fire pulled Jules from harm, turning her with gentle swiftness and keeping her from the paths of mighty creatures. Another held her feet and kept her calm as more Squires rescued George and Olley.

They shared the waters with creatures whose unflawed form found sanctuary from Asham's plan. Those spirits sought homes within them but Enke'loi led a swift counterattack and repelled every fallen member of the First Creation. Rare creatures swam with complete innocence around the Guardians and their Ministers, proving the goodness that still existed in their time.

Enke'loi and her fellow Ministers pulled Guardians and abettor from the flood whilst teams of brass-bodied creatures kept safe every creature designed for the sea and the ice. Even whilst immersed, Tull believed he *heard* Jules's delight-filled laughter. She marveled over these creatures since they met. Now she swam in their waters unafraid. The aquarium exposition teetered as the waters sloshed back and forth, but the facility never plunged into the Forbidden Sea.

Comforting Ministers filled the gaps between their warring counterparts and let their flames dry the sopping clothes of the rescued souls. Upon Jules, they draped a veil that smelled of hyssop and dried her tears. Olley felt the mending touches of his rescuers upon his wounded flesh and spirit for the first time. In all of this, Tull gave thanks.

TULL

A Warring Minister—one whose stature dwarfed Enke'loi—screamed as he descended. Out of one hand protruded a sword of fire. In the other hand, the head of the creature Asham declared a *god*. The defeated Guardian howled at the proof of Tull's word and bowed one last time to an undeserving creation. As the Warring Minister cast down the creature's head, a gathering of Ministers and Squires arose on plumes of fire. A hush fell over the crowd that watched, till even Partakers bowed.

The attacker of judges, who betrayed bride, daughter, and purpose, and who took in the Fallen First, knelt in surrender at the feet of Chief Hont whilst rescue medics treated his harshest wounds. Before the secondkind, he seemed to shrink in stature and ruthlessness. Enke'loi rid him of every foul spirit; still, the secondkind's law demanded trial for his actions and no escape from his soul's failings.

"I thank you for," Tull paused and grinned. "I was going to say *cleansing* him, but that falls rather close to his nose. Simply, I thank you."

The Warring Minister who saved him shimmered.

He kneaded his chest. "She'll see a brighter eve now."

"Remember this season, Son of Mighty Maidens. Be watchful."

As he faced her, he found Enke'loi departed. "Be at peace, cousin."

"I—I never believed in devourers."

"*I never believed in Lucy, of all souls.*"

"She *smelled* her?"

"Devourers smell the air that rakes our skin. That's how they learn of our goodness or our wickedness."

Olley patted Tull's back. "*You found the Devourer.*"

"Anya found her. At the least, she uncovered her resting chamber."

"I—I'd rather give you the credit." She then turned solemn. "I—I saw that creature that Lefty *served* chase Anya till she flung herself to the shores at Ardent Peaks."

"*Pride of the Gierigians . . .*"

For the first time, Tull and his fellow Guardians were treated as *common* souls; even after the events they survived. Onlookers shirked their regard for the outfit and cast adoration upon the Ministers and Squires and the monstrous head; including George, whose paleness did not go unnoticed.

"*How a small token changes much.*"

"From what I—I saw, losing his head was a kind end."

TULL

"That creature could crush every soul in these territories and not suffer a bruise. Asham was no more than an amusement to him."

"They are why you . . ." The pertness of Jules's voice faded but her husband kept her near.

"*Believe me odd, if you must,*"—the light shone through Olley's pearl-hued eyes when he looked upon the head and sent a chill along Jules's spine when he glanced toward the three-lane avenue—"*but I bear a distinct recollection of suffering my end on a cold bed of stones near where we stand.*"

"A cold bed of stones?"

"*Seems to me, yes. My bride alongside me. Nelson stood over me.*"

Tull looked toward the adjacent, cobblestone roadway where Olley met his end in that previous land and along the same route, where Pine met a fiery end. From his past thirty resets, only one other soul spoke to Tull with the knowledge of truths from another land. Given the aftershock of the mending chambers and Pamila Sollars Good's perversions, he considered now Olley made two.

"*You needn't fret, Jules.*"

"I'm fussing, not fretting." She felt the structure of his mended face. "Where will they put Lefty now?"

"*There are places. Those I fear I might see afore my end. My cobbler sent me into the eve. I dread waking in a cold sweat with absolute remembrance why. We've heard of stranger, though.*" He looked upon watchful Tull. "*Have we not?*"

"We have."

"Olley, come back to the loft with us. Hazy will want to tell you of her Hivi'ern feats. Honorine's there. She, or I—I." She exhaled and shut her eyes. "I could look on your wounds. Come home with us, won't you?"

"He will." Tull ended his remark with a gradual nod.

"*As you say.*"

Jules kissed the faces of both souls and held to her husband's arm.

Tull's gaze traced the hem of the sky-fires as he heard Lucy's scream from that previous land. "On the first eve, beneath the Moon of the Sower's Hand, of the hundred twenty-second sowing season, we sought to keep Lucy from raising Vi'emane the Last. The worst of the Seko'tae."

"You stopped her."

"*Now she cannot.*"

TULL

The one who knew their deeds best refocused his heart. "What do I tell Hazy?"

"That misborn Lefty never wanted her, which is good—as he never deserved her."

"Or," Jules patted Olley's forearm and held Tull's hand, "say what no soul said to you when you learned of Patrick's end."

"Heed her advice afore mine."

"By what authority?" Chief Hont's distant voice barked above the squeal of smitten onlookers.

"I confess, I may not—"

Jules squeezed his wrist. "Nelson didn't say a word. Look to your east. There's a glider near the chief."

Olley turned in the direction of Jules's nod but appeared slow to focus. Chief Hont and Asham stood surrounded by souls armed with shock batons; not one of them *official*. The chief's deputies stepped back, away from their superior, and surrendered their lawful advantage anyway.

"Get back!"

Even as the chief inspector held his ground, their benefactor appeared upon seven oval-shaped display plates mounted to a shimmering black rig. Draped in a gown designed for distraction, the territory's advocate scion, Katerena Yvette Mumus, drew gasps from the crowd and the obedience of her father Cyril's agents. Only the Mumus name held the power to dim the sense of wonder the onlookers expressed. Her arrogance kept her from an appearance among those she lived *above*.

"Guardian Gera pledged his purpose to my whims. And,"—she raised a talon-like finger toward Olley, as she appeared in the same manner on every display—"*that* Guardian has benefitted from enough of our ingenuity that he's beholden to the Mumus tree evermore. You will release them into my care, lest—"

Chief Hont proved true to the law. "You'll need to tell of this soul's activity against our judges—and prove how far your whims took him."

"We'll be taking them with us now." Katerena's field envoy threatened, but lacked her influence. "Scion Mumus does not bend—"

"No!"

The sureness in Tull's voice drew attention onto the trio.

"Guardian Tull . . ." Katerena sought to speak as if amused by him; as Sondrea oft did without berating him. "On this matter, I suggest—"

TULL

"You are an advocate scion, Katerena. You have no seat to make suggestions to me. You hold no say over Chief Inspector Hont or these two souls. Claims elsewise demand the decision of our judges, lest you seek to confess your hand maneuvered these two souls you covet."

She laughed as if she found him simple. "By our very custom—"

"Custom is not law. If a law of our kind has changed, let your father and two of our new judges come forward and tell us. Elsewise, by the law, and as headship, I tell you I will uphold the duties of my purpose against any soul who puts a violent hand upon *any* Guardian or abettor."

"You dare challenge—"

"Add to that any fruit of *my* judge's tree or any blameless soul born to this outfit or our new judges." Tull held eye contact with the scion then changed to whom he spoke. "Load your prisoner, Chief Hont. Let our *seated* judges decide his fate."

"You provoke a war."

"My purpose is to defend the secondkind from monsters, Scion Mumus. Defy me, and you'll not find a tower high enough, nor a nest deep enough, to hide in."

"The Guardian who doesn't end his foes!"

"Paralysis doesn't keep a soul from repentance. Amputation doesn't keep a soul from repentance. These are established laws of our judges—like your father. The souls of this age will no longer suffer beneath your tree's prosperity as you redefine and manipulate our laws. Tell the Colonel I say so . . . when his slumber ends."

The scion who enjoyed tremendous extravagance knew nothing of war, so her threat faded with the breeze. What semblance of respect Tull extended for Sondrea's sake faded too. When Katerena faced a loss of how to respond without appearing weak to those subservient onlookers, her glider retreated with a whistle. Tull dismissed her without a conscious blink of his eye as Chief Hont sneered and set Asham into a well-secured rig.

"And you fretted I might shame you."

"No, never you, Lotta Ornery."

"*That's settled.*" Olley scoffed at the likelihood but patted Tull's back. "*You are our headship. I tell you, her timing tows much suspicion. A soul born into alms, authority, deceitfulness . . . yet she turns her mighty ear toward Lefty's whims.*"

"Don't encourage his suspicions, Olley. I—I'm going to melt down that axe!"

TULL

George returned to the fold. "We're to have a peace-filled war with the most powerful name of our kind then, are we not?"

"Make a chain to lock you to any object you cannot move."

"The old judges believed you would rebuke their authority."

"I imagine they had no idea he befriended a Devourer, George."

"I believe Sister Lois knew all along that I would need her help."

"A Reformer's help or a judge's help, husband?"

"The Devourer's help. The Larson Territory's new judge sent me to her"—he glanced toward the territory's former Guardian—"afore the wrong soul found her."

"I—I've oft said she's more cunning than any Partaker."

"I watched her crush a skull the way that Beau Itzal Zeck opened walnuts."

"Sister Lois?"

"Again, the Devourer. She bore a tunnel—cut the glebe with her hands—and fled into the sea."

"And, you sided against the chase?"

"I leapt. I saw the drowned villages beneath and found a chance to doubt my sense; as many have doubted. Then, a Squire took hold of me and returned my feet to the glebe. He likes fools too, I s'pose."

"That's why you smelled of fire when I—I found you here."

"That's why." He admired the veil upon his bride's crown and looked toward the sea with an uncertain breath in his chest. "The Colonel has survived one hundred seventy-four spans."

No groaning, scoffing, or cursing met his claim against a soul who turned gray afore the Accession. Jules looked to him for reassurance and a need for openness.

"He's created a false history; calling son *father* and bride—*first* bride—*grandmother*, lest we wonder."

"Katerena?"

"I first met her the morn after my father's end. She slept in a crib then."

"She is not her mother, my friend."

"No."

"One hundred seventy-four?"

"Even a creature like me asks how that's possible."

"He served in the Last War."

"For the wicked side of the dissenter, no doubt."

TULL

"Quite the opposite. When the first of the Seko'tae appeared, moons afore the First Creation, he ordered the troops he commanded to do their bidding. He's a *conscript*. He arranged and fulfilled their safekeeping, these creatures, and guarded the chambers while those he served hid."

Tull pointed his friends toward the severed head surrounded by new onlookers. "The old fathers feared looking upon them, which gave them power. The Seko'tae awaited a morn, when the warring ended, when they might rule over us. In their hesitancy, the firstkind appeared to our ancestors and upset that plot."

"They've lived beneath all this time?" Jules's voice hinted at sympathy.

"Like the Taotáva?"

"In fear, you can imagine."

"Am I to believe"—Olley leaned on Jules with a sigh—*"that since you're here to speak of these Seko'tae that your time there met an unsavory end?"*

Tull checked the morn's tide and recalled the waves that stood over him in that previous land. "I choose to believe that some of us remain safe there. I believe Katerena learned of the Seko'tae from the Colonel and sent Anya to the Church Amid the Shadows in hopes of seeing her, well, *devoured*.

"'O, the terrane abideth!' I thank you, even more now, for keeping me from Cyril's daughter's clutches."

"I seek another reason for Anya to align her soul with Mumus again."

"You ought to talk to your brother, Olley."

All three Guardians responded, *"Half-brother."*

"A bit less than half now." Jules prodded the cheek of Pine's face.

Olley looked skyward and nodded toward the medic. "Hear her?"

She smiled her best smile and teased his ear with a pinch. "Afore Anya was hurt by that . . . Seko'tae . . . she called out for a soul named Jonas as if she expected him."

"When you have rested," George offered, "I will go with you to see him."

"I thank you, George."

"Olley, who did you see that we've already mourned? You said you—"

"My mind is sane and still. Let us settle, let Hazy rest in your comfort, and we Guardians and our abettors will talk about all . . . if that pleases our headship."

"As you say."

"I must find my abettor, my bride, and my purpose again."

"We'll find them."

TULL

"I may never be what I was . . . to any of you . . . without her."

"A chance I'll take evermore."

"As will I!" George put an arm around Olley's shoulders.

"The new judges could benefit from our obedience for now. We must reconsider our pact against replacements."

"You're bringing in new Guardians?"

"We'll need a wise soul to help train new abettors."

"I believe our headship just denied your remotion."

"I've lost my friends enough times. What we face next, wicked or joy-filled, I must do all I can to see that all of you survive with me."

"Let us leave the princess to cry in her tower a spell. Tell me, George, where you were when our new leader was named, if I heard right, a judge scion."

"I was beneath a stupor!"

"From exhaustion?"

"I believe from shock!" The calmest outfit member's laughter resonated and filled onlookers with surprise and glee.

Because the whole of the territories observed the end of Lucy and Asham's tirade, their former fellows found no reason to keep from their rest till the moonrise. George walked with them till a route toward the rail system intersected the direct path back to Tull's loft. All intended to gather again soon. When they hugged farewell, they heard the sirens of Chief Hont's rig depart with Asham in tow, ending the pursuit of the territories' latest monster. Then, Tull refocused his heart on the worst of all aches.

1721 FRESNEL PARK

THE ARCHIBALDIAN HOME OF JULES BAKER SHANNON AND NELSON JAMES TULL . . .
AS WELL AS HAZEL-SUE LAEL, FOR WHOM THEY SOUGHT A PETITION OF EMBRACEMENT.

The first morn without a father or mother, Tull awoke in a bed nicer than any other he slept in afore and with no memory of how he arrived there. The last peace-filled sleep in his blamelessness preceded the worst morn of his time. A blameless babe slumbered in a crib in this same room and, in a way, established a bond between them.

The way he challenged her afore others this same eve strained, perhaps severed, that bond.

Countess Sondrea Ebbe Conliffe and Judge Leander Jonathan Bromley informed him of his father's end, which claimed a tether to his mother's forsaking, over a gift of chocolate doughnuts. He detested chocolate since. A treat meant for joy, for reward, symbolized evermore a time of painful loss. Even so, he stopped on the way back to the loft and bought a wax sack filled with the oversized, over-frosted treats.

Honorine sensed the Jacobian's hurt the moment he, Jules, and Olley arrived. She hugged them all, though she remained closest to her rig partner. The two souls who stood as witnesses when Tull and Jules wed represented the first who learned the news of their plans to invite a daughter into their home. They found her seated on the couch, amused by another animated reel of hilarious birds.

He who knew Hazel-Sue across many lands cherished her as a treasure and joy. How he shielded her from pain, scooped her up in one arm, and made her laugh proved he knew his role as *her* Guardian, her defender and provider, too. Jules and Honorine basked in the savory sound that filled the loft with warmth; but not more than Olley, who never stood prouder than the moment the blameless soul greeted him with a smile and a wave. Like the loss of light in the race toward winter, they savored her warmth as long as possible.

Guardian and blameless soul watched an animated reel together, with Hazy clinging to Tull's nearness after missing him since he followed Si'an-dro Sa'ähn out of the church on Little Oak Way. She showed no resentment or distance. She never even sought attention from the others. They both ate a doughnut—Hazy faster than Tull—and he smiled every time she delighted in the animated hijinks.

Then, in a moment of stillness, he remembered the morn that followed his father's end and the wisdom his bride offered him. He set the blameless wonder on his knee, brushed her face, and waited till she looked him in the eyes. "I tell you, for as long as I breathe, you will not be abandoned again; nor will your joy."

In the time of truth-telling, Tull spoke to the fears he faced in his blamelessness and all that remained without answer. He spoke of Lucy and Asham's virtues more than their fates, which he explained with honest, simple detail. Hazy slapped his mouth, pounded his shoulders, and buried her face in his neck as she wailed for souls she loved but feared. Tull welcomed the brunt of her pain and wept with her, but he never let her believe this land was no longer safe.

TULL

Honorine departed onto the terrace with Olley, and Jules held her two loves close. Hazy plunged into her arms, weeping all over again, but her right hand never let go of Tull's shirt. Just as she had in that previous land, she relied on him. This time, she of three mothers and two fathers fell to sleep on Tull and Jules without letting one slip from her grasp or lead her away from the other again.

122

THAT PREVIOUS LAND

THE 1ST EVE BENEATH THE MOON OF THE SOWER'S HAND

THE 122ND SOWING SEASON OF THE ACCESSION

IN THE MERCY OF YAH, WHO GIVES THE RAIN, THE SEED, AND THE BLOOM.

THE BELLFLOWER SIGNAL HOUSE

A SITE FROM WHICH MOTHER AND SON VANISHED.
WHILST A BROTHER SOUGHT A COUNTERBLOW.

From an elevated vantage point greater than Tull enjoyed, *another* soul watched the plight of the Jacobian who despised his purpose. The sight of him with a bow in hand excited the heart, but stole warmth from the eve. Any soul who knew the Guardian knew that he never towed a weapon he did not use. That watchful soul, above most, knew well this Guardian.

In response to his presence, Lucy's tendrils of energy clawed at the eve, though an icy blast teetered the vantage point of the unseen without confirmation that she sensed him there. A creature of brass appeared on the bat of an eye and set her hand upon Tull's crown. The daggers of the sea lunged at the fire of her train, but never doused a single flame. True to her purpose, Enke'loi gleamed amid the chaos.

Tull wiped his eyes, peered around the Warring Minister, and drew attention toward a mammoth sword. The weapon crafted for Ministers rose from the debris in a hand so swaddled with darkness that the weapon *appeared* wielded by an invisible foe. Fire burned one edge at such a degree that false shadow fell upon the sword-wielder and brass dripped upon the shore as the Minister's ear suffered a blow.

TULL

Enke'loi wailed against the sword with her mace and roared into the funneling wind. The veil of darkness and smoke screamed back, and the form of a shroud-draped figure appeared in glints of reflective light. A brass-mingled hand wrapped against the hilt as though formed for each other. Tull and Lucy reacted with unheard voices, though outmatched in *presence*.

"Pian Vi'emane horä!"

In retaliation to the scream from Enke'loi's challenger, the wailing voices trapped in the sea emitted a pain-filled shriek.

"Pian Vi'emane nou'see!"

The collar of Tull's shirt ran red and deafness spared him. With regard for his soul, a scarred hand seized the ornamental iron bars that lined the vantage point and flung open the obstruction. Plumes of light filled the sky-fires and a tentacle slammed against the fallen signal house tower. Sparks arose from the iron bars, enough that the observer lost sight for a moment.

Once focus returned, captive vision settled on Tull as he latched two bolts onto the string of a borrowed bow. Whilst on his knees, in a prayer-like pose, a peculiar stillness arose; not unlike a tendril. His unrestrained voice commanded attention from Lucy, the sword-wielder, and their observer. His defending Minister smiled as the first words took flight on the swift wind even as the Guardian set his aim.

"Lord of the Poet King! From Your goodness You have allowed me a purpose of fulfillment. I thank You for Your unending mercies."

As fast as the Jacobian rose, he fell and jarred his knee. In anger's stead, he admired the soft bloom of a small flower. He raised his shoulder, drew back on the bowstring, and held the arrows steady as his instincts aimed into the heart of darkness and smoke. He never feared the wave that rose behind him.

"I thank You, that You stifle—"

Tull's voice disappeared with the roar of the sea. Fire flashed like lightning from within a funnel of snow and the deafened Guardian let loose both arrows. As the sea crashed down, the observer screamed the Guardian's name into the roar and tremble of aftershock. Another great roar shook the coast, disturbed every foundation, and drew every eye. The wailing voices cried out the true name of the Creator and stung the ears of the witness.

Despite how Bliss ridiculed him in other lands, Tull's aim proved clean and accurate as his heart-motive and purpose aligned. The first arrow pierced Lucy's

TULL

shoulder and pinned her against a broken shield fitted for a giant's hand. The second arrow struck the Seko'tae Vi'emane in the chest. Both, who lorded power over Tull, fell by a hand they showed no respect.

As Vi'emane fell unto the Forbidden Sea and Lucy went slack, a ripple of energy uncoiled from the void of debris. Like lightning that uprooted the glebe, a single tendril burst toward the sky-fires and extinguished all sources of energy with a dizzying whine. The sea retreated with Tull's soulless body as Enke'loi roared at the waters and drew a closed hand to her brass breast. Then, as she appeared, she vanished.

A cry of pain drew the observer's eye onto Lucy, whose feet slipped against wet cobblestone till she found crevices that let her push her body and Tull's bolt upright. She thrust hard, roared with the contempt of nature, and snapped the bolt. Her eyes burned with crimson light and bitter ash ran from the wound. Another roar split the corners of her mouth and forced the observer from an exposed setting.

"I thank You, that You stifle the fires of my heart and make me anew."

The observer continued Tull's beloved prayer and gathered a pre-loaded crossbow. The sleek body, encased with iron, ascended into a mechanical apparatus deemed necessary to penetrate an unnatural body and sear the wound without rupturing the flesh. The underside held a mini-quiver of four additional bolts that loaded by spring. Even with the added resources, a steady aim proved difficult and, as a heart beat as loud as the sea roared, a closed eye provided instinctive swiftness.

The second bolt that struck Lucy pinned forearm to breast and knocked her backward. The third bolt—second fired from the crossbow—crippled her defiant gait. No other member of the secondkind, in their established history, withstood the number of wandering spirits she invited into her body. That each of them now sought new hosts provoked the dizzied—and trapped—observer through a breathless prayer.

"Only You return my soul. So I cry out, O Mighty Creator, and beg that You guide this sinner. Hide me in Your righteous robe and let me take root in Your shelter."

A flailing tendril unraveled and cast a lightning storm across the southern territories. Bolts of lightning hammered the banks from along the sea and across the Loy River, with concentrated blasts over the waterway that isolated Conliffe's Landing in the Shelby Territory. The crossbow's bolt-loader cycled without ceasing, even though no more bolts awaited. In turn, he who felled Lucy Bright Moon prayed without ceasing till the storm ceased and not one spirit remained within.

TULL

When the observer's feet reached the terrane, he took a knee and felt the glebe; warmed by tendrils of energy. Even the cauterized ice sparked with bursts of light and color. A scent of fineness, of privilege, spiced the air, like the brisk tap of heels no wider than an arrow's shaft. He looked toward slender legs, sleek hips, and a riding cape that concealed all but the cleavage that an attention-seeker displayed for her own adulation. He abhorred Katerena Yvette Mumus's face, her toothy grin and crazed eyes, and cast his gaze back onto the ice.

"You have ended her?"

"Her scream made less racket than your heels."

"Swipe!"

Another soul, adorned with a tight braid of red hair and tattered clothes that boasted a threatening figure, chuckled at the archer's jab. Her supremacy faded with a cringe when yet another cut off her path. A feral creature—indiscernible by form—crouched in the place where the brass-and-flesh creature last stood and sought a glimmer of him in the sea. Her voice emitted snarls and howls of rejection in fulfillment's stead.

"Who towed Mika's leash?"

Two hands pointed toward the darkness behind the red-headed soul. Till Mika added a third hand, though, the talkative soul paid the approach of a fifth soul no mind. Winded from the broad path he took away from harm, Timothy Todd McCrea still cut close enough that he brushed against Dory Orlean Sevilla and narrowed her proud stance.

"The coward arrives!"

"I was the decoy, you were the keeper."

"You *kept* just fine, from what I gathered."

Privileged Katerena also slung dirt and condemned the deceitful abettor. "You let your fellows face cruel ends and never warned them."

"He wanted this end. Now he believes he has a chance with the medic. I offer to cripple him some, lest she make him for a coward too."

Tim suffered Dory's heckling in silence but cast rocks toward her as he scavenged for a trace of the missing Jacobian's body. So profuse was his search, in point of fact, that the sea washed Buckler's dried blood from his limbs.

"You'll not find trace of him." The archer hung his head. "Our land goes on without his great soul."

TULL

Tim chucked the alms he took from Tull unto the sea. "Cursed, indeed."

Dory's voice pierced the eve like lantern light. "Tell me you mourn the soul who took your arm!"

"I was warned."

The marvel who imbued Lucy with gifts—and last to arrive—laughed at the observer's claim in a manner that bristled the chill on every spine—save he who ended his own bride. With a single hand, Asham Benjamin Gera pulled the scarves from around his face and imagined the sensations that conditions and wicked laughter held, for he no longer felt them. Others clamored around the white-haired laugher, with Katerena and the rest to his left except Mika, who crouched on all fours like a trained pet at his right side. From his wheelchair, adorned with steam engine and lamps, he who finagled the territories into a panic set glassy eyes on the last fallen Guardian.

"One of my better creations . . ."

Asham stepped upon his bride's still hand, lest she surprise him.

"I sought *three* as I recall the, well, *count*."

All endured another fit of his malicious, self-pleased laughter.

"Where is the Last? Where is Tull?"

"They are no more!" Tim made the bold announcement. "The sea claimed them!"

"Prove your claim with their bodies, fool!" Katerena went from vicious to docile. "Did we displease you this eve, Papa?"

Rather than basking in the tantrums of an old fool, Asham hunted for trophies and settled on an invaluable treasure. He pinched his glove between false teeth, slipped loose his scarred right hand, and claimed ownership of the last bolt fired by Nelson James Tull. As far as any soul would learn, the bolt ended the Era of the Guardians. Mika brushed along Asham's leg and sniffed at the bolt, but he paid such oddities no mind as he spoke in a low voice.

"Well-aimed, brother. How time proves dull without you." The voices of the sea and the breeze haunted, but Asham snapped at their taunts. "Say that Nelson James Tull has found his end, but *I* believe. I believe. Soon, I'll see you."

TULL

THE GUARDIAN

THE END

GRIFFIN WRAY

UP NEXT:

107 — TULL & EBBE: SEVEN WINTERS' TIME

SEE WHO RETURNS.

www.ingramcontent.com/pod-product-compliance
Lightning Source LLC
Chambersburg PA
CBHW030548310726
48979CB00010B/2077/J